Chapter 1
Lenton Vicarage, Nottingham

April 1905

The postman was on his way up the path, whistling his favourite music hall tune. Harriet closed the landing window, hitched up her skirt, and ran down the stairs.

"Good Morning, Miss Loxley. A bright one, isn't it?"

"Indeed it is."

She shuffled through the envelopes to the last in the pile, a surprisingly plain cream affair, bearing a red penny-stamp postmarked House of Commons, and with her name and address in Will's handwriting. He'd done it. He'd got her the invitation.

She clutched the letters to her chest, spun round twice and skipped down the hall.

"London, here I come!"

She held the envelope up to the light from the hall window. It was not as ornate as she had expected but was thick enough that she could see nothing of what was inside. She had to give points to her brother. He had very fine penmanship.

When Will had graduated from Cambridge a year ago, his

penmanship, and possibly his intelligence and ability, secured him a position as secretary to Mr James Yoxall, one of the Nottingham Members of Parliament. Ever since then he had been regaling Harriet with tales of the to-and-fro of debate, the discussion of weighty issues and the overall improvement of the lot of mankind that flowed from the Mother of all Parliaments. Change, Will said. Change and progress were what it was all about. Creating a new world in a new century.

Harriet believed herself to be as well-informed and as able to articulate opinions about the way forward as her younger brother. That change he talked about was going to include women voting.

She pulled herself up straight. This modest envelope, her opportunity to attend the upcoming debate on women's suffrage, might be addressed to her but it was Father's privilege to approve all the post. She pulled open the door leading to breakfast.

"Good morning Mother, Father. I'm sorry I'm late down. I have the post."

She made sure her letter was on the top of the pile that she put down at her father's side.

"Mmm," her father said. "Late. Becoming something of a habit."

She apologised again, went to get her food and managed to put two rashers of bacon on her plate before glancing into the mirror above the sideboard. Father was spreading marmalade on toast and not paying any attention to the stack of envelopes by his right hand.

She took some toast for herself.

Emma, Gwen and Eleanor were chatting about the cool spring.

Harriet looked back in the mirror for Eleanor's husband,

Strait Lace

Rosemary Hayward

published by Rosemary Hayward www.rosemaryhayward.com

For Women Everywhere

The argument of the broken window pane is the most valuable argument in modern politics.

— Emmeline Pankhurst

THE LOXLEY FAMILY 1905

GEORGE – ELIZABETH
LOXLEY (AUNT BETH)

ROBERT – MARIA
LOXLEY

EDWARD – ANNETTE
LOXLEY (AUNT LOXLEY)
(deceased)

ROBERT

ELEANOR – WESLEY
BROWN

HARRIET

WILFRED

GWENDOLYN

EMMA

WESLEY
(CHARLEY)

ROBERT
(BOBBY)

Wesley, or the newspaper he would probably be behind. He wasn't there. He must have left for the manufactory early, which meant he was not at the table to exercise discipline over his two boys, or anybody else for that matter. His early start must be why Eleanor was down for breakfast, despite having been unwell for the last few days. Eleanor was pregnant and suffering with it, but she would feel obliged to keep an eye on Charley and Bobby, who right now were kicking each other under the table and about to get into serious trouble with their mother. Harriet caught young Charley's eye through the mirror. She widened her eyes and shook her head. The kicking stopped.

Her father wiped his fingers on his napkin and laid his hand on the pile of letters at his side. Harriet pushed her teeth into her lip.

"Harriet, take more food," her mother ordered. "That's not enough to feed a mouse."

"Yes, Mother."

Harriet picked up three more plate covers and clattered them down before sliding a poached egg onto her plate. She walked towards her chair.

Gwen flashed her one of her you-know-it's-useless-trying-to-escape-Mother's-notice looks. Harriet shrugged and gave her a yes-I-know look back. Gwen was wearing a green-striped blouse, so she must also be going into the manufactory. Gwen didn't believe in displaying anything as frivolous as lace at the manufactory, despite it being a lace manufactory. She used her jet-black hair, strong brows and severe dress to appear indomitable.

Harriet sat down next to her. The House of Commons letter was by her napkin, together with her father's paperknife. He must have passed it down the table unopened. How had she missed that? She glanced at him inquiringly. He winked.

Her mother held out a cup of tea. Harriet had to take it with

3

both hands to prevent their shakiness spilling it. Everything now depended on convincing her parents, and particularly her father, that her going to the House of Commons was a good idea. Perhaps she already had his support, given that wink, but Mother exercised some power here too.

She put down the tea and picked up the envelope.

She felt a flush of pride creep into her cheeks. Who else in the family had ever been invited to the House of Commons? Except Will, of course.

"It must be from Mr Yoxall. To go to Parliament. Shall I read it out, Father?"

He nodded. All conversation ceased.

She slipped the paperknife under the envelope's flap and slit along the top edge, taking care not to tear into the stamp and its postmark. This envelope, dull as it was, was something she wanted to keep. She peered inside. A cream edge, quite thick. She pinched it between her thumb and forefinger and drew out a folded letter. The paper opened up with a reassuring stiffness. An embossed oval at the top had *House of Commons* written around it and a crown in a circle and something she couldn't quite make out. She ran her finger over it. Perhaps if she held it up to the light...

Gwen kicked her ankle.

"Oh, yes, sorry. *Mr James Yoxall, Member of Parliament for Nottingham West, cordially invites his constituent Harriet Loxley to attend the Ladies' Gallery of the House of Commons on Friday, May 12th 1905, at 2pm.*" She looked over at her father, who was watching her intently. "It's the date of the second reading of the bill to extend the franchise to women, Father. I would very much like to go."

He said, "Capital. Yoxall is an excellent fellow and in the best Liberal tradition."

Eleanor pointed her knife towards Harriet. "Wesley says he is too much for the unions."

Harriet's father replied before she could. "Ah, Nell, your Wesley would say that. He has lace to sell. What's more, he has my brother's lace to sell. Wesley needs must support the owners. But I have a duty as a clergyman to speak for the poor. Working people need unions if their conditions are to improve."

Eleanor laid her knife down before she replied. "The conditions at my uncle's factory are very advanced, Father, and the women are not poor. They are working women with wages of their own."

"I know, Nell, but the government has issued report after report about improvements needed in the lace industry. The women's hours are too long and the rooms are too hot."

"They are too hot because of drying the lace. You must dry the washed lace."

Harriet glanced at her mother and realised that Mother was watching her push her bacon around her plate and frowning. Mother complained she was too thin. She needed Mother on her side. Harriet cut off a piece of bacon, put it in her mouth and chewed.

Her mother's frown disappeared and she said, "Yoxall is for the teachers' union, I believe. And the union wants to stop women teachers losing their positions when they marry."

"A married woman has duties." Eleanor muttered, without lifting her eyes from her plate. "Family is more important than work."

"Family is, of course, more important than work." The Reverend Loxley waved his hand as if to encompass his own well-fed family. "How could I say otherwise? But what about a married woman who has no children? Or who is the main breadwinner with a sick or unemployed husband? Or what about a married woman who has other family who can help care for the small children? It makes little sense to discard the skills of these excellent women teachers because they marry. We should leave that decision to them."

Harriet picked up her folded letter and tapped it on her lips. She needed to steer the conversation back to the possibility of travelling to London to watch the franchise bill pass.

"That is a very radical view, Father. Do you also hold that such excellent women should be able to vote?"

"I do. But where will I be when all the women in this household can vote? I'll not be able to get a word in edgeways."

"Oh, Robert, dear, you are quite safe." Mother's voice lilted with amusement, but Harriet detected a hard edge. "You know very well that this bill merely extends the existing franchise for men to women. To vote a man has to own land or rent property to the value of ten pounds a year. We live in a vicarage. We own no land and pay no rent."

Emma looked up and pushed back some stray hair. "But Father votes, doesn't he Mother?"

"Yes, he does." Her mother smiled. "Vicars are an exception."

Harriet smiled too. Mother knew all the ins and outs of the main franchises: freeholder, occupier, university, and lodger. She understood the concept of franchise through ancient rights. She knew how counties differed from boroughs. And she knew Father could vote because he inhabited, by virtue of office, a dwelling house in which his master did not reside. Was it a divine or secular master that was being referenced? The voting qualifications were peculiar enough for it to be either.

Eleanor was looking straight at her, her face hard. Harriet looked back and tilted her head to one side.

"My Wesley hasn't got a vote, Harry. Neither do either of our brothers. Not Robert, not Will. Not Will, even when he works in Parliament. Do you think women should be able to vote when so many men can't?"

Harriet wished Eleanor wouldn't parrot Wesley's opinions. She was surely capable of having her own.

"That question only makes sense, Nell, if you believe the rights of any woman can only be attained after those of all men."

"I believe the reasoning," Mother said, "is that the people who contribute to the wealth of the nation should have a voice in its affairs, which, in our family, means your father and your Uncle George."

"And don't you contribute, Mother? You are a Poor Law Guardian and you undertake half of the work that goes with this parish. What more of a contribution could you be expected to make?"

"Half, Harriet? I only do half the work in this parish?" Her father threaded his napkin through its ring and made to get up from the table.

Had she annoyed him? Was he going to drop all thought of her going to see the bill passed? She needed his permission to travel to London, not to mention the cost of the train fare.

"Robert." Her mother's voice chimed like a bell, just as it did when she reminded her husband to wipe his feet after he had tramped across the lawn between the church and the vicarage. "Robert, please. Harriet needs a decision. May she go?"

"Ah, yes. Of course. The decision."

He sat down again. Harriet held her breath.

Her father spread his arms and turned the palms up, the gesture directed towards his wife at the other end of the table. "I think it a jolly good idea for Harriet to go, do you not Mrs Loxley?"

"Indeed, I do, Mr Loxley."

Harriet exhaled, sharply enough for all in the silent room to hear. Had her parents been teasing her all along?

7

Her father gave her a look that spoke authority. "Only, Harriet, I do not wish you to travel unaccompanied. I will finance a trip for you and your younger sisters. I think I need not ask your brother to give up a day's work at the manufactory to accompany you on the train. Nor need Will come down from London. There are ladies' carriages you may use. You can travel together as far as Will's care and stay with your Aunt Loxley in town. Emma and Gwendolyn, you can take those stricken expressions off your faces. I am not expecting you to spend your afternoon in the Ladies' Gallery of the House of Commons. You may make an early start on Christmas in Bond Street."

Two small heads snapped up from dipping toast-soldiers into boiled eggs and young Charley and Bobby's bright laughter flew across the breakfast table.

Harriet said, "Thank you, Father. Thank you so much."

She was going to see the Palace of Westminster. She was going to sit in the special gallery reserved for ladies inside the famous Mother of all Parliaments. She was going to be involved. She smiled across the table at Eleanor, enjoying her sister's delight in her boys' sparkling faces.

Her father said, "I'm sure Aunt Loxley would love to have Gwen and Emma, as well as Harriet, for the weekend, wouldn't she, Maria dear? And you would welcome some of the burden of Christmas being taken from you."

Her mother's eyes crinkled at the corners as she patted her youngest grandson on the head. "May is a little too early for Christmas shopping, Robert. I suggest the girls get some new dress patterns and fabrics for the summer. Perhaps their aunt could accompany them to Liberty's."

Eleanor gestured to her two wriggling boys to get down. "You may run around in the garden for half an hour."

"Will you come and play cricket with us, Harry?" Charley whispered as he passed her chair.

Eleanor's gaze made her answer clear.

"After your arithmetic lesson," Harriet said quietly. "And in the park," she added, sure Mother was also staring appropriate responses into her mind. Last week she'd had to admit it was her ball that had broken the Drawing Room window, not one thrown by either of the boys.

Chapter 2
Mrs Alice Slack

May 11th 1905

The wood panelling of the booking hall of Nottingham Victoria Station was as splendid as Harriet remembered it from the day that Father had taken them to see the magnificent new building. Emma had been only thirteen years old then, and Gwen fifteen; girls in short skirts and brown boots with their hair looped in white ribbons. Eleanor had leant on her Wesley's arm, heavy with child, while Robert had held little Charley by the hand.

She and Will, at nineteen and seventeen, had considered themselves sophisticated railway-age adults strolling arm in arm across the shining wooden floor. They had fantasised about buying tickets for London and eating an elegant tea in the station restaurant before strolling onto one of the huge platforms and climbing up into a carriage waiting behind its giant, gasping locomotive.

That was five years ago. Harriet had not been in the booking hall since then. Whenever the family travelled to London, the women waited in the Ladies' Waiting Room while Father bought the tickets and one of her brothers arranged the porters. But this time Father had been insistent that she take responsibility for the journey, handing her a copy of Bradshaw and saying that if she expected to travel independently, then she needed to be able to read a railway timetable.

Her speech for obtaining the correct tickets firmly in mind, Harriet left her father looking for a porter and her sisters looking through magazines at the stationery stall and went to stand in the queue in the booking office. As the man ahead of her moved away she checked her coat pocket for the leather purse Mother had given her. She struggled a little getting the clip open.

"Good morning, madam. How may I help you today?"

Harriet raised her head. The booking clerk was a woman. In fact, she was barely more than a girl, about Emma's age, and with a charming smile and fine teeth. Harriet swallowed and said, "Three first-class tickets for the ladies' carriage please, and I need to register one trunk for the luggage van."

She had agreed with her sisters on one trunk and a small portmanteau between them, rather than three large portmanteaus for the weekend. The trunk wasn't full. There was room for bringing fabrics back from London.

The clerk's blonde head bent over the tickets and Harriet's curiosity overtook her nervousness. How had the clerk obtained this job? The only way to find out was to ask.

"Excuse me. I don't mean to be impertinent, but is it common for women to be employed by the railway?"

The young woman looked her in the eye as she handed her the tickets. "You'll need the luggage ticket at Marylebone to claim your trunk. Is it clearly labelled? Trunks are forever ending up in lost property." Then she smiled. "My father worked for the railway and when he died my uncle vouched for me. They took me on so I could help support my mother and the other children. I had to pass the relevant tests in arithmetic."

"I'm so sorry. About your father, I mean. Not the arithmetic tests. Or your employment."

"I enjoy it. Although I get a bit of comment from some people."

"Well, I think it shows how the world is changing for the better. Maybe, one day I'll work for my father's employer. He's a vicar."

The clerk laughed and covered her mouth with her hand. "I don't think we'll ever be seeing that, madam."

Harriet settled into her seat. A family tragedy had opened up life for the young clerk. She had occupation and resources. When and how had her own life taken a turn into a closed-off court? It had been sudden. Look at her and Will. He was two years younger than her and he worked at the heart of an empire making a nation's laws. Although the topics of the day were still discussed at the Loxley table, where she and Will had developed their interest, it wasn't like being in the thick of things. He saw politics from the inside while she played ball with children and drew flowers.

As children she and Will had been inseparable. Even when he played cricket for the school eleven he included her in the local friendly matches. And if the other side laughed he put her in to bowl first. That soon changed their tune. They used to botanise together too, collecting wild flowers from all around, pressing them, finding out their Latin names and creating books of the flora of Nottingham. They had walked so many miles that Mother complained of them wearing through their boots, so they had taken to going on bicycles.

The carriage shuddered as the locomotive started to pull

and Emma put her hand on Harriet's arm. "Here we go. This is so exciting."

Emma, the youngest one of them all, was only recently out of school and now studying art in evening classes. When Harriet had been in the last year of school her biology teacher had recommended she try for a scholarship to Cambridge.

She had been to see her father in his study.

"I honestly don't know if I have the ability to get a scholarship, Father. The competition is high. But set against that the fact that not many women have enough education in the sciences to qualify for the university and maybe I stand a chance of getting a commoner's place."

He had looked at her almost pityingly, as if she had said something foolish, or been something she shouldn't be. She felt the cold touch of doubt. He was going to say no.

"Harriet, even with a scholarship the expense would be considerable. It's not only fees, it's the cost of living away from home. My clergyman's stipend is barely enough to provide for a family. I have some funds set by from the manufactory dividends, but they must be reserved for Will. One day he will have a wife and children of his own to support. He needs his education. It is different for a woman. Someone will support you. I appreciate that you have talent you want to nurture, Harriet, especially at drawing. I can run to some art classes for you. There must be a local teacher we could find. Would you like that?"

Harriet fidgeted in her seat and looked out of the window. The train was crossing the river, leaving Nottingham. Cold shivered down her back. She squeezed her eyes tight to disguise her remembered disappointment; a disappointment not only for herself but for him. He had two more daughters after her. How he must wish he could help them all fulfil themselves.

And then Will had gone to Cambridge. Cambridge had been the dividing point between her and Will.

She looked along the seat, at Emma and Gwen next to her, their heads bent over a copy of the Tatler. She was on a train to London. They were all on a train to London, without any men. That was significant. The world *was* changing, and it was about to change more and in a big way. And when this new suffrage bill passed women would be able to vote on the same terms as men. Then there would be even more changes.

A letter from Will had arrived in the morning post. She pulled it from her pocket.

Dear Sis,

I managed to obtain an interview with Mr Bamford Slack. (The very same who gave his win in the lottery for a Private Members' Bill to the women). He is a very pleasant gentleman. MP for St. Albans. But he doesn't hail from there. He's from Derbyshire, a Methodist lay preacher, and his sister is a vocal teetotaller. Apart from that last fact, I think he and Father would rub along very well. And Mother would get on like a house on fire with Mrs Slack, who is very active in the suffrage movement. I imagine talk at their table is very like ours.

You'll be as delighted as I am that Mrs Slack has offered to escort you to the Ladies' Gallery. I have enclosed a letter from her.

I'm so looking forward to having you here and showing you West-minster, Sis. I'm sure you will be overwhelmed by the termi-nology and all the little rules and protocols. Everybody is, even Mr Yoxall when he first arrived, so here's something to help you out.

The Women's Enfranchisement Bill is a Private Members' Bill and they are always debated on Fridays. It's called a Private Bill because it isn't a government Bill. Rather it's one an ordinary MP has put together. The First Reading of any Bill is a formality.

The Second Reading, the one you'll be at, is what's important.
It's when the Bill can be debated by any MP who wants to speak.
Friday will go like this: Mr Bamford Slack will propose to the
House that the Bill be read a second time. Sir John Rolleston, the
MP for Leicester, will second his proposal. Then the Speaker will
call on other MPs, who will ask to be heard by standing up. They
will give their opinions. The end of the debate will happen when
no more Members rise to speak or it gets to be half past five. If it
seems the debate is going to carry on past the end of the session,
Mr Slack will ask that 'the question now be put'. Whether it will,
that is whether a vote will be taken, is at the discretion of the
Speaker.
By the way, the Bill is timetabled to come on second in the day,
after one for the lighting of vehicles on the road at night.
I'll meet you all from the train on Thursday and spend the night
with Aunt Loxley. Then you and I can have Friday morning
exploring together while the little ones go off to buy ribbons or
whatever they plan on doing.
Toodle Pip
Will

She smiled. Toodle Pip? Really, Will?

Lighting vehicles? That was reassuring. Such a piece of common sense could be debated and voted on quickly before the House went on to discuss the important constitutional business of extending the franchise.

She opened out the sheet of blue notepaper that was also in the envelope. It smelled of Lily of the Valley.

My Dear Miss Loxley,
I am very much looking forward to meeting you. I will wait at the
point where the women assemble. Your brother knows where
that is.

Now to fill you in on the story behind this Bill. Being from Nottingham, I'm sure you are aware of the uproar that surrounded the passing of the Great Reform Bill in 1832. The infuriated mob did, after all, burn down your intransigent duke's castle. But did you know that the very first petition to Parliament to allow women to vote was presented within months of that Bill passing? There have been thousands, literally thousands, of petitions since then. And Bills put before Parliament. At least thirty, I am sure.

No less a personage than John Stuart Mill sought to add women to the great 1867 Reform Act, with a simple amendment. Mill wanted the reference to 'male persons' in the Bill changed to 'men'. The word 'man', as everyone knows, and as Parliament itself has recognised, means mankind and therefore includes women. He failed, although there were many votes on his side.

Women have won many rights since John Stuart Mill's day. Women property holders have the right to vote in local elections and the right to vote for the Poor Law Guardians. And quite rightly, since these women pay local rates and poor rates. But the Education Act of 1898 snatched away the right to elect school boards from the women. After thirty-two years of active service in education women are to be excluded. And how has this happened? Not for any sinister reason but because the new legislation was framed in a way that left them out.

And that sums it up. We women are not considered, not until we assert ourselves. And when we do assert ourselves, and prove ourselves, as we have done by all our service on school boards and the like, we are overlooked in the drafting of new legislation. As if we were of no significance.

We need the vote. We women must be made safe under the constitution, so we can never be left out again.

My husband's Bill, which will be presented on Friday, is exactly the same as John Stuart Mill's amendment. It will allow women

*to vote under the same qualifications as men. Let us hope the
many members who claim they support women's suffrage turn
out to support it.*
Yours in solidarity,
Alice Slack

Harriet stared out at the countryside streaming past the
window. She knew just how long women had been pressing for
the vote. Her mother had been active in the campaign, until
family and the obligations of a vicar's wife had commanded so
much of her attention. It hadn't occurred to her before that
women's position in the world was going backwards; that things
they were accustomed to doing, such as serving as a Poor Law
Guardian, as her mother had done for years, could be whisked
away. If men found they couldn't exercise a right they'd been
exercising for thirty years there'd be riots. Look indeed at the
violence in Nottingham in 1832.

She felt a change of air pressure in her ears and the window
next to her went dark, throwing her scowling face back at her.

"Women," she muttered, "are getting shoved aside because
we are quiet and reasonable. Because we are womanly."

She folded her letters and reached to put them in the portmanteau on the seat beside her, accidentally nudging Emma.

Emma looked up from her magazine. "Harry, do you want
us to hold off D.H.Evans until you can come along too? It says
here they have the best copies of the newest French dresses.
And what about Dickens and Jones? They are the tops for this
season's tea gowns. Gwen and I are going to look at ball gowns
too, even if we can't have them. It says here the black lace craze
has reached a height and garnitures of pearls, groups of tinsel-
butterflies, and choux of velvet are everywhere."

"Plenty for Uncle George to supply to finishing houses,
then."

Gwen leant across Emma. "What's in those letters of yours that's made you so grumpy, Harry? Parliament and men and all their doings?"

She picked up a copy of TitBits from the seat next to her and threw it towards Harriet. "Here, read this and enjoy some beautiful clothes."

Chapter 3
The Women's Suffrage Bill

May 12th 1905

W ill gripped her arm and negotiated their way between the buses, barrow boys and darting pedestrians in Parliament Square. Her ears filled with the clatter of iron-clad wheels and her nostrils with the swampy aroma of sweating horse. Then the noise faded. She was looking up at the walls of Westminster Palace; so many windows, so many statues, so much tracery of roses and thistles and shamrocks.

Will was bouncing on his feet and glancing all around. "Mr Yoxall said he would see us here, in Old Palace Yard, before we meet up with Mrs Slack, so I could introduce you. Ah, look, here he comes."

A man of modest height, about the same as Will's, was pulling on one of his rather large ears and striding towards them. As he got nearer he smoothed his beard, as if making sure no crumbs lingered prior to close conversation. In his left hand he held a portmanteau, with an umbrella strapped to the top.

"Mr Yoxall, may I introduce my sister, Miss Harriet Loxley."

Mr Yoxall touched the rim of his bowler hat and gave a nod. "Delighted to make your acquaintance."

Harriet nodded. "Mr Yoxall."

"Your brother here is a fine fellow. I don't know what I'd do without him."

He clapped a hand on Will's shoulder and Harriet noticed the crease of a smile around his eyes. He meant what he said.

"I hope this young man has explained the procedures for the debate, Miss Loxley. The traditions of Parliament can be quite bewildering."

"I am hoping to witness a momentous event, sir, extending the franchise to women. Or at least some women. Will you be in the chamber this afternoon?"

Did the twinkle and the laughter lines disappear, or was she imagining that?

"The women's cause has my full support, but I'm afraid I have to leave for the three o'clock train for Nottingham. I have Union affairs to attend to. But it should be an interesting discussion." He smiled and tipped his hat again. "Good day to you. Miss Loxley. I hope you enjoy your time in the chamber."

Watching him walk away, Harriet said, "Mother will be disappointed. He's something of a political hero to her."

"He is a specialist in education. Devotes as much time to the teachers' union as he does to Westminster. He knows the ins and outs of every bit of education legislation. There's only so much one man can do."

"But surely some things, like extending the franchise, are important for everyone?"

How many more MPs, supposedly in support of the bill, would be taking early trains home?

"Come on, Sis. Let's find Mrs Slack."

Harriet had imagined Mrs Alice Slack as fifty years old, and a little stern, so she was surprised when she turned out to be no more than ten years older than herself. She was above average height for a woman and quite alarmingly pale, with a tinge of lilac brushing her lips and the area under her eyes. Harriet suspected her new acquaintance did not have a strong constitution.

After greetings had been exchanged and Will had said his goodbyes, Mrs Slack indicated the door ahead of them and Harriet raised her hand to push it open.

"Orders!"

Harriet jumped, her feet almost leaving the ground. The policeman had been standing so still she had failed to notice him.

Mrs Slack put a hand on her arm. "The officer means your invitation."

Harriet showed her paper and the unsmiling policeman handed her a bone disc. She looked at it inquiringly. There was a number on it. He said nothing, and neither did she. She lifted her chin and walked past him.

The room was dark and noticeably warmer than the bright spring day outside. It smelt of too many people. Harriet coughed and quickly covered her mouth, embarrassed to be calling attention to herself.

She needn't have worried since everyone's attention was on a lady standing and waving her hands as if beating time.

"Labouchère! Labouchère has plans to have the House counted and to draw out the discussion of the Lighting Bill for the sake of killing ours! There is nothing that man won't stoop to."

There were hisses from around the room.

"I'm not surprised." Mrs Slack said from behind Harriet. "Although he declares he has equally strong views both in regard to ladies and lights."

Laughter filled the tiny room.

Mrs Slack stepped next to Harriet. "May I introduce my

young friend from Nottingham, Miss Harriet Loxley?" She named several of the ladies present. "And please call me Alice, Harriet. We are comrades in arms here."

Harriet waited for a lull in the conversation, before asking, "Who is this Mr Labouchère?"

She had addressed the room in general. The effort required to open her mouth and speak in this animated company had driven every newly introduced name right out of her head.

The lady who'd been declaiming turned towards her. "He's the MP for Northampton. A fierce opponent of women voting. He's a theatre owner and a journalist. Lived with an actress for twenty years before he married her. He wanted a cabinet position in Gladstone's government, but Queen Victoria herself opposed the appointment."

Harriet said, "Queen Victoria was also against women voting," and blushed as laughter filled the room.

"Good point, Miss Loxley. It's not only men who are our opponents. Some of the most powerful women in the land see no need for others to exercise any rights at all. And as for Labouchère, he's a joke."

"But," Alice raised a finger, claiming the insider's knowledge, "there is a real danger he will succeed in having our bill talked out. He has allies."

Harriet was lucky to have Alice as her guide. She should remember to thank Will for that.

A door opened. An official instructed them to follow him, and to maintain strict silence.

After trooping up three flights of stone stairs and through a swing door into a corridor, Harriet stood twisting her folded parasol and thinking that she didn't know what *talked out* meant and she should ask. But she was acutely aware of the silence around her.

Alice touched her elbow and whispered, "Stay still until I move."

The official a few yards away glared at them, then turned to look away.

"Now!"

Alice slipped through a nearby door.

Harriet grabbed it before it slammed shut. Alice was already far ahead of her, hurrying down a dimly lit staircase. Harriet caught up just as her companion opened a door into a wide space buzzing with conversation. Alice grabbed her arm and manoeuvred them through the crowd and out into an open area lit by leaded glass windows.

"This is the Central Hall," Alice said. "A public space between the House of Lords and the House of Commons. I couldn't risk bringing you here earlier, in case we got shut out of the gallery entrance. I want you to meet Mrs Emmeline Pankhurst and Miss Sylvia Pankhurst, two of the founding members of The Women's Social and Political Union. It is a small group and a new one, based in Manchester, but I warrant these extraordinary ladies will not have their party remain small for long. They have been major supporters of this bill and I have come to know them well. I'll leave you with them for a moment while I catch up with some acquaintances."

The elder Mrs Pankhurst was a slender woman of about forty years, her deep-blue suit well-cut and of high quality. Miss Sylvia Pankhurst wore a light overcoat over a plain grey frock. She shared her mother's fine arched brow and long nose, but not her high apple-cheeks and piercing violet-blue eyes. Sylvia's eyes were grey.

Harriet imagined Mrs Pankhurst's eyes sought to grab her gaze and bind it to her own, while Sylvia's were a door concealing a deep sadness.

Why had Alice Slack left her with them? So they could recruit her to their organisation?

Mrs Pankhurst said, "Loxley is a good north-country name. Where are you from, Miss Loxley?"

"I am from Nottingham, Mrs Pankhurst."

"Ah, the lace industry. What sort of women are the lace workers? Are they women who will support the cause?"

Harriet hesitated to reply. She didn't know the views of the women workers. She only knew the views of her family and acquaintances.

Sylvia filled the gap in the conversation. "Our bill is to be seconded by Sir John Rolleston, the MP for Leicester, Miss Loxley, Harriet. May I call you Harriet? Leicester is very near to Nottingham, is it not? He will argue that modern conditions of industry are the foundation of the country's prosperity and that in England women are free to go to their work, and to receive wages and dispose of them as they think fit. What argument can there then be for withholding from them the privileges of democracy as enjoyed by men? If they had those privileges, they would have the power to demand equal wages for equal work."

Mrs Pankhurst said, "So, the lace workers of Nottingham, Miss Loxley. Do they get paid as much as the men? I am certain they do not."

A sense of trepidation established itself near the top of Harriet's corset. Would her new acquaintances be offended if she did more than nod and agree?

"There are many thousands of women employed in the Nottingham lace industry, Mrs Pankhurst. Three times as many as there are men. They are said to be well paid. But they are not paid as much as the men who manufacture the brown net, the raw lace. And I don't see how the work the women do can be compared to the men's work. The men, you see, the twisthands, work on huge machines in steam-driven factories. Working the machines is heavy work. Even boys are forbidden to be twisthands until they are fifteen years old. The women trim, mend, and embroider the finished lace in the warehouse. They sit and sew all day. It is not the same work."

Why was she being so contradictory? Could she not help herself? Should she not try to agree with these ladies over something? What about Mr Yoxall and his devotion to the teachers' cause?

"Women teachers, on the other hand, they do perform the same work as the men and they have the same education. I see no reason why they should not be paid the same."

"My youngest daughter, Adela, is training to be a teacher, Miss Loxley. I'm sure she would echo your sentiments." Mrs Pankhurst patted her arm and Harriet experienced the same exciting connection she'd had when Alice laid her hand on her arm earlier.

"This attitude towards working men," Mrs Pankhurst continued, "it all stems back to patronage, the medieval sort. The owners believe themselves lords of the manor graciously providing for men who have families to support. Women, they believe, are only bringing in extra money. Pin money, they call it."

Uncle George as a medieval lord of the manor? Harriet tried not to let her amusement show on her face. The effort made her blush.

Mrs Pankhurst's eyes were shining now. "Our bill, as I'm sure you know, Miss Loxley, seeks to enfranchise women in the same way as men are enfranchised. Do you think that is a good way forward?"

"I think it is a step in the right direction. Once one woman can vote the arguments against all women voting will eventually collapse."

"You are a thoughtful young lady indeed. Many women

suffragists desire a wider reform bill, one extending the franchise for both men and women. Such a measure would be bound to fail in this Tory Parliament because the men believe that, since there are more women born than men, it must inevitably lead to men being outvoted."

Thinking men couldn't believe that, could they?

Harriet laughed. "But that only makes arithmetical sense if all men voted the same and so did all women."

Mrs Pankhurst clapped her gloved hands together, a delicate indication of applause. She turned to her daughter. "I shall send a note in to the Prime Minister, to Balfour. He is a Manchester MP, Miss Loxley, and my MP. I shall inform him that the Women's Social and Political Union will oppose every Conservative candidate in the next election unless he promises facilities for further discussion of the women's bill."

Mrs Pankhurst turned away and Sylvia frowned. "Mother claims she is convinced the bill will not fail, but she is manoeuvring to have the government take it on. That would not be necessary if she really believed it will pass its Second Reading today."

So even Mrs Pankhurst doubted the bill would pass. Why? If people supported it, important people like this Sir John Rolleston, why wouldn't it pass? Harriet watched Sylvia's mother wind her way across the hall, a sight as elegant as any ship under full sail, and wondered what exactly having the government take on the bill implied.

She was about to ask when Sylvia continued, "Mother is very emotional about this bill. I hope she doesn't do anything reckless. This morning she suggested tripping up old Mr Labouchère during his constitutional in Hyde Park. It might be done, she said, by a fine wire held by herself and Mrs Montefiore."

Surely two ladies would never stoop to such a thing. It was

quite shocking that they so much as thought it. Harriet laughed nervously. "Not really? You are joking, Miss Pankhurst, aren't you?"

Before Sylvia could answer Alice Slack appeared at her elbow. "Come quickly, Harriet. We must return to our attic or we may find ourselves excluded."

Harriet considered suggesting that they stay. She suspected that many of the significant people in the fight for the franchise were in this lobby, not upstairs. But she had come to see the proceedings of the House and she would not see them down here.

The corridor outside the Ladies' Gallery was empty.

"Oh dear, will we be stuck right at the back?"

Alice held up her bone disc. "These are seat numbers. Places in the front row."

That was reassuring. The seats high in a theatre balcony were excellent, if you had the front row.

The only sources of light were above a sign enjoining silence and the glow from the front of the gallery. It was as gloomy as a theatre with the houselights down. Harriet picked her way, following close behind Alice. And then, in front of her, instead of a wide open space and a rail overlooking a stage, was a twisted brass lattice with four-inch leaf-shaped openings.

The chamber, far below, was long and narrow. Benches faced each other across the width, just like choir stalls in a cathedral but without the dividers. Men leaned back on the benches, or sat with their legs up on them. More were sauntering in, alone or in groups. They lounged and chatted. It was all extraordinarily relaxed.

After apologising her way along the row and taking care not to step on any toes, Harriet pointed and said, "Down there, to the right, just one level up from the floor, there are a lot of men with notebooks and fistfuls of pencils. Are they newspaper reporters?"

"You should speak close in my ear," Alice gestured towards the officious sign. "We will be obliged to leave it we make any noise. Yes, they are from the newspapers and from Hansard. Hansard is the official report."

Harriet sat down. The reporters had a much better view than she did. She had seen other open galleries too, also all filled with men.

She leaned close to Alice. "You'd think that when a debate was specifically about women the women would have been afforded better seats."

She leant forward, gripping the grille with two hands. Below, the stonework swooped as fierce and permanent as a gothic cathedral, although this Moorish design of brass lattice would be more at home in a harem than a place of Christian worship. Were the Honourable Members trying to pretend the women weren't present? Were they afraid they were going to be bombarded with favours, handkerchiefs and bonbons, like knights in a tournament?

Alice leant forward beside her and whispered, "The great discomfort of this grille is that it is like using a gigantic pair of spectacles that do not fit. This gallery is a place for the getting of headaches... Look, there is Mr Slack walking in. Down there, going towards the left."

Harriet turned sideways to get a better view of Alice's husband. Her main impression was of a bald head, a fine wool suit and a stiff collar.

Someone unseen called out for the debate on the Vehicle Lighting Bill to commence.

"The Speaker," Alice said. "He's straight down, beneath us. You can't see him from here. He controls the proceedings."

Harriet gripped the grille tighter. Now it was beginning. All the world-renowned debate.

A neatly presented elderly gentleman with a fine white beard stood and tucked his thumbs in the pockets of his black-silk waistcoat. "I call Mr Speaker's attention to the fact that forty members are not present."

Alice whispered behind her hand, "He doesn't possess a single scruple, does he? Anyone can see at a glance that there are far more than forty men in the chamber. Now, time will be wasted counting."

"Who is he?"

"Mr Labouchère."

Safe from being tripped up in Hyde Park by Mrs Pankhurst, then. It was a relief to know the lady had been joking. Harriet stood and stretched her back.

The Speaker's voice called out, "Two hundred and seventeen members present, which I think even the Right Honourable Member for Northampton can agree is more than forty. I call upon the Right Honourable Member for Middlesex, Brentwood."

Alice said, "That must have been a good fifteen minutes wasted."

Harriet sat and leaned forward again. Her right eye had an unobstructed view. The other could only see a blurred metal bar. She tried closing her left eye. This fence in front of her was beginning to feel more like a chicken coop than a harem grille.

A man was speaking, presumably the MP for Brentwood.

"In moving this second reading of the Vehicle Lighting Bill I am merely asking the House of Commons to assent to a principle which has already been carried out throughout the length and breadth of the land. Therefore, I do not think I need to take up a large amount of the time of the House."

As the gentleman went on to talk about lights and objections from farmers and cycling associations and how he remembered as a young man how his eyes on a dark night were good enough for anything, but they had got beyond that now, Harriet wondered why a simple bill required so much talk. If he wanted less time taken up, he could surely cut down his own sentences.

Finally the seconder stood and spoke, briefly. Then the MP for Brentwood requested that the bill now be read a second time.

Harriet congratulated herself on following events so far. Now they'd pass this bill on lights and move on to the franchise.

Several gentlemen stood. The Speaker's voice soared across the chamber. "The Right Honourable Member for Orkney and Shetland."

"Here we go," Alice said. "Words, words, and more words."

"The Honourable Member who moved the second reading has stated that there might be discussion on this measure for the purpose of preventing discussion on the Women's Enfranchisement Bill, which is the second order on the paper today. I can assure the promoters of the bill now before the House that nothing is further from my thoughts than that. I will be able to prove to the satisfaction of the House that there is a strong and deep-rooted feeling against the bill among my constituents. It is on that ground, and that ground only, that I have given notice that I would move the rejection of the bill."

Alice drew in breath with a sharp hiss. There were other hisses around her. Harriet leaned close to her friend. "What is it?"

"Now they'll have to spend more time discussing this lighting thing."

The Member for Orkney and Shetland was still speaking. "In every county in Scotland farms are divided by the public roads, and farmers have always been in the habit of using these roads for bringing cattle backwards and forwards, and for carrying on general farming operations. This bill would have the farmers arrange for lights every time they move their sheep or cattle. There is an absolutely unanimous feeling against these proposals on the part of the farmers. If any further legislation dealing with lights on vehicles was required it should be limited to vehicles going faster than walking pace."

Somebody behind Harriet said. "You hear how he is doing the exact opposite of what he says he is doing. He is discussing things that don't need to be discussed. Who can possibly have strong feelings about lighting sheep and cattle? At least the proposer kept his introduction short."

Harriet didn't think the proposer had kept it short at all.

Someone else hissed, "As if there were anything other than carts and animals on the roads in Orkney and Shetland, and as if anyone would care if they carried a rear light even if it did become law."

Harriet frowned and sat back in her seat. She wasn't sure the MP for Orkney was being deliberately long-winded. In her experience of reading speeches reported in the Times, MPs generally were verbose. He seemed to have a point. This bill was apparently not about lighting motor cars, or trams, or even bicycles. They already had to carry lights, front and back. It was about lighting wagons and cattle being driven along the roads.

"The Right Honourable Member for Wigtownshire."

"That's in Scotland too." Alice whispered. "Yet more about sheep, I dare say."

"The honourable gentleman proposing the bill made a curious exemption. He drew an alarming picture of the risks incurred by travellers if a cart were left unlighted by the side of a road, but the honourable Member allowed the wheelbarrow to remain without a light. Now, an accident from an unlighted wheelbarrow might be quite as serious as from an unlighted cart. The danger of unlighted carts is in a great degree imaginary, because motor cars, in their own interest, carry a strong headlight. During last winter I travelled as many as a hundred miles by night in a motorcar and I never had the slightest inconvenience from unlighted carts; but I did have some difficulty with unlighted flocks of sheep."

Laughter filled the chamber and Harriet began to sympathise with the frustration of the ladies around her. This seemed to be a particularly silly debate. Requiring lights at night should be a straightforward matter of safety. Why weren't the carters and drovers carrying lights anyway? And what was all this about stationary vehicles?

She felt a surge of anger. Whether they were deliberately trying to take up time for the women's bill or not, they should be showing it more respect.

"The Right Honourable Member for Peckham."

"The term vehicle includes every carriage or conveyance, whether with or without wheels. Now a horse is a vehicle without a wheel. Therefore, a horse comes under this category. Just consider what might happen. Ladies who go to a hunt meet frequently return to their homes in a carriage, leaving servants to take their horses home. Apparently, under this bill, each horse and servant would require four lights, one on the servant's arm, one on his back, another somewhere on the side saddle of the led horse, and a red lamp at his tail."

"I don't believe it," Harriet said. "I truly don't believe it. Is he out of his mind? Or is the person who drafted this bill?"

"The Right Honourable Member for Northampton."

Labouchère again. Another man had stood at the same time and there were shouts of, "Cochrane, Cochrane!"

"Mr Cochrane," Alice whispered. "He represents the government. If he's standing it's to say if the government will take on their bill."

But Labouchère held the floor. "It is all very well to say

Cochrane but this is a significant bill. I gave notice that I would move that the Women's Enfranchisement Bill be read this day six months, and in that way I showed that I am desirous to lay my views before the House. The bill now before the House is an important one, and we have duties to perform to our constituencies in fairly discussing it. Most of the debate has been carried on by Scotch Members, and I wish to congratulate Scotland. I have often wondered why Scotland is so much better governed than England. I believe it is because it has better representatives than England..."

The man's ability to say nothing for sentence after sentence was astounding. Would he never cease? Harriet scowled, sat back, and let the words drift over her.

There were more shouts of *Cochrane*!

The Speaker called out, "The Under Secretary of State for the Home Department." And Mr Labouchère sat down, heavily, and with obvious reluctance.

Harriet sat forward and strained to see. Mr Cochrane looked across the floor, then turned and looked along his own benches before looking directly at Mr Labouchère and saying, "A great deal of the discussion has not been directed to the Second Reading which has been moved. I am afraid that the honourable Member who last addressed the House, who professed to have a single eye to the present bill, protested a little too much."

"Exactly what I thought about most of them," Harriet muttered. "Protesting their innocence while doing their worst. Deceitful and disrespectful and dishonourable."

She forced herself to pay attention to Mr Cochrane.

"I suggest that if the honourable Member for Brentwood succeeds in getting the Second Reading, he should ask the House to send the bill to a select committee, where evidence might be taken and the subject thoroughly threshed out. If he takes that course, and is prepared to adopt amendments, the government would take no hostile view of the measure, but as the bill is at present drafted there are so many objections to it that I cannot for the moment give it any more cordial support."

The gallery was now thrumming with the sound of ladies talking. There seemed to be no officials around to hush them.

"You know the Pankhursts tried to get them to drop their Vehicle Lighting Bill, don't you?"

"There'll be no more than half an hour left for our bill."

"That's how important we are to men, something below a horse's tail."

Harriet was turning to see if she could make out who had made this last comment when Alice grabbed her arm.

"They're standing. They're going through the lobbies. Soon it will be our turn."

"The ayes to my right one hundred and nine; the noes to my left one hundred and eight."

"Really? Half of them voted against?"

"It was a badly drafted bill. The government has agreed time for it to be straightened out in committee. That's what the Secretary of State was saying. The awful thing is they could have worked that out outside the chamber and not brought it to the floor."

"So they *were* trying to delay our bill."

"I think so. So do many others." Alice half stood. "Listen! The MP for St. Albans! Mr Slack is standing."

Alice's husband spoke in a clear, carrying voice that reminded Harriet of her father preaching. "I express deep regret that this measure should have come on at so late an hour in the afternoon. As a comparatively new member, I feel almost appalled at the extraordinary abuse of the forms of the House which this afternoon has witnessed, manifestly, and in some quarters avowedly, with a view to preventing discussion of this bill."

There were roars of cynical laughter. Fury rushed upwards and invaded Harriet's cheeks. She glanced at Alice. Her cheeks were also flushed.

The Speaker shouted, "Order. Order. I will have order in the House."

Harriet laid a hand on her new friend's arm. Alice was trembling.

Mr Slack turned to bring the men around him into his oratory. He was dignified and earnest. He didn't seem in the least new to the business of speaking.

"The law of equal freedom manifestly applies to the whole race, female as well as male. During the generation since the Suffrage Bill of 1867 there has been a great advance in public opinion. Few men can say from their conscience that it is not right to give to women the Parliamentary franchise. The disenfranchisement of women is unconstitutional, inexpedient, mischievous, and unjust."

His words dropped like pebbles into a pool of water. Harriet smiled and turned to look at Alice again. She was smiling too.

When Mr Slack started using open, future-invoking words like *prophesy* and *enlarge*, just as Father did at the end of a sermon, Harriet knew he was coming to the end of his speech. In Father's church a rustle rippled around as people repositioned themselves for the next part of the service. But here, in the Parliament that governed an empire, there were guffaws. These men had no more manners than children in a playground. Harriet clenched her jaw and looked along the Liberal benches for any sign of the bill's seconder.

"The Right Honourable Member for Leicester."

"Where is he?"

"On the other side of the chamber."

"He's a Tory?"

"Yes, but one who cares deeply for working men and women."

Sir John had the languid pose of a man used to being listened to. He waited for the laughter to subside.

"While women take their places in industry side by side with men, their position is by no means secure. They receive lower wages than men, even for the same work. All must recognise the great improvement in the condition of working men since the establishment of trades unions, and probably all would agree that improvement would not have been secured if the members of trades unions had not been endowed with the vote."

This high-class gentleman was arguing for equality for working men and women in a way that Harriet had recently declared to be impossible. Perhaps she should rethink. But she still couldn't see how equal pay could work in the lace industry.

"Women," Sir John spread his arms from his sides as if to encompass everyone, "want the same chance in life as men, and while they do the same work and furnish a large proportion of the labour supply of the country, there can be no reason why they should be denied political rights. The question is not so much that the franchise should be extended but that there should be equality, that one worker should not be denied what is given to another."

His heart was big, this man. But wasn't this far too radical? Sir John was effectively proposing suffrage for all the working classes. Mrs Pankhurst had made a good point about not trying to achieve too much at once in this Conservative House.

"In the past," Sir John continued, "There were great men in the Conservative Party who were not slow to recognise the aspirations of democracy. I hope that the species is not yet extinct and that the next great measure for electoral reform might come from this side and that it might embrace the modest extension of the franchise suggested in the bill."

Harriet looked at Alice. "That's hopeful then."

"No," Alice said, with a sigh, "it means that he knows our bill has little chance of achieving its second reading, but he hopes the government will take it up."

"What does that mean? I've been trying to work it out all afternoon."

"It means the government makes it part of their business for the parliament. They put it on the list of things they are going to do. That's what the King's Speech is every year, the list of proposed government legislation. The government has lots of time to debate its own bills."

The Speaker called on the Right Honourable Member for Northampton.

"Oh, not Labouchère."

"Yes, again. We have a little less than an hour left. We'll listen to him fill it up with objection after objection. Objections for which the Speaker will have to allow time."

Mr Labouchère tucked his thumbs in his waistcoat, pushing back his coat and emphasising his portly frame. Harriet groaned. She was taking a dislike to the gentleman.

Addressing Sir John, he said, "The right honourable gentleman knows full well that there is a difference between women and men in mental equipment. In domestic matters women are much more useful than men, and in certain little trades they might be able to give points to men. But in the consideration of the great problems that come before the Imperial Parliament they are certainly inferior intellectually. Women are nervous, emotional, and have very little sense of proportion. Every man knows what it is to argue with a woman. I have given it up."

"What a horrible little man," Harriet whispered behind her hand as the chamber once again rocked with laughter.

"It is only a few women with masculine minds who take an interest in politics and desire to have votes."

Perhaps she had a masculine mind, by this man's definition, indulging, as she did, in scientific classification, and cricket, and cycling long distances. But Gwen and Emma also wanted to vote, and there was no-one in all this world more feminine that Emma. And Mother wanted to vote. Mother, the epitome of womanhood. And why was she analysing what this man was saying? It was all incoherent nonsense.

"I want freedom for men. I am not going to be crushed under the dominion of women. I am a follower of John Knox, who wrote of the horrible regiment of women."

John Knox! Harriet couldn't imagine anyone less like an ascetic Calvinist than the plump, nattily dressed Labouchère, although he did seem to share Knox's ability to talk forever. Anyway, Knox's famous pamphlet was *The Monstrous Regiment of Women,* which meant unnatural regime or rule, not a horrible army. And Knox had been out of favour with Queen Elizabeth ever after. The Labouchère man was ignorant as well as obnoxious.

Another man stood.

"The Right Honourable Member for Hackney South."

"I, for once, am in full agreement with the Honourable Member for Northampton."

"Why doesn't somebody who disagrees with him interrupt him?"

Alice sighed, "Because that would use up time, and time is what this bill lacks. Nobody is trying to convince anybody of anything here, Harriet. One side wants a division, a vote on the bill, and the other doesn't. If there were a vote it would pass. We have fifteen minutes left."

Labouchère was on his feet again. "Is my right honourable friend, the member for St. Albans suggesting that there should be women judges and women advocates and women members of parliament?"

Why not? Why not women MPs? Harriet hadn't considered the idea before, but now it seemed a very good one. Perhaps if there were, they could change the rules that resulted in this travesty, this pretence of debate.

Mr Slack stood, and the Speaker gave him the floor.

"I am not in favour of assisting you to talk the bill out."

"Talking it out? Is it really supposed that a measure of this tremendous importance can be voted upon after a discussion of a mere two hours? Does it seem desirable to turn this venerable and respectable Parliament into an arena with a promiscuity of sexes? I think it would be most undesirable. There are young men here. In the lobbies I have seen all sorts of political flirtations going on to get the young men's vote. As an old man, I cannot conscientiously countenance placing them or anybody else in the hands of those ladies."

Laughter. Yet again.

Harriet stamped her foot. "What does he believe we are?"

"Shh." Alice gestured towards the sign. "We will be asked to leave."

"Oh, they can shout and yell all they like but we have to shush."

Mr Bamford Slack rose again. "I ask that the question now be put."

Harriet sat forward and gripped the grille. "This is it then? This is the division?"

Alice was shaking her head.

The speaker said, "Assent withheld. It being half-past five of the clock, the debate stands adjourned."

The surrounding ladies erupted in angry conversation.

There was no need now to worry about being ejected from the gallery. Alice put her hand on Harriet's arm. "You have witnessed our bill being mocked, delayed, and thrown into an infinite sequence of future postponements. Welcome to the great fight."

Harriet stared at her, lost for words. She was so angry that she was beginning to wish Mrs Pankhurst *had* tripped up Mr Labouchère early that morning. She followed Alice out of the Ladies' Gallery, down the stairs and back to the Central Hall in time to see Mrs Pankhurst stepping up onto a sofa, shouting across the agitated crowd and calling upon all women to leave the building.

Bright sunshine hit Harriet in the face. The area ahead of her was swirling with women, who all seemed to be heading around the building to the right. She followed them and saw a wizened lady in a dusty black silk dress speaking from the top of another flight of steps.

"That's Mrs Wolstenholm-Elmy," Alice said. "She's been campaigning for women for forty years. They call her the Scourge of the Commons."

Harriet could scarcely hear little Mrs Wolstenholm-Elmy, but those standing nearest to her appeared to be hanging on every word. From behind her she heard men ordering them to disperse. She looked back. Policemen were elbowing their way through the crowd. Women flowed away from them, like a shoal of colourful fish. Ahead loomed a gigantic statue of a knight on horseback. She recognised it from when she and Will had met with Mr Yoxall. Ladies were attempting to climb onto the statue's plinth. Harriet found herself next to Sylvia Pankhurst.

"Is that Simon de Montfort?"

Sylvia laughed. "The founder of Parliament? No, but it

should be. It's Richard the First, Coeur de Lion. Don't ask me why."

Once again the police started pushing women onwards.

Sylvia whooped with excitement. "Mr Keir Hardie is here! Now we'll see the police put in their place. They can't shove an MP around."

Harriet looked where Sylvia was looking. Keir Hardie? The famous, one and only, Labour MP? The Keir Hardie who didn't wear the traditional Parliamentary garb of black coat and pale trousers but dressed like a working man in his Sunday best, because he was proud of being one.

Mr Hardie, in a tweed suit, red tie and a soft hat, took the sombrely dressed Mrs Wolstenholm-Elmy by the hand and led her out of the courts of the Palace of Westminster. The crowd followed. Harriet followed too, her heart beating twice its normal pace.

Then Mrs Pankhurst addressed the crowd, leaning forward, her body starched, those violet eyes boring into Harriet's.

"Thirty-five years ago, this bill progressed further than it has today!"

Harriet was standing near great people. She loved everyone around her. She loved Alice Slack and Sylvia Pankhurst. She longed to embrace them. Only the sight of Will and Mr Bamford Slack apologising a pathway through the throng prevented her.

While Mr Slack greeted his wife, Will whispered, "Sis, you look positively green around the gills. I hate to say this, but you will have to lace your corsets less tightly if you are to take to marching around with radical women."

She loved him dearly, but sometimes he was ridiculous.

"You know nothing about corsets. My corsets support me, they don't hinder me. Have you ever known me not keep up with you because of corsets? You have some peculiar ideas about underwear."

"Sorry! Forget I said anything about corsets. When did you last drink? Either of you? Mrs Slack looks tired out. Perhaps Mr Slack and I can find you somewhere to have tea."

Harriet was indeed light-headed, but there was power coursing through her veins and she wanted to stay and listen to speeches. She could out-walk, out-bike and out-bowl Will. He didn't get to tell her that she seemed worn out. But she looked over at Alice, who, pale and leaning on her parasol, did look like she desperately needed refreshment, and Mr Slack was occupied, surrounded by admiring women all wishing to talk to him.

She said, "It seems Mr Slack may be here for some time, so, little brother, do you know of a nearby teahouse?"

Will offered Mrs Slack his arm. Harriet walked behind them for a hundred yards before looking back at the towering Palace of Westminster and its exuberant decoration. The magnificent Mother of all Parliaments was smudged with soot from the dirty London air. It could, she thought, do with a thorough cleaning, outside and in.

Chapter 4
Daughters

June 1905

The maid was halfway down the stairs. "Wait, Miss Harriet. Wait. Mrs Loxley wants to see you in the Morning Room."

Harriet walked back along the hall.

"Your younger sisters too, Miss Harriet. Do you know where they are?"

"You're in luck, Mabel. They are already in the Morning Room. I just left them. I was about to take the boys for a long walk. I'll go and tell them to play in the garden for a while."

"I'll do that."

"No, no. I'm sure you have other things to do. I have my outdoor clothes on. I'll do it."

Gwen and Emma were sitting together on the Morning Room sofa, Emma telling Gwen about a design she had drawn for a house-frock, in vieux-rose cloth mixed with palest grey velvet and faux old lace. Harriet unbuttoned her coat and walked over to the window behind them. Eleanor's boys were chasing each other round the ancient oak in the centre of the lawn. Fat black rain clouds drifted across the sky. Harriet raised herself up and down on her toes, one hand in her coat pocket twisting a button on her gloves.

Doctor Bardhill was with Eleanor. Was poor Nell going to lose this baby too, the third in five years? Nell had been unwell for such a long time. Secure in her role as older sister, she had always been bossy, but she used to be majestic with it. These days she was mostly fractious. Harriet had snapped back several times. She had found herself less patient with domestic quarrels since she had returned from London, less able to accept things for what they were. She apologised, of course, and offered to take the boys off Eleanor's hands. But wandering the lanes and fields around Lenton was less absorbing than it used to be. She wanted to be in London with people like Alice Slack and Sylvia Pankhurst.

Not that Sylvia Pankhurst was in London at the moment. She was in Manchester, speaking to great crowds at the fairs that were held when the factories closed for their summer breaks. She wrote of standing on chairs and boxes and attracting an audience, of boos and jeers and ribald laughter because she suggested a woman might vote.

The door knob rattled and Harriet turned round. Her mother's expression was grim, her mouth twisted as if her face were fighting its way back into itself. The glove button came loose between Harriet's fingers. She sighed and pushed it deep into the pocket of her coat. Eleanor must have miscarried again.

Mrs Loxley hitched her dress and sat in the armchair. Gwen dropped her book onto her lap. Harriet gripped the back of the sofa. Mother sat with her hands clenched, staring at them.

When she finally spoke her voice was harsh. "Girls. Harriet, Gwen, Emma dear, I am going to find what I have to say to you exceptionally difficult and I beg you to forgive me should I stumble... or weep. Your sister will lose the baby. Doctor Bardhill left the house as I came down."

Emma gasped. Harriet folded her hands in front of her. So far, she had heard only what she had expected to hear, and it was desperately sad, but the news was not enough to explain what she had seen in her mother's face.

Mother was holding up her hand, begging them not to interrupt.

"Doctor Bardhill told me he had conducted a new test entailing study with a microscope and looking for what he called *gonococci*. He believes they might be microbes that have made Eleanor ill." Her mother choked back a sob and wiped the back of her hand across her eyes. "Doctor Bardhill thinks Nell may never successfully carry another child and is in need of an operation to take out her woman's organs. There is a sickness inside her that must be removed before it expands and kills her."

Mother stopped speaking and was staring at them again.

The silence in the room thickened and set.

God help poor Nell. A few moments ago she had been the big sister, reliably ever present, even if unwell and saddened by the loss of yet another baby. Now, she might be dying. And surgery? It meant cutting through the peritoneum. It was done, but it was dangerous.

"Surgery, Mother? To remove her womb, and possibly her ovaries and Fallopian tubes? Where will Doctor Bardhill have her go for something that complex?"

Her mother blinked twice and for a moment Harriet thought she wasn't going to answer. Then she wiped a finger across her eyes and said, "Edinburgh. It's a great centre for the latest techniques. It's where Doctor Bardhill's son is studying."

"Don't worry, Mother, a lot has been learned about keeping

surgery clean and sterile. And there is chloroform. She will feel nothing."

"Don't worry, Harriet! She could die with the surgery. And she could die without it. Yes, she could!" Her mother wiped her eyes again. Her voice dropped into a deeper level of anger and fear. "Doctor Bardhill will send her away to Edinburgh and she may never come back."

She flung her hands over her face.

Emma got up and knelt at her mother's side, laying her head on her knee. Gwen fidgeted. She was uncannily silent and seemed exposed without Emma at her side. Harriet moved round the sofa and sat beside her.

Emma shuddered, her narrow shoulders shaking.

Gwen said, "Is it a spreading thing, these microbes? Is it a thing only women can get? Can we catch it?"

Maria Loxley drew breath, as nosily as an engine sucking back its own steam. She let her hands drop into her lap. Her face was blotched and angry.

"These are particular microbes that can pass from a man to a woman when they lie together."

No-one spoke.

Harriet remembered how she had told them, in this very room, of the intimacies of the marriage bed. How she had said she didn't want her daughters to encounter their future husbands in a state of ignorance and, perhaps not seeking to do it four times over, had informed her three youngest daughters all at once. Emma had been fourteen, and Gwen sixteen, but Harriet had been twenty and if the details of the mechanics of sexual congress had been a surprise to her sisters they were not to her. On the other hand, Mother saying that the habitual bodily expression of love had a deep effect in perfecting the spiritual union that must be the foundation of a lasting marriage had opened a door into thoughts quite unexpected. Harriet had been uncertain about what to do with such knowledge. Now she half-lifted a hand, as if she were still at a school biology lesson.

"It's the closeness of the sexual act that allows the disease to pass from person to person, isn't it, Mother? That being the case, we can't catch it. It's awful to think it, but Nell must have it from Wesley. But where does Wesley get it from? Where can such a disease start? And why isn't he sick?"

Why wasn't he sick? Why should Eleanor be the one suffering? Blue-eyed Wesley. That uncontrollable flirt. That seeker of smiles, with his gifts of ribbons and bows. Eleanor's husband, whom Eleanor loved devotedly. Whose existence made her act superior to Harriet, who had never yet found any man as interesting as her own two brothers.

What sort of a world was it where such microbes existed? Did a God who loved every little thing, including the sparrows in the eaves, also love these vicious microbes? Or were they the work of the devil, spawned in the semen of a man? It was a horrific thought, but only the devil's work could make innocent Nell suffer so.

Gwen said, in a tone that resembled the growl of a chained dog, "Sounds to me like the sources are men in general and Wesley in particular."

You could always trust Gwen to say what others thought better to leave unsaid.

Mother sighed. "Doctor Bardhill says the sources are loose women, mistresses and serving girls, but mostly prostitutes."

Did Wesley have a lover for all the times Eleanor was ill? Harriet felt her face flushing in response to her thoughts. Gwen's dark complexion had revealed no embarrassment, if she experienced any.

Harriet said, "If Wesley is the source of the plague in our house, why skip over him to blame some other woman?"

Mother pulled her back straight and raised a finger, a

familiar gesture. "Harriet, Gwendolyn, I don't know where you learned to be so forthright but please keep those sentiments between these walls."

Harriet glanced at Gwen then turned back to face her mother. "We learned it from you, Mother. Except we say it more directly."

"Well, then, the disease is called gonorrhoea and I want you to know of it. Doctor Bardhill will tell Wesley he must go to a special clinic and not lie with Eleanor until he declares him free of the disease. Your father and Robert will be told. They will talk with Wesley. He will remain part of this family and care for his wife, but he will not touch her until Doctor Bardhill gives him a clean bill of health. He must stay at Loxley Hall until he is allowed back at the vicarage. And I have decided that when any of you girls receive a proposal of marriage your father will insist your suitor undergoes a medical check. Men can be sick and think they have recovered but still carry the disease. As I said, the doctors can now see the infectious microbes and offer treatment."

Harriet couldn't help but smile, despite the horror of the situation. "Does Father know this?"

Before her mother could answer, Emma spoke, and although Harriet could not see her face, she was certain the tears were set to tumble over the ledges of her eyelids.

"Does poor Nell even know about the horrid microbes? Will you tell her, Mother? She loves Wesley so much."

Mother raised her hand. Authority was returning. "We will tell Eleanor it is her appendix. Since the King had his operation, everyone knows of the danger of an inflamed appendix. Eleanor does not need the shame of public discussion. And you, Gwendolyn, Harriet, will do her the kindness of sparing her, whatever your own modern opinions."

Mother's face had resumed its customary calm. It was the

competent face that greeted the parish every day. It was the face, Harriet presumed, that would inform Father of his new duties.

Mother said, "It will break her heart, of course, and she will probably believe the wound from her appendix being removed is the cause. But better a broken heart than knowledge that leaves her feeling sullied and impure."

Gwen stood up and stamped her foot, for all the world like a toddler having a tantrum but with a frighteningly adult gleam in her eyes. "I will never marry. Father need undertake no embarrassing conversations for me. Emma and I are going to design fashions together. We will not depend on men."

Harriet rose and put a hand on Emma's shoulder. "You are formidable, Mother." She didn't take her eyes from her mother's as she continued, "You see, Gwen, what Mother means is Robert and Father will know all about Wesley and his deeds, and, if he doesn't do exactly as they say, so will Uncle George. And then where would Wesley be? Not about to inherit a share of the Loxley Lace business from Uncle George anymore. I can guarantee that."

Emma stood and said, "I'm going to make sure Nell has everything she needs. I'll ask for tea to be taken to her room."

Gwen laid a hand on Harriet's. "May I walk out with you and the boys?"

"Of course. Do you want to walk too, Mother?"

"I would very much like to. I almost desperately need to. But I have to talk to your father."

Harriet waited for Gwen in the garden, one ear tuned to the prattle of Charley and Bobby. They were poking at something with sticks, something out of her view in the flower border. She didn't want to know what dead, living, or disgusting thing they were stirring up. It could be a frog. They were fascinated by frogs. They'd be tapping at it with the stick in order to make it jump. Boys should be taught to leave defenceless animals alone. She should be rescuing the frog from their attentions. She should be training them to observe with respect, and to love God's creatures.

At what point did the forgivable and correctable curiosity of the boy-child turn into the self-centred arrogance of the man? Until an hour ago she had loved the boys' father as a brother, even if his opinions often irritated her. What could lead a man to need gratification so much that it overrode his promises to his wife? She had been there when Wesley made his marriage vows, before God. Forsaking all others. He had said it and Eleanor had said it. What would Wesley's reaction be if Eleanor decided to avail herself of other men?

Appalled that she could even imagine such a thing, Harriet shivered and started walking around the edge of the lawn. What would her new acquaintances, Alice Slack and the Pankhursts, do in Eleanor's situation? Alice's husband, Bamford, was a Methodist preacher. The thought of him being unfaithful was like thinking the same of her father. Something not to be countenanced. Sylvia Pankhurst, who she was writing to regularly, seemed to have no interest in men, which made her letters all the more compelling, for being free of talk of them. Her mother, a widow, also seemed to have no desire to re-marry. And Sylvia's elder sister, Christabel, was studying for a law degree.

The men in the House of Commons had spoken of women as if they were a race apart; as if they were lesser beings, like pets in a household. More than that. They had brayed their contempt, secure in the knowledge that the world was theirs.

Wesley, who had done his own share of braying when it came to opposing women voting, had been welcomed into their house, where all were respected. He had acted like he was one of them and all the while he had been lying, deceiving and betraying trust.

Gwen appeared, carrying two umbrellas. She was shaking, as if she had swallowed down all her moral outrage and failed to digest it. Harriet knew how she felt; she felt the same herself.

They walked until the boys ran ahead, when Harriet broke the silence. "What took you so long?"

"Wesley has books with names like *The Memoirs of Dolly Morton* and *Nell in Bridewell* hidden in his desk. Women having their bare buttocks spanked. There are pictures. Men fully clothed and women naked. It's definitely things respectable women don't do that make our Wesley happy."

Gwen poking around in Wesley's private desk? Did she think the level of his wrongdoing excused any of hers? Eleanor couldn't have known. She would never look in Wesley's desk. But she was no shrinking violet. If she had seen those books, she would have removed and destroyed them. Suppose the boys found them?

Harriet pushed aside her impulse to admonish Gwen and indulged her desire to pin down Wesley's sin. "It's a mistress." She stared at the boys running ahead of her and not at Gwen. "Or prostitutes. Someone prepared to be insulted in return for money... or desperate."

How could Wesley live a double life and not split down the middle? What did he think of when he went to his wife's bed?

"Do you think he goes to the Narrow Marsh for it, Harry? The prostitutes in the Narrow Marsh lean against the walls of the lodging houses, lifting their skirts to show their ankles, and beckoning men into the doorways, but I think doorways is as far as they get."

"That's horrible... And how on earth do you know?"

"The Narrow Marsh is the quickest way to walk to the lace manufactory."

Such a shocking revelation obliged Harriet to resume the part of the older sister. "I don't think you should be walking through the Narrow Marsh. Would you like me to ask Father to provide you with the tram fare?" She paused. "I doubt Wesley goes to the Narrow Marsh. I imagine he likes his pleasures in comfort... indoors."

Gwen half-laughed. "You are wicked, Harry."

Gwen kicked a stone along the path for a while, then said, "It is horrible in the Marshes. But it's brave too, in its way. The women there are always cleaning. You see them scrubbing the streets outside their doorways. Uncle George has given me the money for the tram, but I'm saving it for when Emma and I have our little business. He had Wesley walk me to the tram stop the first day he found out. And, Harry, I had to wait for Wesley to get back from his long lunch. He didn't return until four. Emma and I should be taking over that manufactory from Uncle George, not Robert and Wesley."

That idea was so startling that all Harriet could think to say was, "What's wrong with Robert?"

"Nothing, he just has no fashion sense. Lace won't always be in. The Loxley family needs to look ahead. We need to employ talent. Like Emma. And we need somebody in the family who can watch the books. Siphoning money off from the boss is everywhere in big manufactories. Businesses fail because of it."

"And that someone is you?"

"I'm learning. Uncle George is going to send me to book-keeping classes."

There was a commotion ahead and then little Bobby was running towards them crying, his knee scraped and bleeding. Harriet brushed away the grit with her hand, pulled out her handkerchief, spat, and rubbed vigorously. Bobby's tears petered out in a series of whimpers.

"Can I hold the brolly?"

He ran ahead, triumph at acquiring the umbrella pumping through his sturdy legs.

She called after him, "It's not for poking things, or your brother."

She took Gwen's arm and pulled her close. "Tell me more about your plans with Emma. This is all news to me. Surely you'll need more investment than a few saved tram fares."

There were splashes on the ground ahead and she held out her hand, palm up. "Bobby, Charley, it's starting to rain! We need to head for home. Bring back that umbrella!"

Chapter 5
Deeds Not Words

October 1905

The early October weather was glorious and Mother had decided the family should meet in the garden for tea. Mrs Sheffield had strawberry jam remaining from the summer and the smell of baking had been drifting through the house all afternoon. Harriet took a cloth outside and laid it on the table under the Brambly Apple.

She looked up to see Emma coming down the garden path with a cushion under one arm and Eleanor leaning on the other. Eleanor was dressed in a white tea gown with a high lace collar and a blue sash around the waist. It was over three months since her surgery, six weeks since she had been fit enough to return home from the Edinburgh nursing home where she had been cared for. She had been downstairs, reading and sewing until retiring straight after dinner, but she had not ventured outside before this. Walking this far was clearly a laboured business. But she was alive. That was a lot to be grateful for. And Wesley wasn't here. They could keep Eleanor to themselves.

"I thought I'd join you all," Eleanor said, as she reached the table. "Take advantage of this wonderful Indian Summer, and of those rambunctious boys of mine being away with their friends. When are you picking them up, Harry?"

"At six. I'll leave at half-past five. We'll get the tram part of the way back."

"Thank you, dear Harry. Wesley promised to be here for dinner tonight. He will have time to see them before their bedtime."

Harriet took care to keep her face serene. She had heard from Will, who had heard from Robert, that there had been a noisy scene when Wesley was confronted by her father and Robert. Since returning from the clinic he had been obliged to attend, he had been living at Loxley Hall, and he had been devilish moody. Being in the daily presence of Uncle George should have reminded him of the consequences of reverting to any of his former ways but it didn't seem to have made him good company. Maybe there was a way she could avoid dinner.

Gwen was walking towards them now. Still in her striped blouse, bottle-green skirt and boater, she must have come straight from the manufactory. She was grinning like a cat who had finally found the mouse hole.

She sat next to Harriet and whispered, "I have news. Secret news, for us only. Uncle George mustn't find out I've stolen his thunder. He is going to announce that he has set up a trust for our benefit, for the benefit of all his nieces. That means an income for each of us, to use as we want, as soon as we are twenty-one, or earlier if it's for education."

Harriet stared at her. Gwen's audacity in upstaging Uncle George was one thing. Her uncle's action was quite another. Depending on the sums involved it could mean anything from never having to ask Father for painting supplies again to the freedom to invent a life of her own. Go to London. Be near Will. Visit the Pankhursts in Manchester. Anything.

"How much a year, Gwen?"

"I don't know. I haven't seen the trust. I only..." she glanced nervously at Eleanor, "...overheard a conversation."

"You mean," Eleanor repositioned her cushion, "That you've been listening behind doors, again. Eavesdroppers never hear anything good about themselves."

Harriet was on Gwen's side when it came to overhearing. "You know it's the only way we find out about what's happening in our own lives, Nell. The men never tell us anything."

"Well, I for one am going to wait to find out until Uncle George tells us himself. His kindness and generosity should be respected enough for him to be allowed to make his own announcements." Eleanor fiddled with the fringe of her shawl and sighed. "I think I'll go back inside and lie down for a while."

"Oh no, Nell!" Gwen jumped up from her seat. "Don't go! Emma has some special news for us too. You have to wait for that."

Emma ran back up the path, calling out, "Back in a minute. I'm going to fetch my portfolio. I want to show you all my collection before the tea things arrive."

Eleanor leaned back in her chair and closed her eyes. Her face was drawn and sallow. At twenty-eight years old, after bearing two children and losing four others, Harriet's sister looked twice her age. She hoped the fashionable plump cheeks Eleanor had taken such pride in would return, for her sake.

Gwen said, "Walk round the garden with me, Harry. There are some pretty flowers I can't name. I'm sure you can."

Harriet turned towards her and raised her eyebrows. Gwen had never expressed any interest in plants and all that was blooming in October was Michaelmas Daisies. Gwen jerked her head to the side. Harriet stood and followed her along the path and into the side garden.

"Don't blurt out anything when you see Emma's drawings."

"Am I likely to?"

"You did tell us to stop going into the Narrow Marsh, after, you know, what happened."

What had happened had occurred back in the summer. Harriet had been in the hallway when Gwen and Emma had burst through the front door together, panting and flushed.

Harriet took Emma's satchel from her shoulder. "For heaven's sake, what is the matter? Sit down on the settle, both of you. Get your breath back."

After a few moments of standing in front of them, hands on hips, she said, "Tell me the truth."

Emma looked at her nervously, Gwen defiantly.

Harriet dropped her arms to her sides and tried to smile. "I promise not to tell anyone."

Emma lowered her gaze and looked at the floor. "I went into a court, Harry. The view around the corner, the way the buildings were angled, was enticing. Right in front of me there was a man holding a woman up against a wall, her feet clear off the ground and her skirts pulled up around her waist. I stepped backwards. Then there were these hands around *my* waist. Thank heavens Gwen was there."

Gwen said, "Emma won't repeat it, but I will. *Aye-up, my pretty. I reckons thou likes it up the back end best, eh?* That's what I heard the filthy cur saying, Harry. A foul purring gurgle. I'll never forget that sound. I stuck my brolly in the soft part of his back. You never heard such a screech. He must have thought I was about to run him through."

Emma put her hands over her eyes. "Harry, I could smell his rotten breath and something like a hard metal case pressing through my behind skirts. I thought I was living my last few seconds on earth."

Harriet stared, first at one sister, then the other. "Oh, my

God. You can't keep doing this. Think what might have happened. You have to stop going into the Narrow Marsh."

Emma lifted her head and looked her in the eye. "No, Harry, I need those sketches. I have to be near those people. I have to feel the warmth of the sun on the setts in the street. I have to smell the dishwater thrown across the stone. I have to see the glistening of the light on the water as it runs away. Don't you understand?"

Harriet had understood the determination in Emma's voice, if not the attraction of her subject, and she had agreed to keep quiet about their wanderings, as long as they promised to stay together.

After the incident she had taken Emma aside and explained the nature of the hard case. *Up the back end* had been too much, even for her scientific attitude.

Now she said, "So Emma's been going into the Narrow Marsh to get studies for her portfolio. I hope you sharpened the point of your umbrella."

"I stay close, all the time, Harry. We don't go down any dark alleys. The women around there are starting to recognise us. I don't think we'll be mistaken for prostitutes again."

"I can't imagine why you were in the first place. Not everything is predictable, Gwen. You need to be careful."

Harriet caught sight of Emma leaving the house with her portfolio under her arm. "We'd best be getting back."

"And you won't say anything in front of Nell? She might tell Father."

"I promise."

"Say Emma got the pictures at the manufactory, or outside it."

"I said I'd play along, didn't I?"

Harriet frowned. Deception was taking up residence in the space between the three of them and Eleanor. They already knew things about her, and her husband, that she didn't know herself. Now they were embarking on another deceit.

Emma pushed back the cloth Harriet had spread on the table and put down the unwieldy portfolio. She started laying out a series of drawings and pastels. "My drawing master says I should apply to the Slade School of Art. I might even get a scholarship. You said your friend Sylvia Pankhurst got a scholarship to the Royal Academy of Arts, didn't you, Harry?"

Emma had changed in the last six months. She seemed to have grown six inches, which Harriet knew was not possible, but she was now the tallest of the four of them. She also had a confidence that had not been there before. Was it escaping school, putting up her hair, art lessons, or spending so much time with Gwen? Harriet didn't know.

In front of her now were scenes of Nottingham workers, renderings of daily life that said, *look at me, I am real.* Would the drawing masters at the Slade dismiss the subject of Emma's work as repugnant? They would be fools if they did. Emma had touched on truth.

Harriet looked up. Emma's head was still bent over her portfolio but Gwen was looking straight at her. Harriet nodded her head. "Those are incredible, Emma. You've caught the life within those people."

Emma gathered the drawings into a pile and laid out another sheet, larger than the rest. A pastel; a portrait of a naked woman looking into a cheval mirror. Harriet caught the sensuality and gasped. Eleanor leaned forward to look. Emma was working hard to maintain her confident smile.

The mirror was angled so that the viewer saw little of the woman from the front and what was visible was blurred, but from the back she was beautiful, her buttocks rising to rosy, her figure proud, her spine showing bony as she held her hair up.

The tops of her thighs were imperfect. They had a grainy look. She stood proudly, like she knew she was being watched.

Harriet said, "You can't show that to anyone. How did you ever get to do it?"

Eleanor smiled. "It's wonderful."

"You like it?"

"Don't you?" Eleanor looked straight at Harriet and smiled more broadly. "Of course, you can never show it to anyone, Emma. It is most unladylike to paint flesh like that. Ladies have to work from plaster models. Do they not?"

"It's changing, Nell. The Slade has always let women paint from life. Now, even without drapes. Lady painters don't sit with the men. It's quite decorous."

Harriet looked from one sister to another. Something was wrong here. Eleanor's eyes were twinkling. Harriet would have been overjoyed to see her so happy were it not that she suspected she was the source of her amusement.

Eleanor said, "Don't you recognise the sitter, Harry?"

Harriet stared at the picture. The model's face was not visible. The technique was extraordinarily good. She could not draw like that. The woman's hair, where she was holding it up, was a lustrous chestnut. Her rosy body was not young and unspoiled, but neither was it old, more like used, or better, worked. She was quite thin, but not slim and tender. She was actually rather stringy.

Harriet recognised the cheval mirror. There was a carved rose at the top.

"Oh, Nell? You?" Harriet sat down. "Very funny!"

Emma was laughing. "So, will you apply to the Slade with me, Harry? Your botanical drawings are wonderful and Father is much less likely to object if we go together."

A whole future seemed to open up. A way to get up to London, using the income from that trust perhaps. Then she looked at Emma's work spread in front of her and thought of her own. "I will. But it won't do you any good. Because I won't get in."

Emma stopped laughing and gave her a serious look. "Will you at least try, Harry?"

"Don't underestimate Mother and Father." Eleanor leant back against her cushions. "They only want us to be safe. If you two stick together, you should be safe. By the way, Mother and Father are walking down the path."

Emma cleared her portfolio off the table and headed back towards the house with it. Harriet's father settled himself on the bench next to her. When Emma returned he drew a piece of newsprint from his jacket pocket and unfolded it.

"An old friend in Oldham has forwarded me a clipping from the Manchester Guardian. I thought my five ladies would find it most interesting. It concerns the Pankhursts."

"Pankhurst?" Mother said. "That's the name of the suffrage ladies you met in London, isn't it, Harriet?"

Her father flicked the cutting with his fingernail. "That, I surmise, is why Grimshaw has sent me this. I mentioned Harriet meeting these Pankhursts to him. In case he knew them."

Harriet put down her scone. She was pretty certain she knew what this news was. Sylvia had written to her about events at the Manchester Free-Trade Hall that might not reflect well on the Pankhurst family. She had rather hoped her parents would not find out.

"I met Mrs Emmeline Pankhurst and Miss Sylvia Pankhurst."

"Listen," her father said. "*Arising out of the scenes towards the close of the Liberal meeting held on Friday night in the Free-Trade Hall, Miss Christabel Pankhurst, of Manchester, and Miss Annie Kenney, the latter an Oldham lady, appeared as defendants at the Manchester Police Court, on Saturday, charged with assaulting the police and also causing an obstruction in South-Street.* What do you make of that, eh?"

Mother gasped, "Assaulting the police? How dreadful."

"I'm afraid to say Miss Pankhurst spat at a policeman."

Harriet had to avoid leaving Christabel spitting as the final image of the conversation. "Miss Christabel is the elder Pankhurst sister. You know how shamefully the women's bill was treated in May. Well, the suffrage societies have been working hard since then to get the government, or the Liberals, who will surely be in power soon, to take up our cause. The Pankhursts have also been trying to make it a resolution of the Independent Labour Party. But everywhere, in all parties, there are men who dismiss women as unimportant. Even Mr Yoxall told me he has little time for the affairs of the ladies, as if we are a minority cause, not half the population of the country. It's as if we are not human at all. Men pay more attention to their dogs and their horses."

She looked sideways at her father and he raised his eyebrows. Perhaps she had been a little zealous in quoting things she had been reading in Sylvia's letters.

Emma was wide-eyed. "Did Miss Christabel just walk up to a policeman and spit at him? That does sound rather horrible."

Sylvia had provided Harriet with the events of that evening. "No, she didn't. The two ladies went to a political meeting, where Sir Edward Grey was speaking, and they tried to ask a question about whether a Liberal government would support women's suffrage. They were silenced by the stewards and told to put the question to the platform in writing. They did, and it was ignored, so they stood on their chairs and held up a banner. Then they were removed from the meeting. Not very gently."

"But why spit?" Mother sounded affronted by the idea.

"To get themselves arrested for assault without actually hurting anyone, their hands were restrained and they couldn't slap the policeman. And that gave Christabel the chance to make statements in court. She is training to be a lawyer."

"Ah, yes, it says that here," Father held up his newspaper clipping. "I wonder why. She can never practise the law, as a woman."

"Well," Mother put down her teacup. "I am in favour of the cause, as you well know, Harriet, but that young lady will have to defend that action for many months to come. She's not as clever as she thinks she is."

Harriet didn't know how clever Christabel Pankhurst was, but if her mother and sister were anything to go by it was very clever indeed.

"Mother, you know women have been campaigning for the vote for years, for generations. Did you ever see as many lines in the paper before?"

Eleanor said, "What was on the banner?"

"Votes for Women."

Eleanor smiled. "That is very good. Votes not suffrage. Suffrage sounds so much like suffering. We women suffer far too much."

Harriet smiled back at her. "It's a marvellously simple and clever slogan, isn't it Nell?"

Chapter 6
Crocus Nudiflorus

December 1905

H arriet moved to where she could catch the light from the window and read the letter from Sylvia she had received that morning. She had been in correspondence with both Sylvia Pankhurst and Alice Slack ever since the talking out of the women's bill in May. Over the Christmas period, before the January election, Alice had been working to get her husband re-elected in St. Albans and Sylvia had been pushing the women's cause at meetings in Manchester.

My Dear Harriet,
What a tale I have to tell of men's determination not to let us be heard. Two days ago I was at Churchill's first meeting, at a schoolroom in Cheetham Hill, Manchester. Everyone was firing off questions. I called out mine, "Will a Liberal government give women the vote?" He hedged and hummed and hawed and ignored me, so I repeated my question several times. My brother and other Labour party men at the back of the hall started yelling and there was such a clamour that Churchill could not be heard

himself. I stood, and there was silence, but when I asked my question he still ignored it. The room burst out with shouting and yelling again, and to restore order the chairman asked me to come up to the platform to put my question, which I did. When I turned to go, Churchill seized my arm and pushed me down onto a chair, saying, "You must wait until you've heard what I have to say." Which was that I was bringing disgrace on the honoured Pankhurst name by interrupting him and that nothing would induce him to vote for giving women the franchise.

Then, listen to this, instead of being allowed to return to the hall, I was dragged into a room by two of the men on the platform. They locked me in. Kidnapped me in effect! But I climbed out of a window and somebody brought a chair which I mounted and then I told a fine audience in the street what had happened. The whole story got into the next morning's press and there were innumerable jokes made at Churchill's expense.

Stand firm!

Votes for Women!

Sylvia's adventure must have been in the Manchester papers but not the London or Nottingham ones. Harriet had not seen it in The Times. This morning all she had read about was free-trade and export duties.

She shivered. Despite the coals glowing in the grate, the Morning Room was far from warm. Outside, where rain poured from a leaden sky, the country was in the throes of a general election campaign. She had asked to go about with Will, working to get Mr Yoxall re-elected. But her father had thought it inappropriate for a vicar's daughter to be partisan. Although the same sensibility didn't seem to have applied to the vicar's son.

She looked at her mother, sitting by the other window, wearing her house frock and an old-fashioned mobcap that extended to the edges of her face. An old shawl covered her knees and a stack of newly washed bed linen lay to one side of her, her wicker sewing-basket sat at the other.

"Mother, why don't you sit by the fire? It's draughty by the window."

"I need the light to sew." Her mother held up the pillowcase she was mending. "See how the lace trim on this is torn."

"Are there no visitors expected today?"

"It's not likely in this weather, now is it? And if there should be, I'll leave to have my hair dressed while you receive them. You look neatly turned out, as always."

Harriet entertained a few uncharitable thoughts about sitting and conversing with the ladies of the parish, circled the room and stopped in front of the wall covered with her mother's watercolours, many of them views of the meadows by the River Trent blanketed with the purple haze of crocuses. Her mother's paintings were either detailed landscapes with backgrounds of the city skyline and the castle hill or they were swathes of shining purples that were more colour than form. They called to mind the copies of the modern French works that Harriet's painting teacher had shown her, practice pieces from his years as a student in Paris. He called her own studies of the Nottingham crocuses fine technical work. She pushed the memory aside. She had agreed to apply to the Slade with Emma. She needed to have confidence in herself.

"Mother? The crocuses that grow in Nottingham are crocus nudiflorus and crocus vernus. Did you paint them both? Which pictures are of the autumn crocuses?"

"They are the ones where there are large fields that look like lakes. They were so joyful, the September crocuses. They opened their faces wide to the remaining sun. And those long stamens. Those three golden threads, especially in an evening light. I was very young when I painted those, much younger

than you are now. They are all gone. The railway houses covered the fields."

"Three stamens? Flowering in September? I've seen them,
Mother. They are not all gone. They have no leaves? Yes?"

Her mother smiled. "Children used to call them *naked
boys*."

"I have something to show you."

Harriet hurried from the Morning Room and ran up to the
second landing and her room. She pulled her portfolio of plant
studies from under her bed and went back downstairs more
sedately.

Mrs Loxley put aside her sewing and Harriet put her portfolio on her knee. She turned through the papers until she found
the one labelled Crocus Nudiflorus.

"I found them in a corner of the General Cemetery. See,
pure purple at the edges of the petals, fading to white in the
centre and three reddish-gold stamens. That's your flower.
There are some still."

"Oh, Harriet. When I was a girl, they used to cover all the
land between the Castle Rock and the river. What have we
done to God's creation?"

"Mother?"

"I feel guilty, Harriet. We have a comfortable life because of
the manufactories. But so many hands employed need so many
houses and where there were once fields of flowers there are
brick-filled streets. And what do we create out of God's bounty?
Lace. Frippery. What a waste my time on this earth has been."

Harriet stared at her drawing resting on her mother's knee.
Had her mother once felt as trapped within the four walls of
domesticity as Harriet did today? Did she still? Harriet looked
up. Tears in her mother's eyes reflected strangely red in the fire-
light. Those eyes were seeing something far away, or deep
inside.

"But Mother, lace is beautiful. And the hands have work, and homes. And our family performs many good works. And you are a model vicar's wife, tending to the parishioners and caring for the poor."

"We are part of the Loxley manufacturing family, Harriet. We are cogs in the great machine of industry. No clergyman has ever lived in comfort without patronage or family money behind him. You know, this town used to be surrounded by open land. There were meadows to the south, the common grazing, and there were the great estates at Colwick and Wollaton and, of course, the Duke's house atop the Castle Rock and his deer park below. It was divinely beautiful, once."

Her mother took up her needle again and Harriet removed the portfolio from her lap and put it on the sofa.

Her mother didn't pause in her reminiscing. "I begged my father to use his influence to save some part of the Meadows and leave at least one field of crocuses. He was a man of position in the town, and a man of means, but he wouldn't do it. And I was a mere girl with no money of my own and no influence. I thought about going down to the Meadows to collect crocus bulbs, to where they were digging the foundations of the houses and laying the railway tracks. But I never did. It would have been too eccentric, too outrageous. I failed in courage."

Harriet walked over to look out of the window again. She imagined her mother as a lithe-limbed girl, frustrated by the piled-up streets of the town that spread ever outwards, devouring meadows and felling forests. Her mother, who had never had a bicycle of her own, had allowed Harriet to pedal around the countryside alone and stay out for hours. She had encouraged Gwen in her desire to work at the manufactory and Emma in her art. Her mother, brave in her own way, had tried to give them the wider world.

Behind her, her mother sighed. "I understand why my

father believed they had to build. He wanted better living conditions for the working people. Back when the lands around the town were protected by the old laws, and couldn't be built on, all the space in the centre turned into warehouses and the tenements of the poor. Nottingham became a place of epidemics. Repeated epidemics and repeated riots."

The town out there that her mother was describing had been a volatile and dangerous place, and in many ways it still was. Harriet remembered Gwen and Emma's encounter in the Narrow Marsh and shuddered. There might not be torch-carrying mobs running through the streets, but there were still dangers for women who wanted to walk freely.

She turned back into the room and sat by her mother. "Is there any family history about the riots? The ones that burned the castle?"

"Oh, yes. My grandfather witnessed all that. For three days the mob rushed from one part of the town to another, swinging iron bars they had pulled from railings. When they fired the castle, lead from the roof streamed in rivers down the walls and the flames shot up into the night. He said the smoke was heavy with the scent of cedar wood."

"Do you think they did it because of the Great Reform Bill, or were they just looters out for plunder, like they say?"

"I don't think it was either. They were poor working people, not the middling people who were going to get the vote because of that bill. But they had come to believe it was going to improve things for them, and the Duke of Newcastle, their duke who owned their castle and collected rents from them, was opposing it. It's not what the bill achieved that matters, it's what they hoped it was going to do and how much they hated the people who tried to stop it. They were whipped into fury by their feelings that rich and powerful men cared more about their property than about them. So, they attacked the property." She put her needle down again and looked straight at Harriet, her eyes no longer gazing into the past. "Hope dashed is a terrible thing, Harriet."

"You mean ... about Cambridge?"

The memory hurt.

Her mother lifted her eyebrows and tilted her head. "What about your interest in the franchise, Harriet? Are you going to turn it into action?"

Action was a strange word for her mother to choose, considering they had just been talking about the terror of riots. Or was her mother still thinking of her own inaction over the crocuses in the meadow? Either way, Harriet felt cornered.

"I attend meetings... in the town. I went up to London to hear the debate. I've written to Sylvia Pankhurst and Mrs Slack."

Her mother resumed her stitching. "Your uncle has given you girls opportunity. What are you going to do with it?"

Harriet watched her mother's fine needle flashing in and out, propelled by a lifetime's expertise. Her own life supporting her mother, supporting Eleanor, helping with the children, receiving guests, and visiting the workhouse seemed a useful, loving life. But she wasn't satisfied. She was restless. And her Mother seemed to know it.

"I am going to apply to art college with Emma."

Had Emma told Mother about her suggestion that Harriet apply to study art while actually seeking out a way to study biology? Did they both believe she would never get into a famous art college? She felt she was being pressed to defend a decision she hadn't yet made.

Her mother looked up from her work. "What do you want to do? For yourself?"

Harriet glanced at her portfolio lying on the sofa. Each drawing inside was carefully labelled with the Latin and common names of the plants, where she had found it, whether in sun or shade, the date and the type of soil. Could she tell her mother she wanted to do that? Not as a genteel hobby but scientifically, sharing in the great body of knowledge she knew was out there in the world. She folded her hands in front of her mouth, her thumbs against her lips, and considered what to say next.

Her mother had shared the things she cared about. Harriet was grateful for that. She owed her similar candour. She only hoped she wouldn't tell Father. Women studying sciences might be a step too far for him... and for Uncle George.

She looked towards the window, and the weather that was keeping her indoors. "I would like to study biology, and in particular botany. And, to answer you about the franchise. I very much want to be involved with the campaign for the vote in London, where Parliament is."

"And where Will is. You two were always like two peas from the same pod. I see no reason why that cannot be your plan. You have the means. You are free to use that trust income as you please. Do it. Not to please me, or your father, or Emma, or Uncle George, but because it's what you are being called to do."

Harriet, her mind swamped in surprise, looked back at her mother and saw not a small lady in a mobcap with reddened cheeks and hands showing the first signs of liver spots but a young girl standing at the edge of a muddy meadow with ribbons flying in the wind and tears of loss in her eyes.

"Oh, Mother!" Harriet swiped at a tear forming in the corner of her eye. "I don't know what to say. You don't know how much this means to me. I'm so grateful to you for saying all you have, and for supporting me... But what if Father won't agree to it?"

"When it comes to your father, it is my experience that he is more likely to agree if he is not given a choice in advance."

Harriet sat back in her chair. She had been bumped over a threshold. It felt good, if a little disconcerting.

Gwen edged through the narrow space between Harriet's bedroom door and her bed.

"Harry, can I talk to you?"

"Of course you can. But shall we go down to the Morning Room? It's cold in here."

"I'd rather we talked alone."

Harriet pulled her down to sit on the bed. Gwen was flushed. Harriet wondered if she was feverish.

"Harry, I've been studying the accounting books at Uncle George's manufactory, finding out how the entries work. For practice, I've been tracing the day-books to the double entry in the ledgers and then to the suppliers' accounts, like an auditor does, only I was doing it to see how it all fits." Gwen wrung her hands. "Harry, I think someone is stealing from the manufactory. They are inventing suppliers. It's easy to do. A false name and address and false bank account is all you need. You invent a small lace maker. You create a likely order and send back a likely enough invoice and your invented lace maker gets paid."

Harriet thought through what Gwen had said. "But the manufactory would never receive the webs of net. Someone would notice."

"Someone should notice. But if that someone is the one doing the stealing and the other someone who should notice the strange invoices doesn't—"

"Gwen. What exactly are you saying?"

"Wesley oversees the books and Robert raises the purchase orders. I don't know what to do. Suppose I'm wrong?"

Harriet frowned. Gwen was asking her for advice on a topic she barely understood. "I don't think I've followed how all this works. I thought Mr Gray, Wray, or whatever his name is, was responsible for the Loxley Lace books."

"Mr Wragg. He's the senior officer in the accounting department. He manages all the bookkeeping clerks. The bookkeeping clerks make the entries in the day-books and the ledgers. Mr Wragg reports to Wesley. But Wesley's main job is sales. He doesn't spend much time on accounting."

"I'm sorry. Explain it to me again. What is a purchase order and how is Robert involved?"

"The webs of net are ordered by the production manager. He writes a request to Robert's purchasing department, which writes a purchase order. That's a document. A copy goes to the supplier that the purchase department chooses and a copy goes into the paperwork with the original request. But sometimes supply is short, and the gap has to be filled quickly or production would cease. Then a special order is allowed before the purchase order is obtained. Very often a smaller supplier is used, or even one outside the Nottingham area. That's what this imaginary factory I traced is, a small place in Derbyshire."

"Can any one of the clerks in the purchase order department create an order?"

"Yes, but even the special rushed orders have to be signed off by Robert eventually. The rogue ones I found were all signed by him. Thurman and Co, Number Ten, Burr Lane, Ilkeston, Derbyshire. It doesn't exist. A large building exists, but it's not a factory. It's tenements. Number Ten is one of them."

"How on earth do you know that?"

"I went to Ilkeston on the train to see if I could find the address the cheques were being sent to. That's what auditors should do, you know, check things properly. It's a working family that live there. Lace makers, yes, but there is no Thurman and Co."

Of course, Harriet thought, that's exactly what Gwen would do get on a train by herself.

"Then," Gwen said, "Someone creates a false invoice from Thurman and Co. to bill the manufactory for the net that doesn't exist, and the payment cheque is sent to 10, Burr Lane, Ilkeston. Nobody in production is going to miss the arrival of the net because nobody wanted it in the first place. The people at Burr Lane pay the cheque into a bank account in the name of Thurman and Co, which is actually the bank account of whoever is stealing."

Gwen was crying. Harriet pulled her towards her and held her in her arms. How could Robert be involved in anything underhand? He was so straightforward; so essentially decent.

"I'm not convinced you have reached the right conclusion. I can't believe Robert would steal from the family. It would break Mother's heart. He's the apple of her eye. And perhaps you suspect Wesley because he has shown himself so untrustworthy."

"Such an absolute bounder, you mean."

"I do mean."

"But what should I do?"

"I think you should write all this down, with all the dates and addresses and everything. Then you should see if anything more like this happens in the future. Did you speak to the family in Ilkeston?"

"No, I spoke to the neighbours, just to find out who lived there. I didn't want to risk upsetting anyone. They might be rough, for all I know."

Harriet shivered and put her arm around her. At least Gwen was thinking of her own safety to that extent, even if she did go gallivanting off on trains by herself. As for her suspicions?

Harriet hoped she was mistaken. Perhaps the orders were genuine. Perhaps Gwen was being over-zealous in her application of her newfound skills. But a horrible feeling in the pit of her stomach told her that anyone who could describe a process in detail, like Gwen just had, was unlikely to have jumped to unfounded conclusions. Gwen was as shocked by where the logic led as she was herself.

Harriet reached behind Gwen's back, pulled open the top drawer of her clothes chest and handed her a handkerchief.

Gwen gulped and blew her nose. She snuffled and said, "I think I should take the whole story to Mr Wragg. He likes me. He's so proud of his modern office system, all his files and hole punches. I'll give him the evidence and ask him what he thinks."

Harriet pulled out another handkerchief and handed it to Gwen. A single good blow completely used up one of those delicate lace-trimmed items. She thought back to her conversation with her mother and how unnerved she had felt at the end of it, as if she had been sent to play outdoors. That feeling was nothing to what Gwen must be experiencing right now. She put her arm around her sister and hugged her tight.

Chapter 7
Twelfth Night

January 5th 1906

A s December went by, and Christmas Day passed, Harriet found herself daydreaming about studying biology. She had received an invitation to present her work at the Slade at the same time as Emma but as she worked on her portfolio it was botany, not art, that came to seem like reality.

By January 5th she was glad of the excuse to put her portfolio aside. Twelfth Night was when the vicarage Loxleys hosted Christmas celebrations for the entire family. Her father honoured the ancient tradition of an evening of revels presided over by a Lord of Misrule. His old friends the Bardhills were always invited to the party, and this year Doctor and Mrs Bardhill were bringing all three of their sons: Tom, Joshua and Alfred. Alfred was sixteen, so it would be his first Twelfth Night at the vicarage. Joshua, twenty-one, was down from Cambridge for Christmas, and Tom was making an appearance for the first time in four years, having finished his medical studies in Edinburgh. Eleanor and Wesley's sons, young

Charley and Bobby, would both be in bed, as Harriet and her siblings had once been, each waiting their turn to be admitted to the festivities at age sixteen.

Harriet had not seen Tom Bardhill since he was eighteen. What sort of a young man had he grown into? As a teenager he'd been studious and occupied with piano practice, and not very good at cricket; a washed-out blond who had stayed indoors while she wandered the countryside with Will.

For their share of the preparations Harriet and Emma took charge of the Dining Room, inserting the two extra leaves in the table, retrieving chairs from hallways and bedroom corners and collecting fresh branches of holly and fir from the churchyard to refresh what was left over from Christmas Day. By the time they finished, the smell of roasting mutton was floating up the hall. Harriet followed the scent to the kitchen and walked through to the scullery. Six perfectly turned out jellies and blancmanges graced the marble shelf. There was anchovy sauce and caper sauce and potatoes cut into matchsticks submerged in water in a big cream mixing bowl.

She slipped a mince pie into her pocket for Will, who had returned from a few days in London half an hour ago.

On returning through the kitchen she found the cook in a flap.

"Miss Harriet, the oysters are off."

"Perhaps we could abandon the oysters, Mrs Sheffield. I'll consult Mrs Loxley."

"Miss Harriet, even without the angels on horseback, there are insufficient serving dishes. How am I to serve all these quail pies, stuffed hearts, vol-au-vents, mince pies, marzipan dates, stars of Bethlehem, apple tarts, pistachio creams and sugared almonds and lord knows what else? Though, of course I do know, heaven help me. Why hasn't anyone considered plates?"

Mrs Sheffield was right. The surface of the dinner table would be scarcely visible under its load of pre-prepared and freshly cooked dishes. That much food required a lot of plates.

"I'll get the tram to Loxley Hall and have more dishes sent with Aunt Beth's two maids when they come. Can you manage until then?"

The cook rolled her eyes.

"I can go now and bring some back myself. Would that be better?"

"Well, I wouldn't be so presumptuous as to ask, Miss Harriet, but that would be a great relief."

She commandeered Will to help with the extra dishes.

Handing him the stolen mince pie as they stood at the tram stop she said, "I've got the nicest game planned if I'm Lord of Misrule tonight. It should show up everybody's modern colours."

She had cut caricatures from magazines to pin to people's backs. They would have to ask questions of the other partygoers to work out who they had attached to them. She had Uncle George as the radical Welsh MP, David Lloyd George. Aunt Beth, a gentle soul and proud housewife, was to be Mrs Pankhurst. Gwen was to be the outrageously spitting Miss Christabel Pankhurst.

She grinned at Will, but when he continued eating and said nothing in reply she searched for something that would flatter him for his inside knowledge and compel him to take notice of her. "It's very exciting, isn't it, the election? Do you think there will be a Liberal victory? Will there be great changes?"

He brushed the crumbs from his lip and hands. "More than you jolly well know, Sis. There are plans afoot that will change the entire way government is viewed. No election will ever be the same again."

"How so?"

"Lloyd George, Asquith and Churchill. Watch those three. They intend to charge full tilt at the four horsemen of the economy: casual labour, unemployment, under-nourishment and poverty. They intend harnessing the wind, or rather the taxation powers of government, to upend society and make the health and welfare of the people one of the fundamental duties of a government. Lloyd George has pledged to lift the shadow of the workhouse from the homes of the poor. And he will."

"That hasn't been part of the Liberal campaign. It's all been free trade and the price of bread."

"No, but it's what's going on in the background. It's what the New Liberals will do if they get enough power."

The wind was getting colder and the tram was late. Harriet tucked herself into his side. "Will, you know during the campaign a lot of candidates wouldn't pledge themselves to women's suffrage? Do you think the Liberals will take that up... if they win?"

"Honestly, it's considered more a private view than a party one. They say Lloyd George and Churchill are for, but Asquith is against. It's controversial within the New Liberal group, so they tend to avoid it."

"Wonderful. Women left to last as usual." She poked him in the side on every syllable as she spoke, and not gently.

"Ouch! Do you think we could change the subject before you do me serious bodily harm?"

"Alright... Do you intend bringing your heroes into your games if you get the bean tonight?"

Will laughed and squeezed her arm. "That doesn't count as a change of subject. And you're fishing, Sis."

"You've never got the bean in the King Cake, have you?"

"No, Sis, I haven't."

"That's a lot of plans never carried out."

"Or only one."

"You can't intend to use the game you made up when you were sixteen?"

"Why not? Aren't you?"

She was not. When she was sixteen she had planned something that involved people feeding each other cake with their hands tied.

Harriet didn't get the bean. Tom Bardhill did.

Mrs Loxley rose from the table, the dry rustle of her dress in perfect sympathy with its tones of fallen maple leaves. "Well, we are all very much looking forward to your revels, Tom. Please do not allow the gentlemen to take too long over their cigars."

Harriet was already working her gloves back on when Tom said, "Please do not go, ladies. Stay at the table."

Uncle George, clutching the neck of the port bottle, harrumphed. Harriet noticed how her uncle's beard and moustache seemed to have grown shaggy in proportion to the loss of his hair on his head, which now only covered the back. She suppressed a smile.

"Well done, young Bardhill!" her father shouted from the far end of the table. "Overturning the established order indeed! Ladies, please resume your seats."

Aunt Beth, seated next to Tom and opposite Harriet, said "Oh dear, Harriet, should we put our gloves back on or not, do you think?"

"I think we should leave them off, Aunt. We may get port to drink."

"I suppose we may not smoke then?" Wesley directed his

remark towards Doctor Bardhill but the indignation was clearly aimed at Doctor Bardhill's eldest son.

Tom looked thoughtful for a moment, then said, "No sir, you may not. Smoking has been proved to be productive of serious physical and moral injury, impairing health and weakening intellectual power."

"Well, I'm sure we all have need of our utmost intellectual power. However, given the presence of the ladies, we will be obliged to curtail our conversation."

Tom frowned. "You are obliged to curtail your language, sir. But as to the voicing of your thoughts, I am sure any of the ladies here present are quite equal to them."

"By God, you—"

"Wesley, I am still a man of God! Take care of the Lord's name!"

Harriet almost fell off her seat. Her father had moved so he was right behind her chair. She turned and gave him a reproachful look for startling her like that, before turning back and saying, "Wesley, on what do you wish to exercise your intellectual power? What, for example, is your opinion of the Liberal stance on free trade? Is it better for everyone if we can buy goods from whoever can produce them the cheapest?"

Wesley filled his glass with port, glanced at Tom and made a point of passing the bottle to Eleanor on his left before saying, "Harry, your interest in promoting political conversation amongst women is well known but that does not give you an entry into the intercourse of men."

Harriet swallowed hard before replying, "I believe Tom Bardhill has just given me such an entry. Would the Nottingham lace industry benefit from tariffs on lace imports?"

Her father's hand landed on her shoulder. Was he supporting her or warning her not to go too far?

Wesley said, "The industry doesn't need tariff protection against foreign imports, Harry, because we already produce the cheapest, best quality net at the highest volume. What it needs is protection against the export of the lace-making machines. They are where all our capital is invested. Let the best machines in the world go to America or Germany and we will be in trouble."

"And what about the hands? I understand many are going to France to set up lace-making there."

"Bobbin lace," Uncle George waved his glass in the air. "Luxury goods. It's past technology. Women's work."

Harriet sighed. "Women's work, Uncle? Don't you employ women to finish the net? They are cheaper than men, aren't they, and they sew better."

Her uncle harrumphed again and looked around for the bottle, but it had only got as far as Harriet's mother. He tapped his glass on the table. "Charge your glass Maria or pass the bottle on, there's a girl... Harriet, I pay my women better than my competitors. There is only so far one can go out on a limb without going out of business."

Her mother apologised for not knowing the rules regarding port, passed the bottle to Doctor Bardhill, and said, "The lace-finishers in Nottingham are quite comfortable, Harriet. You know your uncle pays very fairly. I've heard you say so yourself."

Tom Bardhill had the bottle now. He filled his glass and took a deep swallow before handing the bottle on to Aunt Beth, whose round cheeks were looking decidedly flushed.

He said, "The women always look clean and well-presented in the street, but what about the conditions they work in? Damp, dark and dirty, no doubt?"

Harriet wondered if you only got a turn to speak when you had the wine bottle in hand. But nobody had said so. And was Tom Bardhill in earnest in making such an ill-informed statement about the women's working conditions, or was he teasing her? He'd been looking at her when he'd made the remark. His blond hair had darkened a little but he still had an unkempt, boyish look. She liked his smile.

Harriet was still searching for words when Gwen spoke. "You should take a look at the warehouses before you comment on them, Doctor Bardhill. It is Doctor Bardhill now, isn't it? You should add facts to your opinions when you rejoice in a respectable title. The Loxley warehouses, like all the Lace Market houses, are clean and well lit. They have to be or the women could not see to work the lace and they would dirty the large sheets which trail on the ground. Likewise, the employers insist the workers are clean and have facilities to wash. The lace requires it. The buildings are warm, because they are heated by steam pipes. The lace is washed and dried at the warehouse, you see. Nottingham is not a place of wide-open spaces where bolts of net can be hung in the wind and the sun. You must have noticed how cramped a town Nottingham is. You did grow up here."

Uncle George was beaming now, content to have his facilities defended by a woman as articulate as Gwen.

Wesley raised his eyebrows and looked directly at Tom. "See what happens when you allow women into the conversation, Thomas Bardhill. You get treated to a lecture."

Tom threw up his arms in mock agony. "I know. So awful to have an ill-informed opinion corrected, isn't it?"

Uncle George raised his glass in Tom's direction. "You may visit the manufactory any time, at your convenience. And is it Doctor Bardhill now? My congratulations."

"It is, sir," the elder Doctor Bardhill answered for his son. "And very proud we are of him too. He is working in a dispensary in the slums of the East End of London to obtain experience in the diseases to be found there, before going into a proper practice that is."

Harriet saw Tom Bardhill wince at the phrase *proper practice*. He made no comment to follow his father's. Harriet decided to help him out.

"Emma has some fine sketches of the Lace Market and the women who work there."

Her mother sat upright and raised a hand, as if unsure how to interrupt but determined to do so. "And this is a good time to let you all know that Emma and Harriet have both been invited to attend interviews at the Slade School of Art. I am very proud of them."

There were shouts of congratulations and the sound of hands clapping and palms slapping on tables. Will left his place and hugged her. Over his shoulder she could see Emma and Gwen dancing round each other. Emma's blue skirts and Gwen's yellow ones blurring into a whirl of colour.

Will said, "You kept that quiet, Sis."

"Mother wanted to announce it tonight. Very appropriate, don't you think, that it could be when we got to stay for the men's talk."

Aunt Beth stood and stretched a hand across the table. "Congratulations, my dear. Your abilities deserve to be acknowledged."

Harriet squeezed her aunt's hand. She felt a pang of guilt at seeing everyone so happy and laughing for her when she was actually hoping to fail at the Slade and manoeuvre her time in London into applying to study at one of the other London colleges.

But Emma's achievement was genuine. She should say something.

She took a spoon from the table and tapped her glass with it. It worked. The room went silent. Surprised at her own power, she stuttered. "I...I don't know what to say, except thank you, of course, and especially thank you to Uncle George who has made this possible for Emma and I." She picked up her glass. "A toast to Uncle George."

"You need to charge the glasses first, young lady," her uncle called from his end of the table, waving the port bottle in the air.

Glasses duly charged and toasting done, Mother rose from her seat, which also produced silence, although not as quickly as the glass tapping. "And with that cue, thank you Harriet, we will all move on from this part of social inversion and repair to the Drawing Room. Emma and Harriet may bring us their portfolios to view."

Harriet hadn't intended to end proceedings at all, since she was enjoying herself. She made a sorry-didn't-mean-to face at Tom Bardhill. He rewarded her with a huge grin, revealing a snaggle tooth at the front.

He said, "I decree then, that the gentleman leave first."

It was a hopeless attempt at regaining his Twelfth Night authority. He could hardly be heard above the rustling of silk and murmurs of anticipation from the ladies.

Harriet ran up the stairs after Emma to remind her to remove certain sketches. There had, after all, to be limits to the evening's wildness. They returned to the Drawing Room in time to see Tom Bardhill seating himself at the piano in defiance of the custom that an eligible young man ask a young lady to play, not play himself. Not that Harriet or any of her sisters were at all accomplished at the piano. This one was Aunt Beth's second-best instrument, donated to the junior Loxleys. Aunt Beth was a fine pianist.

Tom Bardhill raised his hands high in the air before plunging them towards the keyboard. There was no gentle introduction. No build up. After a few excited chords the tune set off at a gallop. It was a swing going ever higher and higher. It was a fairground ride of a tune. Emma put her portfolio on the table and Harriet added her smaller one. She wanted to move to the music but didn't know the right way to deal with such a looping, plunging beat. Then Will got up and offered his hand, not to her, but to young Joshua Bardhill.

"Two-step? May I?"

First Tom and now Will had cut the women out of their traditional roles in their own sphere of the Drawing Room. Harriet watched and wondered how to reassert herself. Tom Bardhill had a lot to answer for.

The two young men walked jerkily around the room, swinging their legs to the side. Will twirled Joshua around from time to time and Joshua almost collapsed in giggles. Aunt Beth looked horrified at the thumping hands bearing down on her second-most beloved piano but Uncle George was tapping his foot, while trying to appear unconcerned by the whole proceeding. Harriet's parents were standing arm in arm, backed by the ruddy brown warmth of the Drawing Room curtains.

The music came to a crashing halt. Will and Joshua collapsed on the sofa where Eleanor was sitting by Wesley.

Eleanor said, "What, pray, was that?"

"Nigger, whorehouse music," Wesley growled. "The impertinence of it!"

Eleanor put her hands to her mouth. "Dear no, don't use terms like that, please. It seemed most amusing music."

"Noise, rush and street vulgarity. Repulsive dance halls and restaurants."

Will stood up and pulled at his bow tie, sending it askew. "Well, you should know!"

Wesley stood in turn and Mrs Loxley called out, "Quick, Tom, more music. What was that, by the way?"

"The Maple Leaf Rag. Would you like another, similar?"

Wesley strode out of the room, slamming the door behind him.

If things had gone one step further would Wesley have hit Will? Or would Will have hit Wesley. In a normal, well-mannered, Drawing Room Harriet would have expected them to take their disagreement outside.

"Yes, please, Tom," Mrs Loxley called again, altogether ignoring Wesley's departure. "And what is this one called?"

"The Entertainer."

"Very good, then entertain us."

Harriet stepped from the edge of the room. If a man wouldn't ask a woman to dance she would have to ask a man. "Will," she said, taking his hand and kissing it, "may I have the pleasure?"

He stood, and Harriet led him to the centre of the carpet. She glanced around and saw Gwen leading Joshua, her mother laughingly tugging at her father and Doctor Bardhill commanding young Alfred to help him move furniture to the sides of the room. Robert, who'd remained quiet throughout proceedings, had moved next to Eleanor and was holding both her hands in his. She seemed near to tears. Should she go over? No, Robert and Eleanor had always been close. Like her and Will. Like Emma and Gwen. Three sets of two.

"How do I do this?" Harriet whispered in Will's ear.

"One step, then two steps. One, two; one, two; one, two and two..."

Harriet put the candle on the chest of drawers that also served as her dressing table. She didn't light the gas. She removed her dress, taking care not to let the flounces drift into the candle flame. Her room was small and awkwardly shaped, with a sloping ceiling on one side, as if it had been left over during the construction of the second flight of stairs. It was odd that such a cupboard was fitted with gas light at all.

She wrapped her old shawl around her shoulders, sat on her bed, reached for the pins in her hair and dropped them into a bowl. She thought of Tom Bardhill's snaggle-tooth smile. He'd certainly stirred things up.

The evening had shown that seeking more equality between men and women was a more subtle and potentially dangerous desire than she had imagined. But it had also brought the family together. Except for Wesley. He had been moody all evening. Did he suspect that the Loxley women, apart from Eleanor, had ganged up against him? He wouldn't be altogether wrong.

Mabel knocked and edged around the door.

"Ready for me to unlace your corset, Miss Harriet?"

"Yes, please." Harriet put down her hair brush. "What are you planning to do tomorrow, Mabel?"

Her father continued the topsy-turvy world of Twelfth Night into the Feast of the Epiphany by giving all the servants the day off and obliging the family to fend for themselves, although that fending consisted largely of eating up the leftover food Mrs Sheffield had stored in the pantry.

"I'm spending it with me Mam, Miss. She's lonesome now Maisy is wed and Freddy gone off to Canada."

"Montreal wasn't it? How is he getting on? Does he write?"

"Often enough, although I reckons a lot of the letters get lost. He's a jobbing carpenter. Makes good money. He says there's a shortage of honest folk in Canada. A lot of scoundrels: Irish and them that come over from the American side. Once you're known there's plenty of quality work to be had. There, you're done, Miss. Goodnight."

"Goodnight, Mabel. Enjoy your day tomorrow."

"I'm sure to, Miss."

Harriet removed her corset, pulled her shawl back over her

shift and started brushing her hair. Wesley had said something; something about *our* investment in the machinery at the manufactory. Gwen suspected Wesley of siphoning money out of the business, yet he had spoken as if he owned it and nurtured it. She put down the brush, shook her head, and swiftly braided her hair into a single plait. The room was cold. She needed to get into bed and Wesley was not the man she wanted to be thinking about when she got there.

Chapter 8
Caxton Hall, Westminster

February 16th 1906

After two weeks with Aunt Loxley in her Holland Park house, Harriet appreciated how much freedom she had at the vicarage. Her aunt insisted on knowing everything Harriet planned to do and on accompanying her everywhere she went, unless she was with either Will or Emma. Apparently a woman's reputation was a fragile thing and a woman walking alone was in constant danger of all sorts of horrors, of which being thought loose was definitely the worst. Aunt Loxley had allowed her and Emma to walk out together, but Emma's interviews at the Slade had secured an immediate offer of a scholarship and she had returned to Nottingham.

The following Sunday Harriet managed a brisk walk around Hyde Park with Will.

"You missed a fantastic bash yesterday, Sis. The family gave Emma a stack of artist-type materials. Why didn't you come down? Emma didn't say she was upset but she must have been."

When the Slade had dismissed Harriet's portfolio as good quality drawing-room work, lacking in variety and invention, she had renewed her efforts at securing interviews to study biology or botany. The head of the botany department at Bedford College capitulated and agreed to see her, but it had to be that exact Saturday.

"I'm sure Emma wasn't upset. She knew why I wasn't there. I had an appointment at Bedford College. You see, I want to study biology, not art. You only have to glance at Emma's work compared to mine to see what true artistic talent is, but Doctor Catherine Raisin at Bedford said my portfolio showed an admirable interest in the accurate recording of observation."

Will looked both surprised and hurt. She hadn't shared her plans with him. Their closeness was special and she had been heedless of his feelings. She took his arm. "I'm sorry I didn't tell you. But I only shared it with Emma, no-one else. I didn't want to risk anything getting back to Father." She squeezed his arm. "So don't you dare let on."

Will squeezed her back and grinned. "You pair of schemers. The family is so puffed up with Emma's success now that Father can hardly baulk at you two being at different colleges. So, did you get a place?"

"I have been invited to take an exam in July." She paused, "And Doctor Raisin did make some horribly severe comments about the rigour of the courses and their unsuitability for frail, fashionable ladies. Do I look like I wouldn't be strong enough to study?"

He pulled away from her arm, stood back, and looked her up and down, a grin on his face. "You look hale and hearty. A little thin perhaps. Maybe you should eat more and let out your stays. And wear a little less lace. Play the part of the blue stocking if you want to be one."

"You have an unhealthy obsession with my *corsets*. And less lace? Why less lace? I like lace. Doctor Raisin might think the way I dress has an effect on my mind, but I didn't think you did. Perhaps you and Doctor Raisin share the same prejudices."

He flung up his hands in mock surrender. "Enough! I give in. So, when *are* you going home? Will I get to show you round some more of the sights of London first?"

"I'm staying on another week. There's a meeting I want to attend on Tuesday. Sylvia Pankhurst, remember I told you about her? She's a student at the Royal College of Arts. She's been running all over London arranging a gathering at a place called Caxton Hall, collecting a host of women to hear the news from the King's Speech as soon as it is announced. Everyone wants to know if women's suffrage will be included in the government's agenda."

Sylvia, with her full scholarship to the RCA and her radical family, got the freedom of London while Harriet was going to have to resort to subterfuge to even attend a meeting. She was planning to ask Alice Slack to recommend herself to Aunt Loxley as a suitable companion for lunch.

But she did have one special thing that was hers alone. She was the one who had a brother working inside Parliament. "Will, do you know whether the women's cause is in the Speech?"

"Good grief, no. I'm far too small a cog to even overhear that sort of thing. It's all kept very hush-hush."

"Well, you're no use. But seriously, please don't say anything to the family about me going to this meeting. I can't risk Father, or Uncle George, knowing."

"I think Father would be on your side."

"He would worry. And Uncle George might not be on my side. He's far more conservative than Father. I won't get a full scholarship. I need the trust money."

"But you have it, don't you?"

"Uncle George is the trustee. He determines how the trust is interpreted."

"From what you told me, the trust terms say the money can be used for your education. What better education than somewhere as prestigious as Bedford College?"

"The trust says I can use the money as I please, since I'm over twenty-one. As long as I don't give it to you... and Bedford College? Prestigious in whose eyes? Dangerous to some who think women should keep to their proper place. Art is acceptable. Science is for men." She raised her eyebrows and tilted her head to the side. "Science is too demanding for the weak female mind with its frivolous interest in fine clothes, isn't it?"

He gave her a disparaging look, followed by a sniff.

She fixed him with her big-sister stare. "To tell the truth, I'm just not sure what Uncle George's reaction would be. So, I'd rather not test it out."

Alice wiped her fingers on her napkin and pulled on a silver chain descending from her neck to somewhere inside her jacket. At its end was a large and battered steel watch. She opened the lid.

"It was my father's. I find it invaluable, what with trains to catch and the like. So, Caxton Hall at three. An invigorating walk across St. James' Park."

Invigorating it certainly was, and Harriet was glad of her good wool coat and her robust boots as they headed into flurries of rain. Caxton Hall turned out to be a pink-stone and red-brick affair on a quiet road on the opposite side of the park. It made Harriet think of a fancy French cake. Women were milling around the entrance, their voices raised, some saying they had borrowed their maid's old coats and hats to avoid being recognised should they march upon Parliament. It was all promising to be more dramatic than Harriet had expected. Perhaps she should leave before anything happened that might result in being gossiped about. Marching in the street would not sit well with Aunt Loxley. But then neither would abandoning Alice and finding her own way back to Holland Park.

Once inside the hall she fidgeted for a while, then put her hand on Alice's arm. "I never asked what magic you weaved with my aunt to get her to accept you as a chaperone? She'd only just met you and she's very suspicious of new ideas."

"I'm a married woman."

"You think I should get married to secure my liberty?"

"Heaven forbid. No, I think you should use whatever advantage you have and be as underhand as you need."

Singing and laughter drifted in from the back of the hall and Harriet turned in her seat. A woman in the aisle flicked a large rain-dewed blue shawl from her head and shoulders to reveal a mauve knitted cardigan above a dark-grey wool skirt, equally bejewelled with rain drops. She turned to the woman behind her. "We no sooner got out of the station and unfurled our banners than the Old Bill furled them up again for us, didn't they, Lil? But we showed them how we could sing. There ain't no law against singing, not yet."

A woman in a shabby grey coat said, "This way ladies, if you please."

Harriet stood. "Miss Pankhurst? How nice to see you?"

Alice stood and held out her hand. Sylvia's hand, offered in return, was ungloved and looked chapped. Was she so short of money she couldn't afford heat, or gloves? Was that the price of freedom?

Sylvia said, "Mrs Slack. Your husband's bill. The bill that was so shamefully talked out the day that militancy was born. How is Mr Slack?"

Militancy was a powerful word. Harriet was not sure she liked it.

Alice sighed. "I'm sorry to say my husband lost the seat in this latest election. He had gained it in a by-election, when turnout is often low, and I suppose it was to be expected that revenge would be taken in such a conservative constituency."

Sylvia nodded. "I am sorry to hear that. He is one of our staunchest supporters." She smiled and waved a hand, taking in their surroundings. "Mother was peeved that I'd taken such a large hall. She said she was going to be embarrassed by having the press see her address a half-empty space. But look at all these ladies, and only a few of my East End women are seated yet. We'll be glad of seven hundred chairs."

Somebody trying to find out where a new party of women were to sit pulled Sylvia aside. Harriet watched her go and wished she possessed half her certainty and dynamism. She shouldn't be letting thoughts of Aunt Loxley intimidate her. She shuffled her feet and wished she could regain some of the enthusiasm she had felt on the walk here. Sitting and thinking was not good for her.

A lady on the platform rose and clapped her gloved hands. The noise in the hall subsided.

"Mrs Dora Montefiore," Alice said. "From Australia. Has been a fighter for the suffrage since the day her husband's lawyer read his will to her and told her that, since her husband had made no provision otherwise, she would be appointed the guardian of her children."

"He could have appointed someone else?"

"He could, and the wretched lawyer even suggested to her face that he might have been advised to do so, since her husband was Jewish and she is not. In law, he said, there is only one parent, and that is the man. Mrs Montefiore has been paying that lawyer back ever since."

"Wasn't she the one who Mrs Pankhurst suggested might hold the other end of a tripwire to ambush Mr Labouchère?"

"Indeed, she was."

The broad-shouldered, strong-browed lady who was glancing around the hall waiting for its occupants to settle down looked perfectly capable of direct sabotage.

Mrs Montefiore clapped her hands again. "Friends, ladies, members of the press, welcome to Caxton Hall. Caxton changed this country forever when he brought the printing press to our shores and set it up in the heart of Westminster. We, the women of this country, are also going to change it forever." Mrs Montefiore spread her arms wide. "Women of Britain, we await news of the King's Speech. We are here to discover whether the new Liberal government, with its massive majority, will include a bill for us in the upcoming Parliamentary session. We are here to hear what our mothers and our grandmothers listened for in vain. Women, I give you Mrs Emmeline Pankhurst."

Compared to Mrs Montefiore, Mrs Pankhurst seemed slight and soft-faced. The newspapers, those that might have commented on low turnout, were sure to find something to say about her elegance. Her walking suit was a delicious shade of purple verging on pink, like Victoria plums. The skirt was gored and the long jacket was trimmed with black piping. She was clever, Sylvia's mother, taking care to look womanly while also being dressed for the weather and for action.

Mrs Pankhurst spoke in a low voice, with her hands behind her back. Harriet leaned forward, eager to catch every word.

"Women work at home; they work in the fields and they work in the factories. Their work is comparable work to anything men do."

Comparable, not equal. Had Harriet's own conversation about equality with Mrs Pankhurst had an impact?

"Yet women are so often refused jobs in favour of men. They are denied jobs because they are not men and their jobs invariably pay less than men. Because men have families to support, they tell me. And women don't I suppose!"

Harriet rose to her feet with the rest, clapping for all she was worth. Whether this was called militancy or not, it was something she had to be part of.

A woman walked up the aisle, rain spilling from the hem of her oiled coat. From all around the hall voices called out, "The messenger! The messenger from Parliament."

The woman continued towards the stage and handed a note to Mrs Montefiore. Mrs Montefiore unfolded the paper and read. She handed it to Mrs Pankhurst, then took it back and faced the audience.

This could be it. The turning point for the women of Britain.

Mrs Montefiore's commanding tones soared across the silenced hall. "No reference to women's suffrage or a franchise bill in the government's agenda for the next Parliament."

Angry hisses erupted. Some shouted, "Shame!"

Alice grabbed Harriet's hand.

Mrs Pankhurst sprang to her feet and raised her right arm. "We shall march to Parliament and demand to be heard. The time for patience is over." She picked up her umbrella and strode down the aisle and out into the foyer, making it clear she intended the entire gathering to follow her.

Harriet buttoned her coat. Aunt Loxley didn't need to know that she had been here, or that she had marched in the street, calling attention to herself like a trade unionist. Be as underhand as you need, Alice had said. She linked arms with her friend.

Alice said, "The Houses of Parliament are a ten-minute

walk from here. Half a mile at the most. Hopefully, we'll not get too wet in that length of time."

Women filled the road, walking four and five abreast, forcing traffic to pull to the sides. Ahead of her a group of working women had pulled their shawls up over their heads. They were singing, *Don't dilly dally on the way*.

The rain started sheeting down. Harriet's feet were soon wet, despite her good boots. Her woollen skirt ceased to repel water and became twice its normal weight. But she had survived many a country ramble in bad weather and this was only half a mile. Alice shivered and Harriet moved closer to her, hoping to keep her warm. She remembered how worn out Alice had been by their last time spent at a gathering in the streets.

When they arrived at the House of Commons some women in the crowd were shouting for their MPs to come out. Others were in forlorn groups, looking bedraggled. Some of the ladies who had borrowed their maids', clothes were complaining about being treated as if they were their maids.

Men were standing on the steps of the Strangers' Entrance, staring. Officials between them and the women barred the women's way into the building. More men appeared from inside. Someone called out over the crowd that women would be allowed in, in groups of twenty. Harriet swapped her umbrella to her other hand to ease the ache in her arm. That would be thirty-five groups; they could be here for a long time. How was she going to explain to Aunt Loxley that she got wet through to her stockings having lunch with Alice? What plausible lie could she think up?

It was getting dark, and the streetlights were turning what light was left into puddles of confusion. Some men were walking out now, handing out umbrellas to women. Was that Will's walk? Alice, who had been leaning on Harriet for a while, began to slip towards the ground. Harriet grabbed her under one arm and tried to keep her umbrella over them both.

"I've got her, Sis. Come on Mrs Slack. It's time we all went for tea, again."

"Take Mrs Slack's arm. I'm staying here to make my point."

Will cupped his hand and whispered in her ear. "Sis, I need you to hold her up on the other side. She's the wife of an MP. If the press see her looking like this it will be fodder for their fragility-of-the-female-sex stance."

Former MP. But Will was right. Alice was pale and there was a hectic flush high up on her cheeks, where the bone came close to the surface. The skin around her eyes was dark and bruised-looking. The best thing Harriet could do right now was to get her friend to the nearest warm tea-room as unobtrusively as possible.

From the direction they turned upon leaving Old Palace Yard, Harriet knew they must be going to the same place Will had taken them to on the afternoon that the franchise bill was talked out. Then it had been reactionary, stubborn old men who were holding the women back; now it was an entire government and a Liberal government at that, the party pledged to the betterment of the people.

Harriet said, "The logical conclusion is that we women are not people in their eyes."

"What, Sis?"

"We're not people. You don't leave people standing out in the pouring rain."

"People get left out in the rain all the time. Working people work in the rain all day long. You don't leave *ladies* out in the rain."

"Hmph."

A gentleman by the tea-room door stepped back and opened it. She gestured to Will to go in first with Alice and took the umbrella from him. She shook it out and stowed it in the stand before doing the same for her own. Then she remembered she should offer her thanks to the door-holder. Was he still there?

"Why, Tom Bardhill! I didn't recognise you, with your hat pulled down so. What a coincidence. I do apologise, and Will was very much taken up with assisting Mrs Slack. Why ever did you not say something when you saw us coming towards you?"

He blushed and fiddled with his hat. "I'm not here by accident, and when I saw you ladies looking so wet, I felt quite guilty for not having come forward."

"Not here by accident?"

She rather liked the idea.

"I suspected you would go to the Caxton Hall meeting. Many of the women from around my dispensary were going, so I took the train up to St. James' Park with them and hung around outside the hall. Then I followed the march up to Parliament."

He looked as bashful as a child caught stealing sugar lumps. Harriet stared at him for a second. She didn't believe him. How could he simply *suspect* she would be at the meeting? The only people who knew were Alice and Will.

"And why didn't you talk to us in all that time?"

"You ladies are daunting."

"Daunting?"

The waiter was coming their way. "Well, I hope you will join us for tea now."

She smiled to herself and carried the idea of being daunting with her to the table.

Will found a telephone and contacted Mr Bamford Slack at his London residence but it was an hour before he arrived, by which time Harriet was warmed through and assumed Alice must be too. But Alice's husband took one look at her and said he was taking her home.

"I'm feeling much better, dear."

"I insist we have the doctor come to you tomorrow."

"As you wish. Have you heard anything of the reaction inside that self-satisfied pile of stone while we were all being denied our constitutional rights? I suppose you found time to see a few former colleagues before coming to check on me."

The former MP and self-possessed speaker looked abashed and stammered. "I... knew you were in good hands.... In the House? Amusement, condescension, fear perhaps. The women have unsettled the Liberal leaders. Churchill declared that he won't be henpecked into making political decisions."

"Henpecked!" Harriet almost spluttered into her tea. "We are doing exactly what men do. We are protesting. We are questioning. If we do nothing, we are not heard. If we do something, we are criticised."

Tom slapped a hand on the table. "Damned if you do and damned if you don't."

Alice started, then smiled at him and clapped her hands together. She stood and took her husband's offered hand. "Good evening, my friends. May we meet again soon."

Tom stood. "I must be on my way too. Goodbye Will, Miss Loxley." He inclined his head in her direction.

Was that all? Wasn't he going to take her hand? Say something about hoping to meet again soon? She felt her cheeks growing hot.

She nodded her head. "Goodbye, Mr Bardhill. It has been a most pleasant surprise."

His eyes held hers for a moment before he turned away.

They were a deep, sun-shiny blue. The colour of cornflowers.

Will didn't resume his seat. "We should be on our way too,

Sis. You look a little like a drowned kitten, I must say, and I *can* say, since frank talk appears to be the fashion. Although I doubt our aunt will be amused at your appearance."

Moments after she sat down to breakfast the next morning, Richardson, her aunt's live-in lady's-maid-cum-butler, served her a steaming plate of smoked haddock kedgeree. Will was already halfway through his.

Aunt Loxley was wearing her coral-coloured morning dress. With its wide collar and mutton chop sleeves it was ten years or more behind the times. The vivid shade suited the high colour of her aunt's cheeks and brought out the gold highlights in her hair.

Her aunt lowered her gold-framed lorgnette. Holding it in one hand, she waved it as she spoke. "I do like this new Daily Mirror for the pictures it has on the front page. I still take the Times, of course, for your late Uncle Loxley's sake, but this is much more amusing than all those tiny advertisements. Did you see any of this carry-on at the House yesterday, Will? Ladies demanding to be let in."

"We took umbrellas out to them."

Harriet busied herself with her napkin and prayed Will would remember their aunt was not to know about her activities in the street. She had told her she got caught in a sudden downpour and had been drenched by the spray thrown up from the wheels of a cab.

Her aunt put the newspaper down and asked Richardson to bring a fresh pot of tea, waiting for her to leave before saying, "I don't believe in women voting. It is the family that is at the heart of Britain and the Empire, not the individual. Men, as the representatives of families, should be the ones to exercise the suffrage. Women are best suited to motherhood and the domestic duties.

This is undeniable when you consider that God framed men for business, manual labour, the army, and so on. All those spheres beyond the home which it is hard to imagine women accomplishing. Eat up Harriet, dear. Your food will get cold."

Harriet took a forkful of kedgeree and chewed. Yesterday, Will had set her right on how working women were expected to work in the rain. Perhaps he would set Aunt Loxley right now and she wouldn't have to betray too much knowledge of yesterday's events. Her aunt was wrong on so many counts. Did women who were unmarried, or childless, or widowed have no status? Women like Aunt Loxley herself. And there might not be women in the army, but there were plenty who laboured in fields and factories. Was it because their families were so poor they had to? Or did working-class women, being without the restraints of what was right and proper, have more choice?

Her aunt was breaking the mould herself, having a woman acting as both a butler and a lady's maid. Or was she merely saving money by having Richardson play two roles while paying women's wages for a man's job? She told herself she didn't know what her aunt paid and that Richardson, and her aunt, seemed to have made their own decisions.

Will remained silent. Harriet had to speak. "Wouldn't you like to vote, aunt? You are the head of this household and you must pay the taxes, no?"

"I pay the general rates and the poor rates, yes, Harriet. And I could be a Poor Law Guardian, like your mother, if I so wished. Charity is a very proper activity for women."

Harriet had no desire to belittle her mother's work with the poor, but her aunt was missing the point. "The women feel their role is being narrowed. For example, Balfour's Education Act removed the elected school boards that women served on and they cannot be part of the new local authorities. Women seem to gain influence by custom and hard work, only to have it taken away."

Her aunt sipped her tea and said nothing.

Will said, "Harry makes a good point. Women never have influence by constitutional right. That, I believe, is what the desire for the suffrage is about, constitutional rights for women."

"Young man, they exercise their influence through their husbands, sons and brothers. As I see Harriet here is clearly influencing you."

Why was she ignored but when Will said the same thing he got a response?

"Will has his own free thoughts, Aunt, as I would wish mine to be free and acknowledged."

Her aunt's high colour intensified. She put down her teacup and fixed one of those brook-no-nonsense stares on Harriet that she remembered from the many times she had been in trouble for being too unladylike.

"Will is moving in a man's world, Harriet. He is working close to the engine of the Empire. He has understanding that you and I will never have. We cannot have it, because if we did we would lose the essential nature of womanhood. We would cease to be a source of warmth and nurture. We would stop attending to domestic comfort. We would become weaker versions of men."

Harriet looked down and pushed her food around her plate, not daring to oppose her aunt any more than she already had. She wanted to continue living in her house.

Will finished the last of his kedgeree, pronounced it delicious, and laid his knife and fork at the centre of his plate. "Aunt, you do agree that education and the care of the poor are a proper sphere for women, don't you? Do you not think those things are close to the engine of Empire? I think they are. I think they are of the utmost importance if the Empire with its uneducated, impoverished millions is to survive. And I don't mean only in India and the colonies. I mean Ireland. I mean here."

"Survive is a strong word, Will."

"There is revolt in the air of Europe. Socialism is a powerful movement. The union men here are soaking it up. If those of us who are Liberals want to prevent revolution and republicanism, we have to address the working men's, and working women's, concerns."

"Well, I'm sure you know better than I about such things."

Will had his agenda and was getting heard. Harriet had hers and was reduced to silence. She took a mouthful of her rice and fish and chewed it.

But Alice had said to be as underhand as you need.

"Aunt, may we pay a call on Mrs Slack this morning? Yesterday, when we parted, I feared she was becoming unwell. I would like to see if she has recovered."

"I think that an excellent way to spend our morning, Harriet. Bloomsbury, their apartments, I think you said? We could go to the British Museum after. That would appeal to you, would it not?"

"Yes, indeed, Aunt."

"And one day, while you are here, we should take a trip out to Kew and view the botanicals. There is a fine collection of drawings there that you would appreciate."

Their aunt gone from the room, Harriet pushed her congealing plate of rice and fish aside.

"Don't you want that, Sis? Give it here, then."

Will slid her plate to his side of the table and began eating as if there were no tomorrow. When Harriet pointed this out, he claimed that there wasn't, given the meagre portions his landlady delivered as part of his board and lodging.

"Will, just what did you say to Tom Bardhill about me?"

He smiled, a knowing, annoying-little-brother, smile. "And why would you want to know, Sis? Do you want to butter up our aunt by doing something respectable, like considering settling down? You know, marriage, family, all that sort of thing."

She narrowed her eyes and tried to feel cautious and sophisticated. "I want to know if you consider him to be a sound sort of chap."

"He's not one for going out much. Works very long hours in that dispensary of his. He's a good sort, as far as I can tell."

Will was staring at her, a grin plastered across his boyish face. He still had dimples. She felt a blush creeping up her neck.

He said, "I can escort you to the East End and you can visit the Bardhill good works, if you like."

She accepted. Time with the person who thought her interesting enough to seek out and too daunting to approach was exactly what she had been hoping he might achieve for her. Not that she was about to say so.

Chapter 9
A Dispensary in Bethnal Green

March 1906

Harriet sat at the dressing table, contemplated the eyebrow pencil and the pot of poppy-red lip colour and made a face at herself in the mirror. She was planning to apply makeup in order to make an impression at a dispensary for the poor of London's East End. That was hardly normal preparation for a tour of a charity. Would Tom take note, think it unhealthy, like he did smoking?

She had bought the lip colour in the company of Alice Slack, on their first outing after the Caxton Hall meeting.

"I'd like to slip into this chemist's shop for a moment, Alice."

The girl at the counter folded down the top of a discrete paper bag and handed it to Harriet.

Alice said, "You colour your lips?"

"I haven't before. I intend experimenting."

Alice inspected her own face in the mirror on the countertop.

"You know, I can't afford to go round looking like a wilting flower and have my husband rescue me, even if I do wilt now and again."

She turned to the assistant. "Please, may I have one of those too."

Smiling at the memory Harriet was about to dip her finger in the oily red paste when there was a knock at her door.

Richardson handed her a letter with Gwen's writing on the envelope. Harriet tore it open.

Harry,

I need you to come home. I know for certain that Wesley and Robert are skimming the accounts. But it's even worse. Uncle George is taking money out of the manufactory. He has investors who are not family and these drawings of cash are being disguised in the books. He's defrauding his investors. The potential scandal is too much to bear thinking about. Mr Wragg says to keep quiet. He's afraid for his livelihood. What am I to do? I want to have it out with Uncle George. I have nothing to lose, unless he writes me out of that trust money.

Harry, will you help me, please? I don't know what to do.

Another knock and Will calling through the door.

"Come on, Sis! Shake a leg or we won't be there before the caretaker shuts the place up and makes Tom leave."

"Just a minute!"

Harriet stuffed Gwen's letter into her bag and smoothed on a touch of lip paint with the tip of her little finger. She had to talk to Will about Gwen, and as quickly as possible.

"You're finally ready? We should take the two-penny railway from here to Liverpool Street and then get a bus into Bethnal Green. It will be faster than the bus all the way."

As soon as they were outside, Harriet grabbed his hand.

"Come into the garden in the square with me. There's something important I need to tell you."

"Can't it wait? We've got a train to catch. We can talk on the train."

"Please, Will."

Harriet pushed open the iron gate and went over to the bench in the centre of the garden. Checking there was no-one else around, she handed Will Gwen's letter and sat, biting her lip, while he read it.

He went still before saying, "Robert and Wesley work for Uncle George because they are family. The profits of the manufactory are family money and it's family money that pays for us all. Why, in God's name, do they think they should take more?"

"I think she's tried speaking to Mr Wragg, who runs the accounts department. I suspect he knows. But it's not just Robert and Wesley. Uncle George is taking money out."

"And why shouldn't he? It's his manufactory."

"I don't really know. But Gwen says, if the investors found out, the consequences would be huge. She wants me to go home."

"Go home for a bit, then, and sort her out. You are good at that kind of thing. You have a talent for supporting people without undermining them."

He stood and offered her his hand.

She said, "That's Emma. Emma is the one who always considers the other person."

"Emma offers comfort. You offer strength."

"Gwen is strong."

"Gwen is bold. It's not the same thing. Come on, we must go."

The modern railway train was as noisy as she had feared it would be. Will chatted on about how the development of the new underground lines into the East End had required Acts of Parliament that cleared acres of slums which had allowed the London municipality to build tenements with good lighting and ventilation. Harriet half listened, her mind churning over Gwen's letter. Suppose the investors, whoever they were, brought some kind of court case. The whole family's security could be at risk. What on earth did her brothers and her uncle think they were doing?

At Liverpool Street they transferred to an omnibus. Unable to enjoy watching the passing streets as they threaded through the East End of London, Harriet kept her head down and her attention turned inward.

The bus was cramped and her feet were getting cold.

"It would be quicker to walk."

"Some of the streets here are none too clean. It isn't mud, it's churned-up horse droppings."

"I know that."

She had snapped. That wasn't fair.

"I'm sorry. I'm worried about Gwen."

"I know that. I am too."

She had expected Bethnal Green to be narrow streets of back-to-backs, shops and public houses, where women sat outside on kitchen chairs preparing vegetables and a few men idled. That was the scene in the Nottingham Narrow Marsh. But here they got down from the bus into a wide street, bustling and noisy with men and boys hurrying along or assembled in groups leaning against the walls. Newsvendors stood in the gutters, shouting out their latest editions. Carts lumbered past. They passed a pie seller, and the scent of fresh-baked meat pies made Harriet wish she had eaten more breakfast.

Men carrying bundles were dodging down an alley.

She said, "Where is there to go?"

"They are delivering to the sweat shops behind."

"Sweat shops?"

"There are hundreds of little workshops, making clothes and shoes and all sorts of things, where the houses used to have gardens. Those are sweat shops."

"Like the outworkers some of the lace manufacturers use?"

"Like that. Women and children working in their homes."

Uncle George tried to avoid using outworkers and had good conditions at the warehouse. Surely he was honest too. Could she hope that Gwen might be wrong?

Will tapped her arm and waved his hand at a redbrick building with cream coloured facings and tall chimneys. "Tom's dispensary is in part of this hospital."

The building seemed pleasant enough, set back from the road and in its own grounds. Harriet imagined it was attractive when the trees were in leaf and there were flowers in the beds. The woman who answered the door told them that Doctor Bardhill was with his last patient of the morning. She showed them into a room that could have been any dining room in any large house, with chairs arranged around a long central table and lined around the walls.

Harriet sat down and fiddled with her bag. What could she ask about Tom's work? What was she going to say in order to sound intelligent and informed? She should have listened to Will talking about poverty.

When Tom finally put his head around the door, she stood up and smiled. "I'm so looking forward to finding out what you do here. Your last patient, for example, what did you treat him or her for?"

"And good morning to you too, Miss Loxley."

She blushed and nodded her head. "Doctor Bardhill."

"Will."

Will laughed. "Yes, me too, Tom."

Harriet tried to cover her failure of manners by adopting an attentive expression while Tom Bardhill told them his patient was a woman who had scalded her hands from tipping over a kettle of boiling water. The nurse attended to the dressings, but he inspected the wounds to check on their healing.

"But we're closed for the day and I had sent the nurse home, so I had to do the bandaging myself. It took a while. I'm not as good at it as the nurses. Please, come through to my consulting room."

The room was not very large. There was a large bookcase along one wall, a small wooden desk and four straight-backed chairs. Also a high, wide bench along one wall, which Harriet assumed was an examination table.

"There are four rooms like this," Tom said. "For four doctors on duty at any one time."

"And what sort of cases do you get?" Harriet asked.

"Cuts, crushed fingers and toes, infectious diseases. I usually visit those at home. It makes little sense to bring the disease into here."

Will said, "Isn't that dangerous? I mean, aren't people with infectious diseases supposed to be isolated or sent to the fever hospital?"

Harriet detected genuine concern in his voice. The two young men were firmer friends than Will had been implying.

"Someone has to determine if it is a notifiable disease, which is what I think you mean. Wives and husbands, mothers and fathers, they come to me and say someone is sick, so sick they *can't hardly walk*. That's not a diagnosis, not a reason to inflict harsh measures on a person. A common cold can put you in bed for a day or two. A chest infection requires more rest and care than people usually give it."

Harriet said, "Do you catch a lot of colds?"

"Not like I used to when I started here. I take precautions. Use a handkerchief. Wash my hands. I try to train my patients to do the same."

"And will that protect you from cholera and tuberculosis and typhoid? Will has a point. It is dangerous."

"I'm supposed to be a doctor, caring for the sick. What sort of a doctor would I be if I sat in this office and expected people who can *hardly get out of bed* to come to me? Of the three diseases you mentioned only tuberculosis is spread through the air. I cover my nose and mouth with a special mask and I have the patient open the window, if they have one."

"And what can you do for the disease?"

"Damnably little.... Sorry." He rested one hand on his desk and looked her straight in the eye. "Even though Koch's work on the tuberculosis bacterium has taught us much about infection, there is still little we can offer. Quarantine and good hygiene are all we have and they are hard to achieve amongst the living conditions of the poor. The visiting nurses do a lot. To give you a detail, it is important to teach the tubercular patient how to spit, or rather how not to spit on the floor, into the fire or on the public street. The sputum spreads the bacteria."

Harriet swallowed hard. The image of gelatinous yellow sputum made her want to retch. Was she really too delicate a lady, as Catherine Raisin had implied?

"And take the case of typhoid. We know it is caught through contact with the faeces of the infected person. This is a big step because it means we can stop its spread through simple means, such as hand washing, cleanliness around food, and clean water supplies. We can also safely leave patients to be cared for by their families, as long as the families are trained in hygiene. But once someone has typhoid we can do nothing for them that isn't fresh air, and encouraging drinking. One person in five who catches it will die."

Will said, "Cholera, I believe, has been almost defeated because of good public sanitation. Perhaps typhoid will be too."

"And by feeding and housing people better. By abolishing poverty in short."

There was colour rising in Tom's cheeks and his eyes were shining.

Harriet nodded. He was right. Feeding and housing one's fellow human beings should be more important than anything else in the world. Father would say so.

She said, "Why, then, do we invest so much of our national effort in a war in South Africa, instead of putting it into decent housing for working people? Why is the matter of housing left to landlords whose incentive is to make money? Why, for that matter, is medicine left to doctors who need to make money from patients in order to live? Why don't the local authorities pay doctors?"

She caught Tom's eye. His look seemed to contain admiration, and possibly something more. She looked down.

Will said, "Exactly what I was saying, Sis. So, you were listening then?"

She lifted her head and glared at him. "It's not *exactly* what you were saying."

Tom laughed. "Well, the local authorities do employ medical examiners. The one in Nottingham is highly respected for his methods with tubercular patients. Come, I'll show you the rest of the dispensary."

He led them through a door at the back of his consulting room and gestured to his right. "There are the three other consulting rooms over there and a room for the nurses, and on this side there's the dispensary itself. There are two ladies come in to record the medicines we issue and hand out the doses."

He took a key from his pocket and opened the door onto a large room with shelves on all sides and a long, cloth-covered table in the centre.

Harriet recognised the brown-ridged bottles that indicated poison.

"You said there was very little you could do, but there are a lot of different bottles in here."

"Much of it is castor oil or cough syrup. Not bad things in themselves, but they don't do anything for serious disease. There are also pain medicines, like laudanum."

"And the poisons?"

"Arsenic for asthma, skin conditions and rheumatism. Calomel, mercuric chloride, as a diuretic. Those are the main ones. Now, I'll show you the waiting room."

He locked the door behind him.

Harriet looked back the way they had come. "I thought we were waiting in the waiting room."

"That's the subscribers' room. Where the donors' committee meets. Our better class of visitor gets shown in there instead of here."

He pushed open a set of double doors to a stench of stale sweat, spilt food and urine. Harriet held her breath for as long as she could before slowly letting it out. She was determined not to show any reaction.

Will pulled out a handkerchief, held it over his nose and mouth and mumbled, "The consequence of even a cold bath in the bath-house costing a penny?"

"Sorry," Tom said. "The stink does linger here after it's shut up for the day."

The room was filled with backless benches, row upon row. There were plenty of windows, all closed.

Harriet said, "Why so many benches? Do they have to wait a long time?"

"Sometimes all day."

"But they're working people. How do they work?"

He pulled the door closed, looked at her, and shrugged. There was deep pity in that shrug.

"They often don't get seen. I've put a new system in place, where the nurses walk amongst them and assess their needs. That way, the ones with worse wounds than I can tend go straight to the hospital."

They moved on to the nurses' room, which was white-tiled and filled with cupboards, little tables, contraptions on wheels that held bowls, and more straight-backed chairs.

"The nurses can do a lot more than us doctors normally use them for. They learn a lot from working next to us."

Harriet grimaced. "They have to work in that waiting room?"

"After a while you don't notice the smell, believe me. Although, when I get home, I often wish jackets and trousers were as easily laundered as shirts and collars."

When they returned to Tom's consulting room, he pulled open a drawer. "Here are the suture needles and silk thread I use."

Harriet peered at the neatly laid out needles. Some looked like ordinary sewing needles and some were curved and hooked. Will reached out to pick one up. She grabbed his hand.

"Don't touch them. They have to be kept clean."

"Miss Loxley is right. Everything has to be kept clean. I am trying to teach our people here that even the daintiest hand can transfer bacteria."

"There's nothing very dainty about Will's hands, Doctor Bardhill. Nor mine, either, I'm afraid. We have just been on the public omnibus. Perhaps we should have washed our hands before you took us around your dispensary."

Tom blushed. "That's an excellent idea. I should have suggested it to you. But I wouldn't dare say so to most visitors

116

who come in through the subscribers' room. And there aren't the facilities on the other side.

"Where they are most needed," Harriet said.

"Exactly." Tom pushed the drawer of needles shut. "I had a docker with three crushed fingers in here yesterday. After I explained how he would have to try hard to get his fingers moving properly again, he said, *I has to work because I needs the money for the wife and the little uns. There's so much wealth in this country. I sees it coming in the docks every day. But so little of it ever comes our way.*"

Will nodded. "If you go down to the docks, Sis, and I don't suggest you do, you will hear syndicalists preaching their takeover by the workers. They are a well organised bunch and they are infiltrating the regular labour unions. They make Keir Hardie and the Independent Labour Party look like a bunch of pussy cats. And that's why the government must act and improve social conditions, before it all boils over."

Harriet said, "If women could vote, they would vote in the interests of the poor, since the care of the poor has always been their proper sphere, as our aunt would say. And if the poor were lifted up, by improving their health and education, they would become active members of the political classes rather than recipients of charity."

Will put his arm round her. "My fighting sister."

Tom was looking at her in that way she had noticed before as he held open the subscribers' room door. Will followed her out and headed towards the door they had entered by, but she had left her bag on Tom's desk. She turned back and, as she passed through the doorway to his surgery, her hand brushed against his. He caught hold of it.

The sensation, even through her gloves, was like something inside her had started singing. She left her hand in place, too long for him to believe in her disapproval if she withdrew it.

One finger of his slipped in between hers. "Can we meet again soon, later this week perhaps?"

She was on the verge of saying yes when Gwen's pleas flooded back.

"No. No, I'm sorry, I have to go to Nottingham tomorrow."

"When will you return?"

"Probably not until I take my exams in July."

He lifted her hand to his lips and placed a formal kiss on the back of it.

"Then I shall have to come to Nottingham."

He still had her hand. She moved closer to him, wondering what she was hoping for. He pulled her forward and kissed her full on the lips, the softest plunge into pure sensation she had ever experienced.

He said, "You are splendid."

"Thomas Bardhill, you forget yourself."

He grinned.

He couldn't possibly be convinced by her indignation. She wasn't convincing herself.

Chapter 10
Uncle George

March 1906

H arriet knew Robert would be waiting on the platform at Victoria Station. She stepped down from the train with her portmanteau before he could get near enough to help.

"Just look at you! Hopping off like a New Woman. Have you more luggage?"

"My trunk."

She handed him her ticket and he headed for the luggage van.

Harriet had not slept well the night before. On the train her head had nodded over her book, her mind spinning scenes not included by the author. She had forced herself awake and tried concentrating on the view from the window, until she nodded again, this time dreaming of Tom Bardhill, of the admiration in his eyes, the feel of his hand against hers. When her head snapped back up, she sat until the heat drained from her body, then excused herself from the presence of the other ladies in the compartment. She had paced back and forth along the corridor, her legs feeling like bags of sand.

And now here was Robert, walking back from where luggage was piling up on the platform, as tall and as conventionally confident as ever with his smiling brown eyes, carefully cut jet-black hair and neat beard. She knew that face so well. She knew his hair was defiant and his beard attempted to colonise his entire face south of his eyes. Despite all Gwen's suspicions, he was still her own beloved elder brother.

"I've arranged for your trunk to be sent on to the vicarage."

He picked up her portmanteau and she took his arm and lifted her chin. He was a handsome man about town, someone she should feel proud to be seen with. The familiar maroon and cream of the Nottingham Corporation tram hove into sight and she lengthened her stride to match his as he walked faster.

Apart from the screech of metal on metal when it cornered, the tram was a lot quieter than the tunnel-trains in London. Robert asked after their aunt's health and she said she was well. She asked him how things were at work.

"It's looking good. Sales are up on last year. Our four new floral designs for sub-curtains are going like hotcakes, especially the daffodils and irises. Spring, I suppose. Out with the dusty old fabric and in with the new. Wesley's a superb salesman, although it was Emma's suggestion, actually, the flowers. Give credit where credit is due."

"And how is Gwen getting on?"

"Gwen? Gwen is making a huge difference too. She's been right through the Bought Ledger and identified ways we can use it to bring costs down. She has initiative, our Gwen. Wragg is a fine fellow and keeps the books straight, but he has no initiative."

"You've lost me. What's a Bought Ledger?"

"A book where we write down all the net we have bought from a supplier and how much it cost. We don't make enough net in our own factory when demand is high, so we buy from wherever we can. Then when we pay the supplier, we write that in the Bought Ledger too. The thing about Gwen is she went through it all and asked questions."

And Gwen had found answers about her brother Robert and her brother-in-law, Wesley. Why was Robert talking about this so candidly? Was he deceiving himself, or was he about to make a confession?

She said, "What sort of questions?" and decided not to elaborate.

"Well, if we have paid everything, the ledger balance for that supplier should be nothing. If we owe the supplier money, it shows."

"Yes, I see."

"So, it shouldn't ever show that the supplier owes us money, should it?"

She agreed that it shouldn't.

"Indeed," he said, with such a note of triumph in his voice that she wondered if he had only recently come to understand this fact about arithmetic. "But it does, sometimes. And Gwen went back through the entries until she found out where it went wrong and put it right."

"They were mistakes?"

"Some of them were. The clerk had cast the figures badly or he'd written six shillings and ninepence when he meant nine shillings and sixpence. Things like that. But sometimes it was because they did owe us money. One supplier we returned a lot of net to, because of its poor quality. He agreed it was bad and gave us credit against our next order. But we never made a next order because he discontinued that line and we didn't want his other lines. So, Gwen writes to him explaining all this and he sends us the money."

"And this is what you meant by Gwen going through it all?"

"No, even better. She wrote up a little book of comparisons

between suppliers so I can easily see prices, delivery times and number of nets having to be returned. I don't have to carry all that in my head. It's down on paper. I can pick the best deal, and put aside the memory of who last took me out for lunch."

Robert had always been affable where Will was argumentative. Did he even have it in him to be deceitful? Gwen was inclined to rush to judgement. Perhaps it was only Wesley who was stealing. The family had banished him from Eleanor's bed but not from the family business. Maybe he was taking his revenge.

And then Robert was shaking her shoulder.

"Wake-up, Harry. Next stop's ours."

The dullness of the March day had turned to darkness. She stumbled on the tram's steps and was glad of Robert's quickly offered arm.

Harriet woke to a sun much higher in the sky than it ought to be. After several minutes of contemplating its bars lighting her bedroom floor, she realised she had not been called for breakfast. She had been so tired she had gone to bed straight after dinner. She had not spoken to Gwen.

She sneezed, freed herself from the bedcovers enough to get a handkerchief from her drawer, and groaned. A cold was something she didn't need.

A forceful double knock on the door was followed by Gwen saying, "Harry, are you awake?"

"Give me a moment. I need to use the chamber pot."

"I have Mabel here with hot water."

After Harriet opened the door, Mabel and Gwen put the pitchers of hot and cold water on the washstand and Mabel left with the chamber pot.

Gwen said, "Do you mind if I stay? I really need to talk to

you. I told Father about the fraud at the manufactory after breakfast and he's going to Uncle George this morning. He wants us to come."

"You did what? I thought we were going to talk first."

"I'm sorry, Harry. I couldn't hold it in any longer."

Harriet didn't want to think about books of accounts. She wanted to stay in bed and nurse her cold. She stripped off her nightgown, reached for the flannel and scrubbed hard under her arms. She bent to clean between her legs.

"You're so thin, Harry. I don't mean to sound like Mother, but I can see every bone in your back."

"Don't sound like Mother, then. Pass me the towel."

Harriet pulled on her drawers, reached for her chemise and pulled it over her head. "Help me dress. It will be quicker."

Gwen fetched Harriet's corset from her clothes-stand. "I'm not going to lace it tight, mind. Modern women don't tight lace."

"Just lace it, will you. We need to look properly put together if we're to get Uncle George to take us seriously." She glanced at Gwen. "You, by the way, fit the part perfectly. That green-striped blouse always does it."

"I have three of them."

Of course she did. Harriet fastened her stockings to the straps hanging from the corset, trying not to get them twisted in her hurry.

"What exactly did you say to Father?"

"That the books proved, without a doubt, that Robert and Wesley have been taking money and that Uncle George has also been diverting funds to himself without calling them dividends."

"Robert said there were unintentional errors."

"There were. Of course, there were. There will always be errors. These weren't errors. They were large amounts leaving the corporation. The cheques were made out to the Loxley Trust."

"To the trust?"

"Made out to the trust, but booked as payments to suppliers. I checked over and over, Harry. The payments went out of the lace manufactory bank and into the trust."

Gwen was behind her, tying her corset cover. She sighed and Harriet shivered as her breath hit the back of her neck. Uncle George was taking money that he shouldn't. That was clear. At least it was clear to Gwen. But he wasn't keeping it. He was giving it to the trust; to them, the Loxley women.

"What did Father say?"

"He made me go through everything, twice. He was pale and very quiet. Then he asked if I was prepared to say all that in front of Uncle George and I said yes, but I wanted you to come with me."

"He's waiting for us? Not that petticoat, the two on top in the second drawer down. And the white blouse over there. Yes, that one, with the blue trim."

She pulled the clothes on as fast as she could, Gwen buttoning her blouse. They shouldn't keep father waiting. Why on earth had Gwen not woken her earlier? Why had she blurted all this out to Father before they'd had a chance to plan what to say to Uncle George?

She pulled on the skirt she had worn yesterday and fastened the placket. Gwen draped a shawl around her shoulders and started combing her hair.

"Don't make a meal of it. Pin it round the rat, as quick as you can."

"Father said he would wait."

"I just need to clean my teeth. When that's done, I'll be ready. Go and get your outdoor shoes. I'll be down in two minutes."

Harriet dipped her toothbrush in the pitcher of water and ran the bristles over the tablet of paste. How was she going to be able to stand up for Gwen when she didn't really understand what she was standing up about? If there were cheques clearly made out to the Loxley Trust, how could they be listed in the manufactory's books as payments to suppliers? If the payments were as large as Gwen implied, how come no-one had said anything before now?

She ran the toothbrush over her teeth, spat, sneezed, pinned her hat on top of her hastily-put-together hair and stuffed handkerchiefs in her pockets. She checked herself in the mirror. As long as she could hold off sniffing, she looked enough like a person in control. That was the best she could manage. Gwen would have to do the talking.

The red and lime-green porch tiles of Loxley Hall gleamed and the gold lettering in the window above the door glinted in the sun. Harriet squeezed Gwen's hand.

Aunt Beth came to the door herself. "Robert, and Harriet, and Gwendolyn too. What a pleasant surprise."

She looked from one to the other of them and her smile vanished.

Poor Aunt Beth. If only she had been out paying visits this morning, she could have been far away from this unpleasantness that was about to soil her home.

Gwen offered to go through the books with Uncle George, but the more Gwen explained, and the more Uncle George interrogated her, the clearer it became to Harriet that her uncle didn't need evidence. His indignation was not due to feeling falsely accused. It was due to being challenged. He looked as if he might split at the seams.

"I have given you every chance, Gwendolyn. I have installed

you in my office and let you have the run of my financial records. Who do you think you are, a mere slip of a girl, to question me?"

Gwen's voice was choppy, a sign of tears barely held back. "Why would you pay yourself money from the company without putting it properly through the books, Uncle? It doesn't make sense."

Father put his hand on Gwen's arm. "The Ashford agreement is clear, George. The external shareholder is legally entitled to the same dividend as you and I. My signature is on that paper too."

Ashford? Who or what, or where, was Ashford? Gwen had never mentioned anything about Ashford.

Gwen said, "Couldn't you pay dividends to all the shareholders? You and Father and Mr Ashford?"

"No, I damn well couldn't. The contract forbids dividend payments unless profits reach a certain level. Normal practice to suspend dividend payments when times are hard, Ashford said."

Harriet took a handkerchief from her pocket and wiped her running nose. Ashford must be the external investor Gwen had mentioned in her letter. And not just a lender, a shareholder in the company. That made him a part owner.

Her father was scowling.

Uncle George wagged a finger in Gwen's direction. "And do you know what that blackguard Ashford did? He promised he would sell back the shares when the slump was over. We shook on it. A gentleman's agreement. Instead, he's holding on to them. He's buying up shares in the lace business all over Nottingham. I owe that lying cad nothing."

Gwen held her ground. "You signed a contract, not a verbal agreement. Perhaps that was your mistake."

"I signed his wretched paper because he said he wouldn't

enforce the provisions about not paying family salary. He said his lawyers insisted on that clause. Normal practice for family members not to be paid, he said. Boilerplate provision, he said."

The Reverend Loxley wiped his hand across his brow. "And Robert and Wesley, what is their excuse?"

"When Gwendolyn started I wanted to pay them all salary. I was set to moving away from family members being only given spending money out of profits. I'm not the antiquated curmudgeon you think I am, Robert. The young people should have their independence. Beth thinks so. But when I tried, Ashford, that London upstart, that damned banker, had the confounded cheek to threaten me with his lawyers. Me, whose family has been in Nottingham lace for as long as Leaver's machines have existed. Us, Robert. He threatened us!"

"So, you told the boys to steal. Oh, George. Why?"

Gwen said, "Can you buy back his shares from him?"

"Not if he won't sell, my girl."

"And because you don't have the funds. If you had, you would never have become involved with Ashford in the first place."

Uncle George glared at her, his already reddened face darkening another shade. "The money went into the trust. I can't get it from there. The trust is all tied up with lawyers' words too. I didn't anticipate last year's downturn. Nobody did. Except that Ashford, the devious scoundrel. He's starving us out. He's trying to force us to sell more shares to him. And I'm not going to do it. And it's all very well for you, Robert, to come here being all holier-than-thou but your money comes from the manufactory too. You can't keep a large family on the Lenton living. You knew that when you accepted it."

Uncle George, who had been standing with his legs apart and his hands on his hips, sank backwards onto the Drawing Room couch and dropped his head into his hands.

The Reverend Loxley sat down beside his brother. "Leave us, please, Gwen, Harry. I want to talk to your uncle alone."

Harriet followed Gwen into the hall and pulled the double doors of the Drawing Room closed behind her. Her head was swimming. Were things so bad that they could lose the manufactory and all their livelihoods? It seemed they could be.

Gwen pushed open the next door in the hallway, the one leading to the Dining Room and stopped. "Aunt Beth?"

Harriet followed Gwen's gaze. Her aunt was kneeling on the hearthrug. She made a move as if to get up but settled back down, leaving her skirt spread around her in a lake of blue. She put a finger to her lips and beckoned them over with the other hand. Harriet and Gwen knelt beside her, one on either side. Harriet glanced at Gwen and managed a faint smile. It seemed the whole family knew that you could hear everything going on in the Drawing Room of Loxley Hall by listening at the adjoining fireplace in the Dining Room.

Harriet could hear sobbing. She directed a questioning look at her aunt, who whispered, "Poor George. He only wants to keep everyone safe."

Then she heard her uncle say, "I told the boys how to set up the false invoice scheme, Robert. Don't blame them. Blame me. Blame me for it all. It will be my fault if it all comes to our disgrace. I'm so sorry."

Her father's voice, soft, "It's not for me to apportion blame, brother."

But, Harriet thought, her father was going to have to choose between the law and the family. They all were.

Silence.

Aunt Beth gestured to them to get up. Harriet held out a hand to help her aunt to her feet. Her Aunt gave her a wry look, tinged with sadness, but said nothing. Gwen arranged herself on a chair. They were well prepared for the Drawing Room door to open, but it was the sound of the front door closing that Harriet heard. The men had left the house.

Aunt Beth put her hands over her mouth. "It's all my fault." She thrust both arms towards the empty grate as if to expel it from the room. "My fault."

Harriet took her aunt's hands in hers. "What is your fault, Aunt? What do you mean? Come now. The family will find a way through this. We always stick together."

"Harriet, I told, entreated, begged your uncle to create that trust. I wanted the freedom I never had for you girls. I haven't been blessed with children of my own, but I've got you, my four wonderful nieces. I wanted you to study. To go to London. To work. All the things you are doing. And look at what I've done! I've ruined us!"

She pulled her hands away from Harriet's and collapsed into a chair.

Harriet stood still for a minute, then sat down. She pulled a handkerchief from her pocket and blew her nose. "Sorry, I think I have a cold coming on...The trust money? It doesn't belong to us, does it, Gwen? It's from extracting the profits of the manufactory from under Mr Ashford's nose."

Aunt Beth sighed. "It will stop now. Your father will make it stop."

"But, Aunt," Gwen said, "it isn't over. It won't ever be over unless Ashford either gives up or catches Uncle out."

Harriet wiped her nose again. The hankie was sodden. She pushed it back into her pocket and searched for a dry one.

Aunt Beth pulled out a handkerchief of her own and wiped her eyes before saying, "Whatever do you mean, Gwen?"

"Aunt, if Ashford finds out, he can threaten Uncle George with the law and all the disgrace that will bring. He'll do that to force Uncle George and Father to sell their shares to him.

That's what he wants, and Uncle George has given him the perfect excuse."

"Which is my fault."

Harriet said, "No it isn't, Aunt. Will you please stop saying that. You had an idea. A lovely idea. You weren't the one who chose how to make it work."

Father and Uncle George hadn't returned. Harriet could only imagine the nature of their conversation as they walked the streets of Nottingham. She hoped they had forged a way forward. Since her head was throbbing, she suggested to Gwen that they not wait any longer.

As the tram drew away, Gwen said, "What are we to do, Harry? I don't want to lose the income from that trust. We are women. However clever we may be, we can never earn enough to live well. No money and we're back to marrying, or forever living off our relatives. I have found my independence and I like it."

Harriet liked it too. Even the small freedom of having her own tram fare in her own pocket was something she would be reluctant to give up.

"I don't have your head for figures but I think it must be a vast amount of money in the trust if it's going to provide a good income to four of us. How much money are we talking about?"

"I don't know what's actually in the fund, if that's what you mean. I only saw the trust document, not the accounting. But a thousand pounds a year would keep anyone in comfort. To produce four-thousand pounds a year in earnings would require about a hundred and twenty thousand pounds of capital. But I don't believe the trust will give us enough income to live off it entirely. Let's say it's half of that. Five hundred pounds a year each. That would be fifteen thousand pounds of capital for each person. Sixty-thousand pounds for the four of us."

"Sixty thousand pounds! Does the manufactory make the family that much money?"

"In good times easily. It built the new warehouse in the lace market three years ago and Loxley Hall ten years before that. But in bad years there's hardly any profit at all, not if Uncle doesn't lay off the twisthands and the designers. And he hates to do that. They might leave for America. So he continues producing and builds up stocks of net for when times get better."

Sixty thousand pounds into the trust? The new warehouse that loomed over the lace market, Uncle's pride and joy? And Loxley Hall? And the money coming from the manufactory was supporting all their two families in comfort, and Gwen had just said comfort cost a thousand pounds a year. Harriet had never thought of their family as wealthy, but these numbers added up to a definition of wealth.

"You know," Gwen said, "sales are going much better than last year and, if money stops disappearing through Robert and Wesley's little scheme, profits might rise enough to meet that clause in the contract Uncle George was talking about. If Uncle paid and booked dividends properly that would be some money coming out for the family. He would have to pay Ashford his share, of course, even if that does stick in his craw. It might be less money than Uncle's extracting now. But it would be money... I need to see that document."

"Are you planning on staying at the manufactory, then? Wouldn't you be better getting out before there's trouble?"

Could Gwen stand all the pressure if Uncle George didn't stop what he was doing? Would her reputation be ruined if everything went wrong with Ashford? Would she lose her opportunity to become a financial expert before she had even started? She would be far better off using her abilities some-where else, wouldn't she?

Harriet sighed. "Well, my opinion, for what it's worth, is that you should leave before things get nasty."

Harriet sweated and groaned through the next three days. Doctor Bardhill came and told her it was influenza and that she must drink as much as she could, sweetened and salted drinks if she could bear it. It seemed one or other sister was constantly getting her to sit up and lean into a cup of something foul tasting.

The door opened and Gwen backed in, a tumbler in each hand. Harriet pulled herself up to sitting.

Gwen put the drinks on her chest of drawers. "You're looking a lot better." She opened drawers until she found a shawl, which she handed to Harriet. "Do you want the special warm water with sugar and salt added or plain water?"

"Plain water, please."

"I thought that would be your reaction."

She handed Harriet a glass and Harriet swallowed its contents straight down.

"Wonderful. Do you think you could eat something? I'll go and see what Cook has."

Ten minutes later she was back with an assortment of cake and biscuits. Harriet took a bite of shortbread and let it melt in her mouth. Food had never tasted so good.

"So you haven't caught this, then?"

"Not yet. None of us have. But give it time... Will did. He's at Aunt Loxley's."

"Oh, poor Will. I'm so sorry...What day is it? What time?"

"Thursday, about four o'clock."

Harriet slipped back under the covers and turned on her side. She saw Gwen sit down on a chair next to her.

By Sunday she was able to get downstairs and sit by the fire in the Morning Room. Emma was sitting at the table, sketching.

"Emma, do you remember Miss Atkins at the High School, the one who taught biology?"

Emma looked up and tucked back the hair that had fallen over the side of her face. It glinted in the morning sun and seemed lighter than the family chestnut. Was she using something? Lemon juice or even peroxide?

"Oh, yes. Miss Atkins had that dusty-rose coloured trumpet-skirt that looked so dramatic under the black of her academic gown."

"Could you take her a message from me? I need recommendations for books to study for my Bedford exams."

Emma frowned. "Do you think you should be working?"

"Not yet, but when I'm ready I want to have the means at hand. Will you do that for me? And do you still have my old schoolbooks? I should go through them. There will be exam papers in all sorts of stuff, including the dreaded French. Latin too. But I liked Latin, it's logical and economical. But enough of that. Tell me what you have been doing recently?"

Emma laughed. "I would say my feet have hardly touched the ground, but apart from taking the boys to the park I've been sitting. Sitting next to you or sitting next to Gwen, who is upstairs suffering with influenza."

"I know. Poor thing. I'm so sorry."

"It's not your fault, you silly goose. But, you know, we *were* talking about you, Gwen and me, before she got sick. She was saying you thought she should leave the manufactory. Why would you suggest such a thing? It's important for who she is."

Harriet pulled up the blanket that was spread over her knees. Maybe tomorrow she would be able to get properly dressed for the winter weather. A nightdress and two dressing-gowns, an old one of Robert's over her own, were insufficient.

"Has Gwen told you about the financial shenanigans at the manufactory?"

"Yes, she has."

"Has she explained that the family could be in a lot of trouble? And that it might mean no more money into our trust. And what is there might not really be ours, because it was... well... stolen."

"Uncle George can't steal from his own business. That's not logical."

"The way Gwen explained it, it is. There are rules. Contracts. It's the law."

But was it justifiable to circumvent the rules when they'd been manipulated by someone like Ashford? That was what Uncle George had seemed to be saying. Father hadn't agreed. But what was done was done. Morality, law and survival had failed to line up.

Emma drummed her fingers on the arms of her chair and frowned. "The way I see it is that this evil Mr Ashford deceived Uncle George and Father. He's a banker. He could have lent them the money. But he didn't. He came up with this tricky plan to steal the lace manufactory from us. So, Gwen and I have a plan of our own."

"You do?"

"We are going to ask Uncle George to borrow money for us and buy that building in Bridlesmith Gate that's up for sale. He can get a loan if it's to buy a building. He can't get one because he needs to support the family. Crazy, isn't it?" Emma pushed back her straying hair with both hands. "We'll open a shop specially for women. All the extra pretty bits that they love. I'll help Gwen get set up before I go to London. If we open on Saturdays and in the summer, and maybe in the lead up to Christmas, we should have a business. And she can keep working at the manufactory."

Uncle George had taken money from the manufactory and put it in the trust. Now he was being starved of money for the family and the terms of the trust prevented any of the sisters simply giving trust money to him. But there was nothing to stop Gwen and Emma repaying a loan, with interest.

Harriet laughed. "And you'll be repaying Uncle George from your trust income. Full circle."

Emma looked at her earnestly. "And from the money the shop makes."

But Gwen would still be at the manufactory, in danger of getting involved in scandal and all the mental distress that could bring.

"Emma, if Gwen gave up the manufactory she could open the shop all week. She could learn all about finance and business by running the shop, and it isn't as if the manufactory is paying her anything."

"Uncle George has a special job for her." Emma stood, as if to draw a line under the exertions of the conversation. "The others must be having tea by now. I'll go and get us some. Do you want cake? You should have cake. I'm sure Mother will insist, anyway."

She got up and covered the distance to the door in three lithe strides. Harriet wondered when she would feel well enough to move like that again. She stared into the fire and rubbed her palms together. The room was so quiet she could hear them rasping.

Gwen had been distraught when she discovered that Robert, Wesley, and even Uncle George, were taking money from the manufactory. Harriet had believed her in danger of losing her equilibrium if she remained there. How had that reaction changed into a determination to stay? And what was this special job? Why was Emma so cagey? She had a feeling Emma thought she would disapprove.

Emma backed through the door, a tray of tea things in her hands. She put it down, poured two cups, handed Harriet a plate with a slice of fruit cake and said, "Tom Bardhill was down from London. He was here this morning, while you were still asleep."

Harriet breathed in sharply. Emma kept on talking.

"But he had to get back this afternoon. He brought us news of Will, asked after you too. Did you know he took Will to Aunt Loxley's? He went round to Will's digs after he didn't turn up to a meeting they were both going to and found him sick in bed. The landlady was taking up his meals and washing water, but no-one was looking after him. I can't imagine how horrible it must be to be alone when you're so sick. Well, Tom got Will to a Hansom and took him to Holland Park and Aunt Loxley telegrammed us. Now she's saying she's going to get a telephone, in case of emergencies."

"That was very good of Tom." Harriet fiddled with the fringe of her blanket, half relieved that Tom had not seen her. She was in no state to be seen, sitting around the house in her nightclothes. "But I'm not sure our aunt having a telephone is altogether a blessing for us. She'll be able to get in touch with Uncle George and Father far too easily if we step out of line while we're staying with her."

Emma waved her piece of cake at her. "Are you thinking of stepping out of line, Harry?"

Parading around with radical women, wasn't that what Will had called it? Aunt Loxley was unlikely to think highly of that as an occupation. She only hoped Gwen was going to be alright, still at the manufactory, with both her and Emma's support so far away.

Chapter 11
English Botany

July 1906

Harriet rounded the corner and saw Emma waiting by the vicarage gate. Emma was stepping from one foot to another, her white tea gown fluttering in the breeze and her hat, a profusion of white gauze and pink silk-roses, held down with one hand.

"Mother has arranged tea in the garden. And Father will join us, would you believe. Or do you want to wash and brush-up first? I was sure you'd want a cup of tea, but perhaps you'd rather go upstairs?"

"I could drink twenty cups of tea."

"Then leave your portmanteau inside the gate here. You can take it up later."

Gwen and her mother were sitting at the table under the apple tree.

Gwen called out, "How was the exam?"

Harriet walked over to her mother and kissed her on the cheek before sitting next to Gwen. "It was like a big test of all we did at school. Some French, some Latin, some arithmetic, some passages to write comprehensions on, and some drawing, but no music. The French was the hardest and the drawing the easiest. There was an optional biology paper I did, and I believe I did myself justice on the botany but less so on the zoology and not at all well on all the microscopic animals."

Seeing Eleanor and Wesley walking down the path, Harriet covered her mouth and whispered, "Is he living here again?"

Gwen rolled her eyes. "Eleanor was pining and whining, and Doctor Bardhill gave him a clean bill of health."

Wesley must have caught her staring. He looked away. Harriet felt herself blushing.

Her mother handed her a cup of tea. "I'm proud of you, Harriet, and so is your father. We are all proud of you. Look, here he comes. He can tell you for himself."

It was not only her father, shading his eyes from the sun with his hand, it was Uncle George with Aunt Beth, in a hat that defied the sun to come anywhere near her, and behind them Robert with a package wrapped in green tissue paper in his hands.

Harriet stood, "Father."

"Harriet, dear. Our own breaker of barriers. Our very own blue-stocking."

"Father? Are you teasing me?"

"Not at all. You are our aspirant to the new century."

He took the package from Robert and placed it in her hands.

"Congratulations, Harriet, on obtaining a place to study at an institution as renowned as Bedford College, London."

Will's words. Had Will been involved in planning this performance? And she hadn't got a place, not yet, only sat an exam.

Harriet put the package on the table and pulled back layers of tissue paper. A small book, octavo size, but thick, with a scuffed red leather spine. The book boards, marbled brown and red, front and back, were nothing special. Some second-hand textbook? An elaborate joke? She turned to the title page.

English Botany or Coloured Figures of British Plants, with their Essential Characters, Synonyms and Places of Growth. The Figures by James Sowerby F.L.S. 1801.

Sowerby! And a first edition, when the copper plates were new.

Emma said, "The pictures in there are exquisite. They are so like the way you draw plants, Harry. Tender and delicate. Turn to the print of our Nottingham autumn crocus. So crisp. It's as if you could touch the petals."

The page was marked with a piece of card. Harriet stared at the plant she loved, so familiar and so ephemeral. "And accurate. Superbly accurate. Where did you get it? It is an immensely beautiful book by an immensely important illustrator."

Robert said, "There are another thirty-five like that. We didn't think we needed to wrap them all. I certainly wasn't going to carry them all. Will tracked them down in London. Used to belong to the Royal College of Surgeons."

"I...I don't know what to say...A thirty-six volume set? Except thank you, of course. Thank you all."

It was too much. Far too much. The family shouldn't be spending the sort of money a first edition of Sowerby must cost. What must Uncle George be thinking? She looked over at Gwen. Gwen cocked her head to the side. She clearly knew something she wasn't going to say out loud; something that might disrupt this moment of family togetherness.

Harriet pulled out her handkerchief and wiped her brow to clear the beads of sweat that were gathering. She felt grubby compared to her sisters in their light tea gowns. The men had discarded their jackets. She still had hers on.

Her mother picked up the bell at her side and gave it two

hard shakes. "You go and freshen up, Harriet dear. I'll have hot water sent to your room. You look exhausted and we have guests tonight. The Bardhills will join us for a late supper. Will and young Thomas Bardhill are coming down by the evening train."

By the time Harriet got to her room the pitcher and bowl were ready on the washstand, a fresh towel laid on her bed. She took off her jacket. Thomas Bardhill was coming to supper. Could she look at him over cold meats and chutney without blushing? Could she control her glances in the presence of her family? Could she trust herself not to wait in dark corners and fling herself upon him as he passed?

There was a soft knock at the door and Eleanor came in. "I'll help you with your blouse. Will you help me with the ties on my tea-gown? I need to rest too if I'm to keep going into the evening."

"Thank-you, Nell. How have you been?"

"Much better since the surgery, but I still tire easily. That's only to be expected. Child-bearing is hard on the body, even when the children are never born."

Freed of blouse, skirt, petticoat and corset, Harriet pulled her eldest sister down onto the bed to lie next to her. Eleanor didn't know what Wesley had done, and she was the happier for not knowing. The breeze from the open window lifted her chemise and embraced her skin. It was a kind breeze. A breeze to heal her sister.

Will, Tom and Gwen were standing by the French doors, which were flung open to the garden. Warm evening air was drifting through the Drawing Room. When Harriet got near, she heard

Gwen say, "I hope you kept the paperwork for Harry's books, Tom."

"Why would *Tom* have the paperwork?"

Harriet blurted it out before considering that the comment had not been meant for her hearing. She immediately wished she hadn't.

Will clapped Tom on the back. "It was Tom here knew that the librarian at the Royal College of Surgeons was selling off old books and fellows of the college were getting first choice before auction. So, he got a fellow he knew to buy the set. Got them for next to nothing."

So that was what Gwen knew. The amazing gift was a second-hand bargain obtained by Tom. Was it embarrassment at Will's complete lack of tact, not to mention her own, or was it something else that was rushing the heat into her cheeks?

She nodded in Tom's direction. "Well, thank you. It was a very clever choice."

Aunt Beth struck some familiar chords on the piano. Will cleared his throat and took Gwen's arm. "Aunt Beth has asked me to sing *The Trout*. I need an audience. Come on."

Tom jerked his head to the side and slipped out through the garden doors. Harriet stood stock still, astonished at both the brazenness and the conspiracy that had preceded it. Then she left the room by the same door she had come in by and went into the garden via the kitchen, the lilting tempo of Schubert's unfortunate trout following her down the path. Tom was by the table under the apple tree.

She was frightened by her own desire, her desperate need for the sensation of his mouth against hers. They had so little time, ten minutes at most. He came where she led, pushing her back until she was almost lying on the table. His hand ran up the back of her left leg, inside her skirts. She waited for it to travel further but he stood, kissed her cheek and walked backwards, never taking his eyes off her, until he bumped into the trunk of the tree. She choked back a laugh and gestured to him to get back to the house.

Still trembling in places she hadn't known reacted in such a way, she didn't dare return to the Drawing Room. She went upstairs to re-arrange her hair and watch in the mirror as the flush faded from her cheeks.

Next morning, Harriet made no effort to leave her bed. She lay back, feeling the press of the table on her back, the touch of Tom's lips on hers, the roughness of his chin against her cheek and the urgent pushing of his tongue into her mouth. His tongue along the back of her teeth. Her tongue pushing back past his.

Her mother had told her about the pleasure that a man and a woman gave each other, but only that it existed, that it was one of God's wonders and that it might result in a number of things, some of which were undesirable outside marriage and some of which were undesirable altogether, such as disease and the loss of reputation. What Harriet hadn't gathered from either this or her school biology studies was that it involved an intimate exploration of the other. Nor had she suspected how willingly and fervently she would engage in it. Nothing had warned her of the warmth that had surged through her, impelling her to push her body against his, leading her to want his hand on her leg nearer and nearer the warmth's source.

What were his intentions? Could she ask him?

What are your feelings towards me, Doctor Bardhill, because I want you so much that I can't drag myself out of bed for fear mundane events would tear me from devoting every waking thought to you?

How could she be in love with him? She scarcely knew him, despite having known him since they were children.

Will you marry me, Doctor Bardhill, since you have already had your tongue in my mouth and your hand up above the top of my stockings?

She sat up. She was running the course of a courtship right into marriage in the space of half an hour in bed on her own, without even knowing if any courting was going on. She couldn't marry. If she did, she would lose her place at the college, the place she had not yet acquired. Would she give it up to marry Tom Bardhill? The answer was an emphatic no. Men waited until they were established in life before marrying. Robert was still waiting. Why shouldn't women do the same?

She ran her tongue around her lips and the backs of her teeth. She let herself fall back on the pillow. Marriage wasn't her dilemma. Her dilemma was how far above her stockings she should let Tom go, because she wasn't giving this feeling up. Not now she had found it.

Chapter 12
Clement's Inn

September 1906

Sylvia Pankhurst had provided Harriet with directions to the London headquarters of the Women's Social and Political Union.

Turn to the north of St. Clement Danes Church, cross over the Strand, and Clement's Inn is straight ahead.

Now she was outside St. Clement Danes. Only the main church door did not face the Strand, or any road. It faced a piazza. Roads set off in every direction except straight ahead. The church was an island and Harriet had no idea which of the traffic-filled thoroughfares swirling around it might be the Strand.

There was a flower seller by the church doorway. Perhaps she could point her towards Clement's Inn.

"Oh, that's all gone, dearie. When they built all these fancy, wide streets. I think you'd best go up Lincoln's Inn way and ask. To your left, right up that new Kingsway and right again into Lincoln's Inn Fields. I reckons there's still a street called Clement's Passage or suchlike, down Clare Street, right off of the Fields."

The flower seller's breath was laden with a cloying sweetness and an undertone resembling wet coals landing on the fire. Harriet recognised it from accompanying her mother on parish visits. It was the smell of starvation. She wished the woman good-day and gave her a penny for her trouble.

She found Lincoln's Inn Fields easily enough and crossed to the other side of the square. Then, telling herself to take careful note of the street names, she wound along Portugal Street and Carey Street and down Bell Yard, from which she emerged into a noisy thoroughfare. She turned right, walked a few hundred yards and saw St. Clement Danes church ahead and to the left. She had come full circle.

She moved closer to the building towering next to her, out of the way of the people who seemed to know where they were going, and pulled her handkerchief from her bag. Should she be here at all? Perhaps having got herself up to London and into a degree course was enough of a blow for the cause of female emancipation. She dabbed at the sweat on her forehead, then held the handkerchief to her nose, replacing the smell of the horse resting by the kerb with the scent of attar of roses.

She walked on until she was back outside St. Clement Danes. The flower seller with the bad breath was gone.

"Excuse me, Miss."

Harriet turned to see a tall woman with a large leather satchel slung over her shoulder. She was holding out Harriet's lace-edged handkerchief.

"I believe you may have dropped this."

"Well, thank you very much.

"Emmeline Pethwick Lawrence, at your service."

Could this be the same radical Emmeline Pethwick she had heard about from Sylvia, the woman who had only agreed to take her husband's name if he took hers? If it was, this was too much of a coincidence. It must be destiny.

"Miss Loxley, Harriet Loxley. Oh, and if you don't mind, maybe you can help me. I am looking for some offices located in Clement's Inn."

"Which offices are you seeking? They are multitude in our building. I reside there, you see. We have the Fabian society, the Dickensian society. Many worthy causes known to mankind and many not so well known. The way is to the right here, around the edge of the Royal Courts of Justice. A small entrance way. Easy to miss."

She waved a hand towards the building replete with gothic ornamentation rivalling that of the Palace of Westminster. Then she held out her hand, clearly intending Harriet to shake it, just like a man to another man. Her grip was firm and her smile humorous and endearing.

Harriet said, "I'm looking for the offices of the Women's Social and Political Union. I believe they are quite a new organisation. Do you mind me asking, are you the Mrs Emmeline Pethwick Lawrence who is providing the WSPU with its offices? I have heard so much about you from my acquaintance, Miss Sylvia Pankhurst."

"Indeed I am. The very same. My husband, Fred, and I provide space in our apartment. The building is very adaptable, a thoroughly modern construction of mixed offices and full-service apartments. Believe you me, the WSPU will not remain obscure for long. By the end of a year they will be a household name. It is the clarion-call for the twentieth century. Come. These deliveries can wait a little. I'll walk you there."

She led Harriet down a narrow, and malodorous, alleyway next to the building Harriet had imagined as a cathedral or a palace, but which Mrs Pethwick Lawrence had said the Royal Courts of Justice. The passageway opened out into a square laid to lawn, beyond which were three blocks of red brick, fronted by cast-iron railings. Harriet followed Mrs Pethwick Lawrence up a single flight of stairs and along a tiled hallway. At the end go the hallway her companion pushed wide a half-open door to reveal a young woman with her head bowed. She was writing briskly.

"Ah, Christabel, this is Miss Harriet Loxley. She has come to find us, and now she has."

When Christabel Pankhurst looked up, Harriet recognised her mother's apple cheeks and dimpled chin etched in higher definition in her daughter. A breeze from the open window rustled a heap of papers marked with violet copying ink. Emmeline Pethwick Lawrence quickly placed a nearby book on top of them.

"Well, I must leave you with Christabel, Miss Loxley. I want to catch the evening post."

Christabel rose in a movement at once graceful and formidable.

"Miss Loxley. Delighted. Have you come to offer your talents? What are they?"

The daughter had inherited her mother's firm gaze too.

"I'm not at all sure I know what my talents are, Miss Pankhurst. I think I'm in London to find that out. I met your mother and your sister on the day the women's bill was talked out and I've come to see if there's a part I can play. Miss Pankhurst, if I may ask, how do you intend to persuade the government to bring in a women's franchise bill?"

Christabel Pankhurst sat down and gestured to Harriet to do the same. She seemed startlingly young, although she must have been about twenty-six, much the same age as Harriet herself.

"Ah, so you are that Miss Loxley, the well-turned-out scion of Loxley Lace. Good, we need examples of poise and confidence in the movement. We must look impressive, not dowdy, Miss Loxley, and we must make our demands clear. We must not pussy-foot around. We must shout until they hear us. We must take power, because you cannot change attitudes until you have power. We have waited two generations for reason, and justice, to apply. What we need is freedom and citizenship. And the way to that is the vote."

Harriet recalled the protest at the Manchester Free-Trade Hall, the raising of the banner demanding Votes for Women, and the spitting at the policeman. She wondered if Christabel regretted the spitting. She did not appear to be a young lady inclined to regret.

Christabel gestured towards a door to her right. "There is a room full of eager young people next to this one working on tactics. Or there would be if they hadn't all gone to tea." She smiled, a smile that crinkled the corners of her eyes and made her face shine with persuasive power. "Our tactics, Miss Loxley, are to make the new Liberal government aware of us every step of its way. They want us to fade away now the election is over. We will not fade. We will be there, at every by-election. We will question ministers. And if we are refused we will ensure the entire country knows we are refused. Are you willing to disrupt political meetings, Miss Loxley?"

Traceable public action was not what Harriet had antici-pated. Something more like the office work taking place beyond that door would be more easily kept from Aunt Loxley and her newfound love of the Daily Mirror.

"I have no training in public speaking."

"We can provide training. You have presence. Do you have the will?"

Did she?

"I'm afraid I couldn't put myself in a position where I might be recognised. You asked about talents. I can draw passably well. I could illustrate announcements, perhaps."

"Chalk pavements. Start tomorrow. We have a meeting to advertise. Elegant chalking will impress. Be here at two for the instructions."

As she left Harriet wondered what had happened to her intention to do something inconspicuous.

When Will met her by St. Clement Danes he complained that, since it was six o'clock, the buses were overcrowded and the cabs hard to come by.

"It's only four miles to Holland Park, Will. I've walked enough of London now to know it's like going from one village to another. You just need to know the way."

They walked in silence for about fifteen minutes and not until they had left the Strand behind and were striding along the Mall did Harriet tell him about Christabel Pankhurst and Emmeline Pethwick Lawrence and, after some hesitation and diversion into other topics, inform him of her agreement to be back at Clement's Inn by two the next day.

"You can't do that, Sis. You know Emma specially wants to see the Rokeby Venus, and Tom has booked a slap-up restaurant for us."

"I'll be there for the National Gallery. I'm not letting Emma down. If I had known there was a special lunch I may not have committed myself, but I have and I cannot go back on a commitment."

"Why ever not?"

She imagined herself talking to Tom about art, being knowledgeable and charming, with Emma providing some technical input. Could she help with the pavement chalking another time? But it was too late. She had promised.

"Because I want to get involved with this organisation and I don't want to fail at my first attempt. First impressions are important."

"It's them that wants you. They'll be only too happy to have you another day."

"Will, I might be playing a small part but us women must stand up for the vote at every opportunity."

He sighed. "The franchise will be expanded in due course. Patience is what's needed."

"Just when is due course? It wasn't within the lifetime of the last generation of suffragists."

"It's not as simple as you think–"

"It's perfectly simple. The Liberal government has to be made aware of how deeply it is betraying the women."

"The Liberals are your natural allies, not as conservative as either the Tories or the working men of the Labour Party. You women should be supporting the Liberal Party, not opposing it."

"You sound like Asquith."

"Asquith is a clever politician and dedicated to the New Liberal cause."

Green Park was ahead of them. The air was cooling. Harriet wanted to savour the smell of cut grass on the evening breeze, and not argue with Will.

And then he repeated it.

"Women's suffrage will have to wait."

She felt like stamping her feet. She looked down at her boots, robust, with strong heels. She could stamp on his. She could make him yelp.

"Why? Why should it wait? It's been waiting for thirty years. All these politicians say they support it and then they all find something that's more important. How is that? Women are not important? Not as good company as dogs and not as useful as horses. Is that really it?"

He ignored her and carried on, at great length, about the radical nature of the new Liberal government, only stopping explaining proposed legislation for the five minutes it took to negotiate their way through the traffic at Hyde Park Corner and cross into the park.

They were half-way back to their aunt's now and she didn't want to be lectured at for the entire distance. She knew all about the reforming policies, about not sending children to prison and paying pensions to the old to keep them with their families and out of the workhouse. She read the papers. But keeping quiet didn't seem to be stopping his flow. She clicked her tongue. It had no effect.

"And," Will continued, "they will bring in labour exchanges for the unemployed and minimum wages in industries dominated by women, including machine-made lace."

"That won't please our uncle," she muttered, clenching her fists.

"And health insurance for working men. Britain will have, for the first time in history, a healthy population and a healthy army. That's a big point. Should even win the Tories over. They know the men sent to fight the Boers in Africa were a sickly bunch of undersized, ill-educated weaklings."

She grimaced, not that he noticed. They were already half-way through the park. The most pleasant part of their walk was being taken up with him addressing her like she was an audience of schoolchildren.

"That's not a nice way to describe people, Will."

"And all this while fending off the House of Lords, the Irish Nationalists and the bloody women."

"The *bloody* women would be a vital source of support for your progress if you ever gave them the chance."

"Well, Sis, what a firebrand you are becoming. I support the women's cause. You know that. You don't need to get all huffy."

"And you don't need to be so patronising."

Harriet didn't imagine Emmeline Pethwick Lawrence would have put up with being talked at for half an hour, but she didn't imagine she would use intemperate language either. She concentrated on keeping her voice low and steady.

"I don't see why a simple vote extending the franchise enjoyed by men to women would detract from all these worthy causes, or why I shouldn't be allowed to say so. And now I'd like some peace and quiet. If that's alright with you."

They walked in silence for a while, but as they reached the end of the park Will audibly drew in his breath. "At the risk of getting my head bitten off, it's like this, Sis. The Liberals never had such a big majority as they have now and they likely never will have again. The old-fashioned Liberals from the industrial heartland of this country, businessmen like Uncle George, are the bedrock of the party. They vote Liberal because we support free trade, not because the New Liberals plan social reform. Our reforms are far-reaching and long term, and to carry them out we need to win the next election too. Unfortunately for your cause, there are enough MPs who believe that extending the vote to women with a franchise based on property will mean more votes for the Tories. Now I know that's not logical and that if women did vote the same as their husbands, as many politicians claim they will, then there will be as many women voting Liberal as there are men. And if women think for themselves, which of course they do, they should vote Liberal because they care about social change, or they might even vote Liberal out of sheer gratitude for getting the vote. I hear all those arguments, but political thinking is driven by two things: the desire for power and the fear of losing it. Your Pankhurst party is barking up the wrong tree in wanting the limited property franchise. The New Liberals simply can't risk throwing away their chance of real social change for the sake of a few wealthy women voting."

"So you admit those arguments are false and that the government thinks it is their prerogative to dictate when the women are to be noticed. Which actually means Miss Christabel Pankhurst is right, not mistaken. We have to keep harassing the government until it takes heed."

"There are many in the party who believe in the women's cause."

"I know that. They would vote for our bill if given the chance. It's Asquith and your government won't give them that chance."

The end of Aunt Loxley's road was in sight, but Harriet knew she wouldn't be able to enjoy the evening relaxing in the garden now, and she resented it. Will claimed to be on her side but was talking just like the government. After they were let in, she went to greet her aunt, pleaded a headache, and retired to her room.

Chapter 13
The Mud March

Saturday, February 9th 1907

L ying in her bed at Aunt Loxley's, awake in the early morning and dreading the march from Hyde Park to Westminster, Harriet was wishing she had not made an undertaking to Alice Slack. After one and a half terms in London, and well into her course at Bedford College, she was an established member of the Women's Social and Political Union. She was determined to fight for the right to vote. But pavement chalking was one thing; marching in the street was quite another.

After missing their lunch date that first day she had chalked pavements, Harriet had apologised to Emma.

"Don't worry, silly goose. Lunch was splendid. They made a great fuss of me."

"Did Tom Bardhill say anything about my not attending? Was he put out?"

Emma had laughed at her concern. "What you were doing was splendid too, and Tom couldn't stop saying so. How was the wretched pavement chalking, anyway?"

Bending low and drawing on the ground had been harder

than she had expected. It had stiffened her back and cramped her fingers, forced dust and frightful smells up her nose and subjected her to the comments and sneers of strangers. There were more positive comments than sneers, since her lettering was attractive, but it was the sneers that smeared themselves through her mind.

"I was amazed at how the time and date of a meeting could attract so much attention. But I suppose attention is what was wanted."

"I think it must have been you who was attracting the attention. A well-dressed lady crouching in the street and drawing on the pavement. Who has ever seen such a thing? Were you alone?"

"No, there were three of us. And the crowds stood well back. They were noisy, though."

And now she was going to march in the street, like a trade unionist. It could only be a matter of time before someone recognised her and told Aunt Loxley. Then word would get back to Nottingham. What if Mother and Father were scandalised? What if Uncle George decided trust money should not be used to finance her making a public spectacle of herself.

And she had persuaded Emma into this march. She depended on trust money too.

Harriet lit the lamp beside her bed and stared at the glow thrown on the ceiling. There was no point lying here and fretting. She got out of bed, pulled on wool stockings, put on her slippers and a dressing gown and her coat on top of that.

In the downstairs hall the deep silence was only alleviated by the ticking of the clock. She went into the morning room and, hoping to make some impression on the dark, pulled back the heavy curtain over the window. Rain was sheeting through the light cast by the street lamp.

The march had been planned for months. How many people would turn up if this weather continued? And was this march going to be any more persuasive than all the delegations, petitions and bills in Parliament that had gone before it? If she hadn't made that commitment to Alice Slack, if she hadn't convinced Emma to come with her, she could be curled up on Aunt Loxley's sofa with a novel.

She could be seeing Tom.

The morning room door opened and a maid came in, a slight girl in a blue cotton frock and long white apron.

"Beg pardon, Miss Harriet. I didn't know you was in here. I came to start on the fires. I'll have to get this here grate cleaned out and laid. It's going to be a good hour before the room will warm. Shall I have the kitchen get you a hot drink and some toast when I go down for the kindling?"

Harriet watched the girl shovel up the previous day's ashes, screw up newspaper, place it in the grate, lay sticks in a criss-cross pattern and balance a few coals on top. Since she was one of her aunt's three live-in servants, and Mrs Smith, the cook, lived out and wouldn't arrive until half-past seven, requesting a hot drink now would probably get the other housemaid out of bed.

"No drink. That won't be necessary, thank you."

The maid set fire to her construction.

"Ring the bell when the coals start to fall Miss, it will need topping up then."

"Thank you."

Thank you was more than enough but this was an opportunity. Harriet rarely got a chance to talk to the servants in Aunt Loxley's house. At the vicarage they only had Mabel living in and Mrs Sheffield coming in daily, so the family went in and out of the kitchen performing small tasks. Here, Aunt Loxley expected the family to remain in their part of the house and the servants to appear when required. Which, considering the family here was often only Aunt Loxley herself, must make for a lonely existence for her aunt.

"I don't know your name."

"Jane, Miss."

Harriet chewed her lip. Tom had told her he often doctored servants' illnesses in their masters' houses and that he'd found people frequently gave their servants common names so they wouldn't have to be bothered with learning their real ones. Every scullery maid was Jane, a never-ending succession of Janes.

"Is it really? The name your mother gave you?"

"Sure as I've got a mother, Miss."

"And how old are you, Jane?"

"Fifteen, Miss."

"And how long have you been working for my aunt?"

"Since I was twelve."

"Do you like it here?"

The girl blushed. Harriet wasn't sure how the lack of ease had arisen, but she knew her aunt would not want her to get too familiar with this Jane. Maybe Jane knew it too.

"Oh yes, Ma'am, I mean Miss Harriet. Mrs Loxley is a very fair employer. She gives us the cloth to make our uniforms, not like most. And the money's handy, what with five others after me and three still babes."

Harriet was stuck. She wanted to know more, but didn't know how to ask. To Mabel she would have said something like, *And how is your mother, now? Over that cold from last week?*

Abandoned by natural conversation, she continued with friendly formality. "Well, thank-you, Jane. You may go. Don't worry about the fire. I will see to it myself."

"As you wish, Miss. I'll not disturb you with the dusting in here."

So, in her aunt's house, there was Jane, Mrs Smith, Richardson the ladies' maid, and one other girl whose name she didn't yet know. The three she did know had run-of-the-mill names that could well have been imposed, but it seemed her aunt didn't do that. And providing the material for the uniforms? Was this telling her that her aunt was a lot more like the vicarage Loxleys than she chose to appear? Not that the vicarage servants had uniforms. They wore their own clothes.

It felt like they had been waiting at the muster point, in the drizzle, for an eternity. Harriet sighed and shuffled her feet. Emma put a hand on Alice's arm and nodded towards a group of well-dressed women walking towards them. "Who is that over there, in the herringbone tweed, three-quarter length?"

"Lady Frances Balfour."

Alice seemed amused.

Harriet raised her eyebrows. "Really? Balfour's wife? Marching for the vote?"

"Not his wife. His sister-in-law."

Emma said, "And the lady next to her with the long fur stole?"

"That's Mrs Henry Fawcett, Millicent Garrett Fawcett. She's the president of the National Union of Women's Suffrage Societies, and she's been advocating for the vote forever."

Harriet peered round Emma's shoulder. So that fragile looking lady was the famous Mrs Fawcett.

Alice said, "She's written vast amounts, articles in journals, books on political economy and even novels. Doctor Elizabeth Garrett Anderson is her sister and her daughter, Phillipa, went to Cambridge and got the highest score out of all the mathematics students in her year."

Emma laughed. "Well, if people like that can't vote to decide who runs things, I don't see why most men should."

Alice nodded vigorously. "Maybe that's what the men worry about too. And before you ask, the lady next to her, the older lady with the very straight back and the sable jacket that any woman would envy, is Lady Jane Strachey. She has also been campaigning for the suffrage forever. One of her daughters is the chief organiser behind this march."

Harriet grabbed Emma's arm. "Look, over there, Mrs Pethwick Lawrence and Miss Christabel Pankhurst. The Liberal women didn't want the WSPU here today because they keep on heckling at Liberal meetings but here they are anyway. Christabel is the one with the pale coat with the large lapels."

"Miss Pankhurst does seem so very young. How does she get herself heard when she speaks?"

"Force of personality."

Stewards started walking through the groups of women, asking them to line up in sets of eight and follow along behind their banner.

"They wish us to appear dignified," Alice muttered.

Harriet stared at the puddles in the street. "I think we are going to appear wet. Just like the last time we did this together. Is your wonderful husband here to support us?"

"He's going to wait in Piccadilly."

Emma, on the end of their line, turned away from studying the crowd. "Our brother Will and Tom Bardhill are waiting in Piccadilly. Tom is Harry's beau."

"He is not!" Harriet grabbed Emma's arm and pulled her out of Alice's hearing. "Don't go saying things like that in front of other people. If it gets back to our aunt, I'll be sunk."

"You are sunk. I can't imagine how anyone could possibly miss you two making sheep's eyes at each other."

Harriet knew she was blushing. She hoped her cheeks were flushed enough from the cold for the blush not to show. Sheep's eyes were the least of it.

"Look, keep quiet about it, please. The last thing I need is Aunt Loxley getting ideas about lack of propriety, or Mother and Father and the Bardhills planning out my respectable future. I have a degree to finish. I like having a place to use my mind. And so do you. Remember, we are in this together."

A trumpet sounded, a drum rapped a military beat, and the call of the Marseillaise rang across the park.

With the blue silk banner of education billowing above them, Harriet took Alice's hand on one side and Emma's on the other. She sang the bit of the Marseillaise she knew. The bit everyone knew. Except they had changed the marchers into women.

"*Aux armes citoyennes, formez vos bataillions. Marchons, marchons...*"

Harriet walked with her eyes to the front, not daring to look to right or left, mindful of just how exposed to public view she was. Respectable women didn't demonstrate in the street. What was next? Running with the mob?

Mud was everywhere underfoot. Harriet could feel the wet coming through her stockings. She looked down and her green skirt was brown three inches up. That was no way to treat good woollen cloth. She hoped all this was going to be worth it.

She jumped as Alice yelled *Vive la liberté* and started yet again on *Allons enfants de la patrie*. Harriet looked past Emma. The pavements were packed. She looked up. People were leaning out of upstairs windows, flags were waving, things were being shouted. The watching crowds were singing, for the glory of the country, for liberty, for the right to be a citizen and for the vote.

Harriet straightened her shoulders and lifted her chin.

They turned into Piccadilly. Tom was there, as he'd promised, halfway up a lamppost and waving his hat in the air. She didn't wave back. They had been told to remain dignified and not to break ranks. She nodded and smiled and realised the smile had broken into a grin.

She suspected Emma had noticed the grin, although all Emma said was, "There's Will, Harry. With his bicycle. I don't know how he dares ride it in London, with all the traffic there is. He's so brave."

Was it courage? Harriet saw it as freedom. Since bringing the bicycle to London, Will had moved away from his landlady, she of the short rations, and into new digs, further out from Westminster. He had asked Tom to go in with him, but Tom's conditions with the dispensary required him to live in the men's hostel in Bethnal Green. If the dispensary trustees only knew what a hotbed of radical politics that place was they would close it down.

The people in front of them stopped and Harriet risked a look back at Tom. He waved to her and she lifted a hand, trying not to be too obvious.

Last week, he had prevailed upon the landlady of a local public house to allow him private use of the snug so she could meet his fellow doctors. Over pints of brown and mild they had declared their support for women voting, universal adult suffrage, and government subsidised health insurance. As the evening wore on, and Harriet swapped her half of mild for a glass of port and lemon, some started toasting the overthrow of capitalism and replacing Parliament with a federation of worker-run co-operatives. She had become confident and excited, happy to argue with them, even calling them armchair socialists.

She kicked a lump of mud away from her feet. As a respectable woman, she could never have entered that pub without Tom's help. She could never have got back to Holland Park without Will escorting her. Men had freedom she didn't. The freedom to come and go without restraint. The freedom to not just express opinions in private but to demonstrate their support for ideas in the street. They rode bicycles in the London traffic, climbed lamp posts and waved their hats in the air. Tom and Will went down to the docks and listened to working people.

The procession started moving again, and a cheer went up from the crowd.

Harriet rolled her shoulders and pulled herself up straight. She had listened to Jane that morning and discovered something about how Aunt Loxley's servants viewed their lives. And now she *was* marching in the street. She *could* do these things that made her uncomfortable. She could learn to be noticed. It couldn't be any more challenging than arguing with Wesley, or Tom's friends. Just more public.

An hour later the marchers ahead of her filed into a space between the shop fronts of the Strand.

"Exeter Hall," Alice said.

With Emma on one side and Alice on the other Harriet squeezed through the doors and into a whirl of wet coats and furling umbrellas. A wide foyer spread to each side and the muddied crowd split to either go straight ahead or to climb the two staircases sweeping up to the first floor.

Alice headed for the stairs. "I hope we are not too far behind for a seat. Standing throughout the speeches will be trying.

Much as I appreciate the speakers they do tend to carry on rather too long."

From the upper gallery Harriet could appreciate just how many women had chosen to stand. The vast hall, for all the world like a railway station, was buzzing with excited voices.

"The history of this place is linked to the dissenting sects," Alice said. "It was here that all the great anti-slave-trade meetings were held. Famous people stood on that platform down there."

Harriet shook what wet she could from her skirt and settled into her seat. She adjusted her hat, patted her hair into some sort of shape and leant forward, her chin on her hands, waiting for matters to begin.

Lady Strachey spoke, and so did Mrs Fawcett. Mrs Fawcett was a fine speaker, easily heard. Then Keir Hardy took the stage and was magnificent, declaring to resounding applause that the *half angel, half idiot* period of history was over for women.

Alice nudged her and pointed to the programme. "Look who's coming up. Mr Israel Zangwill. He is immensely witty. The Dickens of our day."

Mr Zangwill proved to be a thin man in round glasses, with thick, wavy black hair, a high forehead and a beaky face. He stalked the stage like a magnificent wading bird hunting along a mudflat.

"How do they justify their monstrous proposition that one half of the human race shall have no political rights? Woman is a separate and individual personality; a human soul, and what is more to the point, a tax-payer. Her standpoint, her interests, differ vastly from man's. How dare we then leave her out of the reckoning? Our Constitution would work not only better, but with a fairer balance of powers, if the House of Lords were replaced by a House of Ladies!"

The old hall echoed to the stamping of feet and rang with women's laughter. Harriet stood to cheer with the rest. She was part of this. It would take thousands of women's voices to make themselves heard. She could be one of them.

Chapter 14
I Can't Shout in Church

February 1907

The Wednesday after what the press had already dubbed *The Mud March*, Harriet went to a WSPU meeting at Caxton Hall.

Sylvia Pankhurst took the seat next to her.

"It's going to look like a spontaneous lobby of our MPs. We know the government is going to let us down, yet again. We'll march in groups of twenty and demand to enter. Will you be with me?"

"Demand?"

"Rumour has it we'll be opposed."

All around women were complaining about how the government was not going to include a bill bringing in votes for women in the next parliament. So much, Harriet thought, for the contents of the King's Speech being hush hush, like Will had said. The noise lessened as Mrs Pankhurst called for a resolution expressing indignation over women's suffrage being omitted, only to rise to a ferment when the resolution was passed. The noise was such that Harriet couldn't tell who called for the motion to carry the resolution to Westminster and present it to the Prime Minister but, when Mrs Pankhurst came to the front and called out *Rise Up Women!*, she stood and shouted *Now!* with all the rest.

She wasn't nervous as they poured out of the hall and into the street. She was in the front line but she had Sylvia to one side of her and women next to her and behind her. She joined in *Rise up women, the fight is hard and long* to the tune of John Brown's body, leaning towards Sylvia as she walked in order to learn the words she didn't know. But when Westminster Palace came into sight and she was faced with a line of policemen, shoulder to shoulder, not a gap showing between their bulky greatcoats, she gasped and heard others around her do the same. She glanced from one side to the other. There was no way around the cordon. Her heart was beating fast and she realised her hands were clenched. She forced them open. The women's pace slowed. Some stopped altogether.

Sylvia's voice rang out. "Keep going, ladies! They must step aside."

And they did. Like the Red Sea parting, the wall of blue folded back on itself, leaving a gap wide enough for ten of them to pass abreast.

The lady next to Harriet laughed. A sign of either relief or giddiness. Harriet wasn't sure which. Their pace quickened. At the sound of rumbling, she peered ahead through the gap in the cordon. The rumbling grew louder.

"Horses!" Harriet ran to her right, crashing into the lady next to her. "Oh God, I'm so sorry!"

She hauled her up. The woman ran as soon as her feet touched the ground.

Mud splattered across Harriet's face. She turned to find herself inches away from sweat-flecked muscle and sinew.

Thousands of pounds of horse were about to send her flying to the ground. She stepped backwards.

And then it was gone.

She stood, frozen to the spot, as three more horses came straight for her, then wheeled and continued along the front of the women's line. The animals were so close she could make out the individual hairs on their hides.

Had their riders been wielding sabres her head would now be lying at her feet.

"Whew, that was close."

The speaker was a woman next to her, not the one she had hauled up from the ground.

Harriet shuddered. "A veritable cavalry charge."

"Not really. Cavalry would have been coming at thirty miles an hour. But you still don't want to be in the way of a thousand pounds of disciplined horse flesh."

Harriet had never been nearer to a horse than petting the nose of the milkman's steady old mare. She may have been over-dramatic but she was still trembling.

Sylvia was grabbing her arm. "Come on. Back to Caxton Hall. Regroup. New tactics."

At Caxton Hall tea was dispensed and faces were washed. Resolve was tested. Hats were firmly pinned.

Christabel was on the platform. "We will not tolerate this denial of our right to petition Parliament. Right women?!"

Anyone not determined to carry on must have already left because the cheer that resounded around the hall from women shouting and stamping their feet echoed to the ceiling. Harriet could feel her heart beating in her chest. This was real. This was action.

"But this time we will get through. Split up and run if the horses come at you. If not, make for the line and get through it any way you can. Through any gaps. Under their legs if you have to. Then run for the doors. They will know us! They will know we demand to be heard!"

As they left the building Christabel slipped in behind her sister, next to Harriet.

Harriet stared at her. "What are you doing? I thought you kept away from affrays. The organisation needs you free and in one piece."

"Credibility, Miss Loxley. I must be seen to be exercising my right to petition the King. And I must witness the inside of prison walls myself if I am to encourage others to."

This time they walked in a wide line, straight towards the blue ranks.

When Harriet got near enough she spoke the words from the Bill of Rights she had been reciting to herself as she walked. "I wish to petition Mr Asquith, as the King's representative. It is the right of the subject to petition the King and all commitments and prosecutions for such petitioning are illegal."

She heard a scuffle to her left and turned to see Christabel being hauled through the police lines by two burly officers. This was her opportunity. She yanked up her skirt with one hand and ran as hard as she could for the gap in the line. The way through the gates and into New Palace Yard lay right ahead. She heard shouts behind her.

Something hit her hard in the back of her knees and she fell to the ground. She spat grit from her mouth and pulled her hand from under her to feel her cheek but before she could tell if there was blood she was grabbed her by her upper arms. Breath panted into the back of her neck. She was dragged to her feet and her arms were twisted behind her back.

"Let me go!"

"Oh yeh, and have you hare off again. I don't think so. I've had enough exercise. Move!"

He jabbed her hard in the back and she stumbled forwards. "Move, I said."

She had heard how the police made people move on. He was kneeing her in the back, making her move along like a common street vagrant or drunk. Anger swept through her, but also confidence from understanding who he was and what he was doing.

"I would be able to move if you let me down enough for my feet to touch the ground."

There was a guffaw from behind her and she was lowered several inches.

"Now, move!"

Another jab with the knee. She stepped forwards, out of balance and fearing to fall at every step.

"Faster. I don't have all day."

"I'm going as fast as I can. Why don't you unhand me and let me walk properly?"

"And have you race back to the House? Not on yer life. Think I was born yesterday."

More kneeing followed, but as he manhandled her further away from the Palace of Westminster the blows became less and less frequent. She assumed it was as much hard work for him as it was uncomfortable for her. After what seemed an eternity he grunted and dropped her in a doorway. She shuffled up to the top step on her bottom, leant her head against the wall and closed her eyes. She had no idea where she was.

She wasn't sure how long she sat there before struggling to her feet and walking along unknown roads until she recognised her surroundings. First aid treatment and tea were still available at Caxton Hall when she arrived. The talk was all of both Christabel and Sylvia arrested, of hundreds of women arrested.

Her face turned out to be only slightly scratched. She

borrowed a hat with a veil before setting off to catch the bus back to Holland Park. If her aunt insisted on her coming down for supper, she would tell her she had walked into a low-hanging branch in the dark. Aunt Loxley would be concerned, and would protest at her being out after dark alone, but she wouldn't know the full damage. Neither did Harriet, yet. She intended taking a bath and inspecting her sore shoulders and hips in the mirror as soon as she could.

The next morning, after a night of waking every time she lay on the side that had hit the ground, Harriet made use of Aunt Loxley's new telephone to talk to Gwen. She called through to the accounts office at the manufactory. There was no phone in the vicarage.

"Gwen, my checks from the Loxley Trust are coming in smaller than they used to. Have been for three months. If they stay like this there will be scarcely enough to cover my fees for the next term."

"There's less money going into the trust than Uncle George planned. So less has to come out. I'm sorry. It's the consequence of my meddling."

"You've no need to be sorry. Your meddling saved Uncle George's skin and Robert's and Wesley's jobs. It would have only been a matter of time before that wretched Ashford man found out."

Gwen sighed. "Thanks, Harry. I do hope you'll be able to manage. I really do." She paused before saying, "Are you coming down for our grand opening on Saturday?"

Harriet said she would get there somehow, even if it meant borrowing the train fare from her aunt. The new shop? She wouldn't miss it for anything.

Aunt Loxley seemed only too happy to provide funds. "Harriet dear, of course. It's not a loan. It's a gift. And that skirt of yours will never recover from getting caught in the rain last night. We'll go to the West End tomorrow and get you a new outfit. My treat. I hope there are still some of the new season's clothes in the shops."

"That's very kind, aunt, but it's not necessary, really, it's not."

"I insist. You have Friday afternoons free from college, don't you? We'll leave at two."

The shopping trip meant Harriet didn't arrive at the vicarage until it was time for late supper, but she did have a new blue serge suit, with a long jacket trimmed with braid in a fine modern geometrical design.

Her mother gestured to her to sit beside her. "Will has been telling me about how rough those events outside Parliament were."

"The women," Will said, "were trying to get themselves battered and arrested. It's all part of the publicity. If the police confront them with mounted horses they can summon up images of all sorts of barbarity. The Chronical published a cartoon of a mounted policeman called *The London Cossack*. I kept the cutting for you, Harry."

"Thanks. I'll start a scrapbook. You know, Will, this is not a game. Women were arrested, friends of mine, including Miss Sylvia Pankhurst and Miss Christabel Pankhurst. They are in Holloway prison as we speak. Do you still think the women should be patient? Another year has passed. The entirely peaceful march three weeks ago made not a ha'peth of difference."

Will shrugged and seemed about to speak when she heard Wesley's voice from behind her. "You women are too good for the rough and tumble of politics. You were created to be the ornament of the species, delicate and treasured, the repository of the future. Those who make the laws need to possess the physical force to enforce them."

As if there had been anything delicate and treasured about being forced along the streets with a policeman's knee in her back.

She stood so she could turn and face him. "There is no reason, Wesley, why in a modern world everything should be reduced to physical violence. And I am not any sort of an ornament, thank you."

"But you take great care to look like one. A most fetching one, if I may say so. Is that a new suit you're wearing? Very smart. But if the threat of violence isn't the force behind everything, then why do your militant women friends fling themselves at the police? Seems you women want to both have your cake and eat it."

Harriet said, "Because, Wesley, when we are peaceful nobody takes any notice."

Wesley snorted and turned his back, leaving their conversation without excusing himself.

Harriet watched him go, scarcely believing he could be so rude, before saying, "Mother, it has led to nationwide headlines. There have been questions in Parliament."

Her mother looked round to check that Wesley had moved out of hearing then lowered her voice to an intimate level. "Is that a bruise on your cheek, Harriet? Were you hurt?"

Will was still close enough to overhear. He looked at her sharply and frowned.

If the bruise was coming up and visible, why hadn't he or

Wesley already commented on it? Did men not look women in the face?

Her mother said, "Are there not other ways to get people to take notice? I worry you might put yourself in real danger. Please, Harriet, is there no other way you can contribute to the cause?"

There was. One that scared her even more than the prospect of falling in the street, but maybe now was the time to gather up her courage. There was an army of women travelling the country and speaking to crowds at elections, or outside places of employment as the workers streamed through the gates on their way home. Christabel wanted recruits in that army.

An acquaintance had told her of the dizzying terror she experienced when she first stood on a cart and heard the shouts of derision from the men leaving their work. She said how she kept on speaking, having no idea what she was saying, certain it was nonsense and the only consolation being that there was such a terrible din her nonsense would not be heard.

"I've been asked to give speeches about the vote, Mother, but I don't know if I can. The thought terrifies me."

"I'd prefer you terrified to maimed, Harriet."

Her father spoke to her as soon as she came down for breakfast the following morning. "Your mother tells me you need some lessons in how to speak about the women's cause, Harriet. Speaking in public is something I happen to do quite a lot of. Maybe I can be of some assistance."

Wesley peered round the edge of The Times. "Surely, sir, you are not encouraging this public display on her part?"

"Oh, I am Wesley. I speak out about injustice regularly. Why would I discourage my daughter from doing the same?"

"Because she is your daughter, not your son. And she is not doing it from the safety of a pulpit."

The Reverend Loxley raised his hands in the air. "Guilty as charged. I am not as young as I used to be and maybe courage ages along with the rest of the mortal body."

Wesley folded the paper and stood. "Well, sir, you must do as you wish. I, for one, have a day's work to do."

He stalked out of the room.

Gwen shrugged.

Will said, "That was a bit rich, even for him."

But Wesley had made up Harriet's mind for her. "I'd like to take you up on your offer, Father."

She glanced at her mother, who nodded, a slight but firm dip of her chin.

"Good. Meet me in the hall at ten." He paused, before continuing, somewhat whimsically, "You know St. Paul was terrified of speaking to crowds."

Harriet didn't find that thought very reassuring, considering everything that had followed for St. Paul.

Harriet paced the vicarage hall, the heels of her outdoor shoes clicking on the tiles. Where was he? Of course, it was Saturday. He had probably not finished writing his sermon and would want to be at the shop's opening at two. She knocked on his study door.

"Ah, Harriet. I haven't forgotten you. What do you think about when you hear the parable of the prodigal son?"

"I think how hard it was on the elder son, who was always good. I think Christ is telling us that being good is not enough. We have to be tolerant towards those who are foolish and do themselves harm."

"Well, come on then. I'll finish this later."

As soon as they got through the church door he set off down the nave at a rapid pace, swinging his arms in huge, dipping arcs. Harriet stood still, a smile twitching at the ends of her lips. He turned at the altar step.

"Come on, Harry. You need to warm up. Walk up and down the aisle a few times."

"But I'm not cold."

"Loosen up. Get ready for speaking."

He was back next to her.

"You don't mean that you do this before you take the service?"

"I most certainly do. You are not in the vestry with me or you would know I do. Less room in there, of course."

He set off again and this time she followed, copying his long strides and exaggerated arm swings.

"Breathe, Harry. Breathe."

After three times up the aisle and back he stopped. He was panting.

"Now, take a deep breath and shout. Like this. Haaa!"

The sound sprang all around them, bouncing back from one wall to another. *Haaa! Haaa! Haaa!*

Harriet's throat tightened. She tried to breathe in and made a constricted squeak.

"I can't shout in church, Father."

"Why not? Do you think it's going to fall down? You've opened up your body. Now you need to open up your voice. Come on! Haaa!"

She tried, "Haaa."

A whispery thread ran around the church.

She tried again, "Haaa!"

Breath flew across her tongue.

"Breathe deeper."

"Haaa!" Air rushed through her throat. Dizziness gathered behind her eyes. She shook her head.

"That's it. A few more times."

As she repeated the strange noise it got easier. Her body tingled. This must be what he meant by warming up.

"Go to the altar steps and tell me something about votes for women."

"Not to the pulpit?"

"We can't have ornaments dangling from the pulpit, can we? What is the world coming to?"

Harriet laughed and climbed the altar steps. Her father remained at the back of the church. "Pretend your voice is soaring over the heads of everyone and reaching someone back here. Just like you do when you call those grandchildren of mine to order."

She could hear him perfectly.

"For fifty years we have laboured peacefully for the right to vote and we have been ridiculed, ignored and now battered."

"Good. I'm hearing you loud and clear. But stand up straight. You don't want to constrict your breathing."

"We have stood too long outside the closed doors of the Constitution...Father, how do I stop getting nervous at all those faces watching me?"

"Can't hear you!"

Her father walked up the aisle to where she was standing. "Sorry, I shouldn't fool with you. Your voice is clear and your articulation excellent. Pause a little after each word and a little bit more at the end of each sentence. It gives your crowd time to work out what you are saying after the effort of hearing you. As for the sea of faces, let your eyes go out of focus so you see only blurs."

"And if the men shout out things like, *Go home and do the washing?* Miss Christabel Pankhurst says to answer them back. I don't think I have her wit."

He gave her a wide smile, as if to say he thought she had plenty of wit. "Well, I don't have much trouble with heckling from my congregation, but I would advise continuing with what you are saying. And if they don't give up, have a series of answers ready, like, *I'll go home when I've been permitted to finish, thank you,* and then continue. Don't let them seize the high ground."

"We are demanding our right to be heard."

"Might do the trick."

She put her arm through his and drew herself into his side. "Thank you, Father. You have been very helpful. I wish my brothers would support me the way you do."

"Do you wish them to keep quiet and not say what they think? They expect you to give as good as you get."

"But I am constrained by what is ladylike."

"And they, my dear, are constrained by what is gentlemanly, and that is a reason so many men are afraid of you women. They feel they cannot talk to you as they would to a man, because when they talk in male company they are often complete bounders and your presence would require them to cease to be bounders."

"Wesley *is* a bounder."

"Wesley is a good man who has made some dreadful mistakes."

"How can you say that, Father? We both know what he has done."

"And he has repented, shown remorse and made restitution. He cannot undo the past, and he will not be perfect in the future, but it is our Christian duty to forgive him. A bit like the prodigal son, perhaps?"

Harriet resisted the urge to stamp her foot. This was her father talking, not Will. She had said that people should be tolerant of those who do themselves harm when he had asked her about his sermon. An unwelcome heat rushed through her. Saying was one thing; doing was another.

"It is Eleanor who is suffering."

"Yes, it is. Would she suffer less if Wesley were to leave her? She loves her husband."

Harriet snuggled further into his side. His coat smelled of oily lamp smoke, the scent of a man who worked late into the evening in order to make time for his family in the day.

By the time Harriet arrived at the shop in Bridlesmith Gate, the place was bubbling with women. Gloves and silky stockings were strewn across countertops. Tiny drawers for hatpins and ribbons stood half open in splashes of colour and larger drawers, as if unashamed, displayed less vibrant undergarments to the excited company.

Gwen and Emma had done what they had said they would do, obtained a loan from Uncle George and bought the freehold. Bridlesmith Gate was a narrow street, but it was well situated, near the town centre. They had chosen well.

Gwen took Harriet by the arm.

"We have a kitchen and scullery to the side. And another room we can use for customers behind this one."

She led Harriet into a room where the walls were hung with Emma's familiar pastels of Nottingham street scenes and also a substantial number of water colours of The Meadows, hazes of purple crocuses.

"Mother's selling her work?"

"She has drawers of them stashed away. She felt she had to ask Father's permission."

"I imagine he's very proud of her."

"You should have seen his expression when he walked into this room. Proud is too small a word for it. And talking of being proud, can't I persuade you to show some of your work, Harry? Not the boring studies of groundsel and whatever all those other worts are called. How about some dog roses or cherry blossom? We should have a variety of styles available to appeal to different sorts."

Harriet said she would think about it and walked towards a charcoal and chalk drawing of a young woman sitting on a chair by her front door, a bowl on her lap. She was peeling potatoes. A small child at her feet played with pebbles, lining them up between the stone setts.

"My acquaintance, Miss Sylvia Pankhurst, draws women at work. Her work has the same frankness. A respect for the person. No weeping rags or tattered children."

"That's a nice description, Harry. Thank you."

Harriet hadn't heard Emma come into the room. The last she had seen of her she had been engaged in describing the benefits of the new soutien-gorge from France, an undergarment that supported the bust and allowed the abandonment of one's corset for purposes of tennis playing or bicycle riding.

Gwen said, "Come upstairs to see Emma's special collection. We've got two sets of stairs here. One that goes up to some bedrooms and the attics, and this one here, that goes up to just one room. Perfect for what we want."

Harriet followed up the narrow stairway and into a small upper room. She gasped. There were naked women everywhere she turned.

"You are going to show people these?"

179

Gwen gave her one of her earnest looks. "Only specially invited people. Robert and Wesley have a lot of contacts."

"And if some non-invited spies get in and make a lot of noise about it? You could be ruined."

Emma took her arm. "And we could earn a good living. We are not babies. There is plenty of smut that is being sold in Nottingham. This is not smut."

Emma walked her over to a pastel pink and blue nude lying on her back.

"Look at this, Harry. She is beautiful. Why shouldn't a modern woman's body be beautiful? Why must nudes always be mythological? Anyway, there's no doubt the Rokeby Venus is a real woman, is there? You agreed when we went to see it. If that can be bought by public subscription and hung in the National Gallery, then these can hang in Nottingham."

"The Rokeby Venus is by Velasquez, not Emma Loxley. He painted for royalty, not the middling classes."

"And his secondary-market patrons were discrete. Just as I expect mine to be."

"Suppose Uncle George is on your discrete grapevine. He holds the loan you have to buy this place."

Gwen grinned. "Don't you worry about that. I made sure the contract stated that so long as we make the payments on time the loan cannot be recalled. And we know Uncle George is a bit careless when it comes to reading contracts, don't we?"

She went quiet and shuffled her feet. Harriet looked at her expectantly. It wasn't like Gwen to be tongue-tied.

"Harry, if you are short of money for your fees you must ask us. If we have any to spare it's yours."

Harriet felt a rush of tenderness towards her normally self-assured younger sister. But she couldn't take their money.

"I wouldn't dream of it."

"Don't be a goose. You're out there getting beaten up so the rest of us can have our rights and freedoms. You are working for all of us. I've got my job at the manufactory. Emma's got her scholarship. We both have this shop–"

"You don't know yet if the shop is going to make you money or cost you it."

"That's true. If we haven't got the money you can't have it."

This was the Gwen that Harriet knew.

Emma said, "Please ask, Harry. Don't give up your place without asking. That's all we're saying."

Chapter 15
Publicly Speaking

June 1908

S peaking in public came more easily with practice. Harriet's stomach churned before she mounted her chair or table, box or wagon, but once there she found she had plenty to say and the voice to say it with.

"Women, demand the vote. Demand it not because you are better or wiser than men, but because you are equal to men. If your husband can vote, why cannot you vote? If your sons can vote, why not your daughters?"

A small object flew through the air. She lifted her left hand and captured it. A tiny, soft-furred rodent.

"Ah, *mus musculus.*" She held the mouse up by its tail. "Thank you. In the laboratory where I work we have need of these. You see, ladies and gentlemen, although I'm not sure either a lady or a gentleman would use a dead mouse as a pro-jectile... but I address you as such. You see, this tiny animal has a heart and lungs and a brain. It has a very small brain. But a woman's heart and lungs are as big as a man's. And so is her brain!"

She waved the mouse aloft, then tucked it in her skirt pocket with a flourish to the sound of gasps and laughter from the assembled crowd.

The crowd was mostly men, despite Harriet having positioned herself to catch women on their way home from shopping. Women, ladies, seemed reluctant to draw attention to themselves, even to the small extent of stopping to listen to a speaker in the street. She attracted larger female crowds when she set up her box outside the textile or match-making manufactories.

"Men, is it too hard to see that women should have a voice in the government under which they live and to which they owe allegiance? If a man owes allegiance, he has a right to vote. Then so does a woman, wouldn't you think? But women are not a consenting party to our government. Women have never been consulted. It is a government of men all agreeing with each other. Men legislate for woman and protect women, precisely as they legislate for and protect animals, asking the consent of neither."

She had adapted the speech from one by the American campaigner, Frederick Douglas, and she felt a little uneasy with it, since its argument led to universal suffrage. But already the crowd was breaking up into smaller groups as people talked to their neighbours. She smiled and stepped down from her box. Debate was what she had learned to work towards.

She never went out to speak alone. A comrade from the WSPU had stood below and to the right of her throughout. She was now taking pennies for copies of *Votes for Women*. Tom and Will were to her left. One or both of them often accompanied her, although they seemed pretty frail protection against some of the burly gents that attended her meetings.

She glanced at the cluster of dead mice lying around their feet. "So there was more than one?"

Tom grinned. "Do you want them all?"

She pulled her trophy from her pocket and let it fall to join the rest.

"I'll forgo that opportunity, thanks."

She longed to throw her arms around him and rest her head on his shoulder, but she couldn't even lean on his arm in public and remain respectable. She looked into his blue eyes, sparkling with humour.

"Will you walk some of the way back with us?"

"I'm sorry, no. I have to get back to the dispensary for evening surgery."

"I'll see you there on Sunday, then."

He shook his head. The shaking was followed by a slow nod and widened eyes.

She knew what it meant. He had been asking her for weeks to talk to Will and ask if they might meet in his rooms.

A man was hassling the woman selling magazines. Will left them and walked over to her.

Harriet said, "Can't *you* ask him?"

"You know I can't. He's your brother. He would feel he was... giving you to me. He should be protecting you from the likes of me."

"Doesn't he know?"

Tom shrugged and tried to look away. She walked round so she could look in his face. "You two are as thick as thieves. I don't believe he doesn't know about us."

"Well, yes. If you must know, he asked if I was bedding his sister and I said I was. And he asked if I intended to marry you and I said I did."

"You haven't said any such thing to me."

"Yes I have. I said that if the prophylactics failed I would marry you. Don't pretend I didn't."

"Prophylactics? Oh, the thingies. Can they fail?"

"They can. They do. They're not perfect. Do you want to stop?"

Stop? Give up what George Bernard Shaw had described as the most violent, insane, delusive and transient of passions. Just how transient the passion she wasn't certain, but for now it was improving with repetition and she was not going to give it up.

Will and a colleague of Harriet's from the WSPU walked over to join them.

The woman, whose name was Mary, said, "I'm catching the bus. Could I travel with the two of you?"

Harriet shrugged. "To be honest, I haven't got the bus fare."

Will said, "We can walk with you to the bus stop."

"That would be most kind."

Tom bade them goodbye. His eyes said, *Ask Will.*

Will stepped close to Harriet and whispered, "And to be honest, I don't have the bus fare either. And what I'm going to do when my boots wear through, I don't know."

She was surprised. She knew that when her own boots wore out Aunt Loxley would insist on replacing them. And she would know too, since they were left for her servants to polish every night.

After they'd seen Mary onto the bus she said, "So we're both poor church mice. My trust money is less than it used to be. Father has little to spare since the Loxley Lace dividends reduced and he has a household to feed. Wesley isn't bringing in any salary. God, how I hate that Ashford. Gwen thinks he's closing in for the kill. But you? Why are you low on funds?"

He said, "Do you want to go along the Bayswater Road or through the park?"

"Through the park."

"I've been meaning to tell you, Sis. I think it only fair that the manufactory money supports Gwen and Robert and Wesley. They work for that money. And you and Emma deserve your education. But me? I shouldn't be taking money from Uncle George."

"I didn't know you were. Doesn't Mr Yoxall pay you?"

"A small amount. It doesn't cover my rent. So, I'm going to try for the Foreign Office. Take the civil service exams. Put such talent as I have for languages to use." He laughed. "The French and German will be useful. Not the Greek and Latin." He paused and looked more serious. "I'm taking more lessons in German. And typing lessons too. If I continue as some sort of secretary, I'm going to have to be able to type."

She had thought Will was independent, if underpaid. She hadn't known he was scarcely paid at all.

"Does that mean you have to go abroad?"

"If I get a Foreign Office position, yes. Grunt work in a consulate, probably. But it's travel."

"That's exciting, although I thought it was politics you wanted."

"It is, but it's a rich man's business, unless the unions sponsor you like they do Yoxall. And I could do well in the Foreign Office. The international game is the very best, you know."

They walked in silence for a bit and she noted how their paces fitted together. She never drew ahead. She didn't think he slowed for her. They were already halfway through Hyde Park. She would have to bring up needing a place to meet with Tom soon. They could hardly talk about it in Aunt Loxley's house.

"Will...?"

He said, "What's Archenemy Ashford doing now?"

She had hesitated and missed her chance.

She drew a deep breath. "It's not what he's doing. It's the cumulative effects of everything he has done. Uncle George got around not being able to take out money from the business as he pleased by paying dividends to all the shareholders equally, including Ashford, but that meant reduced income for him and Father and desperately little money left in the manufactory. Ashford guessed that cash was low and put a person of his own in the accounts office to check."

"Is the spy likely to find out about the previous goings on? You know, the apparently illegal ones?"

"I hope not. Gwen buried all the evidence she found. That's what Uncle George wanted when he talked her into going back."

"Is this individual likely to find out anything?"

"No. He gets no help from the staff. He's an arrogant know-it-all. He's upset Mr Wragg and talks down to Robert and Wesley. And as for Gwen, he thinks that because she and Emma come in and talk about clothes and fashions they must have nothing between their ears. Gwen's happy to leave it that way. It means she gets to overhear a lot.

"What Ashford *has* done is force Uncle George to cut the twisthands' wages. Gwen says it was almost essential, since wages have gone down all across the industry. But Ashford wanted to cut the women lace-finishers' rates too and use outworkers instead so they could pay them even less. Uncle has dug his heels in. It's all coming to a head."

"Meanwhile we'll just have to continue being poor church mice."

"We will."

They'd reached the Holland Park side of Hyde Park and she stopped to look back. The trees shimmered with the passionate green of June. The grass was long and lush and driven into silver waves by the wind. To one side a flock of sheep were cropping it short and Harriet felt a longing for the lanes and fields around Nottingham, for her bicycle and days spent seeking out flowers to paint rather than sitting inside diagramming the innards of mice.

"Think what this scene will be on Sunday, Will. Processions from all directions. There will be twenty stands with speakers, thirty brass bands and hundreds of banners. Asquith has said that giving government time for Mr Stanger's current bill is out of the question. He says he intends to introduce an electoral reform bill of his own. For men! Because he doesn't believe there's support in the country for such a great constitutional change as women voting. We are going to show him that support, in spades... I'm going to speak from one of the platforms."

"Well done, Sis! I'm sure you'll be absolutely marvellous."

"Thank you. It means a lot to me, you having confidence in me." She waved a hand at a bench near the park gates. "Let's sit for a while and enjoy the evening."

Will hitched his trousers and leant back, eyes closed. "It's perfect, isn't it? England at its best."

She must have the conversation. There was no avoiding it. Would Will provide his rooms to her and Tom? Could he? What about his landlady? She was a pious woman. But that shake of Tom's head had been clear. There was to be no more meeting at the dispensary. She had to do this or give up that most violent of passions.

Sometimes she was alarmed by the way her feelings captured her body and held her sense of propriety hostage. Tom seemed to have no such qualms. He revelled in mastering the sensations. Not in the sense that he had mastery over them, the sense that she, as a well-brought-up vicar's daughter, might be expected to have, but in the sense that he practised them and excelled.

"Will, I have something very particular to ask you."

"Mmm..."

"You know, don't you...I know you know, that Tom and I have been... well, we've been living as man and wife."

He sat up with a jerk and for a second she glimpsed the efficient secretary with the infinite memory that he hid behind his languid exterior.

"Yes, I do know. Bardhill is a man of integrity, or I would never have kept silent. I supposed you daren't come into the open and marry the fellow because you would be forced to give up your course."

She felt herself blushing. This was so hard, bringing what should be private out into the open. But there was nothing for it now.

"Is there any possibility that we could meet in your rooms on occasion? The people at the dispensary have started to notice me. Tom could lose his position. And his references."

"And his reputation. You're not the only one taking risks."

She shifted in her seat and turned away from him. She felt ashamed and at the same time angry that she was ashamed. She loved Tom. There was nothing purer than love. Nothing closer to God.

"I know, and now I'm asking you to take a risk for us."

She jumped as he put his arm around her shoulders and pulled her towards him.

"Sis, seeing you so much in love is the most beautiful thing and I know you'll be sensible. Sensible is your middle name. My landlady goes out every Sunday afternoon to attend mission meetings to convert the poor African heathens. She's obsessed with the African heathens. And she gives the maid the afternoon off. You can be guaranteed several hours. And I can make myself scarce."

Relief rushed through her and tears filled her eyes. She brushed them away with the back of her hand.

"Thank you."

She said it without looking up.

Chapter 16
We Wish to be Lawmakers

Midsummer Day and after - 1908

Harriet and Emma were about to leave for the muster point for the Kensington section of the march to Hyde Park when Aunt Loxley emerged from the Morning Room.

"Well, you two are prettily turned out, I must say. With everyone in white like this it will be just like a Whitsun parade. And those purple, green and white sashes set your dresses off perfectly."

Harriet said, "Mrs Pethwick Lawrence decided on the colours to give the procession a theme. Purple for dignity, green for hope and white for purity."

Her aunt sniffed. "Knowing their sententious origin doesn't improve the aesthetic, Harriet. I sincerely hope you are not thinking of indulging in such mawkish sentimentality. But, I admit, the idea of colours has been successful. They are in all the department stores."

Harriet smiled. Her aunt had become a devotee of department stores, often spending whole afternoons browsing, shopping, and taking tea in the refreshment rooms.

Emma said, "I do hope you will come to Nottingham soon, aunt. I would love to show you our shop. We have adopted many of the tactics of the department stores. We encourage women to look and to touch and try the wares. And all the prices are fixed. There is no haggling."

"Tactics? Mmm...I suppose it *is* about tactics. Well, off you go, the two of you. Don't be late."

The summer air was fresh and touched with warmth in a way that made Harriet want to spring along the street like a month-old lamb. She laughed and took Emma's arm. "I so want to run and skip, Emma. Sometimes, I wish I'd never left child-hood behind."

Emma squeezed her arm. "Aunt Loxley was surprisingly supportive, wasn't she? Does she know you will be speaking?"

"Heavens no! Her not objecting to us marching is a big enough victory for now, don't you think?"

"I think she's been influenced by the purity of white and the hope of summer, however much she protests."

With dozens of banners and several bands, the Kensington march made the most of its short route to Hyde Park. There was a great deal of noise and shouting from the onlookers too. Many women wore white sashes or favours in their hats. Many men had tied white bands around their boaters. By the time they neared their assigned platform, it was getting hard to manoeuvre through the assembled people. Tom and Will were waiting and Harriet left Emma with them to join her colleagues. She had been assigned the opening speech, always a difficult spot that required warming up the crowd. She moved to the back to review her notes.

Ten minutes later a bugle sounded from the central plat-form, the signal that speeches were to begin. Harriet moved to the front and looked down at the crowd. An ocean of summer hats swayed like a meadow full of ox-eye daisies. She hoped their response to her would be as serene as they appeared. She breathed in and out three times, filling her lungs, and looked over the heads of the people to where the crowd thinned.

"Is there any justification for continuing to exclude an entire half of the community from being admitted within the pale of the constitution? There is no other exclusion from the franchise so absolute as that inflicted upon women. Any qualification of property may, in theory, be obtained by even the poorest of men, but nothing can ever enable a woman to have her voice counted in national affairs which touch her and hers as nearly as any other person in the nation.

"It is, ladies and gentlemen, a very simple question and not one constructed by me but by no less a person than John Stuart Mill. And it was put to the House of Commons on May the twentieth, *eighteen-sixty-seven*. That is forty-one years ago, ladies and gentlemen. And in the forty-one years since then there have been private members' bills put before Parliament almost every year. And there have been thousands of petitions."

Harriet extended her arms towards her fellow marchers gathered around the stand. "As recently as February this year Mr Stanger, the member for Kensington..." she waited, smiling, until the cheers died down. "This year our very own Mr Stanger introduced a bill with these words: *this bill is similar to the one introduced last session by my honourable friend, the Member for North St. Pancras. It is a bill the aim of which is identical to that of the resolution proposed in the first session of this Parliament by the honourable Member for Merthyr Tydfil. This, therefore, is neither the first nor the second time in this Parliament that the principle will have been discussed.*

"Mr Stanger's bill passed its second reading by two hundred and seventy-one votes to ninety-two. Even the government admitted that the argument for ceasing to exclude women from the franchise simply because they are women had been defeated. But would the government give time for the bill to progress? It would not.

"*Three times*, ladies and gentlemen, in this parliamentary session alone. *Three times* this motion has come before the House. I say to this government, *listen to the opinion of the people*. It has been said loud and clear. Remove the disability which attaches to women!"

She gave the cheering crowd its space before delivering her ending lines, lines she had thought on long and hard.

"I say to this Liberal government, and I say to their Conservative and Unionist opponents, and I say to the Independent Labour Party and to the Irish representatives, you cannot go into any election without finding that women are taking part in your politics. You *invite* them to take part in your politics. They run your vote gathering with their political associations, their Liberal Associations and their Primrose Leagues. They *are* your political life. Show them the justice they deserve. Remove the shackles you have placed on women!"

The ocean of heads beneath her broke into a storm of men's hats being waved in the air. Women were clapping and waving. Tom and Will were jumping up and down. Emma too. Harriet raised both arms above her head and shouted, "Votes for Women!"

"Votes for Women!" roared back at her; once, twice, three times.

She stepped back as the nearby band struck up the Marseillaise. This was a cheerful crowd, out for a pleasant Sunday afternoon. There hadn't been a single soft tomato or rotten cabbage to dodge. As the martial music of revolutionary France crashed around her she whispered the psalmist's words, "Truth shall spring out of the earth; and righteousness shall look down from heaven."

On Monday evening Harriet went to the WSPU's at-home meeting at Clement's Inn.

Christabel climbed onto a chair.

"Ladies! After the immense success of the Hyde Park demonstration, and the unprecedented numbers turning out for our cause, I sent a note to Mr Asquith calling upon the government to grant votes to women without delay. Mr Asquith replied first thing this morning. He says he has *nothing to add*.

"The Prime Minister stated it a condition of women's enfranchisement that a popular demand should be made. We have fulfilled that condition by holding the largest political gathering ever known in this country. In spite of this, the Prime Minister, without even consulting the Cabinet, replies that he has nothing to add to the unsatisfactory declaration which he made some weeks ago. Ladies, Mr Asquith intends to ignore the mandate that was delivered to him by the great Hyde Park demonstration. It is now clear that agitation through public meetings will have no effect in inducing the government to grant votes to women. To secure reform we must resort to militant methods. We will march to Parliament yet again and deliver our demands."

It was insupportable. Mr Stanger's bill was still in session. All the Prime Minister needed to do was give it Parliamentary time.

When they got to Westminster Palace Harriet pushed her way forward and demanded entrance to the House, but she didn't make it past the massed, broad-chested policemen. Asquith still refused to see them.

In the months that followed Harriet carried on speaking outside workplaces and in shopping streets. If the police arrived she allowed herself to be led away without protest. She didn't want any visible cuts or bruises for Aunt Loxley to fret over. Her aunt had softened her stance on suffrage activity. Harriet wanted to keep it that way. She didn't want to upset her mother either. She had no doubt that if her aunt suspected any violence her mother would soon know about it.

In September, at a demonstration in Trafalgar Square, she was the warm-up speaker. Standing above the crowd, on the plinth of Nelson's column, she spoke of the death of Mr Stanger's bill.

"There is a new parliament now! This is no time to give up or hold back! The government must be shamed into giving time to a women's bill."

Below her, WSPU members handed out leaflets recruiting volunteers for a rush on the House of Commons the day after Parliament opened.

The day before the planned rush Harriet went to the WSPU's regular at-home meeting, now so enlarged by new recruits to the cause that it had moved from Clement's Inn to the Queen's Concert Hall. Mrs Pankhurst took the stage.

"This morning Christabel, Mrs Flora Drummond and I were summoned to attend Bow Street Police court on the grounds of inciting the public to riot. We have chosen, instead, to attend your meeting. We will appoint our own time to attend the court."

The three leaders called the police to Clement's Inn in the evening. They had photographers present.

The next day furious women gathered outside Westminster Palace in huge numbers. The police were waiting. Harriet tried to force her way through the cordon. She sustained bruises, fortunately none visible. Later she heard that none of them had got through, although Keir Hardy's secretary had flung open the door of the House of Commons and demanded they attend to votes for women. But she had already been in the building. It was her place of work. The government had once again succeeded in keeping thousands of petitioning women out.

Harriet missed lectures for the first time ever in order to attend the trial of Mrs Pankhurst, Christabel Pankhurst and Flora Drummond. Christabel led the defence, cross-examining witnesses to the Trafalgar Square meeting where the incitement to riot supposedly took place. She called upon Lloyd George.

When she had finished Mrs Pankhurst stood.

"I want to ask Mr Lloyd George whether in his opinion the whole of this agitation which women are carrying on would be immediately stopped if the constitutional right to vote were conceded to them?"

"I think it likely."

A cheer echoed around the public gallery. The occupants of the press gallery scribbled furiously.

Then, when Emmeline stood to sum up the women's defence, Harriet knew she was going to hear a speech that would go down in history. Emmeline's regal calm, and talent for picking words that fitted together like fine mortice joints, had already had the galleries enthralled.

"I do not come here as an ordinary law-breaker. I should not be here if I had the same power to vote that even the wife-beater has, and the drunkard has. This is the only way in which women can get the right of deciding how the taxes to which they contribute should be spent, and how the laws they have to obey should be made. If you had the power to send us to prison, not for six months, but for six years, or for the whole of our lives, you would not stop this agitation. We are here, not because we are law-breakers; we are here in our efforts to be law-makers."

The government's strategy of arresting the leaders was far too late. All they had done was create more publicity for the cause, the cause that was in the hands of the thousands of committed members who could fill the public gallery of this court and Queen's Hall for a weekly meeting.

With Christabel in prison, Sylvia Pankhurst took over organising the WSPU agitation at a speech to be given by Lloyd George to a meeting at the Albert Hall. The meeting was run by the Women's Liberal Association and the WSPU had secured seats through Liberal Party contacts. It was a rare chance for women to get into one of the minister's meetings. Sylvia handed Harriet one of the tickets at a gathering for volunteers.

"After you heckle you will be ejected and not gently. Come back here. I will have the press present so they can see how you return dishevelled and hatless, with your hair dragged down and your clothing torn."

A tall, handsome girl called out in a fine Scottish accent. "Surely you do not desire that women submit to that without protest? I will carry a dog-whip and strike the first man who dares to mishandle me!"

Sylvia looked startled. "No, please don't do that. You don't know who might get hurt if you start flailing around with a dog-whip."

Lloyd George had let it be known in advance that he had an important message for the Liberal women. Harriet suspected he would merely reiterate Asquith's proposal to introduce a major franchise bill sometime in the future.

When that was exactly what he did, Harriet stood. She was surprised to find she was shaking but she remembered her father's teaching and threw her voice at the stage.

"What about action *now*? Why should we not vote like men *now*?"

Women on either side of her clawed at her clothes, pulling her back into her seat. She felt a pang of sorrow. These stalwart Liberal women had bought tickets and come to hear their idol speak. He was one of the greatest orators of the day and she was spoiling their afternoon.

She looked from side to side. Stewards were coming for her up each aisle. She was in the centre of the row. She would never get past them unhurt.

Deeds Not Words!

The WSPU slogan flew across the hall in a sweet Scottish brogue. A commotion broke out in the boxes above and to Harriet's left. The stewards in the aisles ran for the door to the upper tiers. From the screams of outrage on high she guessed her Scottish comrade had brought her dog-whip after all. She brushed the ladies' hands away and stepped over toes to reach the end of the row.

She heard the organist strike up the tune of a song familiar from her childhood, *Oh dear, what can the matter be?*, and lengthened her stride. They thought they were being funny. Rage inflamed her cheeks. She was so tired of women's desires being treated like something infantile. It had to stop.

Chapter 17
Wilfred Loxley's Lodgings

September 1909

There was a quick knock on the door and Tom walked in. Harriet stood to hug him. His jacket smelt damp.

"Is it raining?"

"Just a little."

Harriet pulled his face closer and kissed him. It had been a week since they'd seen each other, but it felt like an eternity.

She returned to the sofa. He hung his hat and jacket on the coat stand before sitting down. She tucked her head into his shoulder and picked at the threads coming away at the front edge of the cushions.

Will said, "Leave the sofa alone, Sis. I won't get a new one if you wreck it."

Harriet pulled her hand away from the hanging threads and sat up. She had to tell them. She couldn't just disappear. Someone would have to explain to Mother and Father, and, she gulped at the thought, Aunt Loxley.

Would Tom stand by her? Would Will? Would either of them attempt to stop her? Tell Father? Tell Uncle George?

She looked from one to the other.

"This absolutely must stay between the three of us. I've been selected to be one of the women to break the windows of the hall at Asquith's budget speech in Birmingham.... It's a protest at being kept out."

It would be nice if they would acknowledge what she had just said but they probably didn't realise how many women simply couldn't throw a ball at all, let alone throw hard and accurately.

"But that's not all. Two of us won't run. We'll wait to get arrested."

Will was staring at her with such wide-eyed consternation that she wanted to laugh. She stopped herself in time. It would be unkind to laugh.

"I will survive. I've faced up to insults, and worse. I am ready for this. There is public sympathy for the women being arrested. I need to do my bit."

Will got up and paced around the room.

Tom said, "You are unbelievably brave."

"No, she's not. She's being manipulated."

"I'm not brave, Tom. I've avoided danger all along. I've stayed free while my friends have gone to prison." She put a hand on his knee, to show she cared about what he said, but also to prevent him from speaking further. "And I'm most certainly not being manipulated, brother. I know exactly what I am doing and why I'm doing it. If enough people make enough noise and draw enough attention to a manifest wrong that wrong may be righted... Our games of cricket are going to come in useful."

Will's expression didn't soften at her reference to their childhood. He continued pacing. How much pacing could the worn rug stand?

"It won't happen, Sis. The police presence in Birmingham will make sure you get nowhere near Bingley Hall. Asquith will not have his rally for the People's Budget ruined by the mob. And you do know they are only there for their fun, don't you? Goading suffragettes into battles with the police has become better sport than the Saturday football."

"It will happen. And if we not treated as political prisoners and put in the first division we will hunger strike."

"Are you mad? You have no idea what prisons are like. It could kill you."

"I have every idea. My friends have been going to prison for the past two years."

Tom remained silent, but she saw worry invade his face.

She said, "It's been done before, the hunger striking. They will release us after a few days. They won't let us starve."

Will continued pacing and Harriet bit at her lip. She was sorry to be causing them so much anxiety, even as she was avoiding telling them exactly how the plan would work. WSPU intelligence knew all about the police cordon and the nine-foot high plywood stockades that were going to be erected around Bingley Hall. She was going to arrive two weeks before the stockades went up, along with five other women. They would live in rooms within stone-throwing distance of the hall's windows. When the meeting began other women positioned in the crowd would rush the police cordon. They would be beaten back, of course, but the purpose was to keep the police distracted. Then the stone throwers would take aim, smash the windows of Bingley Hall and the call of *Votes for Women!* would sound loud and clear. Their message would be heard.

Will muttered, "Hunger strike, for God's sake! Don't you worry about her starving herself, Tom? She's too thin to take days without food."

"Thank you, Will. *She* is here, you know. I believe myself capable of not eating. Food has never interested me."

Her nerves were fraying as much as the carpet under Will's feet.

"For God's sake, will you sit down."

He sat opposite her, put his head in his hands and stared at the floor.

She wasn't going to tell Will any more details. He deserved to know that she would be arrested and intended to hunger strike. But he worked inside Westminster and sometimes she wondered how much pressure he might be under to reveal the activities of his militant sister. It wasn't fair to burden him with knowledge he didn't need to have.

Will jumped to his feet.

"I'm going for a walk. I'll be about an hour."

He took his hat from the coat stand and let the door slam behind him.

She followed him down the stairs, not to speak with him but to fetch a pitcher of hot water from the kitchen. Will's landlady was at her Sunday-afternoon church mission meeting and the live-out maid had Sundays off. Will fended for himself until supper. His landlady left him cold cuts of meat, pies, cheese and a huge copper kettle simmering on the range.

She heaved the heavy pitcher onto the washstand in Will's room, took off her jacket and hung it over a chair back, undid her skirt and let it fall to the floor. Tom nuzzled his face into her shoulder as he twisted her blouse buttons free. "Your courage, your determination... it sets me on fire... Oh God, why do women wear such seductive underclothes? I mean, apart from these wretched corsets that take an age to unlace... but under here," he ran his hand down the middle of her back to the space between it and the band of her knickers, "it's all frills and ribbon and pretty lace and invitations."

She lay back in her camisole and knickers to watch him strip off his clothes. So easy for a man. He turned his back to roll on the rubber device, the new-improved penis-sheath-thing her colleagues at Bedford College called a French Letter. She watched him, framed between her knees. She still had her stockings and belt on and left it that way. His shoulders stooped, his arms almost invisible, his back narrowed into his taughtened buttocks. How nice it would be if he would sit for Emma to draw him from life. Impossible, of course. Quite shocking. Had Emma ever had men sit for her? Who knew what commissions Emma was taking, now that she and Gwen had their market established.

She pulled herself up for him to hand her the KY Surgical Jelly, the special potion he brought from the dispensary to make the sheath comfortable for her.

"No, I have another idea. Lie back."

He pushed her thighs apart. She could feel him wiping around her with a warm washcloth.

And then she groaned and her body bucked, and her mind filled with white fire. She reached down and grabbed his hair. Then let go her grip, in case it might make him stop. He pushed her legs further apart with his hands. Her whole body was suspended from this one part and the rest was floating free. Her back arched higher than she had ever imagined possible.

She had wanted him to be there first, before he pushed the camisole up, leaving her knickers in place and approaching her through that gap. But this? This was making feeling inhabit her body in a way it never had before. This was flying in a sky of pure sensation.

He was above her, undoing her knickers and suspender belt, pulling down her stockings, pushing his hands up under her camisole. She lifted her shoulders for him to take it over her head.

"You're so ready, but you're going to wait some more."

"Am I?" she whispered in his ear. She could hardly speak

the words; her mind didn't want speech. It wanted more white fire.

He was fondling and kissing her breasts, arousing the upper half of her like he had the lower. She reached down and palmed his testicles, balls he called them. Balls, she thought, pulling him in towards her, pushing the hard muscle behind.

She couldn't get enough breath. She was gulping in air, swinging her head to the side, seeking more.

But you can't wait anymore, Tom Bardhill. I'm going to make you come in.

Her body bucked again. She groaned. She was so strong.

He was always insistent that they wash and that she use the douche afterwards. It seemed clinical, but sometimes they washed each other softly, like they were handling a new baby. And, if the room was warm enough, they lay back down on Will's bed, quite unclothed, until the time came for her brother to return.

She said, "We will be arrested, me and one other person. Even I don't know who that is. We have a safe house within their planned barricades. We could get away before they come for us, but I won't."

"I am not going to try, my love, in any way, to dissuade you from your chosen course of action, but I do want you to be aware of what the effects of not eating are."

"Go on then, Doctor Bardhill."

She tweaked his ear and snuggled into his side.

"After one day without any food you will feel unbearably hungry."

"I doubt it."

"You will. The feeling will last for three days. And then the hunger pangs will go away. At that point, your body is surviving by breaking down your fat and your muscles. You will be tired, enervated, unable to concentrate. After about two weeks, you will feel weak, dizzy, and cold all the time."

"They won't let it go on for two weeks. The doctors will order our release."

"I want you to be aware of what you are doing. Promise me you will drink."

"I am, Tom. I am. And I will."

He turned to face her, taking both her hands in his.

"Harriet, after you finish your degree, next summer, shall we get wed? If I take up my father's offer, I can establish enough of a practice in Nottingham to support a family within a year. Shall we? It is what I want. More than life itself."

Two things hit her at once, neither of them quite what she might have expected at such a moment. One was that she thought it was his dispensary work he loved more than life itself. The other was to wonder how many women got proposed to stark naked.

"Will you still support me in the suffrage campaign? If I am your wife?"

"Of course I will."

"Even if I'm with child?"

"If you were pregnant, I would advise you to avoid potentially violent situations and hunger strikes."

She knew he'd say that. He was not a man who spoke easily, but when he did, he meant what he said, and he had no fear of saying it.

"Don't go back to Nottingham, not unless you get a dispensary place there. You want to work for the poor in the dispensary system. It's all you've ever wanted. Keep on looking for a paid position. I'll go anywhere you do. You've waited for me for long enough. We'll get wed then. I promise."

She had promised but did she mean it? She loved him. She

thought about him every few minutes when they were apart. He was caring and dependable and they had fun together. But she also liked her life the way it was; sensation in private, and action and study in public. It was necessarily clandestine, but it was invigorating.

Women were beginning to get positions, as laboratory demonstrators and suchlike. Some taught at colleges. They were journalists and artists and factory inspectors. They were becoming independent. But only single women. Married women needn't bother applying for and single women were dismissed if they married.

As Eleanor had once said, a married woman had responsibilities. And the rest of the world took it upon itself to make sure she carried them out. The only solution was to be devious. Or discrete, as Emma would put it.

"Why have you suddenly decided to ask me to marry you? We have been getting along very nicely."

"I want to be with you every day. I want to show the world you are my wife, the person I've vowed to love forever."

"That's very romantic, but a little possessive, don't you think?"

He smiled his snaggle-tooth smile. "Good luck to anyone who tries to possess you."

Chapter 18
Bingley Hall, Birmingham

September 17th 1909

Harriet travelled to Birmingham alone. It would have been pleasant to go down with the other ladies, since she knew two of them from Bedford College, but it was important that they weren't questioned or turned away from the area near Bingley Hall. Christabel said women in groups were automatically suspected by the police and she showed them an example of the note-books policemen carried around with pictures of women agitators pasted onto the pages. Harriet had flicked through the book looking for hers. She had been disappointed when it wasn't there.

Birmingham New Street station was a mass of iron: iron railings, iron bridges, iron lamps and a vast overreaching arch of interwoven iron and glass that spanned at least six train tracks and their platforms. Although it was the middle of the day, the platforms were crowded with passengers and porters seeking customers, whose help Harriet politely refused, since she had only a small, but suspiciously heavy, portmanteau. She intended to walk to King Alfred's Place, which was right by Bingley Hall.

When she left the station she found herself in Stephenson Street, not New Street as she had expected. She had studied the map carefully at Clement's Inn but didn't have one with her. Women reading maps in the street were as suspect as women in groups when there were political meetings about to take place. Mindful of any police spies that might be around, she waited to ask directions until well away from the station.

Her route took her over the top of a vast width of tracks, alongside a goods depot and into a road called Navigation Street. She heaved her heavy bag into her other hand. Where were the houses? There had to be houses somewhere near, because she was expected at one in King Alfred's Place.

King Alfred's Place turned out to be a street running along one side of Bingley Hall, which was a series of pitched slate roofs above brick walls, more resembling a manufactory than the grand meeting place she had imagined. She had also not expected King Alfred's Place to be so wide that four carts could have passed along it side by side. She was going to be lucky to find any windows, let alone hit any with the stones she had carried all the way from London. The building, like the station, must be lit from above. What was needed were people on the roof.

The front door of the address she had memorised was a smart dark green. She turned to look at Bingley Hall again. Here, there were windows at first floor level.

The woman who answered the door was small and spry, with a no-nonsense attitude. Over the next two weeks she kept the London women well-supplied with food and other necessaries. They only ventured out alone or in pairs and returned with reports of high barriers all along the route from the station to the hall.

"Fencing us in," they giggled.

They giggled a lot. Harriet found a surprising degree of

strength in shared silliness with women she barely knew. The college required her to behave like a person with a serious scientific mind. Had she neglected giggling?

One of them, Inga, read out loud from a novel that was all the rage.

Talk not to me of independence. Such words are not for the lips of girls. It is a woman's pride to lean on a good husband. It is her happiness to be shielded and protected by him. The woman who never marries has missed all things.

Harriet felt a stab of pleasure, knowing that she had not missed out on *all* things. She wondered if the same was true of any of the others in the group.

She said, "I am older than Anna in this book, who is twenty-four and considered to be risking eternal spinsterhood. What do you think, ladies? Should we assert our rights to independence, with the prospect of a lifetime's hard work and poverty, ending in loneliness, or should we seize the years of our youth and extend them into education and the professions before marriage consumes us with childbirth and household management?"

One of the two Marys said, "Anna declares she will be a crossing sweeper to earn her own money."

"It is a joke." Inga held up an authoritative finger. "It is saying it is all Anna can do. She has no education."

"And crossing sweepers die young," said the other Mary, the one Harriet knew from Bedford College. "Think of Bleak House."

Inga put the book down, paused as if checking her words before uttering them, and said, "Of course, there are the modern ways of stopping the pregnancies and controlling the number of children. Which must be a good thing. Last century was the massive population growth with the better food and cleaning, so there are more children living. But now is the time for more women to live, by not having many children. There are the, how do you say?... Pamphlets. Modern materials. It is scientific."

Harriet blushed, knowing *it* was messy and required a lot of warm water and wash-cloths. Hopefully, her companions would put this blush down to the sensitive nature of the conversation. She was, after-all, a vicar's daughter.

A clatter of hooves and the sound of men's voices in the street outside drew them to the windows. In the street below, firemen were positioning a tender alongside Bingley Hall. One looked up, grinned and waved. The women drew back.

Mary-from-college said, "Are they worried about fires this afternoon?"

"No." Harriet chewed her bottom lip. "Suffragettes. They'll turn the hoses on us."

Mary-from-college shuddered.

"They won't. They won't do that."

Harriet took aim at the window on the opposite side of the wide street, her arm raised. To her left she heard the roar of the crowd. To her right someone yelled, "Now!"

Her stones flew hard.

One smashed through the glass.

One of Inga's stones arced in a perfect trajectory and destroyed another pane.

Someone yelled, "Votes for Women!"

And someone else, "Run, before they come for us."

Harriet stayed by the window. It was the plan. Two of them would stay to be arrested. Inga was holding onto the edge of her window, as if to stop the sash flying it upwards. She must be the other one staying.

Inga saw her looking at her and pointed upwards, towards the roof of Bingley Hall.

Two women were clinging to a chimney stack on the roof opposite. They had axes. Then the smaller of the two prised up a slate and hurled it into the street.

Where had it landed?

Harriet leant out of the window. The fireman who had grinned at them earlier was arguing with a police officer. She watched him shrug his shoulders and stride away from the canvas fire-hose stretched limply along the edge of the street. A group of policemen surged forward. Some lifted the nozzle. Two struggled with the water valve.

The young fireman refused to come forward to help and his men stood unmoving behind him.

The flat canvas swelled and bucked. Water shot into the air. The policemen hauled up the swollen hose, sending streams of water rushing down the wall of Bingley Hall and cascading into the street.

Then they succeeded in training the jet of water on the women on the roof.

They were drenched in an instant.

Inga grabbed Harriet's arm.

"They will fall. The roof is very steep. They must fall."

"That's Mary Leigh," Harriet gasped. "You know her, the Union's drum-major. She's a firebrand. The tall, fair woman is Charlotte Marsh."

The firemen propped a ladder against the wall and policemen swarmed up it. They were met with flying slates and shouts of *Votes for Women!* Charlotte Marsh staggered and slid feet first to the edge of the roof, a policeman catching her by the arm as she fetched up against the coping. The street was thirty feet below.

Harriet breathed, "Oh my God. Oh my God."

Inga screamed, "They will die! They must die... *Mein Gott.* The other one is coming down."

Mary Leigh had turned onto her stomach and was letting herself down the treacherous slates feet first. Inga's screams were echoed by dozens from the street below. All eyes were on the roof. The firemen pushed a wheeled fire escape against the wall. Two officers started dragging Charlotte Marsh along on her back.

"You ladies need to come with us."

Harriet turned. Three policemen were inside the small bedroom, another was blocking the doorway. One had the bag that had held her stones in his hand.

Stay calm, be polite.

She raised a hand to cover her mouth. "This is it. Good luck."

Harriet heard Mary Leigh and Charlotte Marsh being brought into the police station. She heard them ask for dry clothes. She heard the snorts of derision that greeted their request.

Were they going to break windows on the roof but had been unable to reach them before they were spotted? Or had they always intended to use those axes on the slates? They could have killed someone in the street below. Were they aware of that? Did they care?

She didn't have a chance to speak to them, or to anybody.

She had left a letter for her parents with Emma. She had lied to Aunt Loxley, telling her she was going home for two weeks. A tangled mess of lies. She imagined her mother's distress.

She sat on the hard bench. Her mind churned through the events of the day.

She hadn't anticipated how hard it would be, being alone.

She sang to herself.

Daisy, Daisy, give me your answer do. It won't be a stylish marriage...

When she needed the privy, a policeman escorted her to a door in a yard. It was, to her surprise, a water closet with a wooden seat and a supply of papers.

"Pull the chain next to you when you are done."

She knew to do that, but she supposed not everyone did. Uncle George had indoor water closets installed when he built Loxley Hall, but at the vicarage there was a pail closet in the yard and ashes to layer into the bucket. It was shocking to discover that the privy at the police cells smelled so much less offensive than the one at the vicarage, although it was just as cold.

She lingered as long as she dared in order to escape the lonely thud of the lock of the cell door.

In the morning, she was told she could send one letter.

She wrote to her mother and father, saying that she had been arrested for throwing stones through windows and she hoped they would understand it was for a higher cause. She did not wish to worry them or cause them embarrassment. She expected to be sentenced to months in prison and that the prison she would be sent to was Winson Green in Birmingham. She didn't know if she would be able to send or receive letters there.

The custody sergeant's eyebrows rose when he read the address on the envelope. *How is the daughter of a vicar mixed up in this?* She could hear him thinking it.

Hours later, she climbed the steep steps at the back of a black van. She paused at the top, trying to see through the gloom. There were no windows. But there were ventilation holes up high. Women were seated on benches along the sides, Inga amongst them.

"No talking," a voice boomed from an unseen location.

She sat down and reached for Inga's hand.

"No personal contact," boomed the voice.

She turned towards Inga and raised her eyebrows, unsure if she could see her, but Inga's eyes must have been well adjusted to the dark, because she whispered, "This conveyance. Elegant, no?"

Another woman stumbled into the van. Harriet didn't know her. There must have been other groups, each with their own mission. For a moment she was annoyed at being treated like a pawn on a chessboard, but then she remembered Christabel's words. *You will carry a bag of stones. So will one other woman, in case one of you is caught.*

The others had been safer for not having stones. They were all safer for none of them knowing all of the plan. After all, she had told Emma, Tom and Will something of what was going on. Suppose everyone did the same. It could easily have got to the wrong ears.

Now they were each truly alone, with merely their thoughts of each other for succour.

Another woman stumbled up the steps. Harriet raised a hand in greeting.

She almost fell on the steps down from the van. Someone caught her arm.

"Steady there."

For a moment Birmingham Police Court loomed above her in pink-brick gothic fantasy. Then she was in a narrow passage.

"This way. Follow me."

Up steps, through a door and... Oh God, into the dock, with the magistrate frowning at her and the courtroom air stale, as though used up with the exhalations of hundreds of onlookers. Her knees buckled. Someone pulled her upright.

"Stay standing in the dock."

She grabbed onto the iron rail in front of her, watching the room sway and trying to think of Christabel Pankhurst conducting her own defence in Bow Street Police Court. Christabel had stood up straight, turned her wrist airily toward the assembled crowd, and argued points of law. Harriet would also conduct her own defence. She knew nothing about points of law. What on earth was she going to say? Perhaps she should have been thinking about that last night instead of singing about a bicycle built for two.

Inga appeared next to her. She had thought she would be alone.

Public disorder. That was what they were accused of. A pretty accurate description.

She answered the magistrate that, yes, she had thrown a stone that had broken the window of Bingley Hall on the afternoon of September 17th. A rustle of response rose from the crowd. Was it shock, support, or relish at the spectacle she was making of herself? And then she heard herself saying, "If I had been allowed a ticket to attend the meeting and if I could have been assured of my questions being taken, and of my not being forcibly and brutally ejected into the street, I would have had no need of making my presence known in such a manner."

From the corner of her eye, she saw Inga stand up straighter beside her. Two weeks ago, Inga had been a total stranger. Then an amusing temporary companion. Now it was as if they had known each other forever.

She took a deep breath and summoned up the Harriet who had stood on wagons and chairs and addressed crowds at political rallies; the Harriet whose father had trained her in public speaking in his church.

"Men today would have us request the vote politely, using women's ways, but women's ways have been ignored for far too long. Since we women cannot obtain our freedom using soft ways, I am going to throw my stones with the best of the men."

There was a cheer from somewhere behind her, followed by a scuffle and a distant shout of *Votes for Women!*

She was ready to take whatever was coming next. She was sure it would not be a reprimand and a request to go home.

The magistrate shuffled his papers and wrote something down before looking straight at them.

"Three months in the second division for wilful destruction of private property. That should give you both time to seriously consider your actions, which could not indicate more plainly your lack of fitness to be entrusted with the exercise of political power."

Inga spoke up, "We respectfully request, as political prisoners, to be placed in the first division."

"Request denied. Take the prisoners down."

Chapter 19
Winson Green Prison

September 1909

"This one is yours. Mind you wash thoroughly. When I say, get yourself dried and put on the clothes you see in the corner there."

The bathwater seemed clean enough. Harriet had heard of new prisoners at Holloway having to bathe in cold, dirty water. She put a hand in. The water was warm.

The apple-cheeked face appeared above the low door to the cubicle.

"Get on with it. We haven't got all day."

Harriet began pulling off her skirt to show willing. Not offending anyone here, until she had to, was an important part of the strategy she had worked out after talking to other suffragettes who'd been in prison.

"I'll need help with the buttons of my blouse and the laces of my corset."

"Oh do you? I'll be sending for her ladyship's maid, shall I?"

But the wardress entered the cubicle and helped her. Harriet removed the rest of her clothes, folded them in a pile on the floor, as far away from the water as she could get them, and stepped into the bathtub before giving herself time to think about it further. There was a lump of brown soap on the side of the bath. It smelled of carbolic. She lathered all her limbs she could raise above the water, stood up and did the rest of her body, sat down and rinsed off.

"Good."

The apple-face above the door was smiling, almost. Harriet hadn't realised she was being watched. All the talk that had gone on while they were planning the stone throwing, all the advice, had boiled down to this one thing: stay true to your inner self. Don't be defined by others. Know that you are a good person and deserving of God's love. She told herself not to be ashamed of her body. She forced herself not to reach for the towel to cover herself before getting out of the bathtub.

The face above the door disappeared.

Harriet took a deep breath and rubbed herself vigorously with the thin towel. It seemed to be incapable of soaking up water.

She inspected the prison clothes. They weren't stained, as some women had complained, but they were made of coarse cloth and really did have arrows stitched on them, like cartoon prison garb. When she put on the stockings they fell and bunched around her ankles. She couldn't find any garters in the heap of undergarments.

She put everything on, aware that the cell might be cold, rolling the skirt over three times at the waist to keep the hem off the floor and tying the front of the blouse in a knot. The ensemble was completed with a white apron and a white cap that tied under her chin. Whoever had thought this up must have had an eye for the grotesque. It made her mother's outdated mop cap look stylish.

The mock prison clothes that suffragettes wore to march in

fitted the women. These garments were simply ridiculous. Was that part of the point? Removing a person's clothing and dressing them in something humiliating was all part of saying, *you are not your own person anymore. The outside world does not exist for you. You are ours.* But bunched-up stockings and a skirt two sizes too big? Was that part of the humiliation or mere incompetence? She decided on the latter.

As for her self-respect? Perhaps she had invested too much of that in dressing well. Perhaps a lesson in humility would be good for her soul and make her all the stronger.

Apple-face returned.

Ask if the clothes are wrong, they'd told her. You might be lucky with your wardress.

"There weren't any garters, or a suspender belt. Could I have some, please?"

"I'll look into it."

"Also, I am a political prisoner. I should be allowed to wear my own clothes."

"I don't make the rules. I carry 'em out. Take these."

The wardress handed her a pile of bedding topped with a folded nightdress, a towel, a washcloth, and a brush and comb.

Ask for a toothbrush. That was something else they'd said. For some reason you had to ask for a toothbrush.

"Please, may I have a toothbrush?"

"I'll see to it. Now, follow me."

Harriet followed, shuffling along the ground to prevent the ill-fitting shoes escaping from her feet. Her cell number was twenty-three. It was written on the door.

"In here, twenty-three. They'll be bringing supper in half an hour."

There was a chair, a table and a wooden plank hung on the wall, which on investigation proved to be a bed that swung down on chains. She moved her pile of linen from where she had put it on the table to the bed. Then, mindful that she had no idea of the time or when she might be expected to go to bed, she organised the pile into something that looked a bit like a place to rest.

There were four books on the corner of the table: the Bible, the Book of Common Prayer, a publication of the Religious Tract Society, called *The Thorny Path*, and a book titled *Heroines of the Faith* by a Frank Mundell. Harriet picked up the Frank Mundell and inspected the cover, a sentimental wash depicting a childlike Christian martyr, neatly dressed and strapped to a post in what was, she supposed, a tidal river. She smiled. Was this self-immolating martyrdom the sort of moral improvement the authorities should be putting in front of women determined to protest against their sentences?

She stood with the book in her hand. Time stretched out ahead of her. Three months, a quarter of a year, before she would see Tom again. And what would she look like when she emerged? Not like some graveyard angel. More like something terrible to behold.

No. Not three months. A few weeks. They would let her go once she showed the determination not to eat.

She sat down on the wooden chair and bent to yank up her drooping stockings.

"Father, Mother. I'm sorry. Please forgive me for being a worry to you."

Sobs erupted from somewhere buried deep within her. She bent double, head in her hands, and let the tears come. There was no comfort, only the cell floor staring back at her.

"Supper, twenty-three. Bring your platter and mug to the door."

A thin wardress with raked-back black hair, one she hadn't seen before, stood at the door holding a tub and a pitcher.

Then she had understood correctly. She had been addressed as a number. Miss Loxley had left with Miss Loxley's clothes. For a moment she was stunned. The feeling was followed by a rush of indignation. The degradation was deliberate. She was a human being in the process of being turned into a caged animal.

But she was a human, all the same. She possessed a self, and she needed to hold on to it. Even the animals at the zoological gardens had their names on their cages.

Homo Sapiens Viraginis. A warrior woman.

She picked up the tin plate and mug, that were stacked, together with a bowl and spoon, on the opposite side of the table from the books, and took them to the door. The black-haired wardress deposited a small slab of grey meat and a lump of something that resembled suet dumpling on her plate.

"Hold your mug up, steady like."

Black-hair filled the mug with steaming cocoa poured from a pitcher. As it settled, flecks of grease floated to the surface. If this was the sort of food she was going to get, refusing it would not be hard. She turned away good food all the time. It was one of her strengths, like throwing balls.

"Please, would you inform the governor of my request to be placed in the first division. I am a political prisoner. I have the right to my own clothes and the tools of my trade, so I may usefully occupy myself. I will not be taking any food until my rights are acknowledged."

"Take the food. I haven't the time to stand here all night. Lights will go out at eight o'clock. Make sure you are in bed by then."

Harriet put the plate and mug down in the corner of the cell, turned her chair away from them, and opened the Bible at the beginning of the Book of Genesis. What better place to start than the beginning?

How was she supposed to know when it was eight o'clock?

There was the sound of the key in the door. Harriet opened her eyes. She had not realised she had them closed. The black-haired, stern-faced wardress was there, holding out a tin mug.

Harriet got up and looked into the cup. It was water.

"Thank you."

Black-hair left. Harriet took a long draught, and then another. She emptied the cup. It was a big cup, probably a whole pint.

There was only one blanket in the pile of bedding. She changed into the nightgown, pulling it over her shift and leaving her stockings on.

She wondered how Inga was faring.

The next morning the routine began. Get up. Dress. Empty chamber pot at sluice. Wash at communal sinks. Make bed, rolling up bedding in standard fashion. Scrub floor. Attend chapel. Have breakfast.

She didn't eat breakfast, making it twenty-four hours since she had last eaten. The wardress she had first met brought a small loaf of bread, a pat of butter, and a boiled egg. She poured hot milk into her mug and brought another filled with tea. She also left a jug of water on the table. The bread was simple brown bread. A good quantity. The egg was a friendly mottled brown.

She was hungry. Tom had been right. Why wouldn't he be? Why had she scoffed at his predictions?

The day wore on. They brought her sewing to do. No communal labour for her if she wouldn't eat. No outdoor exercise either.

The wardresses left the food where she had piled in it the corner, even though she asked them to take it away. The little brown loaf was quite an attractive thing. The butter collapsed as the day grew warmer.

Lunch was a four-inch piece of fried fish with a pile of cabbage and a boiled potato. The smell of the fish was nauseating. It helped her avoid eating it. But the potato looked harmless enough. She quickly moved the plate into the corner, pulled the chair next to the table, and turned back to the book of Genesis. Temptation was to be resisted. Resisting temptation had been important since the beginning of time. The flesh was weak.

Forty days and forty nights Christ went without food in the wilderness. Couldn't she manage more than two for the sake of getting women rights they deserved as human beings?

She got up and paced across the cell, counting. "One, two, three, four, this way. One, two, three, four, five, the other way. One, two, three, four, five. Once I caught a fish alive. How many beans make five? Five times five is twenty-five. Am I glad that I'm alive?"

She sat down again. The Book of Genesis.

This is now bone of my bones, and flesh of my flesh: she shall be called Woman, because she was taken out of Man. Therefore shall a man leave his father and his mother, and shall cleave unto his wife: and they shall be one flesh. And they were both naked, the man and his wife, and were not ashamed.

The second story of the creation of man. One creation story straight after the other. She liked this one. Perhaps she should stop here, with not being ashamed.

There was the sound of the key in the door. Black-hair was there, holding out a plate and a tin mug. On the plate was a slab of grey meat and something that looked like suet dumpling. In the mug was steaming hot cocoa.

Had she slipped back in time? Was it yesterday?

Was she hallucinating? Already? Should she yell, *Get thee behind me?*

How could she get behind her? There wasn't room to swing a cat in the cell, let alone conduct a metaphorical dance with evil.

Black-hair put the food on the table, picked up the water pitcher, looked into it and said, "Wicked, it is, if you want my opinion, wasting good food when there's plenty hungry through no fault of their own."

She left. Harriet couldn't see what was good about the piece of grey meat and equally grey pudding on the tin plate, or even how she was supposed to eat it with only a wooden spoon for a utensil. The old food was still in the corner. Harriet tipped the remaining water from the jug into her cup and drank it. Black-hair returned with a fresh jug of water.

"Eat your dinner twenty-three. You're all skin and bones as it is. Refusing to eat isn't going to get you anywhere."

The cocoa steamed on the table. It smelt good. Why had she thought of it with revulsion yesterday? Maybe yesterday's had been a bad batch.

She sat on the chair and stared at the plate of food as if mesmerised by it. Two ounces of meat, she guessed, and four ounces of whatever that lump of starch was. A carefully calculated nutritious diet.

She got up and paced around the cell. Her nightgown was rolled up with the blanket. How long had she got to undress and get into bed? When was eight o'clock?

She stood still. She had to stay calm. She was a modern woman and, despite what she had said in court, the modern woman must be less emotional and less hysterical than the men had been in their franchise struggle. Women must prove themselves stable and responsible, since the presumption of men, and many women too, was that they were not. She had not been party to anything like the violence and destruction of the franchise riots eighty years ago. She was not going to burn down

Nottingham Castle. She had merely broken a window. And now she was merely going to forgo drinking this cocoa that seemed so unbelievably tempting.

She might have named herself a virago on her imaginary cage-sign but she was no warrior. Quite a different type of fighter. She was suffering to get her suffering noticed. The papers would be full of women emerging emaciated from prison. The suffrage debate would be kept in front of the public. If enough people, enough politicians, saw how much the women cared they must come to see the righteousness of the cause, or at least stop resisting them.

How did women voting hurt them? What was the real reason for the stubbornness of their resistance?

She sat down with the Bible open, but all she could think of was cocoa and how much she would like to drink some. Tom had said she must drink. Not cocoa though. Cocoa was more foodstuff than drink. Cocoa was milk and chocolate and sugar. And delicious, said something in her brain. She swallowed. Her mouth was very dry.

Her stomach growled. In fact, it twisted and howled and sucked at her insides. If she put a hand anywhere near that cocoa her hand would reach out and put that tin mug to her mouth without her being able to control it, just as Eve's hand had reached for the apple. The book of Genesis didn't say how long Eve had resisted, nor was there anything to indicate she was other than well-fed in paradise, just as she, Harriet, had always been well-fed. She had never known real hunger, although she had thought she had. She had never missed more than one meal in a day.

Was she putting herself in unnecessary danger by not taking a small drink of that cocoa?

If only she could leave this room and take a walk around the corridors.

She rubbed her arms as if she were cold. She should undress and go to bed. But the bed was a lonely place.

She had always slept alone, in her little room in the vicarage or at Aunt Loxley's. Why was she anxious about getting undressed? Why did she feel desperately lonely, when she usually valued her own company? Just one visitor, one silly conversation with Emma about clothes or one discussion about how the boys were getting on at school with Eleanor. Just some trivial chatter. That was all she wanted.

She wrapped her arms around herself. This hunger had come on faster and was stronger than she had imagined possible, but this prison sentence had a limit and the limit would be nearer if she persisted with not eating. She needed to remind herself of that.

She stood up, yanked the prison clothes off as fast as she could, put on the scratchy nightgown and folded the clothes, neatly, since they seemed obsessed with tidiness and cleanliness in this place.

She lay down on the plank they called a bed, stretched out on her back, and told herself to sleep and not to think of food. She repeated the Lord's Prayer, until she drifted into a scene where her father was teaching the prayer to her and Will as they sat next to him, their heads tucked into his sides, the smell of church-candles on his clothes.

Whenever she pulled her knees up, she pulled the blanket and left a strip along her back where the icy air crept in. When she stretched, her feet stuck out. If she lay on her back, her shoulders froze. The night spun through to dawn in a frenzied quarrel of cold versus arms, legs and neck.

The next day she saw other prisoners, Inga included, at the wash basins and in chapel. They exchanged looks and whispers. For liberty, they said. For justice, she replied. She went through the routine of making up her bed and scrubbing out her cell, as if it was not something alien but a reasonable backdrop to the drama of her hunger.

Apple-Face said, "Don't you know nothing about how to wash a floor, twenty-three? Here, give me that cloth. You wring the water out like this, see. Or else the floor will be wet until midday."

At lunch time, Black-Hair brought her a pork-chop with mashed potato and apple sauce and green beans and took away the pile of food that had accumulated in the corner. This new plate wasn't second division food. Perhaps it was from the governor's own table. It smelt heavenly, seductive, bewitching. Her mouth watered in enthusiastic response to the aroma of grilled meat. It continued to water well after the fat from the chop congealed. Black-Hair left it, even after she brought supper and cocoa.

Saliva dribbled into the space between Harriet's cheek and the sheet. She dreamed of breakfast in the vicarage: of covered plates of kedgeree and scrambled eggs, of toast and marmalade. She lifted a lid from a dish on the sideboard and there was a face, the apple-face of the wardress who had watched her bathe.

"Wake-up. You still have to go to wash, for all your silliness. No slacking off on hygiene in here. When you're done, you can do your sewing in here. No chapel for you. The chaplain will be coming by."

Her hips ached. Her mouth would hardly work for dryness. Her stomach wasn't there. There was a hole between her hips and her ribcage. What was connecting them together?

There was a plate of toast and marmalade on the edge of the washstand. Freshly made toast. Crisped bread. Melted butter, with little solid dabs still clinging around the edges. Bitter-sweet, thick wedges of orange peel. Sugar on her tongue.

"What's your name?" she whispered.

"Stych."

Harriet hadn't expected an answer.

"Thank you, Miss Stych."

"Just Stych. There's water in the cup."

Harriet took the offered cup and drank a mouthful. Her throat loosened.

"Do you want the vote, Stych?"

The woman didn't answer. She must be breaking some rule about getting involved in a conversation with a prisoner, but then Stych folded her arms across her stomach and said, "I work as hard as any man, and any gent, I don't see as how I shouldn't have a say in how things are done."

Stych picked up the cup. "Here, come on, drink. It was you threw that stone through the window of Bingley Hall, weren't it? Mighty powerful throwing that."

"You were there?"

"Happen I was."

She managed a few whispered words with Inga at the wash-basins. Inga's face was ashen, her black curls falling in unattractive lumps from under the ridiculous cap and her brown eyes staring out on either side of the sharp line formed by her nose.

"Keep going," Inga said. "This is the hardest day. They will let us out if we keep going."

Harriet didn't know if she was strong enough. She wasn't full of the power of hate for the wardresses, the politicians, or men in general, like some of the others. She looked at the floor and shuffled off in her ill-fitting shoes.

The toast was still on the table.

Her head was throbbing, her eyes clouded. She had to empty her slops and fetch the hot water and lye to scrub the floor. She lifted the night-bucket and retched.

If she just licked the marmalade off the toast that might settle her stomach, stop it screaming.

Stych would know she had done that.

So what? Stych wanted her to eat. Stych would be pleased that she had eaten.

Stych would know she had licked up the marmalade like some sort of savage.

Harriet grabbed the plate and threw it across the cell. A loud clang rang back at her. Her head reverberated. She bent double. Nothing. Then a vicious squeezing of her stomach. Her head splitting apart. Her stomach leaping, throwing itself through her throat. A stream of yellow bile. And another. And another.

"Get her out of here. There's an empty cell down the way."

Back in her scrubbed down cell, someone brought her soup, salt-fragrant chicken soup, steam rising to the ceiling. She concentrated on stitching a neat hem on a sheet. She wasn't hungry. She was calm and focused. Thinking of Tom made her happy. They would be together soon, when they let her out.

Next morning, when she stood up to dress, she knew she was tipping backwards, but she couldn't stop. Her back hit the table and she slid to the floor. Stych had her take sips of water before helping her back onto the bed.

"What did the chaplain say when he came to see you?"

"That I should be using this time to contemplate the wrong I had done and to consider how I might make reparation."

"Well, I'll have to be getting the doctor to you now."

"He'll tell me to eat."

"He'll listen at your heart to see how long you'll last not eating. None of us wants a corpse on our hands."

They sent in another prisoner to empty her slops and clean the cell. She couldn't see her very well. Her eyes didn't seem to be working properly. She thought she was a young girl. The girl sang as she scrubbed the floor.

She couldn't get up off the bed unaided. She couldn't concentrate to read. She didn't want to read. She wanted to sleep. Sometimes it was light and sometimes it was dark. Sometimes there were people.

"Lift her onto the chair and tip it back."

"Wouldn't it be better on the bed?"

"I can't get the right angle with her against the wall."

They were lifting her, putting her in the chair. The doctor, it must be the doctor, was standing over her. He had a long rubber tube looped in his hand.

"Nose is too small. We could damage the septum. Open your mouth."

Who was he speaking to? There were four wardresses around her, two holding her arms, two her legs. Stych whispered in her ear, "Open your mouth, twenty-three. Don't make him force it open."

She tried. His hand, thrust up against her lips, reeked of carbolic soap. Her stomach heaved and her jaws clamped shut. He held her by the chin and twisted something metal into her mouth, bracing it between her teeth, jamming her jaw open. She tried to scream but no sound came. She flung her head to the side.

"Keep her still, dammit."

He leant over her. She could see up the tunnel of greasy hairs sprouting in his nostrils. Her head was gripped between powerful hands. Her mouth was stretched until it must split at its seams. She looked to the side, tracking the tube swinging in his hand. His thick, soapy thumb pushed down down onto her tongue. The pipe came nearer and nearer, until her eyes could no longer focus on it. His face wrinkled into concentration, then into a smile.

A shaft wormed, then thrust, deep into her body. Her throat boiled and heaved. The shaft shot through her centre and nailed her to the chair. Her chest caught fire. Her bladder throbbed. She pulled herself tight, her eyes on the man's face and the satisfaction in his pursed lips.

He snapped his fingers. Someone handed him a pitcher. He poured white liquid into the funnel at the end of the tube. The shaft swelled.

Her back threw itself up in an arc. Her head jerked from side to side. The vice on it tightened. The doctor continued to pour, his nostrils flaring.

A slither. A squelch. The tube out. The chair tipped back to the vertical. She was lifted to her feet.

Her stomach squeezed and a stream of white mess shot onto the doctor's coat and feet.

"Ye gods! Clean her up! The Jezebel!"

M

A burning arc stretched from her throat to the bottom of her ribcage. She curled up tight on the bed, her back to the room.

Did you know about this, Tom? Did you know this could happen? They'll keep doing it if I don't eat, Stych said. I don't know if I can stand it.

Do you know how to do this, Doctor Bardhill? Have you done it to people?

There was a scream and the sound of furniture crashing to the floor. Someone else having the tube thrust down their throat, someone who was resisting. Was it Inga or Miss Marsh? Miss Charlotte Marsh would put up a fight, no doubt about that.

Harriet knocked on the wall. Someone knocked back.

Chapter 20
Trees Coppered for Autumn

October 1909

On the other side of the gate a band was playing the Marseillaise. Had they received word of what had been going on? How had the outside world of sunshine reacted?

Harriet could scarcely put one foot in front of another. Stych and the black-haired wardress offered to carry her out in a chair, but sitting was even more painful than walking. Kneeling, uncomfortable as it was, had become the easiest position. Everywhere else, her bones were too close to the surface.

She had spent a lot of time kneeling on folded blankets, elbows propped on the edge of her bed. At least the chaplain had been pleased. The thought brought a twisted smile into her mind. Was it reflected on her lips?

Inga said, "It is almost worth being in the prison for the relief of getting out."

Six weeks. Half their sentence. The doctor had told her she would die if he didn't recommend her release and he wouldn't have her blood on his hands. Perhaps he was fed up with her vomit on his shoes. She hadn't got the impression he cared much about her well-being. Stych said the authorities were releasing her because they didn't want her death on *their* hands either, and they considered the women's actions to be blackmail.

Harriet had expected to fast for four days and be released. Instead, she had endured five and a half weeks of being held down and forcibly fed twice a day. How had it been possible? But she had done it. She had struck a blow for the cause.

The gate opened. Harriet forced her head up and looked towards the cheering crowd of women waving their banners of purple, white and green. She flinched at the flashes of press cameras.

Inga said, "Sunny and cold. We can be grateful those policemen at the Bingley Hall let us get our coats and hats before taking us away."

"They wouldn't do otherwise, would they, the policemen? They wouldn't arrest us and make us go in just the clothes we were standing up in. That would be barbaric."

Inga said nothing. She either hadn't understood the rough croak Harriet's voice had made through her torn throat or Inga was reflecting on the nature of barbarism.

Inga was gaunt, her nose a sliver, her cheeks fallen in, her eyes staring out of deep hollows. Worse, her face was bone-white and so were her gums. If Inga looked such a fright, what did she look like herself? There were no mirrors in the prison. Perhaps it was as well not to know. She hoped any newspaper photos would be too blurred to be usable.

This was not how she had imagined this would end. In her mind, there had been a picture of strong young women striding out to freedom, independence in their step.

Suddenly Inga was surrounded. She was one of five sisters, and it seemed they were all here and all talking at once. Harriet registered the shock on their faces before she lost her grip on Inga's arm and fell backwards, with no power to alter the descent, no ability to bend, to curl or to throw out her hands.

Then many arms were bearing her up. She could hear Emma, Gwen, and Will. And Tom? Was Tom there? She turned towards them and saw she was only a few steps away from the fortress-like gates of the prison.

"Oh Sis..." Will's voice broke.

Emma was crying.

Gwen was trying to look like she wasn't.

Gwen said, "Tom has hired a motor carriage and driver to take you to a convalescent home until you are well enough to get the train home."

"No," she croaked. "No institution. Home."

"As soon as you can, Harry dear. As soon as you can."

Tom was standing by the back door of the motor, in a dark-blue lounge suit and a black Homburg, which he took off as she approached. She tried to walk faster, but it was not possible. Her legs wouldn't answer to her mind. He was looking at her with neither a smile nor a frown, the breeze lifting his fine blond hair, which was cut longer than she remembered, with a parting off-centre. And he'd shaved off his moustache.

When she got within speaking distance, he replaced his hat and took her hands. "Welcome back, dearest."

She still couldn't fathom the expression in his eyes. She stopped trying.

Her knees buckled.

Somebody caught her. Will, possibly. She heard Tom say, "Here, let me lift her in... She's as light as a feather."

Now she was sinking into a thick eiderdown laid over the back seat of the motor carriage. Emma climbed up, padded her round with cushions, tucked a rug around her knees and kissed her on the cheek. She tied a long net veil over her hat and under her chin.

"We don't want your hat blowing away, do we, Harry? I wish I was coming with you, but we all have to return to Nottingham. Tom will stay near the nursing home and visit every day."

Harriet clasped her sister's hands in her own. Was Emma as horrified by these bony claws as she was? Was Tom?

Tom climbed into the front of the vehicle. The driver got down and turned the crank handle until the floor beneath her shuddered and the body of the carriage vibrated. She held on to Emma's hands.

"Tom's so sad he can't be in the back with you," Emma whispered. "Propriety, you know."

Emma pulled her hands away and backed down onto the roadway.

Propriety? They were obsessed with propriety in the prison. Propriety was one more tool in the box of humiliation.

The motor carriage trundled over the cobbles of the streets, every bump lancing through her. She set her teeth together, braced against crying out and fixed her eyes on the nape of Tom's neck, looking for the little tuft she would hold on to and pull when they came together. Sometimes she pulled so hard that he would squeak. The little tuft was gone, covered by the longer hair.

She sighed. Why did both Gwen and Emma have to go back to Nottingham? They had the shop, but surely one of them could manage. Will had his work at Parliament, of course. Why couldn't the motor go all the way to Nottingham?

Too many questions. Too hard.

The sounds around her changed. The air was sweet, free of the reek of burning coal that was the constant smell of a city.

She leaned forward to peer around the hood. There were green meadows on either side, trees lining the course of a stream, cows with their heads down, a fox running along the hedgerow. One by one, she withdrew the pins for her hat and loosened and removed the scarf. She stuck the pins back in the hat, clutched it to her breast and lay down on her side on the cushions. Propriety be damned, damned to all hell.

She woke to the squeal of gate hinges. Pulling herself upright and leaning forward, she could see a brick-built, two-gabled building with a gothic-arch doorway. She groaned. Not another fortress.

She decided not to replace her hat.

But here were trees, coppered for autumn, and rolling green grass and people walking freely in coats and boots, mufflers wrapping their throats. The air she breathed in filled her lungs with joy. That was it. That sensation. Joy. She had not felt it in a long time.

Tom helped her down. Not by lifting her in his arms, but with a proffered hand, which she leant on gratefully. He lingered a little over the disembarking and whispered, "It won't be long here. Only until you are fit again. I promise."

One of the establishment staff retrieved her hat and scarf from the backseat. Another was carrying a bag.

Tom said, "Your sisters packed some things for you."

She didn't want him to go, and he walked in with her, but the home's sister-in-charge introduced herself and explained that Harriet must rest. Rest was essential to recovery.

After Tom bade her goodbye, with a bow and a smile, not with an embrace or a kiss because of ever-be-damned propriety, nurses helped her up the stairs to a sun-drenched room overlooking the green lawns.

Here were smooth sheets and fresh air pouring through an open window. Here was peace and time to not think.

It seemed an eternity of sleeplessness as she lay on her back, her side, her other side, but in reality, she slept for hours on end. The nurses came every hour and, if she was awake, they got her out of the bed and walked her around the room, stretching the sheets back tight until not a wrinkle dare show. Twice a day they rubbed oil into the bits of her that stuck out, the shoulders, the hips, the buttocks, the heels; sticking-out bits she had not realised she'd had before.

We have to prevent bedsores, they said, by way of explanation. Bedsores are horrible.

The windows were always open. How she had longed for fresh air in the prison.

Some of the other women had broken their cell windows.

Fresh air is a vital element in the healing process, they said. They wrapped her in shawls while she sat in the chair by the window.

Five times a day they brought little meals; drinking cups with spouts, filled with Bovril or chicken consommé, teaspoons of honey, oat porridge with a dab of cream.

After a week, they helped her down the stairs and into the sitting room with its French doors facing the parkland. The doors were open, despite the autumn cold. They wrapped her in blankets. She began to want occupation and asked for books. They asked what she would like and all she could think was anything but the Bible. They brought her a volume called Five Children and It, by E. Nesbit.

Tom came three times a day, for half an hour only. Sister refused to let her be tired out. "Edith Nesbit," Tom said, "one of the founder members of the Fabians."

She couldn't read more than a few pages at a time. But she liked the Psammead, the sand fairy that the children found buried in the gravel pit. Ugly, grumpy and occasionally malevolent, perhaps that's what she would be when she got back into the world.

"Tom, how come you can be here every day? What about your work?"

"I have no work at the moment. I'm going to take up my father's offer and go into his practice. The dispensary trustees fired me when I asked for the time off to be here. Relatives only, they said. Well, not just that. Someone told them about the meetings."

"I'm sorry. That's my fault."

"No, it's not. It's entirely their doing."

"They fired you? How could they fire you? You were a volunteer."

What right did an employer have to demand another human's entire life be put at their disposal? A labourer, and Tom was a labourer in that dispensary, sold his time worked. The rest of his life should be respected as his own.

"What meetings? Meetings at the docks? The syndicalists and anarchists? Isn't that dangerous?"

No sooner had she said it than she appreciated the irony of her asking the question.

"I go there sometimes, to listen. How would I know what it's all about if I didn't find out? But the meetings they objected to were the Fabians."

"Edith Nesbit?"

"And Sidney and Beatrice Webb and George Bernard Shaw and other well-known people. The intellectual arm of socialism. The part that doesn't advocate the violent overthrow of the ruling class or consider themselves anarchists. They want a civilised life for the poor. They want sufficient nourishment and training for the young, a living wage for the able-bodied, treatment for all when sick, and a modest but secure livelihood for the disabled or aged."

"Who wouldn't want that?"

"Exactly. Who wouldn't? I was seeking answers to poverty, just like the government is. Benevolent philanthropy, wonderful as it is, will never achieve it. It is simply insufficient. The poor teem in the millions in their slums. Only the power of government and of government's ability to raise money can ever hope to effect real change."

"Don't socialists say the ultimate aim is the extermination of the bourgeois classes?"

Tom blushed. A very pretty state for him. She liked how she could see more of his face now he was clean-shaven.

He said, "Yes, they do. I'm not sure socialists like the Fabians really mean it."

"Then they would do better not to say it."

She didn't want to acknowledge her increasing tiredness. This had been a delightful reawakening of her brain. But he had to go. His half hour was up.

She received letters. She was surprised, and saddened, that none were from her mother or father. Had she hurt them that much?

Inga sent a postcard saying she had taken a house with her sisters on the south coast and was recovering in the sea air.

From Christabel Pankhurst:

No mere words can possibly express the feelings of the Committee towards you and the other comrades who have so nobly, and with utter disregard of self, suffered the pangs of the hunger strike at the promptings of duty and loyalty to a cause you passionately love, and which is dearest in life to us all. When you and the others are sufficiently rested we shall hold a special cele-bration breakfast at the Savoy to present you with a medal for valour.

She wrote to Alice Slack, who wrote back that she loved receiving letters but had little energy to reply. She was still in mourning for her husband, who had died in February, aged only fifty-two.

Tears invaded Harriet's eyes as she recalled the day they had perched above the House in the Ladies' Gallery and watched Bamford Slack's bill fail.

She hadn't told Tom about the effect the force feeding was having on her mind. It was too like having to admit to having been raped. A word she could barely think, let alone say. But the violation, the penetration and the degradation, they were what she imagined rape to be. And the shame. A completely unjustified sense of shame, since she had not been the perpe-trator of the violence. The doctor had. The man with the white coat, who had sworn to do no harm.

But there was one worry she could expel by voicing it. Although even that was hard to bring into the light of day.

"Tom, when you warned me about the consequences of refusing food did you know about the feeding tube?"

"It's a method of last resort used only on lunatics."

"Then you did know? Do you know how to do it?"

Had he stood over some poor person being held in place, while he poured liquid into them, like filling a jug?

He looked down at his hands, as though accusing them of actions he had never sanctioned.

"I have witnessed it. I never for one moment imagined it would be used on the women."

With this said, she could go further. "Tom, when I was

alone in my cell, I kept thinking about how awful it would be to die alone without all your family around you."

To her surprise, he stood up and walked over to the French doors.

After a few moments, he returned to his seat at her side. His face was flushed.

"The reason, Harry... the reason your sisters went back to Nottingham..."

She waited for him to find words.

"Harry, your father, Robert, Wesley and your Uncle George are all very ill. Enteric fever."

"Typhoid?"

A deep shudder ran through her, throwing her far away from Tom and the restorative sitting room and into a place of fear. How could this have happened? Even if many people recovered from typhoid, it was a ghastly, long fever. Her father and uncle and brothers must be suffering terribly. And her mother and sisters? She should be there to help. That's what family was about. Nobody with a fever should be left alone. A fever must be kept down.

And how could this have happened at the vicarage or Loxley Hall? Typhoid was spread by dirty hands onto food, Tom had said so back when she had first visited the dispensary. Typhoid wasn't something you caught by breathing the air. Her mother kept a model clean house. The pail-toilet always had fresh ash next to it to cover their business. It was washed all over every evening; seat, walls and door handle. Her mother had taught her to always seek out water after and to wash her hands thoroughly. It wasn't as if they didn't know how enteric fever was spread. All the same, Tom was passionate about the need for the city's pail-toilet system to be replaced with water closets, as was Nottingham's Medical Officer of Health.

They had water closets in Uncle George's modern house. The infection couldn't have happened at Loxley Hall.

Why had her sisters not told her? Why had Tom not told her? He was supposed to be the person she would trust most, for the rest of her life. Her father and her uncle and her brothers were at death's door, and she wasn't even praying for them.

Suppose her father died without ever seeing her again.

"Tom, I need to be with them. I need your help to get there."

"Harry, if you went there, you would be one more person to be cared for. They are overburdened with care. And you are too weak. There are measures regarding cleanliness that have to be carefully carried out. If you forgot, you could fall sick."

"I won't forget."

She sat back, exhausted by the emotions that rushed through her. She should reach down into the truth and tell him that. He deserved that.

"I am afraid I might never see my father, my brothers, my uncle, again. Can you understand how awful that would be?"

She was shaking, a shaking she couldn't control.

Sister's voice flew through the door. "Doctor Bardhill, I have to ask you to leave immediately. My patient is distressed."

Tom stood up and stepped back.

"Tom, please. Take me to Nottingham. I can't get there alone."

"Harry, it's not a good idea."

"Doctor Bardhill!"

"I'm leaving, Sister. Goodbye Harry."

A nurse helped her to her feet, telling her to come upstairs and lie down. She grasped the stair rail to haul herself up each tread. Even if she needed to take things easy, she should still be in Nottingham. She reached the top of the stairs and held onto the landing wall. Tears dripped from her chin. She concentrated on holding onto the nurse's arm. She couldn't spare a hand to wipe her face.

"Stop crying, Harriet Loxley." She said it out loud, causing the nurse to start.

The nurse arranged her pillows and pulled the curtains over the window, exhorted her to rest and to try not to think about it.

She turned on her side and pulled a pillow into her chest.

In prison she had been forbidden to write to her family. She assumed their letters to her had been returned. Why had her family not written to her since then? Was Mother setting her aside because she was causing the family trouble when what they needed was help? Mother wouldn't approve of self-starvation.

No. The family must be overwhelmed. Mother and Eleanor, Emma and Gwen; one for each bedside. No, one more, Aunt Beth. Poor Aunt Beth. She must be beside herself with worry. And if all the men were ill, would not Gwen be going into the manufactory to look over the books? No wonder they had gone straight back to Nottingham. She must have been too self-absorbed to see the strain in their faces. She *was* one more burden.

The next day she was still anxious but filled with pent-up energy. One of the nurses took her for a walk in the grounds.

"You must have been an active one, I reckon. You are recovering that quick."

"I liked to walk and bicycle, and I used to play cricket."

"Well, we'll not overdo it, but maybe in a few days we could get out a ball to throw. As long as we stay well clear of the windows."

There was a glint of laughter in the nurse's eye. They clearly knew more about her than she had thought.

In the afternoon she wrote to her mother.

Dearest Mother,

Tom has told me the dreadful news from home. I cannot fathom how awful it must be for you all. I understand why you have decided I should be here instead of with you, but I implore you to let me come home. I am recovering well and each morning brings improvement. There is colour in my cheeks and I walk further every day. I can surely be of some use to you all in a week's time, even if I have to rest a lot.

I'm sorry, Mother, for the anxiety I have caused you and Father. It is a terrible consequence of the actions I decided to take. I hope you understand my reasons, even as the results distress you.

I love you, Mother. I hope that gives you strength, as your love does me.

I am praying with all my strength for Father, Uncle George, Robert and Wesley. May He hold them in His saving hand.

Four days later she was in the sitting room attempting to read Five Children and It, but the tale of the children's ill-advised wishes and the Psammead's grumpiness was slipping past unabsorbed. Was Tom so determined that she rest that he felt he couldn't even see her? Not for half an hour? Had she frightened him away with her desperation? If he wasn't going to visit, why hadn't he written?

Tom appeared in the doorway. She started to speak, but he put his finger to his lips.

She saw Will pass behind him and go towards the stairs. She raised her eyebrows.

Tom came into the room and pulled up a chair.

"We have a motor carriage outside. Will is going to pack your bag and put it in there, and then I'll carry you out."

She could feel her eyes widen.

"Your mother got your letter. She asked us to fetch you. Will was reluctant but I told him he couldn't overrule the wishes of two ladies, especially not his mother."

She kept her voice low, like his, "What about Sister? Does she know I'm leaving?"

"After the last time I was here she banned me from visiting. Your mother has written to her but I doubt the letter has arrived yet."

"So, it was Mother who arranged this place?"

"Yes. Didn't you know?"

No, she didn't know. It was astonishing what people thought she might know when they didn't actually tell her.

He leant in close. "I have a plan for dealing with Sister. Once Will is back at the car, I'll carry you to it so fast that she doesn't have time to argue. She can't stop us by force."

"I hope no-one catches Will in my room. That would cause a furore. How does he know which one it is?"

"We worked it out from the times you have waved to me from the window. First floor, second from the right." He stroked her cheek with a finger and looked into her eyes. "I'm sorry. I should have taken more care of your feelings."

He stood.

"I'll nip out for a minute to see if Will's finished."

Harriet sat back and imagined Will sorting through her clothes and attempting to fold them. Heaven knows what state they would be in by the time she got home. The thought of home passed like fragrant wine over her lips and trickled strength down into her belly.

But what would she find there?

She shivered and pulled the blanket on her knees up around her shoulders.

When Tom returned, Sister followed him into the room and stood hands on hips. "Doctor Bardhill. I thought we had agreed you would stay away. I trust you will not be upsetting our patient."

"No indeed, Sister. I intend to take her home."

He swept Harriet up into his arms and carried her to the door. She handed Sister the convalescent home's copy of Five Children and It as she was borne past her and mouthed a thank-you.

Will was in the front of the car, by the driver. He wasn't exactly scowling but he wasn't smiling either. After greeting her, he said nothing. Tom helped her into her coat and she positioned her hat and looked for the pins. Will had not brought her hat pins. They would still be on the dresser in her room. She sighed, said nothing, and tied her veil tightly over her hat and under her chin.

The walk from the car to the station concourse was twice anything she had undertaken at the convalescent home. Her knees were trembling by the time Tom left her on a bench with Will and went to buy tickets.

Will clenched and unclenched his fists before saying, "There have been questions in Parliament. There has been an open letter of protest signed by over a hundred doctors. But there are other doctors who say the procedure is quite safe and exists to stop you being a danger to yourself."

"That depends on what you mean by safe. It hasn't killed me. I'm still here. But it's indescribably horrible. A form of torture. Something done to force me to eat when I had chosen not to."

"Which you did to force them to do something they didn't want to do. Treat you as a political prisoner. It's all about the public perception, isn't it? Now *Votes for Women* can run articles about women being tortured by the government."

"And the government can stop it all by the simple act of supporting one of the many franchise bills that have come before Parliament."

"And until then Christabel Pankhurst will continue to use you as cannon fodder."

She saw Tom returning with a porter and swallowed down the retort she was about to make.

The porter tipped his cap and loaded her bag onto his trolley. Tom handed him a coin and picked up the bag himself. She stayed sitting and watched. She wasn't sure why two men needed a porter to carry her one bag.

Tom handed the bag to the porter.

"I'd like you to carry this while I take the trolley."

The porter, a young man with a shock of black hair and broad shoulders, put the bag on the ground and seemed about to push Tom's hands away from his precious equipment.

"Don't concern yourself, man." Tom handed over another coin. "You walk alongside with the bag. Miss Loxley, please stand on the trolley, facing me, and hold on tight."

She had recovered some strength while sitting on the bench. She stepped on the trolley, facing Tom and gripping the sides. The porter grinned widely, showing gaps in his teeth.

Tom tipped the trolley.

"Keep up, Will, old chap. There are only two minutes until the train leaves, or we'll have an hour to wait."

He dodged through the concourse, providing her with a view of open mouths over his shoulder. She whimpered every time she knocked an elbow or a knee onto the sides of the trolley but she was filled with fierce energy. When he bumped her down the steps to the platform, she held on for dear life.

Will dashed for a carriage door before the guard could close it.

She laughed. Propriety had received a severe drubbing.

"You're a right trooper, ma'am."

The young porter tipped his hat. He handed Will her bag and Tom lifted her up into the carriage and placed her on the seat. She didn't know where all that energy had come from but it was gone.

She said, "Well, that was exciting. Perhaps the WSPU should employ you two to organise jail breaks."

Despite her attempt at humour, she was shaking. She untied her veil, removed her hat, and sank sideways across several seats.

"I think I'll rest a bit, if you don't mind."

Chapter 21
Loxley Hall

November 1909

Harriet held on to Tom's arm as she climbed the steps of Loxley Hall but let go when she reached the top. She didn't want to be leaning on anyone when the door opened. The red and lime-green tiles in the porch were dull, as if they had not been washed that morning. She remembered how they had sparkled the day she and Father and Gwen had come to confront Uncle George over the embezzlement at the manufactory.

But Will didn't ring the bell. He opened the door and went in. Of course, he'd explained while they were on the tram. They were all here. Father had fallen ill here. And the others had moved out of the vicarage so it could be disinfected.

The hallway was empty and silent. Four people fighting for their lives and everything was quiet.

"You'll be sharing a room with Gwen and Emma," Will said. "I'll take your bag up."

Tom pulled his watch from his waistcoat pocket. "Five

o'clock. Might still be tea time. Let's see who is in the Drawing Room."

He opened the door and gestured to Harriet to go in first. Eleanor rose from a chair.

"Harry! Here at last. It is good to see you. Was the journey very tiring? I'll ring for fresh tea. No, Tom you ring, please." Eleanor took her hands in hers. "How thin they are, Harry. We must feed you up. Did you eat well at the nursing home?"

"Very well. But I am not to eat too much at once, not until my digestion recovers. But less about me! How is Father? And Robert? Uncle George? Wesley? Are they recovering? Is it bad? Please don't spare me, Nell. Tell me the truth. I am desperate for the truth."

"Come sit. Has Tom not told you how things are?"

"Yes, but his news is days old."

"Well, it's been ten days since Father fell ill. He was the first, but the others were feverish by the next day. That's ten days of fever now."

Tom walked over with a slice of cake on a plate and handed it to Harriet.

He said, "After two weeks of fever we should be able to tell if there are complications. If there are none, then another week and they should start to recover."

Harriet drew a sharp breath. "Three weeks of fever. That's enough to exhaust the strongest person."

"Yes, but it's not the real danger. Secondary infection is. We have to be patient and vigilant. It's all we can do."

Harriet tried to eat some of the cake, but it tasted like dust in her mouth. When would they let her upstairs? Only after Tom had taught her the hygiene measures she must take, she supposed. He had made it quite clear how important all the hand-washing was.

The door opened and Will came in.

"Ah," Eleanor said. "Perhaps you could go to the kitchen for tea. No-one has answered the bell."

As the door closed behind him, she said, "The servants are overworked, what with all the daily cleaning of the sick rooms and bathrooms and all the nagging they get about keeping themselves clean. Water is being carried about everywhere, all the time. It's a wonder someone hasn't fallen."

Tom said, "I shall go upstairs and take a look at our patients, if you'll excuse me, ladies. I'll probably relieve one of the sitters for a while."

When the door closed behind him, Harriet put her plate aside. Maybe she would be able to swallow more cake with some tea. Maybe the worry that was clawing through her stomach would recede a little and allow her to eat. He was right. She wasn't going to be much help if she didn't maintain what strength she had.

Will returned and Aunt Beth's cook bustled in behind him, bearing a tea tray.

"Begging your pardon, Mrs Brown. I was up to my elbows in flour when the bell rang and the maids were about the house cleaning. I'm so sorry Mr Wilfred had to come to the kitchen. I do hope the cake is to your liking, only I'm finding it hard to bake much and I've not seen Mrs Loxley at all today and I need some instructions for luncheon and dinner tomorrow so I can get the orders done in the morning."

Eleanor said, "You are doing splendidly, Mrs Elliot. It is a very trying time for us all. Maybe our Mrs Sheffield could take over the baking." She paused and Harriet guessed there was tension with two cooks in the kitchen. "Or some of the other kitchen tasks. At your discretion, of course. And I think we could help with planning for tomorrow, couldn't we, Harriet? How many are we?" She counted on her fingers. "You, me,

Mother, Aunt Beth, Gwen and Emma, Will, and maybe your Tom."

Your Tom? When did he become *her* Tom in Eleanor's eyes?

Eleanor went to the bureau that stood in a corner of the room, flipped down the top, and came back with a pencil and a notepad. "Eight to feed then. But we don't really know. Gwen is coming and going to the manufactory and Emma goes into the shop. And what about you? Do you need special food?"

Harriet said, "Let's have a side table of cold cuts and winter salad for luncheon and perhaps a jam tart. Then we needn't worry about who is here."

"Good idea. And, Mrs Elliot, perhaps you could prepare a veal and ham pie so we can do cold luncheon the next day too. And tomorrow, some steak and kidney pudding, carrots and boiled potatoes. And order cod for dinner the next day."

"Begging your pardon, Ma'am, what with the deserts, that's a lot of pastry to be making."

Harriet smiled, "Yes, it is, isn't it? No pastry for deserts then. Let's have stewed apple for dessert, with custard. And we might have rice pudding the next day. With strawberry jam dolloped in the middle."

"Nursery food," Eleanor said. "Very comforting. Well, that's done."

She handed the list to the cook, who nodded and left.

"Thank you, Harry."

"For what?"

"For being here." She wiped a tear from her eye, a sight Harriet had rarely seen.

"All this talk of food has put me in mind of the boys and how they can eat. Oh Harry, I've never been so relieved to have my boys away at school as I am now."

Will said, "Have you told the boys? Or the school?"

Eleanor wrung her hands together. "What is there to say that will do anyone any good? If everyone recovers we can tell them there's been illness. If not... if not..." She lifted her chin. "If not, I'll do what I have to do."

Weariness was creeping up on Harriet, not a deep, soul-sore weariness like Eleanor's but still a sensation she needed to respect. If she didn't it would put her out of action for days.

She said, "I think I will need to rest soon, but I'd like to speak with Mother first. Do you know where she is?"

"She's with Father," Eleanor said. "I'll relieve her so she can come down."

Will stood. "No, you stay here. I'll go."

Her mother sat in the chair between her and Eleanor. Harriet had never seen her look so worn down. She was a slight woman, but had always been strong. Indefatigable would have been the way to describe her. Now, her face twisted in an attempt to hold back tears.

"Thomas explained to me how distressed you were that we chose not to make you aware of the extent of your father's and your uncle's illness."

Harriet knelt at her side and her mother took her hands in her own.

"I don't know what to feel about what you have done, Harriet. Part of me is horrified at seeing a child of mine look this ravaged. Your hands, your cheek-bones..." she removed her hand and tucked it under Harriet's chin. "I brought you into this world. I cared for you and nurtured you. My one desire was to see you grow fat and bonny. And look at you. You are like an unfledged bird that has fallen from the nest."

"I had hoped to be thought of more like a grown bird that had flown the nest, Mother. One with feathers."

She was looking her mother in the eye as she said it and caught the brief flash of shared humour. Underneath all the steadfastness, her mother had always taken a delight in the absurd.

"I am sorry to have caused you and Father distress. I never thought the refusal of food would be necessary for more than a few days, but once I'd started I couldn't, in conscience, give up. Not when so many others around me kept going."

It was becoming uncomfortable kneeling on the floor. Harriet stood and went back to her chair. Eleanor was looking at her with concern and something else. Was it perhaps admiration? Or despair?

Her mother said, "My whole adult life I have waited for someone else to secure my right to vote. I could not do what you have done. I'm not sure I can even stand being the mother of someone who has done what you have done. But in that I have little choice. I'm glad you came, Harriet. I'm sorry I kept the truth from you. That was wrong of me."

"No, Mother," Harriet wiped away a tear with the back of her hand. "You were trying to do what was best, as you always do. I am here to help."

"It is you who deserve to be cared for, but I can't care for you as I would dearly wish. We are at our weak and mortal limits here."

The doorbell rang and Eleanor said, "It will be the visiting nurses come to wash our patients and change their linen. That means the others can come down for a while. I'll go up with them and see what's become of your Tom."

Harriet got up and rang the bell for yet more tea. It seemed that eat and drink whenever possible was the rule in the house and Tom had not eaten since breakfast.

It was Will, Gwen and Emma who appeared in the Drawing Room, not Tom.

"He's staying to talk with the nurses," Will said. "Aunt Beth has gone to her room."

"The maid will be bringing tea soon," Harriet said. "We can ask for some to be taken to her."

"No, she doesn't want to be disturbed. She needs to sleep."

"How long has she been sitting with Uncle George?"

"Eight hours," Gwen said. "We each do eight hours."

"Well, I can do that. It will be one more person to take a shift."

Will flung himself down in a chair. "Don't be ridiculous, Sis. You can barely stay standing for half an hour."

"I assume I'd be able to sit."

"You won't survive."

"It is very cold in the rooms," Emma said. "Doctor Boobbyer, the medical officer, you know, he sets a store by fresh air."

"I love fresh air, Emma. You know that. Fresh air was one of the things I yearned for most in the prison."

Emma looked deflated and Harriet was sorry for being rough with her. Emma was, as usual, thinking of others before herself.

Her mother said, "If Harriet wants to help, I think we should give her the opportunity. The care of her body is her own right."

"Mother!" Will sat upright in his chair. "You can't mean for her to push herself beyond endurance. She's more than capable of it. Just look at her!"

"I have been looking at her, Wilfred. That is something *I'm* quite capable of doing."

The use of his full name silenced her brother, as it always had.

Gwen said, "Good. If you're going to be here, Harry, you jolly well should muck in. Now where's that tea? Who's going to the kitchen this time?"

The time when Harriet should have gone to rest was well past, but if she mentioned it she would be making Will's argument for him, so she said, "If you will all excuse me, I have some clothes to unpack. I believe I'm sleeping in with you and Emma, Gwen. Which room is it?"

"Go right at the top of the stairs. Third door down on the right. Don't be too shocked. It's an empty room with three camp beds and a box for a wash stand. We found a screen and rigged up a pole across it to hang clothes. Aunt Beth never got all the upstairs rooms furnished."

An improvement on the prison, then. Somewhere to hang her clothes.

Chapter 22
Enteric Fever

November 1909

Harriet must have been dozing, the sort of dozing in which she remained aware of sounds that tricked her into thinking she was paying attention. She rubbed her neck, shivered and rescued her shawl from where it had fallen down her back. Cold streamed through the open window. Did every doctor consider fresh air the cure to all ills, or was it the remedy of desperation?

Her father was moaning. She took the cloth from the bowl by the bed and gently wiped around his eyes and nose. He moaned a little more. His beard, always dark, was showing on his cheeks.

His eyes snapped open.

"Father? Father it's Harriet."

"Harriet. Darling girl. Always breaking things."

His eyes closed again. Harriet shivered, pushed herself to her feet with a groan, and walked to the open window. The trees in the garden were coming into view, glittering with hoarfrost; the grass a silver carpet, as if God had woken to a world of black, barren cold and breathed purity across it with a morning's sigh. A crow cawed and she turned back towards her father's bed, the cold penetrating somewhere deeper than her bones.

They took something from me in the prison, Father.

She said it in her mind, not aloud. She didn't want him to hear a litany of self-pity. She had brought her suffering on herself.

She went back to his bedside and turned down the lamp. The memory of prison was sharp-edged but the fear over whether he would improve was dulled by waiting and kept at bay by hope.

Her shift went from six in the morning until two in the afternoon. At two, she looked in on her brothers and her uncle before going to lie down. It was seven o'clock when she woke and went downstairs.

She found Tom and her mother in the Drawing Room.

Tom took her hand in his own and turned it over a few times. "How is your recovery? Are you sleeping well?"

"I toss and turn. It's hard to be comfortable."

"You need more flesh on your bones. Have you been eating while you've been taking your turn sitting?"

He was looking her straight in the eye. Should she say that she could no longer stand the thought of marmalade, or cocoa, or fish? It had been fish for lunch.

"I make toast when I get up in the morning. Aunt Beth's cook showed me how to do it on the range. There's this large wire thing, a bit like a tennis racquet, that you can open up and put the bread inside. Then, you sandwich the bread," she made an up and down closing motion with her hands, "and put it on the hottest part of the range. You have to be vigilant because it cooks quickly, much quicker than on a toasting fork by the fire. The toast comes out with a sort of grid pattern on it." She was gabbling, she knew. She smiled at him enthusiastically. "Then someone brings me a boiled egg or the like from breakfast, around about nine. And I have whatever's left from lunch at two."

"Your mother said you didn't come down for lunch today."

"That's true, I–"

The door flung open and banged against the wall. Aunt Beth rushed in, her hands flapping at the air.

"Doctor Bardhill! I'm so glad you're here. Come up and look at my husband. Please! There is a dreadful change come over him."

Tom dashed past her and into the hall, calling over his shoulder, "Harry, do you know how to use the telephone?"

"Yes I do. Aunt Loxley had one installed."

She ran after him.

"Then, call Nottingham 456. It's my father's number. Ask him to come immediately."

A scream echoed around the hall. Tom turned back and said, "Ask him to bring morphine and syringes." He took the stairs two at a time.

Doors opened. Footsteps thundered along the landing. Harriet grabbed the phone from its table in the hall and cranked the handle. She took a deep breath. "Nottingham 456, please."

Tom's father promised he would be with them in half an hour.

Harriet put the phone down and stood, anchored by indecision, as if she had grown roots. Should she go upstairs to Tom or return to the Drawing Room to reassure Aunt Beth?

A maid backed through the kitchen door. A second followed her. Another bloodcurdling scream swept around the hall and the second maid dropped the tureen she was carrying, sending orange liquid and shards of white china flying across the tiles. The girl ran back the way she had come, as fast as if a thousand devils were chasing her. The other stood stock still, staring into

Harriet's face. She couldn't be older than fourteen. Then she turned and ran after her companion.

The orange puddle spread at Harriet's feet.

Mabel, their maid from the vicarage, burst out of the kitchen.

"Oh Lor', Miss Harriet, I'm sorry. Them two's not got a pennyworth of sense between them. I'll send them straight back with a mop and bucket."

Another shriek from above, and Mabel's body stiffened but she held her ground.

"Mr George Loxley," Harriet said. "Young Doctor Bardhill is with him."

Mabel nodded. Harriet wondered if she had given the impression that Tom was inflicting the pain.

"He took a turn for the worse, a little while ago."

"The Good Lord help him, and us. I'll get this cleared up." Mabel turned to go, but stopped and came back. "And what should we be doing about dinner, Miss Harriet? It's all ready."

"Bring it through. I'll let the family know. But keep those young girls in the kitchen."

Feet pounded the stairs.

"Uncle George!" Emma sobbed. "It's Uncle George screaming. We went in and Tom said it's ab... something or other."

"Abdominal sepsis," Gwen finished for her sister. "It's one of the complications the doctors didn't want to happen. Tom and Will are trying to get him to swallow some laudanum but–"

"Doctor Bardhill will be here soon," Harriet said. "With morphine he can inject."

Gwen grabbed Harriet's arm. "What on earth is this all over the floor?"

"An accident with the soup. I'm surprised Mother and Aunt Beth didn't come out to see about the crash. One of us should go to them. Where's Nell?"

"She was with Wesley," Emma spun round, towards the stairs and back again. "She came running with the rest of us. Won't Mother want to be with Father? Suppose this is happening to them all!"

Harriet grabbed her by the shoulders. "Come on, Emma, buck-up. Go and tell Mother and Aunt Beth that Doctor Bardhill is on his way and try to get them to have some dinner. Gwen and I will go back up to Father and Robert."

Now was no time for hysterics. They had to find the strength to be a part of whatever was coming. She gave Emma a gentle push towards the Drawing Room door and turned towards the stairs.

Aunt Beth returned to her husband immediately after Doctor Bardhill's visit. She slept in an armchair at his side and refused all offers to relieve her. Almost twenty-four hours later the Reverend Robert Loxley, with Harriet at his side, screamed aloud and threw off his bedclothes.

"Get away! Begone! Filth of Satan! Get away, I say! You shall not hold me down."

"Oh Father! Oh, my God! Father!"

Harriet ran to the door, looking for Tom. He had slept in Will's room last night and had promised to stay for as long as Uncle George needed the morphine injections, which every four hours. Tom was already running up the stairs, medical bag in hand. He didn't ask her to leave, so she followed him back into the room. She stood inside the door and watched him draw morphine up into a syringe. She tried to slow her breathing, which was coming in shallow gasps. Tom pulled her father's sheet across his upper body, pinning his flailing arms.

"Harry, I want you to hold this sheet tight, like this, so I can inject the morphine."

She walked to the bed and bent over. It took all her strength to pull the sheet tight. A pungent smell rose from her father's body. She felt dizzy and realised she was holding her breath.

"You cannot bind me, Satan! You have no power over me!"

Tom flicked the vein on the inside of her father's elbow and injected the drug. Her father flung his head from side to side. Then, suddenly, he was still.

"Oh God, Tom, is he–?"

"It's the morphine. It's very quick." Tom took a step back from the bed. "The nurses are here somewhere. Will you be alright if I go to find them, Harry? The sheets need to be changed."

Uncle George died two days later, his hand in Aunt Beth's. Tom and Will cleared space for the coffin in the Morning Room. Aunt Beth retreated into her bedroom and would see no-one but Mother.

Mother was like a winter leaf, only her structure remaining.

Harriet ran her finger across the stubble on her father's cheek, even though she knew she should touch his face as little as possible. Will had been tidying his beard every morning. He should be coming soon. He would have hot water she could use to wash her hands.

Her father no longer screamed and cursed the demons that surrounded his bed. He lay still, beads of sweat the only indicators of the disease that was sucking out his life.

This was death then; no profound summation of a life, no coming into greater glory, merely a ghastly limp extension of ghastly illness.

"I don't know if you know I'm here, Father, but I love you

with all my heart. I'd beg you not to leave, but I fear it is too late for that and you are already halfway towards wherever you are going."

Could he hear her? Did her voice reach across whatever threshold he was crossing? Did her love?

She picked up his hand and lowered her forehead onto it.

"I'm sorry that your last thoughts of me must have been concerns, Father." She remained, head down, for several minutes. "No, you mustn't believe I think I am no more than a worry to you. I am strong, Father. I am going to fight on. I am going to preach the way you always preach, determinedly and repeatedly, until the world improves. It was you gave me the courage, that day you had me shout in church."

He moaned, and she wondered if she should fetch Tom. It was only three hours since the last morphine.

"Oh God," she whispered, "why can't you grant him some peace? He has defended and praised you all his working life. Why not a little peace?"

His breathing changed, and she lifted her head. Each breath was catching in his throat. She took his hand again. He squeezed hers, just a little. She was sure he did.

"I love you, Father. I love you so much."

Cold stole through the open window and surrounded them both.

"Don't go. Please, God, don't go."

When she had to acknowledge that his hand was limp, she got up and kissed his forehead, still damp but already growing cold. A handbell stood on a table by the window. Three short bursts were the prearranged signal for the family. If she accidentally dropped it, so it fell into the frost below, would it delay their pain? Could she, by throwing away the harbinger of death, stop the anguish?

She lifted the bell and rang.

Will came through the door, too soon to have been summoned by the bell, holding a water pitcher and the cloths for shaving. For a long moment he stared at her, unmoving, until she took the jug from his hand and put it on the washstand. When she turned back, he still hadn't moved. She went up to him and flung her arms around him. He buried his head in her shoulder and her own sobs racked her chest.

When Emma entered, her outdoor coat over her nightdress, Harriet released herself with a whispered, "Go to him, Will."

She went over to the window. The garden was still dressed in white. There was no thaw, no warmth in the risen sun. She pulled the window to, until only a thin sliver of cold air brushed her face.

When Mother arrived, she asked Harriet to relieve Eleanor at Wesley's bedside and Will to send Gwen from Robert's. Harriet took Will's hand as they left the room.

"God help me," he whispered. "For all those years of childhood I longed to be an adult and now I don't like it so much."

She took him in her arms and squeezed him hard, her own tears welling up again. Then she drew back and walked towards the room where Wesley was fighting for his life, wondering how she would be feeling if it was Tom who was at death's door. Eleanor had lost a father and might lose a husband too. How could anyone bear that?

Harriet stayed with Wesley while Eleanor went to her father. After half an hour Gwen came in and she stood to hug her.

"Mother wants to know if you want to see Father again before she sits alone with him."

"I said my goodbyes."

"That's what I thought. Tell her on your way down. I'll stay with Wesley."

"What time is it?"

264

"A little after eight."

Harriet stepped back and took her sister's hands in hers, reluctant to leave her. Gwen was wearing grey woollen gloves with no fingertips, like a market trader. Her sister followed her glance.

"I wear them at the manufactory. Office too cold, factory too hot. Nothing's ever right, is it?"

Harriet had experienced pangs of annoyance with Gwen for her coming and going, sometimes arriving late for her turn at a bedside. Now she saw how Gwen must be holding the manufactory together. If Wesley and Robert were to die, she would be the only family member left there, responsible for all their welfare.

"Gwen's a whiz with the numbers, Nell."

Gwen jumped at the same time Harriet did herself. Harriet hurried back to the bed. Wesley's startlingly blue eyes were open, ranging around the room. She pushed aside his damp hair.

"Nell?"

"It's Harriet, Wesley. I'll fetch Nell for you."

His eyes focused on hers.

"Harry? Have you saved the world yet?"

Gwen handed her a cloth, and she wiped it around her brother-in-law's face. He was cool. The fever had gone. A surge of joy crashed through the grief filling her mind. How could two such opposing emotions exist at the same time?

She passed the cloth to Gwen and went to find Eleanor.

Mother had asked them to leave her alone with her husband until she rang for them. Only she never did ring and eventually Harriet went up to tell her that the nurses needed to lay him out and the undertaker was at the door and ready to measure up for the coffin. She didn't know who had sent for him, but there he was. The Morning Room, already set aside for Uncle George's coffin, would now hold two.

Harriet arranged for a fire to be laid in her mother's room. She led her there and persuaded her to lie down until lunch.

In the Drawing Room, Eleanor was listing people to be invited to the funeral.

"How is Wesley, Nell?"

"Sleeping peacefully. Oh, Harry, I'm so happy. Is that very bad of me, with Father gone only a few hours ago? How can I dare to be happy?"

"I'm happy too, especially for you."

Tears ran down her cheeks, belying her happiness.

"Oh, move the cards. You'll get tear stains on them."

"I think that would be most appropriate."

Eleanor said, "I have to contact the school, so the boys can be home for the funeral. I suppose I should use the telephone. The thought of those boys having to take the train home, knowing they will never see their grandfather or Uncle George again... I don't know if I can do it. Perhaps you could be next to me, Harry?"

Harriet took the pen from Eleanor's hand and pushed the cards aside. "Of course. Let's think about what you should say."

There was a tap on the door and Tom came in, together with a gentleman Harriet didn't recognise. Eleanor rose to her feet and Harriet did the same.

Tom took Eleanor's hands in his own.

"I know how much your father meant to you all. I don't have words to convey my feelings. He was a wonderful man, dedicated to improving the lives of everyone around him."

Harriet swallowed and studied the unknown gentleman who was keeping a polite distance by the door, looking at the floor with his hands folded in front of him. He made a striking presence. He was beyond the middle years of life but quite athletic looking, with silver-grey hair cut short and features dominated by a nose so startlingly Grecian it would have astonished the ancient Greeks.

Tom said, "Ladies, allow me to introduce Doctor Boobbyer, Nottingham's Medical Officer of Health. Doctor, this is Mrs Wesley Brown and Miss Harriet Loxley."

The gentleman by the door stepped forward and bowed slightly.

"Good morning, ladies. I am sorry to be intruding at this tragic juncture for you both. First, may I offer you my deepest condolences? Mr Loxley and the Reverend Loxley were profoundly respected."

Harriet, as she had grown accustomed to do, offered her hand to shake. Doctor Boobbyer, looking bemused, paused before he took it.

Eleanor nodded her head.

Eleanor said, "I'm afraid my mother and my aunt are indisposed, Doctor Boobbyer. I hope we may be able to assist you."

The medical officer looked from her to Harriet and back, as if unwilling to do what he had come to do. Eleanor sat down. Harriet remained standing. Tom took a step closer to her side.

After an audible intake of breath, Doctor Boobbyer said, "Well, I'm sure you ladies know that I am obliged to research the history of possible contacts and sources of contagion in cases of enteric fever. I have come to see if Mr Robert Loxley and Mr Wesley Brown are well enough to answer a few questions."

Eleanor said, "My brother has not come through the fever yet, but I will go and see if my husband is awake."

Harriet sat down at the table and sighed.

"Doctor Boobbyer, is the pail closet at the vicarage perhaps to blame for the typhoid?"

He gave a sad smile, a fleeting bend of the lips.

"In a way I wish I could say it was, because then I could put pressure on the diocese to modernise the accommodation. But, if it were the source of infection, the cases would have been spread out more. Also, only your father and Mr Wesley Brown were living at the vicarage, as I understand, and there are water closets here at Loxley Hall. Since all four of the patients have shown an identical disease pattern, it is more likely they were infected with contaminated foodstuff at a common meal than through the pail closet at the vicarage."

Gwen came into the room.

"This is my sister, Miss Gwendolyn Loxley, Doctor. Have you met before?"

"I have not had that pleasure."

This time he didn't hesitate when Gwen offered her hand.

"My brother-in-law is awake and will be ready to see you in ten minutes, Doctor."

Harriet said, "Doctor Boobbyer thinks they may all have eaten the same bad food, Gwen. Was there a family dinner or similar?"

"They had a meeting at Johnson's dining rooms. All of them. With Mr Ashford."

Doctor Boobbyer nodded slowly. "Mr John Ashford, the banker?"

"Yes."

"Mr Ashford also passed away yesterday. Do you happen to know the date of the meeting, Miss Loxley? Or even what they ate?"

"I certainly do, because I was there. We all ate the same, except I refused the oysters. I cannot abide oysters."

Harriet stared at Gwen. Since when had she been invited to shareholders' meetings and been permitted to talk with the arch enemy? Harriet said nothing. The arch enemy was dead.

Eleanor returned to take the medical officer to interview

Wesley, but it seemed he already had his answer, at least according to Tom.

"Either the oysters were contaminated, which happens, because sea-side towns pump sewage into the sea alongside the oyster beds, or the person who prepared the oysters at Johnson's is a typhoid carrier."

Gwen dropped down onto a chair.

"How can something as petty as an oyster have ended the lives of three healthy men?... Nasty, slimy things."

Tom sat next to Harriet. She felt tears about to brim over. Tom squeezed her hand.

The door shuddered open.

Eleanor.

"Good news amongst all the bad. Doctor Boobbyer looked in on Robert and said there still seem to be no complications."

"Thank Heavens."

Harriet started to stand, meaning to embrace her sister, but no sooner was she upright than she felt dizzy and fell back into the chair she had been sitting in.

Eleanor and Gwen rushed to her side.

"I'm alright."

"You clearly are not."

Was Gwen wagging her finger at her? Really?

Tom put his hand on her forehead.

"There's no fever. I'm sure it's just the strain on the body from lack of nourishment and sleep. Not that these are minor things, but food and rest will put them right."

Gwen said, "She's thin. She's weak. She's vulnerable. We have allowed her to do too much. I knew this would happen if she came here. I sincerely hope you're right, Tom. This isn't the Harry I know, and I want that one back."

Harriet's head was swimming.

Tom got up and rang the bell. When the maid came he asked for hot sweet tea and a slice of cake.

Cake again? Was her life destined to revolve around cake?

"What kind of cake would you be wanting, sir?"

"Any kind! Whatever you have. Just make it quick."

He sat back next to her and took her hand.

"When we are man and wife, Harry, we will have cake every day."

Harriet lay back in the chair, hot tears gathering behind her eyes, forcing their way to the front. The cat was out of the bag now. This wasn't right. Her father should have been the first to know.

"Tom, when we are man and wife, you will learn that if you want food from the kitchen quickly, you fetch it yourself."

She tried to smile, but there was a gripping feeling at the back of her neck. Heat was exploding all over her body and was prickling under her clothes. She wiped her hand across her forehead.

When her tea and the ever-present cake arrived she consumed it under Tom's watchful eye, then agreed to go upstairs to lie down. Gwen went with her. Harriet stripped down to her shift and crawled under the covers.

Gwen sat on the floor by the low camp bed and held her hand. She held it for a long time, only the gentle changes in pressure sharing her pain.

Eventually Gwen shifted and said, "Is it true, then? You plan to marry Thomas Bardhill?"

"I do. We are very much in love."

"Well, only a blind man could fail to see that. So I suppose it can't be helped."

"Congratulations would be nice." Harriet dropped her head back onto the pillow.

"You were always so good at fending off those boring suitors, Harry. Emma and I looked up to you."

"Perhaps Tom isn't boring."

Gwen withdrew her hand, gave her a hard look, and changed the subject.

"I saw the expression on your face when I said I was at that meeting. It was true. I was there."

"I don't doubt it. But why were you there?"

"Uncle George insisted the manufactory needed a family member with a head for numbers and Wesley should be spending all his time on sales. And to think Emma and I once thought we could be the advisors on fashion. Seems fashion isn't what makes profits. What makes profits is everyday things, like..." Gwen paused and pulled out a handkerchief to wipe her eyes, "...like the lace corners on handkerchiefs."

"That Ashford," Gwen blew her nose. "He kept his hands clean, while his soul was black. He bought up distressed businesses all over the town, fired the workers and sold the assets. The Loxley warehouses in the Lace Market are valuable, and the machinery in the out-of-town factories is the most up-to-date money can buy."

"Did Uncle George start paying you a salary when you went back?"

"Eventually." Gwen blew her nose and tucked her handkerchief away. "He put Robert and Wesley on salary too. That's what the meeting with Ashford was about. He threatened us with legal action over the salaries."

"Well, Ashford is dead, God rest his soul. What will happen to the manufactory now? Wesley expects to inherit it jointly with Robert."

"There's no point worrying yourself about that. We'll find out soon enough. Meanwhile, I'll take care of family interests at the manufactory, just like I have been since all the men fell ill."

"Well, perhaps you'll allow me to worry a little bit, since there's no income from the shares and none from Father's stipend and we will have to move out of the vicarage because Father is no longer a vicar..."

Gwen sobbed, shuffled closer to the edge of the bed and laid her head on it. Harriet put her arm over her shoulder.

She was almost asleep when Gwen backed out from under her arm, went over to her own low, canvas-slung bed and pushed it across the floor until it was next to Harriet's.

Gwen lay on her back and stared at the ceiling.

"Thanks to Uncle George, us women will never be destitute, even if he should never have taken the money out of the manufactory like that." She blew her nose, turned on her side and pulled herself to the edge of Harriet's bed. "Please hold me, Harry. I can't bear it. Father being gone; Uncle George being gone. I can't."

Chapter 23
Lenton Vicarage

Christmas 1909

The whole family was crammed into the vicarage Drawing Room, except for Mother and Aunt Beth. Harriet had last seen them with their chairs pulled close together at the dining table.

Will was on the floor by Harriet's feet, hands curled around his brandy glass, peering into it as if it contained answers. Gwen, at the other end of the sofa, was methodically biting her fingernails. Robert, by the fire, was as pale as his dark complexion could allow, almost as pale as the honey-cream fabric of the wing of the armchair he was leaning against. Wesley, on the other sofa, was bent into Eleanor's side, as if his own back wouldn't support him.

Uncle George was not harrumphing about something.

Father's chair was empty.

The end of Christmas Day and two vast holes had buried them in silence.

Harriet took the cushion that had been behind Tom's back before he left to fetch the port and tucked it under her. She pulled Inga's letter out of her pocket. It had worn soft at the edges with her repeated reading.

Dearest Harriet,

It is a pity that you were not able to come to the festive breakfast and the award ceremony. Your name was read out to great applause. The medals are wonderful, no?

I understand why you couldn't be there. Your family must suffer much. I prayed for you. I believe we have the same God, although He has not confirmed it.

Mary Leigh's case against the Home Secretary and the Governor and Medical Officer of Winson Green prison has failed. There was much said about her condition after hunger striking and legal arguments about assault but, in a nutshell (that is the right expression, I think), the Lord Chief Justice ruled that it was the duty of the Governor and the Medical Officer to take all reasonable steps to keep the prisoner in health. We looked the pictures of health when we came out, no? The jury had to determine that the steps they took were reasonable, and they did it without leaving the room. Perhaps they should have experienced those steps for themselves.

When shall I see you again, my dear Harriet? Christabel is organising speaker pairs for the election in January. I want to share these trips with you. Are you yet ready?

Many greetings

Your comrade, Inga

Tom backed through the door with port and glasses on a tray. Harriet folded Inga's letter and tucked it away. Emma came in behind Tom, carrying one of the rattan-seated chairs from the hall. Tom handed port to Harriet. It smelt warm and nutty.

Emma dropped her chair by the small table at Harriet's end of the sofa and said, "It was almost unbearable, wasn't it, Harry, being in church for Christmas this morning and Father not giving the service? It was as much as I could do not to blub all the way through. I'm so glad you were there this morning. You are a tower of strength."

Harriet didn't feel like a tower of strength, more like scaffolding holding up a ruin. She had imagined a few days without food, a triumphant exit from the prison, Tom's arms around her and a few good meals putting everything to rights. Instead, although she wasn't a living cadaver any longer, she still couldn't face certain foods without feeling nauseous, or eat much at one meal, and she couldn't sleep because when she closed her eyes she heard the rattle of the cart bearing the jugs and the feeding tube as it approached her cell. No place she was alone felt safe.

Once she had accepted that Tom never had believed that force-feeding would be used outside of an institution for the insane, she had explained about the man, the doctor, the person with all the power, standing over her and forcing objects into her body. Tom had to know, because the visions that kept returning had crept into the intimate space between them.

But she hadn't been able to tell her sisters, her mother, or Will. They were sufficiently upset over seeing her in that dreadful state. If they ever found out about the lasting nature of the horror, they would combine to persuade her out of suffrage activity altogether.

She probably never would tell them. Why should all that suffering go to waste?

She looked around for Tom and made him out in an ill-lit corner of the room, perching on the piano stool. He saw her look and waved. Was he hinting that some music might substitute for conversation, since nobody seemed to have anything to say? Or was he over there simply because there was not enough furniture in the vicarage Drawing Room for them all to sit? She had, after all, taken over half his space on the sofa with her cushions.

She said, "Tom, dear, would you play for us, please?"

He opened the lid and sounded a note with one finger, letting it linger.

"As long as it's not any of your damned blackamoor stuff," Wesley muttered, without lifting his head from Eleanor's shoulder.

Tom pulled himself in and played the note again. Then a bar of Psalm 23, slowly and soulfully.

Eleanor started to sing, her voice soft and maternal.

"The Lord's my shepherd, I'll not want."

One by one they joined in, except Robert, who lay back in his chair with his eyes closed and Wesley, who was weeping.

Harriet did not sing, but she mouthed the words and sang in her heart. They were words they had all grown up with. They bound them together, and to Father. He would have loved to have heard them all singing together. She looked sideways at Emma, whose voice rang out with a bright tone, silver to Eleanor's gold.

Tom played straight into Abide with Me, and by the time they reached the last line everyone had tears on their cheeks.

Tom lifted his hands high from the keyboard.

"Anymore?"

Eleanor said, "That was lovely, Tom. Father would have been so happy."

Emma folded her handkerchief, put it in her pocket and said, "He really would. Father loved Christmas. Are we going to do Twelfth Night this year? I'm sure he would want us to."

"Oh yes, we should." Eleanor clapped her hands. "And, we

should have the Bardhills over. Maybe there'll be a prospective Mrs Bardhill to toast by then."

Harriet shifted her weight on her cushions.

"Tom and I thought there should be a year of mourning before we marry."

This wasn't true. Tom had said a summer wedding would be quite the thing to turn the family around. He had also said that, since they acted as man and wife when they were in London, following social niceties over mourning periods while in Nottingham seemed somewhat hollow. She had told him, tartly, which she regretted, that the niceties weren't for him, or her, they were for everybody else, like Mother. In truth, she couldn't yet cope with things that required decisions.

Will said, "I'm afraid I don't have the heart for games. Maybe next year."

Tom squeezed back in between her and Gwen and Gwen shuffled into the edge of the sofa muttering, "If there is a next year. Who knows where we'll all be next year."

Eleanor clapped her hands together again. "It's decided then. No revels on Twelfth Night. But we'll have a dinner party, perhaps less elaborate than usual."

Will swallowed down the remains of his brandy and got up to get another.

"Are you sure you won't have a little one, Robert? It's medicinal, I'm told."

Robert pulled himself more upright in his chair and shook his head.

Eleanor said, "There's a letter, addressed to you, Robert, that's been on the hall table for a week. I'm going to get it. I don't know why nobody took it to you at Loxley Hall."

Eleanor bustled out of the room and back again, handing an envelope to Robert, and a paperknife to open it with.

Had they all been speculating on what that letter said, imagining it must be something to do with Father? Yet none of them had made sure Robert got it. Were they paralysed by grief?

Robert slit the envelope open and read for only a few seconds before saying, "It's notice from the diocese that we must vacate the vicarage in two weeks, so the new family can move in. That's two weeks from the date of the letter, so in four days." He let the letter fall on his knee. "I'm sorry, I should have seen to this."

Harriet groaned.

She heard Will curse.

Robert said, "I shall write and request more time."

Gwen banged her glass down. "Who on God's earth gives a family notice to leave their home at Christmas?"

Robert smiled a thin-lipped smile.

"The church, apparently."

Harriet noticed Emma go round the back of the sofa and leave the room. She must be upset. They had all been born in the Lenton Vicarage, lived there their entire lives. Could it be gone? Just like that, with one short dismissal.

Gwen got up and took the letter from Robert's lap.

The door opened and Emma came in, followed by Mother and Aunt Beth. Tom stood and Will struggled up from the floor. Wesley sat up straight and Robert had pushed himself half up on the arms of his chair before Mother said, "No, no, please, you all stay where you are. Beth and I are only staying a moment. We won't sit."

Robert and Wesley sank back. Tom and Will moved to the back of the sofa.

How would Mother feel about being forced out of the home she had cherished for nearly forty years? She seemed remarkably calm standing there in the green silk she always brought out for Christmas, her hands, in their lace gloves, folded in front of her.

She laid a hand on her sister-in-law's arm. "Beth and I have been having some long talks about what is to become of us once we can no longer stay at the vicarage. I was waiting until the diocese informed me officially that we would need to move, but it seems they have seen fit to write to Robert and not to me."

So that was why Emma went out. Had she known about these discussions all along, with her quiet solicitude and ability to win confidences?

"That wasn't very clever of them, Mother," Gwen said. "Given that Robert doesn't actually live here."

"Quite. Anyway, your aunt has something to say."

Aunt Beth put her finger tips to her lips and looked around them all, as if committing each face to memory.

"I am so very sorry for the predicament you are in. I love you dearly, more than I can say. What has happened is terrible. It is very much my fault and the result of things I said and I persuaded your uncle to do. I suggested the trust to George and I nagged him until he set it up, even though he said there were difficulties taking the money from the business. I told him the men should be getting salaries, that Wesley had a family to consider, and that when a person works they deserve to get paid. I wouldn't let go of it."

Gwen shifted her position on the sofa. "Aunt, our predicament is due to oysters. Whatever happened, or why, pre-oyster, does not make any of this your fault."

Mother said, "Shush, Gwen, hear your aunt out."

Aunt Beth lifted her chin and raised her arms as if embracing them all.

"You must all come to live at Loxley Hall. George and I always wanted to fill it with children, but we were never blest. But we were blest with you. Loxley Hall has enough room for us all."

Tom put his hand on Harriet's shoulder and squeezed.

Next to her, Gwen whispered, "That is the obvious solution."

Eleanor went towards her aunt, arms outstretched. "You can't believe how worried I've been, dear Aunt. Thank you. Thank you so very much."

Robert pulled himself to standing. "Thank you, Aunt. That is very kind. But are you sure you want your house filled with us all?"

"She does," Emma said, a smile lighting her face. "I do believe she wants it more than anything." Her smile faded. "Except getting poor Uncle George back, of course."

Harriet got up at the same time as Gwen and joined in the hugging and thanks. The grey light in the room seemed be turning to gold.

"Well," Eleanor said, returning to her seat, "Loxley Hall might have sufficient rooms but some are quite bare. We can bring in furnishings of our own for the spaces that need it. I assume the diocese expects us to clear the vicarage. Hand me that letter, Gwen."

Mother, looking somewhat nonplussed at this usurpation of her role, took Aunt Beth's arm.

"That's settled then. Beth and I are going to bed and you young people can do the rest of the organising."

Eleanor read through the letter.

She said, "There are eight bedrooms on the first floor of Loxley Hall. Aren't there, Robert? How many are being used?"

"Aunt Beth has one. I have one. Will uses one when he comes down from town. And Uncle George used one as a study."

"And we are..." Eleanor counted on her fingers, "Mother, Wesley and I, our two boys, Harriet, Gwendolyn and Emma. That's six more spaces needed. Not enough, even if we make the study into a bedroom."

"There are third-floor rooms. At least another six. Small, but the boys could have one each."

Wesley snorted. "My children are not going to sleep on the servants' floor."

"I have no such qualms, Wesley." Will returned to sit on the couch next to Harriet. "I'm in London most of the time anyway."

"And very proper that would be. There are no separate male and female sections up there. The staff are exclusively female."

"Oh, been up there have you?"

Eleanor got up and stood between the two of them, her cheeks flushing. She extended her arms in a gesture of separation.

"This is not helpful."

Gwen said, "Emma and I can live above the shop. We enjoy our little space."

"Good idea," Will said. "You need to keep an eye on your secret room. All Nottingham knows it's there. Won't be long before the constabulary sneaks in to take a gander if the place is left empty."

Gwen turned to face him.

"Do you think you might take this seriously?"

Emma put her head in her hands and moaned a long howl.

Nobody moved. Maybe they all wanted to howl. Maybe they were working up the courage. Harriet turned the glass in her hand several times, lifted it, and finished the port she had been holding onto. The dark warmth made her feel stronger, but also distant. She heard Eleanor saying that there seemed to be plenty of rooms, and Gwen telling Robert that if the diocese didn't grant them more time they'd simply stay anyway and what were they going to do about that?

Harriet adjusted her cushions and laid her head back. She was dimly aware of Eleanor touching her cheek and imploring her to go to bed. She muttered something like *goodnight* in return.

Will pushed against her leg.

"Hey, wake up Sis, or go to bed. Which is it to be?"

She jerked awake. The sofa and chair opposite were empty. Both Wesley and Eleanor must have gone up, Robert too. Tom was still wedged between her and Gwen, Will leaning back against his knees.

Gwen lent forward and ruffled Will's hair.

"Leave her be. She's old enough to decide when to go to bed. What are your plans, Harry? Are you going to stay in Nottingham for a while?"

"I intend to go back to London to finish my degree. I'll be living with Aunt Loxley."

Three years ago, Owen's College had obliged Christabel Pankhurst to stay away from politics after she had been arrested. But that was three years ago. An institution's stance on women's rights was a matter of public scrutiny now. Bedford College had kept Harriet's place without conditions. It was an institution promoting the rights of women. How could it expel a woman who fought for those rights?

"I want to be in London to speak on platforms in the election in January. We're going to shame the Liberals into votes for women."

"Save your strength, Sis. There won't be anything in the Liberal agenda except getting Lloyd George's People's Budget through the House of Lords. The Liberals are creating the most meaningful measures to combat poverty this country has ever known. The women will have to wait."

She pulled herself up straight. "A *people's budget* in which half the money is going to build eight dreadnought-class battleships in an arms race with Germany. Your hero, Lloyd George, is typical of men everywhere. Social reform is noble, sabre-rattling is manly, but women will wait. It's a major constitutional crisis, brother, that *people*, due merely to the chance of being born female, don't get any opportunity to give their opinion on your very worthy budget. And who is it who suffers most from poverty? The women and the children, that's who."

Tom leant forward.

"I can vouch for that, treating, as I do, the consequences of poverty every day. If the women get to vote, they will oblige governments to spend the people's money on the people's health and less on wars and dreadnoughts and the posturings of empire."

"We're not on different sides, my friend. It's a matter of priorities."

"Exactly, dear brother. And the priority is votes for women."

"Good for you, Harry." Gwen clipped Will around the ear. "You tell him. You get out on the hustings. Emma and I can look after ourselves, can't we, sweet girl?"

"Yes. We can. We will."

Emma got up, bent, kissed her on the cheek, and wished her sweet dreams. Will unfolded himself, bounced on his toes a few times, and wished them all goodnight with a theatrical bow. Had Harriet offended him? If she had, he deserved it.

Gwen moved to the chair by the fire.

"You're not going up, Harry?"

Harriet sighed and shook her head. Sleeping was hard. Either she tossed for hours or she woke in the middle of the night and couldn't chase away the demons that had trailed her from the prison. She looked at Gwen, who was staring into the fire and chewing her fingernails. Maybe being honest with her would help. Out of all her sisters, Gwen was the one who most often shared her feelings.

"It's hard for me to sleep, Gwen. As soon as I close my eyes, I'm back on that chair in the prison, that doctor's face close to mine. I need to be so tired that I sleep as soon as my head hits the pillow. And I need some nice thoughts to take to bed with me."

Gwen surveyed her mangled fingernails.

"What you have done, Harry, amazes me. It's more than I could ever face. But I have a nice thought for you. At least, I hope you'll think it's nice. I want your advice."

"You want my advice on manicures?"

"No, silly. Uncle George left the lacework's voting shares equally between Robert and Wesley and I."

"That's wonderful. What's the problem with that? You deserve nothing less."

Dear old traditional Uncle George, proving himself untraditional once again.

"But, nothing for Aunt Beth?"

"Aunt Beth is provided for. Don't worry. But it feels like I'm getting both the men's share and the women's share. Should I give up my share of the trust?"

"Don't you even dream of it. The trust is there to keep us all secure, so we won't depend on our husbands and brothers. Few women are so fortunate."

Gwen pressed her lips together and slapped her hand on the arm of her chair.

"Thank you. You don't know how much I needed you to say that. I can use the trust money to pay the loan back on the shop. And the money will go to Aunt Beth, which seems quite appropriate since she will be housing the family. As for the manufactory. This is my opportunity. I'll show them what a woman can do. Make it clear I have been doing it. I'll get Robert on my side. Robert, of all people, understands how everything has been turned upside down."

"You said it. A topsy-turvy world will open up a gap for a

woman to squeeze through, and squeezing is what we'll have to do until things improve."

Gwen glanced at Tom and smiled.

"Are you two getting wed in the summer or not? I detect a certain level of disagreement on the matter. At least you, Tom, won't have to face Father's medical examination. Although you, Harry, will be breaking your solemn promise to have nothing to do with men."

How much any such promise, which she hadn't made anyway, had already been broken was something Harriet had no intention of sharing with Gwen.

"What my sister is alluding to, Tom, is not a solemn promise, just a fancy of hers that she has persuaded Emma to go along with. However, what I'm going to say next is important and it must stay in the family, although your father already knows a part of it."

She stopped. It was dangerous to drag such things into the space between people, but she couldn't keep the awfulness from Tom. Not anymore.

"The reason, Tom, for Eleanor's ill health, before her operation, was that she suffered from gonorrhoea, contracted from Wesley, who spent his afternoons frequenting the whorehouses of Nottingham when he should have been selling the warehouse stock."

She watched his face for a reaction. He only nodded.

She continued, "Wesley had to go to a clinic and stay away from Eleanor until he could prove he was free of the disease. What's more, Mother made Father promise to demand a clean bill of health from all his other daughters' suitors. So Gwen vowed never to marry."

Tom nodded again. "The disease is, unfortunately, quite common and sexual health depends on both partners remaining faithful. If that's what the Reverend Loxley would have wanted,

I'm happy to abide by his wishes. I promise I'll take the test, Gwen."

He was still water. It was no wonder she was so much in love with him.

"Not marrying is a promise I intend to keep." Gwen got up and made as if to leave but stopped by the door. "And not only because Emma and I don't want to catch a disease from a man who can't contain himself, but because we want to do things in this world. Things married women can't do because they're tied to a husband and children."

Harriet shot her a look.

"Emmeline Pankhurst does plenty and is a widow with four children."

"Widows have always had it better. But a husband's death seems a high price to pay."

Gwen left the room with a rustle of skirts, leaving Harriet to wonder just how she summoned up that sound exactly when she wanted it.

Chapter 24
Black Friday

November 18th 1910

Harriet looked up at the now familiar pink-brick façade of Caxton Hall and shivered. She longed to get out of the wind but she had arranged to wait for Alice and Inga outside.

She smoothed the front of her skirt. Despite all the sponging it had received, shadows of egg and vegetable matter mottled the dull black. She had spoken all over the south and the midlands during the January election. She no longer felt dizzy and sick when she mounted her box. She trembled with energy, not fear. And she no longer dreaded the missiles. They weren't dangerous and were rarely well aimed. She sensed her father standing beside her, urging her to show she had plenty of wit.

When the election had resulted in almost equal seats for the Liberals and Conservatives only the support of the Irish Nationalists and the Labour Party had allowed the Liberals to form a government, and the King's Speech in February had included only the budget and new legislation to redefine the relationship between the House of Commons and the House of Lords.

However, during the campaign, Asquith had promised to set up a committee to write a bill giving votes to women. The WSPU suspended all militant activities and Christabel turned its formidable powers of organisation to holding massive meetings and demonstrations around the country, including another one in Hyde Park, this time with forty platforms for speakers.

Harriet had spoken in Hyde Park. The press had reported on the solemnity of the crowd, saying it took something significant to keep half a million people quiet.

A Conciliation Committee on women's franchise had been duly formed, with members from all parties. It met throughout the summer and, after many months of discussion, formulated a Conciliation Bill.

Churchill and Lloyd George voted against it. Lloyd George managing to say, within the space of a few sentences, both that the last shred of argument against women's suffrage had disappeared and that he agreed with Churchill in condemning the bill. It would, he claimed, hand votes to the Tories. In his turn, Churchill declared that he supported a wider franchise bill for increasing all adult suffrage.

Despite their opposition, the Conciliation Bill passed its Second Reading with a majority of one hundred and ten. Then, unbelievably, instead of letting the bill proceed to a standing committee, the Liberals carried the vote for it to go to a committee of the whole house, which required the government to give it time for debate.

So now Christabel was sending women to Parliament to lobby for *The Bill, the Whole Bill and Nothing but the Bill*. It was the same slogan, Harriet recalled with a wry smile, that had accompanied the fight for votes in 1831. The fight that had resulted in the burning of Nottingham Castle.

A gust of wind caught her hat, and she re-pinned it. It was a cheap, black-felt affair that she had trimmed in WSPU purple, green and white. She could afford to lose it, but perhaps not yet.

The black clothes wouldn't have to last her much longer. This was the final week of mourning for her father. She had kept it up for the traditional full year; a period set aside for grieving, not in the sense of weeping, but in the sense of putting aside life's decisions because the mind was not to be trusted while the heart was sore. Although Tom kept saying that sharing the same bed every day would be the most wonderful thing, she thought marriage must inevitably lead to a new stage of life and she liked the stage she was in. She had her own purpose. Anyway, she told him, she couldn't marry until she had finished her degree.

Inga arrived at her side, in a plain brown suit with a WSPU sash, her shoulders straight and a bloom in her cheeks. Harriet could see the shadows of the hollows left by their prison ordeal, but she doubted anyone else noticed. Will was with her. There seemed to be a bloom on his cheeks too.

"Will, I thought you had to be at the House today."

"I do. I took some time to escort Inga, but I must shoot off or I'll be missed. Good luck with your lobbying. I will watch out for the march."

When Sylvia Pankhurst appeared, in a threadbare coat and with a battered satchel on her shoulder. Harriet waved her over.

"Are you marching today?"

Sylvia tapped her satchel. "No, I'm reporting. I have a taxi-cab meeting me. I will be racing about following events as they unfold. It could be dramatic. There are already police drawn up three-deep in Parliament Square."

Harriet caught sight of Alice Slack weaving her way between the crowds of ladies gathered outside the door to the hall. Her throat was wrapped round with a fur collar and she carried a white muff. She seemed smaller and more stooped than when Harriet had last seen her, which was over a year ago. As she introduced Inga she thought how the cause brought such unlikely people together: Inga the daughter of a wealthy Jewish brewer and Alice the widow of a teetotal Methodist preacher.

Sylvia greeted Alice warmly, calling her an old comrade before setting off at a run to her cab.

As she watched her go Harriet said, "You know, Alice, according to the property and residence rights defined in this Conciliation Bill we are going to fight for, neither Sylvia nor I would be able to vote. Both my aunts could, and my two younger sisters, because they all own houses. But my mother and older sister couldn't, and neither could my elder brother or brother-in-law. I'm starting to think that perhaps the real trouble with the property franchise is not the way it's defined, but that it exists. It's impossible to reconcile it with justice. Perhaps it *should* be one person equals one vote, instead of one's property equals one's vote."

Harriet hated to hear herself saying it, since Churchill had said the same thing.

Alice shook her head. "The subordination of women to men is the evil we are fighting. We mustn't lose sight of that. Enfranchising even one woman would be momentous. That single vote would forever sweep away sex as a barrier to suffrage."

They were in the fifth group to go out. Men and boys filled the pavements to either side, pressing in against them. It made it hard to keep walking. Shouts rose like waves.

Silhouettes of mounted policemen loomed in front of the buildings of the Palace of Westminster. Colourfully dressed women whirled and twirled in the street. It was so like a stage set that Harriet imagined a space cleared for dancing.

"Keep walking," Inga said. "We have nothing to lose but our chains."

They were close enough now for Harriet to understand why she had fancied the women were dancing. They were being pushed into the arms of the crowd and the crowd was pushing them back, like bagatelle balls.

She linked arms with Inga and Alice, and, when she got close enough to the waiting ranks of blue-coated police officers to speak without shouting, she took a deep breath and said, "Excuse us, please. Let us through. We wish to petition Mr Asquith."

"And who are you to be talking to Mr Asquith, then?"

"We are citizens of the British Empire with a right to petition. Kindly let us through."

At a sudden jerk of her right arm, she turned to see Alice being wrenched away and thrown to the ground. A rush of indignation swept through her and she turned back to remonstrate. Two thick arms came up under hers from behind. Two hands thrust inside her coat, gripped her breasts and twisted hard. She screamed. A rough chin rasped against her cheek.

"That's what you're wanting, ain't you? You stuck up whore? That's what you're missing."

She gagged in the stream of foul breath. She kicked backwards. He thrust his knee up between her legs and lifted her from the ground. When she tried to force her legs down, she only pushed his knee harder against her.

"Enjoying it, are you? Want some more?"

She heard Inga scream somewhere to her left.

Her unseen attacker laughed, thrust upward with his knee, lifted her clear off the ground and threw her into the arms of the officer she had so recently spoken to.

"Want to see Mr Asquith, do you? How about you see these gentlemen over here instead?"

The policeman twirled her round as if she were a rag doll and threw her towards the jeering crowd. She caught sight of Alice lying crumpled on the ground nearby. But where was Inga? She hoped Alice would lie still until it was safe to move.

She was facing into a chest stinking of onions, its owner gazing upwards, as if seeking rapture in the heavens. His hand tugged at the placket of her skirt. She pulled backwards as hard as she could. Behind her, someone yelled like seven demons and four fingers stabbed upwards under the man's chin and into the soft part of his throat.

He screamed and spittle spattered her face.

"Quick, run." Inga was rubbing her right hand with her left and grimacing with pain.

"Alice?"

"They carried her away. Arrested. Run!"

They ran some twenty yards before being surrounded by the crowd. "This way." Harriet panted out the words and seized Inga's hand, turning her away from Westminster Cathedral and the heaving mass of hostility and towards St. James Park. It was the wrong direction for Caxton Hall, but Harriet knew her way around these streets after her years of living in London and working with the WSPU. The times of wandering around hopelessly lost were a mere memory.

They had slowed to a walk when Inga said, "I must go back. We mustn't give up."

She turned to retrace her steps.

Harriet stepped in front of her. "There is a nasty split below your eye. You need medical attention."

"I'll get it later."

Harriet's soft private areas were swelling up like rubber balloons. She needed Inga with her back at Caxton Hall.

"I need medical attention. I need cold compresses for a part of my body I can't name. I need you to get some and pass them to me."

"Oh, my God. What did that brute of a policeman do?"

"It was a policeman? I couldn't see. I thought it was some thug from the crowd."

"Yes, a policeman, with his hand reaching into your skirt. Oh, God, Harriet, I understand. Of course, I will come back with you."

Harriet could smell onions. She retched and vomited, only turning away in time to avoid Inga's shoes.

Harriet's head was throbbing. She was alone, sitting on a hard chair in Caxton Hall, with a wad of wet rags stuffed high between her thighs. Her drawers were sodden and her breasts ached. She had asked a man to step aside and let her make her point, and he had thought he could savage her. A man had tried to enter inside her clothes and force himself into the intimate part of her.

She shifted on her chair, lifting the weight from her sore areas. This must be what soldiers experienced at a field hospital. The walking wounded were left to get themselves to the next level. Except she didn't know how she was going to do that. It was a four-mile walk back to Aunt Loxley's house and every step she took now tore into her centre. She couldn't get a Hansom alone. She couldn't face being alone with a man. She couldn't get a public omnibus when her clothes were splashed with vomit.

She had known she wouldn't be marching in a colourful parade. The rumours had been that the crowd would be hostile and the police out in force. She should have had a back-up plan. Inga was God knows where. Perhaps she had been arrested after returning to the fray.

More limping and sobbing women were staggering into the hall. They fell into their rescuers' arms, collapsing on chairs and grabbing proffered cups of water.

This was the price of freedom and independence.

Water. She needed water.

Suddenly Inga was beside her, pressing a cup to her lips. She took it in her hands and gulped, looked up and saw Inga smiling, actually smiling. The cut below her eye, so recently cleaned with carbolic, had burst open afresh and blood smeared her face.

"Look who I found by the door. I think he was scared to come in."

"Hello, Sis. You look a proper mess."

Will sat next to her and took her hands in his. He leant forward and kissed her on one cheek and then the other. They used to do that, she remembered, when they were little. When they would pretend they would grow up to marry each other.

He said, "I've never seen anything like what I've seen out there. It's shocking, truly shocking. Whatever the women have done to annoy the politicians, there is no excuse for treating them like this. It's barbaric."

"It's propriety."

"Propriety?"

"Propriety builds a cage around us. If we leave the cage we are out in the wild and we are free to be hunted down. And to be insulted, derided and assaulted."

He blinked and said, "For what it's worth, if anything, there was no reason that bill couldn't go to standing committee."

She squeezed his hands and attempted a smile. "Did Asquith see Mrs Pankhurst?"

"No, he turned them away. They were trapped in the St. Stephen's entrance, behind the police cordon, on the steps, watching it all. I eventually found a way through. I've been so worried about you. About you all. Where is Mrs Slack?"

"We think she was arrested."

"She should be safe then."

"You think so?"

She had said it bitterly, and she knew he understood.

It was Richardson who opened the door of the Holland Park house, but before she could show them upstairs, Aunt Loxley appeared in the hallway. Her aunt was wearing a soft-pink tea gown, with a train and beige lace trim. It was a fashion from at least ten years ago. A shimmering red and gold paisley shawl covered her shoulders. Harriet knew she had inherited that shawl from her mother. Aunt Loxley radiated tradition, stability, and propriety.

"Wilfrid Loxley, how could you allow two young ladies to get into such a state? If young ladies are what they are. Young hooligans might be a better term. And who is this other person, anyway? This is not one of my nieces so blood-stained I don't recognise her, is it?"

Harriet said, "This is Miss Inga Rheinhart, Aunt, a friend of mine. Would you be kind enough to offer her hospitality for the night? Her family resides in Brighton and it is late and not very safe out for a woman."

"Of course, Miss Rheinhart, you are welcome. Please forgive my reaction. Your appearance is a little disturbing. Richardson, please see to hot water and see if Cook left enough cold cuts for our extra guests."

Harriet was leaning on Will's arm. Her aunt gave her a searching look and clearly chose not to say what she was thinking.

What she did say was, "Remove your shoes and coats and

come through to the Drawing Room until the water is ready. I will have fires lit in your rooms."

Harriet felt even unhappier, if that was possible, as if this sympathy from an unexpected quarter had breached her defences.

"Can we have some water to drink, please, Aunt?"

Her aunt rang the bell, and Richardson reappeared.

"A pitcher of water in the Drawing Room, please, and some warmed wine too. Come on through, all of you. I will have my doctor come to see to that cut in the morning, Miss Rheinhart. First, we'll get it cleaned up."

Harriet slept badly, her bruises forcing her awake every time she moved. She came downstairs early, hungry but dreading breakfast. She did not feel up to a dressing down from her aunt.

As soon as she sat, her aunt passed her the Daily Mirror.

"I'm shocked Harriet, deeply shocked. I find myself unable to believe such things can happen in this country, and yet I must believe that they did. The camera does not lie."

The photograph on the front page was of a woman, tumbled on the ground like a heap of rags. A burly policeman and a tall man in a top hat stood over her. Alice had looked like that the last Harriet had seen of her. It was not possible to tell if the woman in the picture was Alice. Many women must have fallen.

"They are calling it Black Friday," her aunt said. "You can't go on like this, Harriet. Think of your poor mother. Stick to throwing stones. But only in circumstances where you can run away. I never thought I wanted to vote, but now I think I do. What can I do to help?"

"Oh, dear Aunt, you are helping. But if you want to do more, join one of the suffrage societies. Membership counts for a lot. And would it be possible for Miss Rheinhart to stay a few days? We have a meeting at Caxton Hall on Tuesday, to hear if the Prime Minister has granted the Conciliation Bill the time it needs."

"If that is what you want. But I implore you both to take care. Faces are not easily repaired."

Chapter 25
The Battle of Downing Street

Tuesday, November 22nd 1910

The messenger from Westminster handed her paper to Christabel Pankhurst, who stood and addressed the hall.

"The government is calling another election to get the mandate for the reform of the House of Lords. If they are still in power, they will give facilities in the next Parliament for a bill widening the male franchise and frame it so as to admit free amendment to include women."

There was a brief silence, then murmurs and groans arose from the assembled women. Feet stamped on the floor. Someone shouted, *Disgraceful.* Sylvia Pankhurst, in the seat next to Harriet, leant forward.

Inga, on the other side, whispered, "Is this a bad thing?"

Inga had acquired a blue-satin eye patch to cover the cut she had received on Friday. It made her look like a comic-opera pirate.

Harriet said, "It means the Conciliation Bill is dead, like all the others that have been brought in, year after year. Now we have to wait, yet again, on an uncertain outcome. We've wasted our time with putting our hopes in compromise."

"They have betrayed us?"

Sylvia hissed, "Lloyd George. That manipulative, scheming, double-crossing, Welsh wizard."

Mrs Emmeline Pankhurst stood.

"I am heading for Downing Street. Come along, all of you!"

Sylvia grabbed Harriet's arm. "I have a taxi waiting outside. We need to get there before the police bring in reinforcements. Their spies will be running off to alert them right now."

Harriet gathered up her umbrella and her muff and followed. She walked slowly, with her legs wide, protecting her bruises, and attempted to button her coat with one hand as she went.

Sylvia was leaning through the side window of one of the new motorised cabs, gesturing at her to hurry. Harriet climbed in, next to Inga. Sylvia tapped the glass and the vehicle lurched forward.

"Brace yourselves. I told him as quick as you like. These things are enough to rattle the bones out of your body."

The taxi drew to a jerky halt. Police constables lined up in front of the entrance to Downing Street were rapidly being joined by others. Sylvia got out and climbed onto the taxi's roof.

Inga called, "Are you going to make a speech?"

The driver poked his head out of his window. "More power to your lungs then, missus."

"I'm only reporting. I need to see."

Other cabs were drawing up. Women piled out of them.

Sylvia shouted, "Here comes Mrs Pankhurst, ladies. Be ready!"

Harriet got out of the taxi in time to see Emmeline

Pankhurst descend from a Hansom. A large police officer approached her. His bulk made her seem as vulnerable as a flower underfoot.

In a rush of indignation Harriet flung her umbrella and muff onto the seat of the cab. They were going to be stopped by force, yet again.

The line of constables was now two deep.

Someone nearer to the police line yelled, "Shove along, girls."

Harriet's lungs filled. All stiffness vanished. This time she would not ask nicely. This time she was going to act. Deeds Not Words was the WSPU slogan and deeds needed people to do them.

She raised an arm and shouted, "What are we waiting for? If Asquith is in there, we need to get to him while we can. We must make him listen to us."

The crowd surged. She heard Sylvia shout, "Push forward!"

The line of men broke. Harriet was in front of Numbers Ten, Eleven and Twelve Downing Street. Policemen ran alongside, trying to outflank them.

Harriet yelled again, "It's the green door!"

Herbert Asquith wasn't going to hide behind doors any longer, even if she had to break one down. Together, they could destroy that door. They had numbers and the power of justice on their side.

She felt a tug on her skirt, as if someone was dragging her backwards. The wet pavement flew up towards her. Her head crashed onto the stones and all went black.

A smell of leather. Harriet groaned. She opened her eyes. Her nose was pressed into the back of the seat of the taxi-cab.

Cautiously, she turned over, levering herself with her elbows. Her head swam.

"Ah, you're moving, are you Miss? We was about to take you to the hospital, only I said give it a minute, we'll never get through this lot without causing more damage."

Inga's face appeared above her.

"Thank the heaven, you are awake."

"What happened?"

"You went down in the rush. I think maybe someone grabbed you by your skirt. It is nearly ripped from the waistband."

Harriet pushed herself up to sitting and gathered the torn fabric of her skirt around her. Women's clothing had brought her down. And she had missed all the action. She felt sick and hoped it was going to remain only a feeling.

Inga said, "A policeman picked you up and carried you here."

"A policeman?"

"Yes, they seem a different breed from the ones of Friday. Asquith came out, by mistake, I think, and the police pushed him into a car before we could reach him. Then they brought in the horses and most of the women fled. But one went right up to some police horses and walked them away. Charmed them, I think. They arrested her, of course, and Mrs Pankhurst, but I think Sylvia escaped. Anyway, she is not here."

Harriet's face throbbed all down the left side. She pulled off her glove and touched her cheek. When she brought her hand down again, there was blood on her fingers. She was going to have a bruise there, no hiding that from Aunt Loxley.

The driver said, "What do you ladies want to do? There don't seem no point in stopping here now the road is clear."

"Holland Park, if you can. We'll go to Holland Park."

"Holland Park it is. And, for what it's worth, I'm all for what you ladies are doing. I can't vote, mind, 'cos I don't pay enough rent, but I don't see why the government don't just give you ladies the vote since you wants it so bad. Better than causing all this trouble saying no."

Richardson's mouth remained open for a good few seconds before she spoke.

"Whatever next, Miss Harriet! Come down to the kitchen before your aunt sees you. Let's get those cuts cleaned out with carbolic. And your skirt. Good heavens. That will be beyond repair."

Harriet followed her towards the stairs and gestured to Inga to come too. Harriet had never been in the working areas of her aunt's house. At the vicarage, where they had insufficient servants, she often ran into the kitchen. At Loxley Hall she did the same, partly because it had become a habit and partly because she had become uncomfortable with ringing a bell every time some little thing needed doing. Aunt Loxley, however, believed the upstairs people only got in the way of the work downstairs and should keep to their own sphere.

Richardson led them to what Harriet assumed was the servants' dining room and disappeared through a door. A narrow sideboard, stacked with plates and bowls, stretched along the long wall. Eight hard-seated chairs surrounded a rectangular table that almost filled the central space. With windows only at shoulder height, the room was already growing dark in the waning November light. She sat on one of the two chairs nearest the door. Inga took the other.

Richardson returned with an oil-lamp, followed by the girl Harriet knew as Jane carrying a bowl, a pile of clean rags and some tweezers.

Inga said, "I'll tend to Miss Harriet."

Jane nodded and left the room, but Richardson sat down at the table and took up a confiding attitude, owning the space as hers to gossip in.

"Would you be kind enough to explain to me, Miss Harriet, Miss Rheinhart, what this Conciliation Bill is? I gather it won't pass because the government won't support it, but I'm unsure what it says. Could I vote? Could Cook? Not Jane, I'm assuming, her being only nineteen."

Harriet winced as Inga made preliminary pats across her grazed cheek. It was disconcerting, Richardson staying with them and initiating a conversation. It was upending things. But hadn't she and Inga been upending things for years? Four years ago, she had been terrified of marching peacefully. Today she had run screaming with a mob, as if she were storming the Bastille.

"Ow, that stings."

"I'll stop with the carbolic and pick out this grit. This will not be quick."

The tweezers approached her face. Harriet put her hand on Inga's. "Wait a minute, so I can answer Richardson's question."

Inga put the tweezers down.

Harriet said, "It depends on property. My aunt could definitely register to vote. I could not. Anyone living in their employer's household, as you do, could not, I'm sorry to say."

"Could Cook? Her husband's a butcher. They've owned the premises for generations."

"I suppose that would be the case."

A cook would be able to vote when her mother, a Poor Law Guardian and vicar's widow, wouldn't. That was ironic since Churchill and Lloyd George had opposed the bill on the grounds that it enfranchised only upper-class women. But nobody had ever claimed the bill was perfect. It was a foot in the door. Or would have been if it wasn't for those two turncoats.

Inga lifted the tweezers with a questioning look, and Harriet nodded. Time and again, the metal approached her face. Little specks of black lined up on the rag Inga had spread out on the table.

Richardson coughed gently. "It's not too bad. Nothing deep. You can see the bruise coming up, though. What happened?"

"I fell onto the pavement. My skirt got caught up, some-how."

"Lucky you didn't break your nose."

There was silence for a few moments, then Richardson said, "Concerning this business of women voting. I've heard it said that as women don't contribute to the economy they shouldn't vote, and as people who don't own property don't contribute they shouldn't vote. But these people, men and women, work hard all of their lives and never own anything. Where would the country be if they stopped working? It would grind to a halt, that's what."

Inga was dabbing at her with the carbolic again and Harriet closed her eyes in the hope it would reduce the pain. It didn't, but she kept them closed. Today the country was miles further from Richardson voting than it had been only a few months ago. Asquith, Churchill, and above all Lloyd George, had nipped progress in the bud. The Conservatives would have accepted one million women who met the current franchise.

She heard Inga say, "How long have you worked for Mrs Loxley, Richardson?"

"Since I was fifteen and I'm sixty now. She's a very fair employer is Mrs Loxley. When Cook came here looking for a daytime only job, she took her on and said she could leave at four every day, since Mrs Loxley only ever eats a light cold supper of an evening and Cook could put that up before she left. And most people won't even employ married women in service."

"Why did Cook want the work if her husband has a butcher shop?"

"Not want, need. It's the way life is, see. You earn money when you're a single woman. You live with your parents and you contribute to the housekeeping. You're all comfortable then. Then you marry, leave home, leave your job, have children and you're poor. There's only one income and many mouths to feed. Then all the little mouths grow up into beings with useful hands and the family has money again. The husband has help in the shop, he expands his deliveries, maybe goes into pies as well. But then the young people leave, join the army, or go to America, or something just as silly, and the husband and wife and one son can't run the shop without help, so business falls away until there's work two men can handle but not enough income, at least not enough to put some by. You get my drift?"

"Yes," Inga said. "That is Cook's life, but what about you? Will you be able to get the new pension?"

"Me? I have a little put by and, when I'm seventy, I can have Mister Lloyd George's five shillings a week. But when I get too old to work, I'll only have somewhere to live because Cook has been kind enough to say to go with her when she moves out to Finchley. They'll leave the butcher's with the second son when he marries and get a little house out there where it's cheap and the air's fresh. Finchley's a clever choice. All the Jews moving there keeps the rent prices down."

Harriet opened her eyes. Richardson was smiling, clearly unaware that Inga's family was Jewish. Inga didn't react. Harriet supposed she was schooled in not reacting.

Harriet wasn't sure, from Richardson's little speech, whether her aunt's maid intended to retire soon or join the cook at some later date. Her aunt would be bereft without Richardson. She'd had her all her adult life.

Inga said, "All is done. Do you have a court plaster in the

house, Richardson? I think the grazing should be covered over, at least for the night."

Harriet resisted the urge to touch her sore cheek. She knew she was lucky to have got away with a mere plaster. Inga had silk stitches in her face, administered by Aunt Loxley's doctor the morning after Black Friday. That's what was hidden under the blue eyepatch. Six hairy knots, like black spiders sitting on her cheekbone.

Richardson left to look for the plaster and Harriet said, "She deserves to vote before she dies. I deserve to vote before I die. Richardson thinks so, the taxi driver thought so, and sufficient Members of Parliament thought so, but this infernal government ignores us all." She raised a hand and brought it down hard, as if to slap the table, only swerving away at the last moment. "We can't give up. It could be another generation before there's any change."

"We," Inga said, "should do what we're good at. Go back to Downing Street and throw stones through the windows."

Take the fight to the enemy's door? The door she had been unable to reach because of her skirt. If they were caught it would mean prison again. Could she stand that? But could she stand stopping now? It was essential to get those million women voting, because as soon as that happened, and the Liberals introduced their wider franchise bill, they would have to include the women in that bill.

And in a calm space she would be able to take aim and hit her target.

She pursed her lips. "That's it. Since they care more about their window panes than they do about us, we'll smash a few for them."

Chapter 26
The Argument of The Broken Pane

Wednesday, November 23rd 1910

T he lamplighter moved out of sight. Harriet eased along the wall of the Colonial Office, and peered around the corner. There was no-one in view. Touching Inga on the hand, she walked out into Downing Street as nonchalantly as she could. The stone in her other hand was round, smooth, and exactly the right weight; the weight of a cricket ball.

When the road widened they quickened their pace, Inga heading for Number 10, Harriet for Number 11. Harriet started to run, swinging her right arm behind her. She heard glass breaking. Inga's stone had hit its target. She was at the top of her swing, her heart racing. This was going straight through Lloyd George's window.

Pain shot along her arm. The grip on her wrist was steel-jawed.

"Drop the missile, Miss."

She gripped the stone even more tightly.

"If you drop it, it'll only be two weeks you'll get, I warrant, and you're not going to hit anything now, are you?"

She dropped the stone. The policeman loomed above her. He must be six-foot-three at least. Not heavily built, quite slim in fact, and impossibly young. An older, more stolid looking companion was picking up her stone.

"Unhand me. You are hurting my wrist."

The older officer juggled her stone from one hand to the other. "Like you was about to hurt Mister Lloyd George's windows and whoever happened to be on the other side of them."

The taller one loosened his grip.

"If you agree to walk calmly with us to the station, we can take you softly by the arm. But try to flee and we will restrain you."

She had no doubt that they would.

She looked towards numbers ten and eleven Downing Street. There was a gloriously large hole in one of the windows but no sign of life in either house. Were the occupants in other parts of the building? She wondered how far those seemingly modest dwellings went back

She hoped Inga had run far enough.

As if he could read her mind, the tall officer said, "The staff have instructions to stay away from the front windows and doors in the event of a disturbance, until we tell them it's safe. We guessed you women might be coming back."

The policemen steered her to the right, past the spot where she and Inga had recently been standing.

"Who was your friend?"

"What friend?"

"Who broke the window of Number Ten?"

"I don't know."

"I don't believe that."

Don't argue. Change the subject. Get the conversation on your terms.

"Where are we going?"

"Cannon Row police station."

Not a long walk then.

"Do you believe women should be able to vote, officers?"

There was no reply, but after a minute the tall one said, "Why do you do it, Miss? There's more and more are on your side. Even Constable Murphy here thinks women should be voting in a modern country. But you start behaving like hooligans and you put peoples' backs up."

"I was not behaving like a hooligan. I was protesting, in exactly the way men have always protested."

He said, "I know there were riots and near revolutions in the past, but we don't behave like that these days, do we? This is a civilised country."

They turned a corner, and she caught sight of the street sign, Cannon Row.

"I wasn't rioting. You need a group of people to make a riot. But do you think women should vote, constable? Will you vote against the Liberal in our cause?"

"I can't vote, Miss. I don't meet the property qualification. And, for what it's worth, I think votes for all, men and women, is what Mister Lloyd George and Mister Churchill want."

"If that's true, why are they so against us?"

They were inside the police station now and Constable Murphy was handing her stone to the desk sergeant. The tall officer left without another word or glance. She started to shake and tried to stop by breathing deeply. Ahead lay a police cell, the court and prison. She handed her possessions over in response to the demands of the unsmiling man behind the desk and clenched herself against a strong desire to urinate.

Sleepless in the cold cell, she wondered if Inga had made it back to Aunt Loxley's. It had been their plan should they become separated. She had warned Tom of her stone-throwing plans, using Aunt Loxley's telephone, and told him she would confirm in the morning that all was well. When she didn't call in the morning, Tom would realise she had been arrested and Will would be on his way to check the list at Bow Street Police Court.

Always plead not guilty, they said at the WSPU training sessions. Plead not guilty because then the magistrate has more discretion over sentencing. Use your time in court to make the case for women.

But what exactly should she do? She wasn't prepared to shout out a speech throughout the entire proceedings like some women did. She wished to appear dignified. She should try to turn the questioning to her advantage. And at all costs resist implicating Inga. Say as much as possible; and as little. And stay completely calm.

Dignity and calm, she thought, might be a little hard to achieve unless they gave her facilities to wash, tidy her hair and clean her teeth in the morning.

Despite her dishevelled appearance, a great cheer went up from the public gallery when she stepped into the dock. The charge was read. Loitering with intent. She resented that. She had been walking, and at the end running, with purpose. Loitering sounded underhand and sinister.

"Not guilty. I was protesting, your honour. I have a right to protest."

The magistrate looked at her over his half-moon glasses. "You will have your opportunity to speak, Miss Loxley. Please restrict yourself to answering questions until then. What were you doing in Downing Street on the evening of November 23rd?"

"Protesting against the government's sabotage of the Conciliation Bill."

"Did you have in your possession this stone?"

He held up the cricket-ball-sized pebble she had found in Aunt Loxley's garden.

"I did."

"What did you intend to do with it?"

"I intended to throw it through the window of Number Eleven Downing Street, as a protest against the perfidy of Mr Lloyd George."

There were hisses and shouts of support from the gallery.

"Silence, please. You are not at the pantomime. If there cannot be silence, I will have the court cleared."

He waited for the hubbub to die down before fixing his eyes on her again. "Who was your companion, Miss Loxley?"

"I had no companion."

"Who was the lady who threw the stone that broke the window of Ten Downing Street?"

"I don't know."

She tried to keep her eyes on his. She hoped her voice was firm and her cheeks pale.

"I remind you that you are under oath, Miss Loxley."

"Yes, sir."

"So, your friend ran away before the officers could apprehend her?"

She pressed her lips together against her answer and remained silent.

"Please answer the question."

"I'm sorry. I thought it was a statement, in the nature of a conclusion, not a question."

"Did your friend run away?"

"No. No friend of mine was there."

It was lying under oath. She could only justify it to herself because she believed the cause was greater than the wrongdoing. Would her father have thought so?

The two police officers were the only witnesses. The magistrate told her she would have the right to question them after him. They said they had come up behind her and another female. They had seen the other female throw a stone through the window of 10 Downing Street while still too far away to apprehend her. They had prevented Miss Loxley from throwing a stone herself.

When her turn came she asked the tall young policeman, "Did you see or hear me speak to this other female?"

"I did not."

"What did you see me do?"

"I saw you run and raise your arm above your head in a manner good enough to bowl for England."

He seemed to be suppressing a smile. She glanced at the magistrate. He had lowered his head, but she was sure he was also smiling.

"Do you have anything you wish to add before I pass judgement, Miss Loxley?"

She took a deep breath and concentrated on the wall behind him. "Indeed I do. For over fifty years the women of this country have been asking for an extension of the franchise and they have been ignored. They have raised petitions, and they have been ignored. They have sent delegations, and they have been ignored. They have mustered demonstrations in the hundreds of thousands, and they have been ignored. They have had a bill pass its second reading by an overwhelming majority, and they have been ignored. I have broken one window and this public gallery is full and the press are busy scribbling notes for tonight's edition as fast as they can. The women of this country have been driven to the argument of the broken pane against their will. We want to make laws, not break them."

A huge cheer swelled up from the gallery and there was the sound of feet stamping.

The magistrate ordered the public gallery cleared.

"Now I can hear myself think, Miss Loxley, I remind you that you have a right to protest peaceably, not to destroy property. The evidence of intent to cause harm is clear in the presence of a large stone, of a smooth and rounded form that could not have been picked up from the ground in Downing Street. I sentence you to two weeks in the second division for loitering with intent."

Her vision blurred, but she pulled herself upright and breathed deeply. The sentence was light. The magistrate came back into focus and she was sure he was smiling again.

It was Holloway for her this time, the women's prison that had seen so many suffragette inmates that the WSPU had rented a house nearby, where they offered beds to released hunger strikers and where women sang the Marseillaise from the roof in the evenings. She took heart from this, but the rest of her body didn't respond to the encouragement. She walked with her head down, hearing nothing but doors slamming and seeing nothing but the floor in front of her feet.

She lifted her chin as the door from the prison waiting room swung open. The bosomy, red-faced, woman facing her allowed it to close behind her before she spoke.

"Please remove all your clothing except your shift. You may lay your clothes on the chair here."

One eye kept wandering to somewhere over Harriet's left shoulder.

Harriet did as she was told, the wardress helping with the

buttons at the back of her blouse. Harriet didn't resist. There was no need to make this process more unpleasant than it was.

"Your drawers too."

She did as she was told and stood by the chair in her shift and stockings. The woman came up close and without speaking ran her hands down the sides of her body, then into the space at the top of her legs.

Harriet screamed and pulled away. Was this why they were alone? Was this why she had taken care to close the door?

"There's no need to take on like that. If I pat you down, you don't need to strip."

Harriet clenched her jaw. Endurance. She could survive this with endurance.

The woman continued down each leg, sliding her hands slowly along her stockings.

"Beautiful, these are. Silk, are they?"

The hands went back up, close to where she couldn't bear them to be, and then ran down her legs again. There was nothing she could possibly have concealed inside her stockings. She closed her eyes and prayed those hands would not be coming up again. She forced her feet against the floor, gripping it with her toes. The room was cold, but she could feel sweat dripping between her breasts, which had fallen, one to each side, when her corset was removed.

The stockings must fall down now her corset was gone. This must end.

The hands smoothed the stockings upwards and then they were gone. The stockings were still on her legs.

"Good. Now go into that cubicle on the right and bathe. You may put your shift and stockings back on when you have finished."

When she had dried herself, as well as she could with the tiny towel provided, and had wrestled the stockings back up her damp legs, Harriet straightened her back and walked back into the reception area. Her clothes were still on the chair. The wardress was by the far wall. She showed no sign of coming any nearer to her.

"You may dress."

Harriet seized her drawers and dragged them on, fingers fumbling the ties. Her stockings were clinging to her legs, held up by her inadequately dried skin. Thinking about them made her shiver. She wrapped her corset around her.

"Here, I'll tie that for you."

She wanted to say, *No thanks, I can do it myself.* But the words wouldn't come out.

To keep her mind from those reddened, agile hands, and whatever perverted thoughts might be guiding them, she said, "Are we considered political prisoners? Can we wear our own clothes?"

"Rule 243A. You're in the second division, but you get some privileges of the first. Mister Churchill did it."

"And I can keep my hat and coat and gloves?"

"You can."

Harriet pulled on her petticoats and then the green serge skirt. She reached for the matching jacket. It was the WSPU colour she had adopted after discarding her ruined mourning clothes.

"Beautiful lace on these petticoats, if I might say so. My sister sews petticoats. I have an eye for a well-made petticoat."

Harriet bent to tie her boots, an action which had the advantage of avoiding the wardress's wandering eye.

"My sister has my little boy while I work here, me being a widow. She watches my boy and three of her own while she sews. Her husband is a docker. It's good work when it can be had, but it can't always be had. My money's regular. So, what I want to say is, I'd be standing in the streets with you ladies, but I daren't risk my job."

Harriet's boots were secure, but she waited a few moments and let her terror ebb before straightening up. Perhaps what she had interpreted as molestation had merely been a clumsy interest in fabrics. Had the force feeding led her to fear assault from the most unexpected source?

She stood straight, willed a smile onto her lips and looked into the wardress's mismatched eyes. "What is your name?"

"Ainsley."

"Well, I can't say I'm glad to meet you, Mrs Ainsley, given the circumstances, but I promise you I will continue to fight for our right to vote as long as I have freedom and ability."

This time her cell number, her prisoner number, and her name, was 41D. There was a small white loaf and a tin-pot of milk on the table. About a pint of milk. She sat on the chair and stared at it. Holloway policy was confinement to the cell and silence for the first four weeks of the sentence. Ainsley had told her that on the way to her cell. But, due to rule 243A, she would be able to take an hour's exercise a day in the yard and have books or the tools of her trade sent in. She should write to Tom, and to Will and have him send the books that were at her aunt's.

"Can I have pen and paper to write to my brother, please?"

"After four weeks. No letters or visits for four weeks."

That was that then. One prison rule trumped another.

Harriet broke off a hunk of bread and stared at it. No refusing food this time. The women's protest had been in order to secure first division status, and they had secured it, in all but name.

Doors were slamming throughout the block, the eternal sound of prison. She had listened for Inga at the police station, straining at every female voice. There had been no sound of her. She had to assume she had made it back to Holland Park. The burden of explaining to Aunt Loxley would have fallen on her.

I wish you luck, friend.

Harriet chewed on the white bread. It was soft and stuck behind her teeth and to the roof of her mouth. She swallowed a long draft of the milk. It was cool, as was the cell. It was dark outside now and the electric light was on. She looked around for the switch to control it. There was none.

At least this time, she would not return to her family as an emaciated wreck. If all the meals were of this quantity, the greater danger was swelling out of her only set of clothes. She worked her way slowly through the loaf, going through her family one by one and sending them messages in her mind.

Emma, you are a true radical. Your paintings will last long after I am forgotten.

Gwen, you are at the coalface of women making their mark. You are as good at running the manufactory as ever Robert or Wesley were. Don't let them hold you back.

Robert, don't let caring for us all overwhelm you. Eleanor can shoulder more of a burden than you think.

Will, you're an argumentative little brother but I know you will always have my back. I hope what I saw was what I thought it was. You and Inga deserve each other.

Mother, your gentle watercolours will delight your grand-children. Please unpack them and put them on the walls of Loxley Hall. I'm sure Aunt Beth will love them.

Father, may you rest in peace, you will always be with me.

Tom, dear patient Tom, please don't worry about me. I love you so much.

The overhead light snapped off. She groaned. Lights-out had caught her by surprise. Hopefully there would be enough light from outside to lay out her bed sheets and change into her nightgown.

The woman in front of Harriet in the queue for chapel was tall, with red hair escaping from a bun, and she moved as if she wished to take longer strides than the pace of the line allowed.

Harriet turned and looked back along the line. None were wearing prison garb. Every one of them must have been imprisoned for campaigning for the vote.

The chaplain read from the First Letter of St. Peter.

Likewise, ye husbands, dwell with them according to knowledge, giving honour unto the wife, as unto the weaker vessel, and as being heirs together of the grace of life; that your prayers be not hindered.

He looked up from the text and surveyed the women seated in front of him.

"Although you are but the weaker vessels of the text, read your Bible even if you don't understand it. The failure in understanding is entirely due to the natural weakness of the female mind. It is not for the female to decide the affairs of the nation. Christian women allow their husbands to lead and guide them. Thus the leaders of the nation guide us all."

Harriet stared ahead, thinking of her father and how he took a Bible passage and lit up the truth of it for all to see. But some passages, he said, were of their time and not to be understood as applying to modern lives. God has given us the grace to know better, he said.

Tears threatened to escape her eyes, and she wondered if she should blink and let them fall.

"A man can control his emotions. A woman can't. A person who is subject to the whims of emotion cannot be entrusted with political power."

Harriet raised a hand to brush the offending teardrops away but before she did a voice inside her said, *Emotions are the direct route to all that is pure and good.*

"Father," she whispered.

You are hurting because you are being bullied. A decent man would stop bullying.

The tears spilled over.

Something was being pushed under her cuff. Harriet risked a glance in the direction of the woman to the right of her, the red-haired woman. She was looking at the preacher, giving no sign of having done anything.

Once she was alone in her cell, Harriet drew a small piece of brown toilet paper out from her sleeve. The writer must have had access only to a pencil stub, or a bit of pencil lead, since the letters had been formed with great difficulty.

Emily Davison – ball for yard – be prepared to run.

So the red-haired woman was the infamous Emily Wilding Davison, she who had torn out her bed planks and barricaded her cell door against the doctors when they came to force feed her. The prison authorities had reacted by smashing her window from the outside and turning a fire-hose on her until the cell was six inches deep in freezing water. Miss Davison had spent the rest of her sentence in the prison hospital. Six months later, she sued the prison and was well compensated. Emily Wilding Davison was a legend within the WSPU.

What sort of ball game was being planned? Should she go without her hat? It was unlikely there would be a suitable place to lay it down. And a coat? Should she wear her coat? It was November. No-one who had a coat would go out without one in November. She should definitely wear her corset. She had no support for her breasts otherwise. She couldn't run around in her blouse and jacket with her breasts hanging loose.

The ring of watching wardresses were doing nothing to stop the ball game. Harriet stepped nervously beyond them.

It was football, the game played by men in factory yards all over the north of England. The women's hair was flying out of their pins and their faces were flushed red. The game had none of the grace of cricket. Could she do this?

"Go on, forty-one." A voice sounded softly behind her. "You won't often get the chance. Once the governor finds out, he'll put a stop to it."

She turned. It was Ainsley, the first time she had seen her since her admission. She nodded, took off her coat and laid it on top of one of the piles that were marking the goals.

Emily Davison ran up close, panting. "You're on my team. Do what I do."

The game seemed simple: kick the ball between the other side's goal posts. Except other people got in the way and some of them could kick the ball along in front of them while running. Harriet was soon hot and out of breath. Emily Davison ran up and down the yard with the zeal of the newly converted. Other women seemed to have played the game before. One was acting as a supervisor, reprimanding, in signs, women who pushed or tripped others, which was apparently not allowed, although frequently done.

Harriet had the ball. There was a clear view of the goal. She kicked hard, and fast, before anyone could get between her and it. The ball flew to the side, well away from her intended target. She bent over, laughing. Who knew kicking a ball straight was this hard? Someone clapped her on the back. There was no talking allowed at exercise time, but who needed it?

The ball was coming her way again. This time, she tried the business of kicking it along in front of her. She got three kicks in before someone came at her, chipped the ball to the side, and ran it back the opposite way. She turned and ran after them, panting. Now, someone on her team had the ball, a young woman with her black hair flying free. She shot past Harriet, the ball obeying every little nudge it was given. She drew back a leg and kicked.

"Goal!"

The young woman's shout had gone up unthinkingly. Harriet looked round at the wardresses stationed around the perimeter of the yard. They were making no move. Indeed, they appeared to be smiling.

The bell rang. Exercise time was over. Women swirled around the piles of clothes, laughing and clapping each other on the back. The young woman with the loose hair winked at Harriet. She grinned back. Emily was pulling on her jacket, sweat running down her face in a manner Harriet would once have believed unladylike, but today seemed empowering, heroic even. She hoped they would be allowed to keep the ball for another day.

A week later, Emily was not at chapel, nor in the yard. By this time, Harriet's name was known to all the women, and she knew theirs. The opportunities for passing notes and whispering were many; in the washrooms and the slop rooms, at chapel and in the yard, and, for those not confined to their cells, at communal work. The loose-haired young woman slipped her a pencil stub and Harriet soon knew she was Lydia and that she was from Yorkshire and a fustian cutter. From the age of fourteen she had walked the length of bolts of cloth spread on long tables, cutting through the tiny loops of cotton with a sharp blade to create the ridges of corded cloth that was fashioned into working-men's trousers. She walked miles, day in and day out. It was no wonder she was so fit. Confinement was hard on her.

Through a note Harriet learned that Emily Davison was on

hunger strike. Three days later, she heard banging and screams from further along her corridor. She lay on her bed and pulled her pillow over her head, but still a white coat loomed over her and she stared into a pair of nostrils lined with greasy hairs. She muffled a scream of her own.

Four more days to go, Tom. Only four more days.

The wardresses don't want to do it, Tom. Most of them, at least. They are women who have to work. The doctors? I don't know. I think they could afford to refuse. I think some of them enjoy it. The women have been usurping their power and they are taking it back.

Why did she do it, Tom? Emily, I mean. We got the concessions we wanted.

They're singing the Marseillaise throughout the block. It's a wonderful tune and a powerful declaration of unity, but the words are hateful, filled with violence and gore *pour la gloire et la patrie*. I'm starting to hate the sound of it.

Harriet walked out of prison for the second time with her head held high, although her thoughts were racing between the triumphs of female companionship and a fervent desire never to see prison walls again.

She fell into Tom's arms.

"Propriety be damned," she whispered in his ear.

"I love you." He whispered back.

Chapter 27
Propriety

July 1911

Harriet lay back on her pillow and watched the net curtains fluttering in the breeze. The Loxley Hall guest
bedroom had been fitted out prettily since she had last seen it.
The curtains were new. Probably Emma's doing.

1911 had held so much promise. When Asquith had called
the second General Election of 1910 to get a mandate to curb
the powers of the House of Lords, Harriet had campaigned with
the WSPU. The election returned a result almost identical to
the one the previous January and the Parliament Bill ending the
Lords' veto passed its second reading in the Commons on
February 27th, 1911.

Will had been ecstatic.

Three members of the Conciliation Committee had won
places in the private members' ballot and the Conciliation Bill
was revived. The bill passed its second reading with an even
higher majority than before. Notable members of the government were absent from the debate, including Asquith and
Churchill, but Lloyd George voted for it.

The WSPU continued its suspension of militant action.

On June 22nd Harriet walked with over forty thousand people from Westminster to the Albert Hall in a women's version of the new king's coronation procession. She was one of seven hundred dressed in white and wearing their prison medals.

The next week she graduated with a degree from London University.

Doctor Raisin strode over. "Well, you made it Miss Loxley. I must admit I wasn't sure you had it in you, but here you are with a degree and a reputation for causing trouble. Well done. What next? A position in one of the better girls' schools, perhaps?"

"I intend going back to work with the WSPU to fight for the Conciliation Bill."

"Good choice. Take action while you can."

She might never see Doctor Raisin again.

It was a fine morning. She should get up. But her limbs felt like they were made of lead. An hour of cricket with her nephews yesterday shouldn't have exhausted her.

There was a knock at the door. Harriet pulled herself up to sitting, put her hand over her mouth and swallowed down the now familiar dry retch. She had been down to breakfast three times since arriving back at Loxley Hall, and each time she'd had to flee the room. Mother had looked upset.

She had told no-one about her suspicions, not even Tom. It might really be exhaustion. She had only missed one bleed and her times had never been predictable since her hunger strike.

Eleanor walked in, followed by Gwen and Emma. Harriet reached for her shawl and wrapped it round her shoulders. Emma was carrying a tray with a plate and a glass of milk.

Emma said, "We brought you rusks. They're very good. Cook won't tell what she mixes in the milk when she soaks the bread."

Harriet grimaced. "No, thank-you. I feel a little sick."

Eleanor took the plate from the tray and handed it to her. "You'll feel less sick if you eat at least one and then get up. Believe me, I know. And feeling sick is a good sign."

Harriet stared at her, lost for words.

"Harry, you're with child, aren't you? I know it, Gwen knows it, Emma knows it, Mother knows it–"

"For pity's sake, Nell. Who doesn't know it?"

"Apart from Tom? Wesley and Robert."

"Wesley and Robert?"

Gwen laughed. "Robert's too innocent and Wesley's too self-absorbed."

Eleanor gave Gwen a reproachful look and sat down on the edge of the bed.

Harriet glared at them, each in turn. Emma smiled back. Had they come to sermonise? If so, they could get on with it and leave. She put the plate of rusks on the bedside table and folded her arms.

Eleanor said, "You have to get up. You have to tell Tom and you have to arrange the wedding you've been putting off all year for no good reason."

Harriet took the milk from the tray and drank it slowly, spinning out the minutes until she would have to answer. They had burst into her room and interfered in her relationship with her own body. She had been putting off the wedding out of respect for Father. And because she couldn't have married while she was still at college. They knew that. She swallowed the last of the milk.

"I have been very happy not being married, thank you."

"Hmm, so are Emma and I," Gwen said. "But we don't have a child to consider."

Harriet knew she was wanting the impossible. She wanted to go back to the time before she graduated, to when working with the WSPU was a wild adventure, and having relations with Tom was a sweet secret. She longed to wriggle below the bed covers and pull them over her head until her sisters gave up and went away.

She wanted Father to be alive, even if this news was something she would have to confess to him. She wished she could confess it to him. He had always known how to raise her up when she failed.

She muttered, "I want things to be like they were."

"Don't be ridiculous, Harry." Eleanor reached over and took the empty glass from her hand. "Why wouldn't you marry Tom? Everyone can see how much he adores you and you obviously adore him too or you wouldn't be in the position you're in. Once there's a child involved, things are never the same again. You could try being grateful for what God has given you."

Harriet saw Emma wince, and Gwen looked at her feet, avoiding Harriet's gaze.

Harriet's stomach rumbled. She looked at Eleanor and tried to smile. Eleanor smiled back, a fleeting twitch of the lips. Coming in here to talk so frankly must be torture for her.

Harriet took a rusk off the plate and nibbled it. Malt was Cook's secret.

"As you wish. I'll get up and I'll talk with Tom today."

She swung her legs off the edge of the bed to convince them she meant it. She did mean it. They were right. The only way was forwards.

Tom was at Loxley Hall for a late supper, but it was not easy to find a quiet place to talk. Supper had been served in the Drawing Room, but that didn't mean the Dining Room was empty. Emma had used the table to spread out paintings for everyone to see; Mother and Aunt Beth were playing a board game with the boys in the Morning Room. Harriet was beginning to wish she and Tom *were* married, so they could go upstairs together without offending anyone's sense of propriety.

"Come into the garden with me."

"It's still raining."

"Only just. Bring a brolly from the hall."

He grinned, and she felt a prickle of mischief at wondering how he thought they were going to manage the umbrella. This expedition was not going to be what he was hoping.

She pressed herself into his chest. Drops of water were gathering on the shoulders of his jacket.

"I think I may be pregnant."

She had imagined him responding with, *How do you know? Are you certain?* or *How could that have happened?* Instead, he pulled away from her so he could look into her eyes.

"Crikey!"

"You're happy?"

"Couldn't be more happy."

"I suppose it would be cheeky of me to suggest we should get married?"

"Downright hypocritical."

Harriet insisted on being present when Tom met with Robert.

Robert stood. "This is a strange carry-on. Very formal, arranging a meeting. What can I do for you two?"

Tom said, "I have come to you as the head of the family, Robert. Harriet considers it an unnecessary formality, but since we will depend upon your family's goodwill, I am here to ask your blessing. I am afraid I am not yet in a financial position to support your sister and provide her with a household of her own but–"

"I am with child, Robert–"

"We want to marry and... well... I know about the stipulation that any of the suitors for the hand of one of the Reverend Loxley's daughters must undergo a test for a sexually transmitted disease before he would give permission and since—"

Robert's smile drained away, and he sat down with a thud. Tom hesitated, as if he thought he should remain standing to attention. Then he sat on the sofa next to him.

"Everything alright, old chap?"

"I get these turns whenever something challenges me. It's like my mind is cowering."

"It's normal. You're healing. Healing from illness and healing from grief."

"Neither Wesley nor Will seem so unmanned for so long."

"Will was not at death's door. And bear in mind that you don't know how anybody else is feeling inside."

Robert wrung his hands together, put a hand on Tom's knee, then quickly withdrew it.

"Thank you. Now, what was it? My thoroughly modern sister, one of my thoroughly modern sisters, is pregnant and you are going to marry her? I suppose you would have married her if she wasn't pregnant?"

"Yes, sir."

"And you don't, and never have, had physical relations with another woman?"

Harriet glared at Robert. "Of course he hasn't."

Tom said, "You did insist on being here, Harry. And no, I haven't."

"Well. I'm not completely naïve. You must get on with it. Marrying, I mean. The new Vicar at Lenton is a man of the world. Go and get the banns, man. And as for the other thing. You're the doctor. You know more about that than I do. I really don't want to act as if you can't be trusted. I have enough trouble

I've inherited with having to remind Wesley to get tested every year."

Chapter 28
Great Sacrifices to Preserve Peace

July 1911

T he wedding was a quiet affair. Just the two families. Eleanor helped Harriet alter the blue silk dress she had worn for Twelfth Night the evening Tom had been the Lord of Misrule. With a new wide collar of cream lace and a long net veil, she felt she had made a good show, even if she hadn't had a fashionable white dress. Funds were not abundant. Gwen had made that clear. Surpluses from the manufactory were being used to buy out the Ashford heirs and Harriet had no trust income saved. It had all gone on her college fees. Tom was treating poor people for pennies but not getting wealthier patients. They truly hadn't been in a position to marry.

Yet here they were, at breakfast the day after.

Wesley shifted his chair back and folded over the top of the newspaper. The morning sun flashed on the spectacles he had taken to wearing. They suited him. Made him look responsible.

He slapped his hand on the breakfast table and his cup rattled in its saucer.

"Lloyd George has come out for action. Britain will not

stand for German battleships threatening Agadir. He's thrown down the gauntlet."

Harriet reached for the paper.

"Let me see."

Tom laughed. Ever since she had attempted to hurl a stone through his window, Tom had joked that she had become obsessed with the doings of David Lloyd George. She kicked him on the ankle.

"Robert hasn't seen the paper yet," Wesley said, handing The Times to Robert, who had shown no interest in it when Wesley had taken it from its place beside him.

Heat rushed to Harriet's face.

"Wesley, who are you to determine who gets the paper?"

Did he have to take every opportunity to put her in her place, or what he believed was her place?

Mother's voice swooped down with an authority Harriet had not heard in a long time.

"Robert, dear, perhaps you could read out the article to us, since I'm sure we are all interested."

The room fell silent. Everyone was waiting for Lloyd George's famous oratory, the pleasure of rotund phrases and measured cadence. Harriet expected ulterior motives and bombast.

Robert glanced at the article. "It's a speech given at the Mansion House last night."

He stood up, tucked his thumbs into his waistcoat, and looked around his audience. Emma laughed. Harriet scowled. She found nothing amusing about David Lloyd George.

"I would make great sacrifices to preserve peace. I conceive that nothing would justify a disturbance of international goodwill except questions of the greatest national moment. But if a situation were to be forced upon us in which peace could only be preserved by the surrender of the great and beneficent position Britain has won by centuries of heroism and achievement, by allowing Britain to be treated where her interests were vitally affected as if she were of no account in the cabinet of nations, then I say emphatically that peace at that price would be a humiliation intolerable for a great country like ours to endure. National honour is no party question."

Harriet gasped, and so did Will. Tom stiffened at Harriet's side. Robert glanced at them before reading through the rest of the report. When he finished he folded the paper and put it down.

"What do you think, Will? You are the one close to affairs."

"I'm surprised, as must be Berlin. There was no advance whisper of this in the corridors."

Harriet said, "Not amongst your new Foreign Office friends?"

Will glared at her. His new connections were supposed to be a secret until he had told Mother of his plans to go to France. Remorseful, she lowered her eyes.

Will spread his hands. "The surprise is, as I'm sure you are all aware, that Lloyd George, the erstwhile outspoken opponent of the Boer War, should wield the language of national honour in the context of a colonial dispute between Germany and France."

Wesley grabbed the folded paper from Robert's side and waved it at Will.

"Britain cannot allow the German navy a port on the Atlantic coast of Morocco. It's insupportable."

"And Germany will not achieve one with one small gunboat like The Panther, which is all they have sent to Agadir, not a fleet."

Harriet tried to speak but fell silent upon hearing Emma.

"What do the Moroccans think? I mean, why are France

and Germany, and now Britain, arguing over Morocco? It's not their country."

"Well," Will cleared his throat. "It's true the Moors are an ancient and proud people, who have maintained their liberty for a thousand years, but France has long had interests in Morocco. In modern times, it has been an unstable state and is now on the verge of civil war. The Moroccan government asked France to send troops to Fez to help get things under control–"

"Where they behaved with unconscionable ferocity." Tom's hands were clenched next to his plate. "France, believe you me, will take over Morocco completely in the next few years, despite all the treaties that have been written. The Great Powers, Emma, have no respect for other people's countries. They regard them as places to control and exploit."

Wesley half stood. "Arrant socialistic nonsense–"

Will said, "The balance of power–"

Harriet raised her voice above them both.

"Lloyd George is speaking of *peace* being a humiliation. *Peace,* the greatest blessing we all pray for. What hope is there for us if the Great Powers come to the edge of war in their own territories? And," she glared at Wesley, "for all we know, this could be it. This could be the crisis the politicians don't defuse."

"If it comes to war, then men will do their duty."

Wesley didn't bang his fist on the table, but Harriet got the distinct impression only Mother's gaze was stopping him. His moustache seemed to have taken on a life of its own.

"Germany mustn't be allowed to get power over the seas. The British have to control the English Channel. We stopped Napoleon and we'll stop the Kaiser. We've got the ships and we've got the money."

Wesley's words flew like banners. Harriet saw Robert nodding. None of her sisters, nor her mother, nor Aunt Beth, seemed about to protest. Even Will was looking down at his plate. It was as if she were the one who had climbed over the warning signs, not Wesley.

If only Father were here.

Tom said, quietly, his hands still clenched, "I don't see any value in putting anyone's life in danger for the sake of French control over Morocco, Wesley. Not mine, not yours, not your sons'. My wife and my unborn child are the dearest things in the world to me. I would defend them to the last, but in my life, my work, I see death and suffering every day. I won't inflict those real things on real people for the sake of notions of national honour and standing in the world."

There was silence. Was it because of the open reference to her pregnant state, one day after her wedding? Such things, common enough as they were, were not talked about at table, even amongst family. Or was it Tom's damning of accepted ideas about patriotism?

Wesley looked like he might boil over.

Harriet looked towards her mother, who wiped her lips with her napkin before saying, "Well, that was all very interesting. Now, since we are all together, I propose a little excursion. I suspect we could all do with walking off the excesses of yesterday's wonderful wedding breakfast. We are not as well situated for the grounds at Wollaton Hall as we used to be at the vicarage but we can get the tram out to Lenton and save our energies for the park."

"Topping idea, Mother," Robert folded his napkin and rose from the table. "We seem to have a lot of energy to work off." He slapped Tom on the back as he passed behind him. "You've landed a fine one in my sister, old man. Don't underestimate her."

"Did you mean it, Tom?"

Harriet had waited to ask until they had fallen behind the rest of the party. It had been charming to walk in the park and be introduced as Mrs Bardhill, and to take people's hands and feel the warmth in their greetings, but now she wanted to talk about what had happened at breakfast.

"About not fighting, I mean. I'm sure the baby and I are the most important things to you, but aren't duty and country and empire important too?"

Tom frowned. "It depends what you mean by duty. And no, empire is not important to me. The supposedly noble concept of empire is nothing more than Britain taking over other people's countries, appropriating their resources and telling them how to run their lives."

The anti-colonial view had been voiced many times at the dispensary hostel, but Harriet was glad Tom had not gone so far at breakfast with her family.

Tom squeezed her hand so tightly it hurt.

"Harry, we are living in a precarious world. Every time there is a standoff like this Agadir Crisis, there is talk of a war. Our politicians are only too happy to tip us as far over the edge as they dare. One day they will tip too far, and then all the talk will be of honour and greatness and victory. France, Russia, Germany and the Hapsburg Empire also value honour and greatness and they have conscript armies and reserves that vastly outnumber ours. If Britain joins a fight, conscription is inevitable."

She said, "Conscription was a concession the Tories asked for in return for their support for the Conciliation Bill. The first round of talks broke down over it. The Liberals wouldn't accept it. The British people will never accept conscription."

"Believe you me, in a modern war it *will* happen. The people in power will retreat from high ideals of social justice and treat human beings as resources and bargaining power. This country's men will march away to glory, and rapid firing artillery will cut them down in swathes, casting entrails on the ground and blasting limbs from bodies."

He must have felt her recoil, although she had tried to suppress it. He drew a sharp breath.

"I'm sorry, my dear. I'm sorry, but the war between the American states and the Boer War sucked in doctors in their droves. Shot designed to maim, exploding shells, repeat firing contraptions like Maxim guns. Those dreadful things have improved what the profession knows about amputation by leaps and bounds."

The bitterness in his voice was hard to bear. Harriet raised her gaze above the ancient trees, their leaves fading from the fresh greens of June to the dusty shades of July. The Conciliation Bill was still waiting for the week of government time that Asquith had promised, and even if one million more women were suddenly able to vote there was no guarantee that they would be against a war. They weren't the ones who would be sent away to fight. People like her aunt's cook's sons would go. Changing the franchise a little now so it would change more in the future was a rational strategy, but suppose the future wouldn't wait for change.

There was no answer to be found in the expanses of the sky. Harriet sighed and looked ahead. Eleanor's sons were spread a wicket length apart, a cricket ball flying between them. The sun glinted on their blond hair as they leapt to catch it. Would her daughter, if the child was a daughter, be able to run freely and throw balls like those boys? Would these boys, would her son, have to die in a war, for... what?

Mother was beckoning to them. Some fifty yards away, their party had stopped to talk to a couple she recognised as parishioners of her father's. She pulled Tom's arm.

"We must catch up. We have duties."

Chapter 29
Nottingham Castle

May 1913

The doorbell rang. Aunt Beth jerked upright, her hands clutching her embroidery frame as if to deny she had ever dozed. Harriet wrenched at her skirt, a movement that sent Sylvia's building blocks skittering across the carpet. She struggled to her feet.

In the hall, Mabel was saying something about a crate being on the doorstep and getting it moved. Harriet picked a piece of white lint off her skirt.

The Morning Room door opened.

"Mrs Bardhill. Miss... er... Rine...at."

Harriet gave Mabel a stern look, worthy of her mother. Mabel was quite capable of saying Inga's name correctly. To her credit, Mabel avoided her eyes and shuffled her feet.

Harriet held out her hand. "It is wonderful to see you again, my friend. I hope the journey was not too tiring. Allow me to introduce my aunt, Mrs Loxley."

Aunt Beth put her embroidery frame aside and stood. Had she also noticed the maid's discourtesy?

"It's a pleasure to meet you, Miss Rheinhart. My niece speaks of you often."

"The pleasure is all mine, Mrs Loxley."

Inga was the picture of health, her burgundy travelling dress complementing the high colour in her cheeks and bringing out the raven-gleam of her eyes. What must it be to have such fair skin and such dark brows? And that suit? A double skirt of plain cloth and matching jacket over an ecru lace blouse, trimmed in the same rich red as the jacket. It was a suit to die for.

Sylvia was clinging to Harriet's leg. She hoisted her up onto her hip.

"Mabel, could you please bring some cold lemonade, if Cook has any."

Mabel nodded. Was it curtly? Harriet couldn't tell.

"Not for me, thank you Mabel," Aunt Beth said.

She waited until Mabel left the room before continuing with, "We have a room prepared for you, Miss Rheinhart. I hope you will be comfortable."

Inga gave a slight bow, a bit more than a nod of her head.

"Thank you, Mrs Loxley. I am very grateful for your hospitality."

"Please, call me Beth while we are at home. I believe it is all the modern fashion. And it can get so very confusing with two Mrs Loxleys in the house. The servants distinguish us by Mrs G and Mrs R. At least they do when they think we can't hear them. That was my husband, George, and Maria's husband, Robert. God rest their souls."

"I was sorry to hear of your loss, Beth. And of yours too, Harriet. A terrible blow for the family. I trust everyone else is well."

Harriet said, "Yes, we are all fighting fit. My mother is at a meeting of the Poor Law Guardians. You'll meet her and my sister Eleanor at lunch. The others will be here for dinner, including my two boisterous nephews. They are down for the holiday. They arrive on the three o'clock train."

"And Will? Is he coming back from Paris?"

Harriet raised her eyebrows in Aunt Beth's direction and smiled at Inga. "Yes, we are expecting Will."

With the house full for the Whitsun Holiday, Will would be occupying one of the small servants' rooms on the attic floor, as would her two nephews. Aunt Beth had put her foot down and overruled Wesley's objections when it had become necessary to turn over a room to Harriet and Tom, plus another for a nursery for Sylvia.

"If you will excuse me," Aunt Beth said, "I shall go through to the Drawing Room and leave you two young people to talk. I must get in my piano practice before luncheon."

As soon as they were alone, Inga kissed Harriet. First on one cheek, then the other. "Oh, how I have missed you, my dear companion in arms." She put two fingers under Sylvia's chin. "And what is your name, *kleine mausi*?"

"Sylvi."

"And mine is Inga."

Harriet kissed Sylvia's cheek.

"You're a weight, Sylvi. Down you go."

"How old is she now?"

"Twenty months."

"She's a pretty little mouse, all blond curls and those big brown eyes. She has your eyes."

"We named her for Sylvia Pankhurst. Tom and I both like that name. And Maria, for my mother. Sylvia Maria."

"I saw Sylvia Pankhurst recently. She is looking very worn down, but there's a fire in her eyes. She is much occupied with her East London Federation. Mobilising the working classes."

"She has been writing to me. I don't know how she finds the time or the energy. I have lost count of how many times she has been in and out of prison, now they have that horrible Cat and Mouse Act."

Inga sighed. "There is no escape. Like the mouse on the run, hiding in the corners."

Harriet smiled and raised her eyebrows. "Like my daughter?"

"Oh, that is a little German term of endearment, Harriet. You know that."

"Yes, I know that. But now it seems like all women fighting for change have to scurry around in dark corners, only coming out to make trouble. The whole Union is in hiding."

"Or in prison."

"Or in France."

Harriet gestured towards the sofa.

"Please, do."

Inga sat, spreading her skirts in front of her. Harriet took the seat next to her thinking how Christabel Pankhurst had managed her daring escape to France.

Christabel had been in her own flat when the police arrested her mother and Frederick and Emmeline Pethwick Lawrence at Clement's Inn. Fred had slipped a cheque to an assistant, transferring all the Union's funds out of his control. The woman ran to Christabel for its second signature. Christabel, realising the danger she was in, fled to the nursing home that Emmeline used to recover from her hunger strikes. She left there in a nurse's uniform, burnt her favourite, distinctive pink hat, and took the boat train and cross-channel ferry to France.

Harriet said. "The damned elusive Christabel!"

"Your British press is so very humorous."

Mabel returned with a tray of lemonade and ginger biscuits.

"Cook says, would Miss Sylvia like to come down and help clean round the mixing bowl?"

"Do you want to lick the mixing spoon, Sylvi?... Look at her.

She's already halfway across the floor. There's nothing like the lure of Cook and the kitchen. They adore her."

After the door closed behind them, Inga said, "You don't employ a nanny?"

Harriet had fielded this question many times, usually talking about a changing view of childhood and her belief that the child learned much from contact with her own parents. To Inga she said, "To be truthful, Tom and I can't afford to hire a nanny. His practice is not taking off as we had hoped. I don't know why. He is a good doctor. Tom always wanted to help the needy, but he can't seem to build up a list of enough wealthy clients to subsidise working with the poor. It's as if he's tainted. He's starting to believe that associating with the socialists has permanently damaged his reputation."

Inga frowned. "From what Will said, it was more than the socialists. Your Tom has gone to some very dangerous meetings. Suspicious Russian exiles hold gatherings in London because anywhere else the secret police will catch them. These people are not limited to demanding fair working conditions in return for fair labour. They want the industry to be taken over by government. Some even want the industry to be taken from the owners and given to the workers to run. There are many such movements in Germany. They are everywhere, I think."

"He only went to listen. He was attracted to the Fabians."

"I sincerely hope so, Harriet, because these other people are revolutionaries. If they are caught arming themselves, they will be executed."

"I don't believe Tom would countenance armed revolution. He's scathing about the Ulster Volunteer Force and their threats to fight the government's plan for home rule for Ireland."

Harriet frowned. The failure of the plans to give Ireland its long sought-after autonomy was yet another reason women's rights were being pushed into the background. What's more, the

Protestant Irish, unlike the leaders of the WSPU, were not being arrested and jailed for conspiracy and insurrection, despite arming themselves and threatening rebellion.

She pushed such bitter thoughts aside.

"Come, have something to drink. My aunt's cook makes excellent lemonade. Not too sweet.... Now, tell me the truth. What is the understanding between you and my brother?"

Inga gripped her hand. "He is lovely, your Will, but he is in France now, and you know my father is moving us to America."

"I was grief stricken, believe me, when you wrote. Is there no way you could stay in England? Just you?"

Inga shook her head. "We can't stay here, Harriet. The Russians and the French have agreed to support each other. Germany is encircled. And we can't trust England not to side with the French. Your Sir Edward Grey is making promises to the French. Us Germans will not always be safe here."

"How do you know that? About Sir Edward Grey. There's nothing in the papers about any alliance with France... Ah, Will."

It was no secret that the German plan, if Russia were to threaten Germany in the east, was to attack France first. There were only two ways they could move their huge armies into France: through Belgium, whose neutrality the Great Powers had agreed to respect, or by sea via the English Channel. The border with France was well fortified. And the Royal Navy had agreed with France that it would protect the channel. There was no news of any other British agreement with France.

Inga said, "German troops practise war games every year. The Belgians build *große Betonfestugen*... castles. This is not the right word, I think. Big concrete buildings. On the border. And the Russians construct eight-wide railway lines to Germany's eastern border. And me? I depend on my father. I must go with him."

A breeze billowed Aunt Beth's delicate cream curtains into the room. Harriet shivered and said, "Tensions are less than they were back at the Agadir crisis. No-one will attack Germany. Why should they? And the Germans won't risk an attack on France. It's all bluster. Anyway, Germany has given up trying to match the size of our navy, once it got its wretched dreadnoughts."

"The French hate us. They want their Alsace and Lorraine back."

Inga sighed, got up, and walked around the room a few times. Harriet watched her but said nothing. It was a moment beyond words.

Inga returned to her seat.

"Do you know it is over a year since we last saw each other? I was such a long time in Germany. It is not since that meeting with Asquith and Lloyd George, I think. I was so surprised to see you with the delegation that went in, when you were so ... how do you say? Near to the birth."

"Christabel asked me to be there. She felt a need for people from the early days of the cause. I think it gave her strength."

It had been November, 1911, long before the conspiracy charges and Christabel's flight to France, and just a month before Sylvia was born. The women's Conciliation Bill had been pushed aside, once again. All the suffrage societies were outraged, not just the WSPU. Asquith agreed to receive a delegation but the Prime Minister only repeated what he had said before, that his proposed universal bill would be framed in such a way that it could be amended on a free vote to include women.

Harriet had been heavy with child and Tom had taken the day to accompany her on the train and through the streets.

Christabel had been magnificent in a long coat with wide lapels striped in the purple, green and white of the WSPU. But she had been uncharacteristically nervous. She had read out her speech and it had been stilted. When it came to the back and forth of opinions, however, she had regained her self-possession.

"When Christabel demanded that nothing less than full womanhood suffrage should be included in any measure for full manhood suffrage. Asquith replied that he could understand and respect her argument but *he* was the head of the government and *he* was not going to make himself responsible for the introduction of a measure which *he* did not believe to be in the interests of the country.

"Asquith was so supercilious it defies description."

Inga clapped her hands and held them together, tightly clenched. "They would prefer the women to sit back quietly and wait to be handed out treats. The women will make them care. We must keep breaking the windows."

Harriet smiled grimly. Two hundred and twenty women had been arrested when they marched that afternoon. Then, in the evening, women broke windows all over London.

She and Tom had caught the early train home.

Inga said, "I was with Charlotte Marsh in the Strand. Remember her? She was one of the women on the roof of Bingley Hall, in Birmingham. Charlie knew what to do. Hit the plate glass with the flat of the hammer, then the claw doesn't get caught in the hole. And on to the next one. No rocks. Rocks bounce off plate glass. We sped down the street like we were playing hockey. I broke six windows. Then I ran."

Women emerging from the shadows, spiriting hammers out of their pockets and sleeves and smashing windows all over the West End. The argument of the broken pane in millions of shards of glass. Harriet felt a shiver of the same righteous power she had felt as she had raised her arm to send a stone flying through the window of 11 Downing Street.

She chewed on her bottom lip. She didn't want Inga to think she had abandoned the fight.

She said, "Why do you think Emmeline and Fred Pethwick Lawrence left the WSPU? Were they against this new militancy?"

Inga put down her glass and waved her hands impatiently. "They were a danger because they are wealthy. The government seized their country house to pay the costs of their conspiracy trial. They couldn't be wholeheartedly behind the campaign when they could lose so much. An army must be united."

A military metaphor? Given what Inga had said earlier? To be as organised as an army was perhaps useful, and had been dramatically successful in the case of the great window breaking. But to be as unthinkingly obedient and as dispensable as a soldier, especially a soldier who's general was no longer on the field of battle?

"And Christabel fled to Paris? That's a good thing?"

"She would be in prison too, if she hadn't escaped. The sentences were... how do you say... Draconian? Are you no longer behind the cause, Harriet?"

Harriet clenched her teeth. She believed in women voting as much as she ever had. She also still believed that if women sat quietly nothing would happen, but ever since Sylvia's birth she had drifted around the edges of the Nottingham WSPU branch and had steered clear of their attacks on pillar boxes and telegraph wires.

A sullen silence filled the room. Inga, her trusted friend and beloved comrade, was scowling. They had come through too much together to fall out now.

Harriet licked her lips. "Did you know Charlotte Marsh is the branch organiser in Nottingham now? She is a gifted artist. She has taken lodgings near my sisters' shop and they have some of her work on display."

Inga's frown relaxed. "I would like to see the famous shop.

When shall we go?"

Harriet glanced at the clock. "It's time for Sylvia's sleep. I'll fetch her from the kitchen and show you to your room on the way up to the nursery. You can freshen up from your journey and then we'll head for Bridlesmith Gate. It's only a quarter of an hour's walk."

On Sunday morning Harriet arranged for Eleanor to look after Sylvia so she and Inga could take the bicycles and explore Nottingham. She ended their tour at the embankment by Trent Bridge and spread a blanket on the middle steps of the flight of seven. She laid out bottles of ginger beer and slices of veal and ham pie. The sun was warm on her back.

Inga said, "I was surprised at the Nottingham Castle. An impressive rock, but a modest house. Didn't Christabel Pankhurst once tell Sylvia to burn down Nottingham Castle?"

Harriet nodded. "So Sylvia said. And a drawing of the Castle burning was on the front of one of the issues of The Suffragette. It's a symbol of the fight for the franchise."

"But why this little house? That cabinet minister, that Hobhouse, he said something about Nottingham Castle and eighteen-thirty-two. He said it was men demanding rights in a way that women don't, or can't. What happened in eighteen-thirty-two? Was it a real castle then?"

"No, it was a house. A different one. It belonged to the Duke of Newcastle, who opposed the Great Reform Bill. That bill," she said, when Inga looked puzzled, "was the first major extension of the suffrage. There were riots, and the mob set fire to the castle. They hanged a lot of the rioters after. It's one of the most dramatic parts of our history."

Harriet searched in the basket for more food, thinking that it was typical of Christabel Pankhurst to have made such a suggestion. The woman seemed to revel in the shocking. She found, and unwrapped, a paper packet of sandwiches.

"We have some ham here. And I know we packed cucumber. Which would you prefer?" She put the packet down on the rug. "You know, Inga, Hobhouse is a provocateur. Women haven't demonstrated the passion men showed over the Great Reform Bill? That's arrant nonsense. Women today have generated more popular sentiment than any mob last century ever did."

Inga said, "Remember that time at Downing Street? And afterwards your performance in court. It was masterful."

"You were there? In court? Why did you never tell me? That was such a risk. What if I had let your name slip?"

"I'm sorry that I haven't thanked you, comrade, but I dared not mention it in letters. They could be opened."

Harriet shook her head. "When I was still working in the office at the WSPU, women were writing and offering to undertake militant acts in their droves. The government could have had them all arrested if it had been opening the post."

Over Inga's shoulder, Harriet could see boats moored by the steps down to the river. She could hear the water slapping against the embankment's concrete. Summer was coming with its peaceful days.

Inga used her napkin to pick up a piece of pie and waved it in the air, as if signalling a new direction to the conversation. With her other hand she drew a letter from the pocket of her skirt. "I had this from Miss Christabel Pankhurst a week ago."

Harriet laid her sandwich down on the rug and focussed her attention back on Inga. The sickle-shaped scar under Inga's right eye, left there by Black Friday, had faded to a pale lilac.

"Christabel wants us to burn Nottingham Castle."

For a moment she couldn't reply. She was as winded as if she had fallen from her bicycle. Then words came.

"No! Not ever. The castle belongs to the people of Nottingham. It's a fine art museum. It houses lace patterns going back centuries. We love the castle. And, anyway, what's this *we*? When did I become involved in this?"

Inga smoothed out the letter. "Listen to me, please. Please, for the sake of our friendship. Christabel says, *The cost of repairing government windows has fallen on them too lightly. The blame for our actions lies not with us but with those who fail to lobby government for the women's vote. Society does not value women, so we have to attack the things society values, which is not women but money, property and pleasure.*"

The crate Mabel had remarked on when Inga had arrived?

"That was yours, wasn't it, the crate? For God's sake, what's in it? Paraffin, candles, rags? Anything explosive?"

Inga fiddled with her ginger beer bottle. "Nothing explosive."

"The boys are down from school. They could find that stuff at any moment! Don't you realise how dangerous that is? It's a ridiculous idea, anyway. No hearts and minds will be won by burning the castle. All Nottingham will be set against our cause. The Castle is not a symbol of power. Not now."

Inga bowed her head and said nothing, but Harriet could feel how she longed to be heard. When Harriet had raised her arm to smash Lloyd George's window, she too had been on fire with anger. She had burned to break what men cared about. She had believed in the depths of her being that men deserved to have their ears opened by the sound of splintering glass.

Inga remained silent. Harriet turned her attention back to the river. Two women at the water's edge were talking with the man who hired out rowing boats. She knew him of old. He always had some snide comment to make when women went out on the river. "Will's my brother!" she had once said, and he had laughed at her indignation. What was going on today was too far away for her to hear, but the women seemed agitated.

Inga took a ham sandwich and pinched it between finger and thumb, keeping the buttery edge well away from her gloves. "Have you heard anything from your friend Alice, Mrs Slack?"

Hoping this signalled the end of the discussion about the Castle, Harriet replied at length, explaining how, after the brutality of Black Friday, Alice had lost her nerve for marching and confined herself to attending meetings and writing.

"I always wondered," Inga said, "if that picture in the newspaper was her. You know, the one with the woman lying on the ground like a heap of rags and the man in the fine coat and top hat standing over her. You were right by her. Have you seen this man?"

"I saw her on the ground. I didn't notice any man. But I was somewhat occupied with being thrown from one assailant to another." Harriet hoped she had said it wryly rather than bitterly.

Two young men strode down the steps next to them, so close and fast that there was a draught as they passed. Harriet looked past Inga to see what the rush was about. The men headed towards the two women on the river bank. One handed something to the boatman, who walked up the steps and returned with two sets of oars, handing one set to each of the men.

"That's it," Harriet said. "The women were attempting to hire from him."

Inga turned to look.

The men stepped into a moored boat each and extended hands to the ladies. Harriet laughed out loud as they let the women step behind them, passing them the oars after they were seated.

"I wonder if those men wanted to impress independently minded women, so they suggested this stunt, bearding the misogynistic old boatman in his den. The ladies are experienced boaters. There was no wobble."

"Or the men are , how do you say, trying their luck with the ladies."

"No, they clearly know the women."

Inga laughed, "Men will do anything to impress the women, as long as it is as easy as teasing an old boatman."

But whatever had been proved, the only way those women had been able to row was through the intervention of men. Just like Harriet had only been able to go out in a boat or play cricket because of Will.

She heard the sound of a boat club rowing eight, the cox shouting the rhythm. The slim boat was cutting through the water, the oars lifting only the slightest sparkles into the air.

The Nottingham boat club was closed to women. It had even stopped women forming their own club. Harriet pushed her teeth into her lip. Men would go on excluding her, her daughter, and her daughter's daughter and women would sit and watch and wait forever, unless someone did something about it.

She said, "This river belongs to everyone, not just the men."

Inga didn't reply and Harriet watched the boats for a few minutes more before saying, "I played football in the prison yard, Inga. It was fun. It was freedom. I want my daughter to have that freedom. And not be held back by damned propriety imposed by men."

Harriet picked up her neglected sandwich and bit it savagely. She looked at Inga, at the set of her jaw and the way she was staring into the distance. If she refused to help Inga attack Nottingham Castle, she might act alone. If she were caught the authorities were bound to come down hard on a German national sabotaging an English monument.

Swallowing down the last mouthful, Harriet said, "Let's use

your paraffin on the Rowing Club's boathouse. It's just along the river from here. The area is deserted at night."

Inga turned back towards her and looked her in the eyes. She nodded, a slow, deliberate movement of her head.

Harriet swallowed hard and reached for something to drink. She could be separated from Tom and Sylvia for years. Or she would have to hunger strike to get released on a Cat and Mouse licence. And not everyone was being released immediately. Many were forcibly fed first. Could she stand that?

Could she stand being shut away from Sylvia?

Chapter 30
Nottingham Boathouse

May 1913

Harriet pulled back the curtains enough for the street lamps to light the room. Inga was lying on her back, fully clothed and fast asleep. One of the pairs of trousers Harriet had taken from Will's room was for Inga, but there was no need to wake her yet. They had agreed on avoiding all sound.

If her heartbeat got much louder it would wake Inga and the rest of the household too. Although it wouldn't wake Sylvia. The child could sleep through anything. If Harriet were caught, Tom would find her note explaining what she had done by Sylvia's cot. She shuddered as she pulled on a pair of Will's trousers and imagined the empty future opening up before her husband and her daughter.

In these trousers, and front buttoning blouses, she should appear masculine enough to fool casual observers, at least under cover of dark. If there were less-casual observers near the boathouse, such as a policeman or a watchman, the plan was to continue riding the bicycles along the Trent embankment, as if they were young bloods engaged in a night-time jaunt.

Young men. So carefree. Off they went, without leaving notes for anyone, to ride bikes, to go to work or become soldiers. It was all the same to them. Someone else would take care of things at home.

Harriet shrugged braces over her shoulders and put on her own jacket. Will's was too broad across the shoulders. Men's boaters were the final touch. To get two of these, Harriet had raided the hatstand for Robert's and Wesley's. She hoped that if their absence were noticed, Wesley's mischievous sons would get the blame.

She shook Inga's arm. Inga sat up with a start, her eyes wide, as if she was still seeing the land of her dreams. Harriet put her finger to her lips.

She coiled her braided hair around her head and secured it. The boater was sturdier than a woman's boater. The straw was thicker. She pushed a hatpin into it experimentally. Having the pin jerk through and go into her scalp because she had applied too much pressure would not be a good idea. Any squawk could scupper their plans.

The pin shuddered through the thick straw and scratched her finger. She stuck it in her mouth to stop the blood dripping on her clothes and gave Inga a rueful glance.

She watched Inga dress. It was strange how, having laid down a rule not to talk, talking became so desirable. In Holloway they had believed that not letting you talk forced you into contemplating the evil of your ways. They had clearly never tried it. It led to you talking to yourself.

Was Inga still on board with the plan? Had she been completely deterred from the idea of attacking the Castle?

Inga gestured towards the door. They crept down the servants' stairs, through the scullery, and out into the side yard by the shed. It had been Inga's job to get the bicycles ready before dark. Harriet had kept watch outside the shed door.

They each had a can of paraffin, a bundle of rags, a candle and a box of matches in their bike baskets, all tucked beneath a flour sack. She saw a jemmy poking out from Inga's.

"Get that under the sack," she whispered. "We don't want to look like burglars."

The side gate creaked as she opened it. Inga touched her shoulder. Harriet shook her head free of worries about being heard and wheeled her bicycle into the road.

"This way," Harriet said, speaking slightly louder now they were clear of the house.

The way to the river along Castle Boulevard was longer than going through The Meadows but promised fewer people, not that there should be many anywhere at two in the morning.

"Be careful of the tram lines. It's very easy to trap a bicycle wheel in a tramline. Cross them straight, not at an angle. Ride slowly."

"Two young bloods out for a night-time lark are unlikely to ride slowly."

But Inga didn't know the way and Harriet set a sensible pace until they reached the river, where Inga pulled ahead of her onto the embankment where the smell of damp from the river mingled with the sickly aroma from the paraffin can bumping around in her bike-basket. There was no sign of anybody, not even a tramp. Somewhere distant an owl hooted.

Harriet stepped off her bicycle. Cold air flowed over her buttocks and between her legs. She felt as exposed in trousers as if she were naked from the waist down and cast up on the river bank, like some monstrous reverse mermaid. Shivering, she wheeled the machine down the side of the boathouse, turned it, like Inga's, so it faced the way home, and propped it against the wall.

Inga pulled the jemmy from her bike basket, inserted it between the door and the jamb, and pushed. The dry wood splintered with a shriek of nails and the door burst outwards. Harriet hurried back to the river and checked along the bank. There was no sign of activity, no lights, no raised voices, no movement on the bridge. She strode back to the boathouse, collecting her paraffin can and rags on the way. Heat rushed through her veins. She was going to turn their delicate phallic vessels into delicate ashes.

She marched over the broken door, her face hot. Inga's candle was lit and wedged upright in the centre aisle of the shed and Inga was already splashing paraffin over the lower racks of boats hung on the opposite wall. Harriet piled her rags under the boats on her side, unscrewed her can and threw paraffin over the boats. Inga returned to the centre. Harriet flung aside the empty can, walked over to Inga and lit her own candle. She watched as Inga returned to the far wall and planted her candle in her stack of rags and left the boathouse, then Harriet turned towards her rags and bent down.

Searing, stabbing pain shot through her calf. She dropped the candle and screamed. Her trousers. She must have dropped paraffin on her trousers. What a fool. What a goddamned fool. She staggered towards the boathouse door.

Inga was rushing back towards her. She was wrapping something tight round her leg. Inga was dragging her by the arm. She was sobbing. They were both sobbing.

Flames were sweeping over the boats, licking up and revealing the rafters.

There was the doorway. There was the outside. The bicycles were ahead. Inga let go of her arm and ran towards the river, a flour sack trailing from her hand. She wanted to shout, what are you doing? We need to go! But she mustn't call out. Had anyone heard her scream? Her leg pulsed. The pulsing rose and invaded her centre.

Inga pulled away the first sack and wrapped the one now

dripping with water around Harriet's lower leg. She struggled out of her jacket, removed her blouse and tore it into strips which she used to tie the sacking in place.

Air rushed around Harriet's ankles, away from the river and towards the flames. She could smell the varnish sizzling on the carcases of the boats. Something crashed to the ground.

Harriet swung her throbbing leg forward, towards her bicycle, suppressing the urge to cry out when it took her weight. Cycling had to be easier than walking. She could push a pedal with one leg.

The planned return route wasn't the road they had come along, where people might already be running towards the burning boathouse, but along the dark embankment. She needed to show Inga the way.

Harriet buried her face in the pillow, trying not to groan every time Inga picked at the pieces of cloth and sacking stuck to her calf. She attempted to concentrate on the cool air blowing in through the open window.

Sylvia would wake soon and Tom would go to her. Tom would find the note she had left by Sylvia's bed. The note she had intended to retrieve if they got back without being apprehended.

"Inga, I need you to go to Sylvia's room and–"

There was a soft knock at the door. Harriet sat up and crossed her undamaged leg over the wounded one.

"Miss Rheinhart?"

Tom.

"Is Harriet there with you?"

Inga looked at her, eyebrows raised. Harriet nodded. Inga opened the door and stepped back to let Tom in.

He stopped a few steps inside, his face thrown into shadows

by the low morning light. His nostrils seemed to flare. Harriet couldn't think what to say, so she said nothing.

"Miss Rheinhart? Harry? What's going on? I can see you are in pain, Harry. I can see it in your face. Please, tell me what's happened."

She turned back onto her stomach to let him see the damage to her calf that she had been unable to see for herself. She heard a slight intake of breath.

"I'm going to fetch my medical bag and get supplies from the kitchen. I suggest you wash and make yourself respectable, Miss Rheinhart. I will need your help."

The door closed behind him. Harriet sat up and stared at Inga.

"Perhaps it's his doctor voice," Inga offered. "But I have no hope of becoming respectable in the time it will take for him to return from the kitchen, not even if he has to stay to heat water."

There was genuine fear in Inga's eyes. Fear Harriet had not seen at any time during their assault upon the boathouse. Harriet knew where it came from, from the white coats and disdainful voices that had loomed over them in the prison.

But Tom had appeared in his red and grey tartan dressing gown over his nightgown.

"He's my husband, Inga. You can trust him."

Inga sat beside her on the bed, holding her hand for what seemed more than long enough to change her clothes, before shrugging, walking to the washstand and starting to wash her face and hands.

The door opened, without a knock this time. Tom was dressed in trousers and a white shirt now, with the sleeves rolled up above the elbows. He had two of Cook's aprons in one hand and his medical bag in the other. He handed one apron to Inga and put his bag on the bedside table. Then he returned for the kettle of steaming water he must have put down outside the door. He took it to the washstand.

As he fastened an apron around himself, he said, "You'd have done better to have washed before you touched the wounded area, Miss Rheinhart. Dispose of that dirty water, please. I suggest you use the bathroom on the landing. Then we will both scrub with hot water and carbolic soap."

With Inga out of hearing, Harriet hissed, "Why are you being so wretchedly pompous? She's our guest, not our enemy."

Tom sighed and sat on the edge of the bed. "Sorry, Harry. I wake up and find you gone and you're not with Sylvia. There is a note by Sylvia's bed telling me that if I should find it you have been arrested. This room reeks of paraffin and soot. You are both covered in smuts like a pair of sweeps. You have a nasty looking burn on your leg. And neither of you has told me what happened. A doctor needs to know how a wound was caused, if he is to treat it."

"And you think the best way to get that information is to be unpleasant?"

"To be firm."

She grimaced as she moved away from him towards the centre of the bed. She longed to lie on her stomach and free her calf from the rasping bedclothes.

"We are not the ignorant masses you treated in your East End dispensary. You should treat us with respect."

The bed heaved as he stood up.

"Respect, Harry? What respect have you shown me? Sneaking off in the night without a word. Putting yourself in God knows what danger. What about Sylvia and—"

The door opened and Inga returned with the empty wash-bowl. She had taken off her jacket and wrapped Cook's apron around her.

Harriet closed her eyes. Tom had never spoken so harshly to

her before. It hurt. But he was worried and upset. Who could blame him.

"I'm sorry," she whispered.

She didn't think he heard. The deep stabs that had gone once Inga stopped pulling at the cloth stuck to her leg reinvented themselves as sickening waves. She whimpered.

"Roll onto your front, Harry. Inga, I want you to cut away the clothing until we can find firm edges to hold on to. About there should do. Now, please tell me what you two were doing."

Harriet spoke as clearly as she could, given the pillow in her mouth and her unplanned gasps.

"We used paraffin to start a fire at the boathouse. I spilt some on my leg."

"God Almighty! You could have killed yourselves. How long were you in the smoke?"

Inga said, "We got out fast. We didn't breathe in much smoke. We coughed a bit at first, but not recently. I threw one flour sack over Harriet's legs to put out the fire and soaked another in the river to wrap around the wound."

"That was quick thinking. You saved her from more severe burn damage. So, we have possible contamination from soot, flour and whatever filth was in the river. Harry, I'm going to soak the burn area in cold water and try to peel off the rest of the sacking in one piece. It's going to hurt."

The cold water felt good. The muscles in her back relaxed. She heard the door to the stairs to the attic rooms open and bang shut and young Charley and Bobby trying to talk quietly and failing. Their footsteps faded as they reached the downstairs hall. Going to forage for food in the kitchen, most likely. They were always hungry. What about Sylvia? Was she awake yet? Was she hungry?

There was a tug on the flesh of her calf, then a tearing, layers separating, sticking, then splitting and ripping apart. She screamed into the pillow. Her leg must be flayed, skinned like Cook skinned a rabbit; one quick jerk and the entire pelt turned inside out, leaving a pink, vulnerable corpse devoid of all features belonging to the breathing creature. She screamed again. She hoped the sounds were muffled into the pillow.

"Good. I'm glad that hurt. Just a few stray fibres to pick off."

She struggled to turn over, but Tom pressed a hand into the middle of her back. "Not finished yet."

"What," she spat the word sideways into the room, "do you mean by saying you're glad it hurt?"

"If the burn had gone deep into the flesh and destroyed tissue and nerves, you wouldn't have felt any pain. See here, Inga, the wound is pink and wet. It looks nasty, and it is, but it would be a lot worse if the area was dry and hard."

Throbbing all along her leg, but not of screaming quality. Tom had seen a lot of burns at the dispensary. She understood now how he was using her friend as a way of talking to her; a less personal, less alarming way of letting her see what he could see.

But what about what other people in the house might see?

"Would you get more hot water from the kitchen, Tom? It will look less odd if you do it than if Inga does. If we both reek of paraffin, we are going to have to wash thoroughly, including our hair. We can't have the servants gossiping all about town."

Inga said, "I'll get your clothes from your room and help you wash and dress."

Harriet felt Tom draw a line with his finger on the back of her leg. "First I need to paint the skin around this area with Gentian Violet and you need to watch me, Inga, so you can do it when I am not here. There will be a lot of bacteria waiting to get into this open wound. It is imperative it is kept clean. Who knows what contamination was in the river water."

"What shall I say is wrong with my leg, Tom? Everyone is bound to ask."

"Say you have an ulcer. Ulcers take time and care to heal. Can you lift your leg? Bend at the knee so I can wrap the bandage round. This will need changing every two hours, Inga. Do you think you will be able to do that throughout the day?"

"It is the least I can do."

Harriet groaned. "What about these clothes? We can't return them. The smell will give us away. We can't put them in the waste bins here, either. They'll be noticed."

"I'll take them into the surgery. When I go in later."

"And the boaters? I'm afraid we've dirtied them too. We didn't think this out too well. Did we?"

"No you didn't." Tom sounded angry again. "The police are likely to raid the Nottingham WSPU office, aren't they? Then they'll have their hands on the names of all the local members."

Harriet raised a placating hand. "The office is no more than a front. Ever since the raid on Clement's Inn important documents have been hidden away from the office."

Inga said, "I thought you were going to let the boys take the blame for the boaters disappearing."

"I was. But one is Wesley's. He'll question the boys and they'll deny it. I don't trust Wesley."

Tom wrinkled his nose. "I'll take the boaters into Nottingham, Harry. I can buy new ones. Might as well get fully involved in your damn silly plot, since I'm already implicated."

"That won't work, either. They'll be too new." Harriet imagined the boaters on the hatstand. The boys borrowing them, and taking them where? "I know. Inga, you take them into the bathroom and scrub them with soap and water as much as you can. Then carry them down the garden and leave them on the table. Someone will find them and bring them back in. Or you could bring them in later and give them to Eleanor. Tell her you wouldn't want to get the boys in trouble with their father because they left them outside all night to catch the dew."

"We're involving even more people."

"I know, Inga. But I think only Wesley and the servants are a danger. Not that I think even Wesley would report me to the police, but he's a gossip."

"And the boys," Tom said. "Boys gossip too." He sighed. "But if that's the best we can do, let's do it. You need to get back to our room, Harry. And, by the way, the skin around the wound area will be stained purple for a while. It's nothing to worry about."

WSPU purple. That was funny. Purple skin was the least of her concerns.

She said, "Will you check on Sylvia? What time is it?"

"It's only five o'clock. I'm sure she's sleeping soundly."

"So why were Charley and Bobby up so early?"

"Going fishing? Who knows? They're boys."

They were young men, really. It seemed only yesterday she had been holding their hands and leading them on adventures. Now they were almost as tall as her.

God, what had she done? If anyone found out, Sylvia could be a young woman before she ever saw her again. A choking sob thrust up into her throat. She remembered Emma howling that Christmas, when Father wasn't there anymore. If only she could howl right now.

Chapter 31
The Poor Boats

May 1913

Harriet was reluctant to write a note claiming WSPU responsibility for the burning of the boathouse. The more evidence there was, the greater the chance of someone in the family connecting Inga's visit with the arson. It was Mabel, after all, who had carried the crate of materials into the shed. Mabel was quite capable of putting two and two together.

"We have to write the note, Harriet. And do it this morning. Or it is all a waste. We are taking action, making a point. For the cause. The right information has to be in the papers."

"Alright. You're right. But let's make it quite unlike us. Let's imagine ourselves two of the hoydens that are doing most of this stuff. One of the holy crusaders who likes to vaunt herself. Mary Richardson, for example."

"Her? Yes, her. Everything she says is from the soapbox. She is more stage character than person."

"How about this?" Harriet pulled the sheet of plain paper towards them and wrote:

We could not help being sorry for the poor boats.

"A whiney-clever tone, see."

She picked up the pen again,

Please don't be angry with us for what we've done.

"Ha," Inga said. "We need explanation."

Harriet thought for a moment and added,

But you understand, don't you? We can't possibly let any property be safe so long as we haven't votes. Be thankful that we haven't gone further. Of course, you know how to stop this sort of thing. If not, allow us to tell you, induce the government to bring in a bill giving women equal voting rights with men.

W.S.P.U.

Inga held out her hand for the pen and wrote,

If we had been men, life would have been taken ages ago.

"Let me write it all out," Inga said. "Your handwriting might be known to somebody. What should I write for the address?"

"Chairman, Nottingham Rowing Club, Nottingham. The post office will deliver it to the right person. They are astonishingly obliging. Will you walk into the central office with it?"

The door opened and Will came in. Inga turned the envelope over.

"I'm glad I've caught the two of you together. I'm back to Paris tomorrow. Do either of you have anything you'd like me to fetch from the fashion capital of the world?"

Will settled himself in an armchair and leant back, looking very much like he intended to stay.

Harriet said, "If only I could afford it."

"Well, I'd love to be able to buy you something, Sis. But, you see, I am two pairs of trousers short, which leaves me only one. Quite a mystery, don't you think? Two pairs of a chap's trousers disappearing one night. And then a chap meets with some old school friends for a stroll early on a holiday morning and hears that someone has set fire to the Rowing Club's boathouse.

Suffragettes are getting the blame, of course. No doubt it was deliberate. Paraffin cans left behind, you see."

Harriet put her elbows on the table and her chin on her hands and stared at her brother. He looked angry.

There was no point in lying. It was yet one more person involved. But he'd already guessed.

"You'll keep our secret?"

"I've kept a host of secrets for you already."

"Are you counting?"

"I'm worried, damn it. Arson isn't a two-week sentence. It's years. What about Tom and Sylvia? Does Tom know?"

She nodded. Inga slipped the envelope under the blotter. Will raised his eyebrows. He was too astute to be fooled.

He said, "I am exasperated. I'm constantly exasperated. I want you safe but I can't stop loving your passion and your courage. Will you marry me?"

"What?"

"He means me, Harriet."

"Say yes and come to France with me."

"I cannot go to France. Come to America with me."

"We've done this before, Sis. Can you tell? She's so stubborn. Right-o, I'll come to America when my two-year stint in Paris is up. How about that? This is a big step for me. Will I survive?"

Inga went over to Will's chair, sat on the floor, and laid her head against his knee. Harriet clapped her hands together and made to get up but as soon as she put pressure on her calf muscles pain shot through her leg. They looked so sweet sitting there together. She longed to embrace them both. Instead she sank back down onto her chair and groaned.

She said, "Are you serious? Both of you?"

"Never more so, Sis. Never thought the snares of love would capture me, but they have."

The door banged open and Sylvia rushed in with Eleanor behind her.

Harriet lifted her carefully onto her knee and kissed her head.

Eleanor said, "I was wondering if Miss Rheinhart would care to accompany us for a walk."

Eleanor looked down at Inga, on the floor next to Will's chair. There was a quizzical expression on her face, but she said nothing.

"We are going to visit the Boots library, Harry. Do you have anything to return?"

"On the table, over there."

Eleanor picked up the book on the little table by the window.

"This one? *Roughing it in the Bush or Life in Canada?* Botany? Can I get you another one? Is there anything else you'd like while I'm out?"

Botany? That was funny. The book was a humorous account by a woman who had gone to Canada with her husband, enticed by the cheap land and homesteads that were being promised in the British press.

"Would you see if the library has something amusing?"

"But anything else? Some chocolate for the invalid, perhaps? And how is your leg, Harry? When you weren't there for breakfast, Tom told me you have an ulcer. That sounds unpleasant."

Harriet avoided Eleanor's eyes by turning her attention to retying Sylvia's hair ribbons. Marching, chalking up pavements, even throwing stones through the windows of public meetings were actions she could share. Destroying property, while seeking not to be found out, was not. Lying to her family did not sit well with her conscience.

She said, "Tom says it will be a long time and dependent on constant renewal of the dressings. He taught Inga how to do it."

"Well, we are grateful that you are able to remain with us, Miss Rheinhart. Will you be ready to leave in fifteen minutes? Once I have this active young miss dressed to go out, it's hard to hold her back."

Harriet nuzzled her face into Sylvia's neck. She smelled of talcum powder. "You go with Auntie Nell to get your hat and your boots."

"I want Mama."

"I'm sorry I can't go. I have a poorly leg."

"I don't want—"

Eleanor picked the child up from Harriet's knee, positioned her on her hip, and took Harriet's book in her other hand.

"Now, that's quite enough of that, young lady. You are coming with me or you're not going at all."

The door closed to the sound of Sylvia's wails. Harriet twisted her hands together and bit her lip. This imposition on Eleanor was her fault.

Inga got up and said, "Is it far to the lending library? Will Sylvia walk all the way?"

"A mile or so, I suppose." She smiled at Inga. "Eleanor will take the perambulator. Discovering she can pile quantities of books in it has cured her of the embarrassment of being mistaken for a nanny."

Inga smiled back, dark eyes shining. "And I should hurry myself to join her before I get my marching orders."

She picked up their letter and bent to kiss Harriet on the cheek, leaving behind the heady scent of honeysuckle. Then she went and kissed Will. Full on the lips.

Harriet laughed. A new woman indeed.

But yesterday was the last time she was going to risk a prison sentence. From now on Inga would have to act without her. New woman or not, her time with Sylvia was too precious. For both her and the child.

Chapter 32
The Shop in Bridlesmith Gate,

June 1913

Harriet pushed the shop door, but it was locked. She shaded her eyes and peered through the diamond panes, then rang the bell. Emma appeared and unbolted the door at the top and bottom.

"Do you usually close in the afternoons?"

"Half day closing. New laws. All shops have to close at midday on Wednesdays, to give employees time off."

"You don't have any employees, do you?"

"No, but all the shopkeepers are closing. So we don't compete unfairly with each other."

Harriet followed Emma across the sales floor with its wooden drawers and glass showcases and into the room to the side that should have been the kitchen. A huge wooden contraption supporting a thick white stone dominated the small space. Harriet took off a glove and ran her fingers across the polished surface. It was deliciously smooth.

"I've brought my bookplates for you to see. Thirty-six. A different plant for the front of each of the thirty-six volumes of

Sowerby. I had a lot of time to sit and draw, what with this leg. What is this contraption?"

"It's the machine for lithographs, prints. Would you mind not touching it, please, Harry. You see, your fingers will leave grease and I have just cleaned it off."

Harriet withdrew her hand and put her glove back on.

"I'm sorry. It is a most seductive item."

"It is, isn't it? I can use it to make copies of your ex libris plates. I imagine them a little more special than the mass-produced plates you can buy, and with more subtle colours. And you are sensible enough to leave plenty of room for people to show off their names and their fine writing. We are getting some quite sophisticated custom in here these days."

"All passing through on their way upstairs?"

"Don't tease, Harry. It's art."

It was, indeed, art. Emma portrayed living women, flowing their spirit through her pastels and flooding it onto the paper, making their bodies beautiful. Harriet had no idea how she did it. It was a talent, and she was making money from it, even if she did have to be circumspect about the market she had entered.

Harriet opened the satchel she had brought with her and handed over her drawings.

"Oh, I love this honeysuckle one. It's so energetic. May I copy this one onto the stone?"

Emma picked up a tool that looked like a pencil with a fat black tip and drew on the smooth surface, producing something that more resembled the artful shadings and divisions of stained glass than the crinkled, twisted shapes of Harriet's hedgerow woodbine. Harriet's work was the detailed diagram of a scientist with a bit of artistry thrown in. Emma's honeysuckle was fluid and sinuous.

"Art Nouveau, Emma?"

"Yes, but more realistic."

Emma's version of honeysuckle wasn't remotely realistic, but it was enticing.

"Does the print come out as a negative? Does the ink run off the greasy areas?"

"No, I use chemicals that react with the grease in the drawing and with the stone. Then the ink sticks to the drawing. It comes out the same way you draw it. Wonderfully easy, no?"

"And what are these chemicals?"

"Gum Arabic and Nitric acid."

Harriet winced.

"Please be careful with strong acid like that."

"Of course. This is a little demonstration for you. To see if you like the idea. I'm going to have to clean this stone off before using it because it will have your fingerprints on it."

"I'm sorry about that. So, I can't get to see the print today?"

"No, it takes time, and it's quite messy." Emma put down her crayon and stepped back to survey her work, head tilted to one side. "Yes, something like that will serve. With pale green and charcoal grey, not black, and white for the highlights. Now, would you like some tea? Come through to the kitchen."

What Emma called her kitchen was the room beyond the one she had set up as a print shop. It was a tiny space, with a deep fireclay sink to one side, that must have been intended for a scullery. Emma clattered a copper kettle onto something that looked like a stove, tiled in white with a leaded iron grill on top.

"Is that a gas range?"

"Yes. We had it put in a few weeks ago." Emma struck a long match and twisted a knob. Flames shot up. "You have to be careful not to lose your eyebrows, but it is so much cleaner and easier than coal."

Harriet sat at the table, reached down, and rubbed the back of her calf.

"Is the ulcer still bothering you?"

"Tom says the itching is a good sign."

The kettle rattled on the stove and Emma turned off the flame and poured water onto the tea leaves.

"Tom's such a lovely man, only, tell me to mind my own business, but is anything upsetting him? He doesn't seem his usual self. Is he missing the political hotbeds of London stuck in provincial Nottingham?"

"He's joined the Independent Labour Party branch here, and the Peace Society. He doesn't lack stimulation. No, the problem is he's worried. It should have been easy to take over part of his father's list, but somehow it isn't. I do wonder if people have taken against his politics."

Emma collected a jug of milk from the meat-safe near the back door and sniffed at it. "Have to be careful. It goes off so quickly this hot weather. You know, this is a radical city. There ought to be plenty of people in Nottingham who sympathise with his politics. And we are leaders in the prevention of disease. Think of Doctor Boobbyer and all the work he's done for the health of the people here." She sat opposite Harriet, poured their tea, and put Harriet's cup in front of her. "Help doesn't all have to come from the medical officer, does it? Or charities. What if our lace manufactory could employ Tom as a doctor for the hands. The hands must need doctoring."

It was a marvelous idea. Clever too. Exactly what she might expect of Emma.

"I'm sure Tom would love that. He could work with people who might not go to a doctor."

"And the manufactory would get a healthier workforce. I'll talk to Gwen about it when she gets home. It'll be better coming from me than from you. That way she can appear magnanimous instead of beholden. She's a bit full of herself now she's stepped right into Uncle George's shoes. But the shoes were there waiting. Wesley never wanted that sort of responsibility and Robert has not really recovered his strength. If Tom works there too, they will all be working together. It was what Uncle George always believed a family should do."

Emma put down her teacup and clapped her hands together.

"Do you want to see my latest studies of the wealthy wives of Nottingham before their husbands come to cart them off? Or are they all too racy for you?"

Harriet swallowed down the remains of her tea.

"I'm not going to know how racy they are unless I see them. Lead on."

Harriet blinked in the bright sunlight outside the shop. It was going to be a fine evening. She should take Sylvia to the park.

"Wait, Harry! Wait."

Gwen was running up the street, her skirt held clear of her boots.

"I can't wait for long. I have to be back for when Sylvia wakes up."

Gwen thrust a newspaper at her, folded back to the inside pages. Harriet took in the headline.

Shocking day at the Derby. Favourite disqualified. Chance wins at 100 to 1. Suffragette hit by King's colt after running onto track.

"Oh my God! I wonder who it was."

"The article doesn't say. But it does say there was newsreel taken and it's expected in the picture houses tonight, which is pretty gruesome. The woman is badly hurt. She's in hospital."

What had possessed this person, whoever she was? Horses thundering along at thirty miles an hour. It was mad. The whole movement was going mad.

"I'll walk with you, Harry. You've turned pale."

Had her own actions had anything to do with it? Since the boathouse there'd been a flurry of attacks on men's sporting preserves.

"Do you think it's all gone too far, Gwen? Do you think Father would still be behind me being in the Union?"

He'd helped her learn to speak in public. She doubted he would have helped her plan arson.

Of course he wouldn't. How could she even think such a thing.

Gwen said, "Suffragettes are burning down churches. I think he'd take a dim view of that, wouldn't you?"

Chapter 33
The New Woman

June 5th 1913

Harriet waited on the front steps for the paperboy. Wesley was not going to get to the news before she did, not this morning. Father had always read the paper before anyone else. Wesley was not Father. Wesley had no position, whatever he might think. Robert was the senior Loxley man and Aunt Beth was the senior member of the Loxley Hall household and, what's more, it was Aunt Beth's house and she paid for the paper.

The boy was still out of sight, but she could hear him whistling. She went down the steps, rounded the corner, and slipped a penny into his hand.

"Thank you, missus. And a topping good morning to you."

She spread the paper out on the wide top step and knelt to turn the sheets.

"Emily. God, it was Emily Davison."

The text danced in front of her eyes. She forced herself to pick out the facts. In hospital. Not regained consciousness. Injuries to skull. Horse fell, then got up. Jockey thrown and injured but recovering. Spectators, including a doctor, rushed to help.

"Emily. Emily, you great big-hearted bolt from heaven. You were bound to go too far."

Harriet folded the paper as well as she could and put it on the hall table.

"Breakfast time, Sylvi. What do you think Mabel will have for you today.?"

"Eggy."

"Eggy bread?"

While immobile and resting her leg, Harriet had started paying Mabel four shillings a week for the extra help she provided looking after Sylvia. With her work on the bookplate designs for the shop Harriet had needed Mabel more than ever, and having Sylvia eat a light breakfast in the kitchen was better for everyone.

She noted the absence of the newspaper on her way back across the hall. She chewed her lower lip, lifted her chin and walked into the Dining Room.

Wesley was behind the paper. Eleanor was next to him. Robert was still at home, and eating heartily, which was good to see. Mother and Aunt Beth were not down for breakfast.

Tom looked up and gave her a reassuring smile. She had told him about Emily as soon as she had gone back upstairs.

She sat down next to him and concentrated on eating and staying calm. She was halfway through her first oat cake when the explosion came.

"This malignant suffragette, this Emily Davison, has run under the feet of the King's horse and almost killed the horse and the jockey. The insufferable lunatic."

Harriet put down her oatcake and hid her hands in her lap

to prevent Wesley seeing how much they were trembling, should he emerge from behind The Times.

She said, "I think, if you read the article carefully, Wesley, you will find that the horse is quite unharmed and the jockey is not seriously hurt."

He lowered the paper and glared at her. Everyone else had fallen silent.

She held his gaze. "But Miss Davison is in Epsom hospital and unconscious. She may never recover."

"And serve her jolly well right. If she does, I hope they send her to the lunatic asylum where she belongs. She's forty and single, it says here. Probably deranged by the change of life and lack of a husband."

Eleanor shot a frown in his direction and said, "This is dreadful news. What has happened?"

"This suffragette, Emily Wilding Davison, ran out between the horses and was hit by the King's colt. That's all there is to say, really. She could have caused a lot more damage than she did."

"I knew her." Harriet forced herself to keep her voice low. "She was a highly intelligent woman, God-fearing and kind. She was a steadfast supporter of the women's cause."

Wesley snorted. "She obviously has several screws loose."

Eleanor laid a hand on his arm.

"What do you think she was trying to achieve, Harry?"

"I don't know in detail. Of course I don't. But it would have been to get the most publicity possible for the way just about anything from horse racing to getting letters delivered is considered more important than allowing women to vote."

Wesley snorted again. "And why should women vote when they behave like felons and lunatics?"

Eleanor said, "We are not all felons and lunatics, dear."

"Eleanor, my love. It is only a matter of time before all this setting fire to buildings and vandalising post boxes kills some-one. A postman was wounded by sulphuric acid being put in a pillar box. It burnt his hands. Strong acid does that, you see. These harridans think they are so very clever with their elemental knowledge of chemistry."

Harriet winced. She didn't want anyone to experience the pain of burns. She was all too aware of what it was like.

Wesley waved his knife in the air.

"I can't vote. Robert can't vote. Why should the likes of this lunatic Emily Davison vote when we can't?"

Those blazing blue eyes. Harriet held their gaze. She took a deep breath and determined to stick to facts.

"If the government had given time to the Conciliation Bill, which, I remind you, was voted for massively by the House, Emily Davison would not have been able to vote, because she was not a householder. But Emma would. And Gwen. And Aunt Beth."

Wesley held her gaze.

"Your precious bill didn't pass last time you tried, did it? It didn't pass because everyone's fed up with your violent behaviour. People have realised just how dangerous it would be to give votes to women."

"It didn't pass because twenty-five Labour MPs thought supporting industrial disputes in their constituencies was more important than staying for the reading and because the Irish MPs were afraid Asquith would resign if it did and that would end their chances for their Home Rule Bill."

"You see. Priorities. Men are capable of distinguishing priorities."

As if *he* were in favour of striking workers or home rule for Ireland. She watched him. His lips thinned and his eyes narrowed. There was silence in the room. It was as if they were alone.

"But the bill wouldn't have done anything for you, Harry. You wouldn't be able to vote... And nor would your husband."

Tom half rose from his chair. "I could vote if I set up my own household. As could you, Wesley."

"Fat chance of that for you, then. You need some decent work first. And, Harry, why should you vote when your own Mother can't? She does far more good in the world than you do. All you do is prance around with banners and throw stones. You act like a common criminal. What exactly do you believe, Harry?"

Tears pricked behind her eyes. She closed them and pushed her fingers hard into her eyelids. She mustn't allow tears to fall. If she did, he could accuse her of being irrational, hysterical and manipulative. When she opened them again, Wesley was still glaring at her.

Robert cleared his throat and folded his napkin in a gesture reminiscent of Father winding up a discussion. He smiled sweetly at her, and all her damned-back feelings burst out.

"I don't know what I believe anymore! Or what is for the best!"

She pushed her chair back so hard it fell over. She heard Tom say, "You're a despicable bully, Wesley Brown," and the scrape of his chair as he got up to follow her. She was shocked by how much she needed him to follow her.

She stood outside the Dining Room door, shaking all over, not knowing what to do next.

Tom wrapped his arms around her and pulled her head into his shoulder. After she stopped trembling, he said, "If such things were still done, I'd call him out. Pistols at dawn."

"No you wouldn't."

"No, I wouldn't. Come, let's get away from here. Go for a walk. I'll make sure Sylvia is alright with Mabel."

"No, bring her. The fresh air will be good for her too."

The small park at the centre of the Park Estate was the perfect distance for Sylvia to walk. Tom could carry her home on his shoulders.

Life would be much calmer if she didn't have to contend with Wesley. Why did he and Eleanor still live at Loxley Hall? Cheaper than setting up their own place and a nicer area than they could afford for themselves? Eleanor having all the family support that she had become used to? It was emotional support as well as practical help for Eleanor. Her sister loved Wesley dearly, but what would life shut up alone with him be like for her?

Harriet would love to be shut up alone with Tom. She could have her own newspaper. She could get the Manchester Guardian instead of The Times and pick it up from the hall table every morning and be the first to read it. Perhaps she should do that anyway. She should at least find out how much it would cost.

They reached the little park and Harriet led Sylvia to the grass.

"Look daisies. Pick some and I'll make you a daisy chain."

She went to sit on the bench with Tom. Wesley's attack had forced her own disillusionment into the open. Not about the suffrage cause itself, but with the policy of obtaining justice from men in power by becoming more and more strident, and more and more violent.

She said, "It's enough. It's too much, in fact, the destruction. There'll be something organised for Emily, I'm sure. After that I'll remain a member but I'll not do anything dangerous."

"Are you frightened of Wesley?"

"No! I've never been frightened of Wesley. Infuriated by him, but not frightened of him. He won't give me up, even if he does call me a criminal. Wesley is quite fond of me."

"He doesn't seem to be too fond of me. Never has been."

Sylvia toddled over and dumped a handful of crushed daisies in Harriet's lap. Harriet pulled out three with long stalks, split the stalks with her thumbnail and threaded the flowers into a loop.

"Give me your hand. Look a bracelet. Find some more and I'll make you a necklace."

She watched the child until she sat down not too far away. She had taken so many risks that could have separated her from that little person who depended completely on her. A hollow space opened up within her. She moved closer to Tom and grasped his hand.

"I will miss the Union, Tom. There are other suffrage societies, but they are dreadfully calm and ladylike."

"You have your bookplate project with Emma."

"Yes, and I have an idea for a whole series called The New Woman. But it's all so...sedentary."

"I support you in what you do, my love. I always will. But please don't run in front of any horses. And I worry about Sylvia. It changes everything, doesn't it? A child, I mean. It puts another life in our hands. I don't think I ever knew what awe meant before I had a child to care for."

Chapter 34
The Funeral of Emily Wilding Davison

June 15th 1913

Harriet found Alice and Inga at the muster point near Victoria Station, where Emily's body would arrive from Epsom. Harriet and Inga were to be near the front of the march, with the prisoner suffragettes. Alice would be further behind. They arranged to meet afterwards, at King's Cross, where Emily's coffin would be loaded onto the train for the north.

Alice was shaking. Harriet knew exactly how she felt, because her own inner self was bidding her walk right back across London to Marylebone, get on her own train, and go home.

Marching today was the only thing Harriet could now do to thank Emily. Emily, who had given her the freedom to run around a prison yard in pursuit of a ball. It was not hard to imagine her rushing out onto a racecourse. What *had* she been doing at Epsom that day? Not intending suicide. The Emily Harriet knew was a committed Christian. It was true that she was fervent, self-sacrificing and dramatic, but her fervour was motivated by a connection to the sufferings of others. She had thrown herself down the prison stairs hoping that one woman driven to desperation by the prospect of the feeding tube would lead to the end of the torture. That was not suicide. It was risking your life for your comrades. This racecourse thing? Was it a stunt gone wrong? Emily trying to attach WSPU colours to the King's horse, so it would fly over the finishing line trailing them behind? That would have sent a dramatic message. Instead, Emily had paid the ultimate price for her fearlessness.

For two hours Harriet put one foot mechanically in front of the other. Sometimes they marched fast and sometimes they stood still. Over the years, she had become used to processions being that way. But she was not used to silence. As the cortège passed, the crowds quieted and the only sound was the funeral music drifting on the wind. There were some exclamations at the sight of Mrs Pankhurst's empty carriage. Word must have gone round about how she had been arrested and returned to prison as soon as she had stepped out of her nursing home. Otherwise silence.

All the women in white. The lilies. The mounds of flowers on the carriages. The massed crowds. Was Emily Davison a pure angel ascending to heaven, like Christabel had portrayed her on the front page of The Suffragette? Was she a martyr for the cause? Was she a crusader for the one true way? Were suffragettes walking a pure road anymore with so many leaders in prison, Christabel in Paris, and all hope of a suffrage bill including women swept aside?

The procession ground to a halt. People peeled off to the side. St. George's Bloomsbury, with its six Corinthian columns and steep steps, was ahead of them. Spectators were being pushed back by the police. Harriet reached for Inga's hand and they found a place by the railings. She hoped Alice would cut away and make for King's Cross.

The wind ruffled Harriet's skirts. She ran her tongue around her lips and wished she could take the water bottle from her bag without appearing disrespectful. Inga seemed withdrawn. Harriet pulled herself upright and stood attentive for the duration of the familiar words she could hear through the open doors of the church.

Then the coffin was being carried down the steps. The women lined up there saluted. The crowd heaved and surged towards the coffin and its pall. They seemed capable of slicing off purple, green and white relics from whatever part they could reach.

Harriet whispered in Inga's ear. "King's Cross is a twenty-minute walk from here, but we can be faster than the cortège by cutting through the back streets."

She pulled the bottle of water from her bag and offered it to Inga.

Alice was on a bench on the station platform, just as they had arranged. Now that they were free to talk, they sat in silence. Inga was set to leave for Chicago in a week. Alice was withdrawing from her association with the WSPU.

Eventually Harriet said, "I think this is the last time I will be in public for this great cause. It has taken all I have to give. Perhaps I am tired, but I feel as though we have achieved nothing but hardship and suffering for ourselves."

Alice put her hand on her arm.

"You have a family to care for. That is great cause enough."

Was it? It was precisely that belief on Eleanor's part that she had always chafed against.

They waited to see the coffin being loaded onto the train, then walked out of the station together.

"You will write, won't you Alice? You too Inga?"

Alice took her hand. There were tears in her eyes. It was time for tears. The day had required so much endurance that the tears had been kept too long at bay. Her friend turned away and crossed the Euston Road.

Harriet put her arms around Inga.

"Safe passage, my comrade-in-arms. Soon to be sister-in-law. Love you."

"Love you, too."

Inga raised her arm to hail a cab. Harriet turned right along the Euston Road, for the half-hour's walk to Marylebone Station and the journey home. She was so tired she could hardly lift her feet to put one in front of the other. After the train, would be the walk to Loxley Hall. Nobody would meet her at the station. There was no way to let them know when she would be arriving. This is what independence meant. Standing on her own two feet, even when they tried to refuse to do her bidding.

Chapter 35
Doctors who are Revolutionaries

June 1913

Harriet had a bookplate design roughed out in pencil: a woman reading in front of a circular window, three borders of flowers and fruits, *Ex Libris* at the top and a matching framed space at the bottom for the owner's name.

It was, she thought, a little too much like an Annunciation. Motherhood is announced to you. Take it. Leaving it is not a choice. It will change your life forever.

Not what New Women had in mind.

The door shuddered and Tom stumbled through, his face red and his hair over his eyes.

Her drawing board crashed to the floor as she stood. Sylvia had been with him when he left.

"Where's Sylvia?"

He fell forward, forcing her to sit back in the chair. She gripped his shoulders.

"For God's sake, Tom, speak to me. Tell me it's not Sylvia."

She heard something that sounded like, *I'm sorry*. What was he sorry for? She moved her hands to his head, ready to grab a fistful of hair and yank him up until he looked her in the eye. She took a deep breath and said slowly, leaving a gap between each word, "Is there anything the matter with Sylvia?"

A gulping gasp, and he looked up. He swept his hair from his eyes.

"I'm sorry, Harry. I'm behaving like a great booby. Sylvia is with my mother. She's fine."

She had never experienced panic like this, not any of the times she had put herself in danger. Letting the fear drain away, she smoothed Tom's hair with her hand, just as she did when Sylvia came howling to her for comfort.

"Do you think you could tell me what has happened?"

He got up, went to sit on the edge of the bed and pulled a handkerchief from his trouser pocket. He rubbed his face. The flesh around his eyes was red and swollen.

"He finally told me. Today. He's lost half his list. He can't carry on like that. Half a list is not enough."

"Your father?"

"Everybody's leaving, because of me."

"Because of the socialism thing? That's amazingly unfair."

He looked around as if searching for something.

"Where's that book?"

"What book?"

"The one about Canada."

"The book went back to the library weeks ago. Are you saying that you have no work, that we have no income?"

"You have income. I'm parasitic. I need to go to where nobody will know me. I'll go to Canada and make a new life for us. There are doctors there who are revolutionaries. They believe in a new world. They'll admire me for my principles. When I'm settled, I'll send for you and Sylvia."

Tear their little family apart? How could he suggest such a thing? He was distraught. He either didn't mean it or he thought he had to fix everything, all alone. He was not alone. He was overcome with anguish because he saw his father suffering as a result of something he had done. But she was not overcome.

She went over to the bed, sat next to him, took his hands and squeezed them.

"I will come with you to the ends of the earth if necessary. Don't you dare speak of leaving me behind. But that book made it quite clear that life in the Canadian Bush wrecks your body and destroys your mind. If we go to Canada, we go to Ottawa, or Montreal, even if I do have to work-up my French."

"Montreal! Yes, Montreal! Montreal teems with poverty. I can do good there."

She waited until his breathing was something like normal and the high-red on his cheekbones was softening.

"But first, please, please try to find a position in this country. Edinburgh or Birmingham or Manchester?"

She pushed the hair away from his face. A ghost of a smile. Did she see that?

"You need a haircut. You look a complete fright."

"I am a complete fright."

"No, you are my dearest husband and I will love you always."

"I'm sorry, Harry. I must have alarmed you. I was, I think I am, overwhelmed. I will go round the dispensaries, I promise. I'll give it another year. Things might settle down."

She tipped him back on the bed and drew him into her arms. He rested his head on her shoulder. His breath tickled her ear. She had never seen him so dominated by emotion, and she loved him for it. All along her body she felt the heat of him, except where their legs dangled over the edge of the bed. Intimate and ridiculous at the same time. But who could see them? This space, this closeness, was theirs alone.

Chapter 36
Deeply Personal

March 1914

Harriet pulled a chair up to Emma's kitchen table and lifted Sylvia onto her knee.

"Look, Auntie Emma has got you a nice cup of milk."

Emma chucked Sylvia under the chin.

"Did she walk all the way here?"

"She did. She's a great little walker. I might have to carry her on the way back, though. Can I leave the portfolio with you? There are five new designs. Feel free to improve them anyway you wish."

"I'll bring it back this evening. Gwen and I will be at dinner." Emma pushed an envelope across the table. "Your share of last month's sales. The New Women are very popular." She paused, her hand resting on the evening newspaper on the table in front of her. "Do you know a WSPU member called Mary Richardson?"

"She's notoriously militant. Has been arrested many times. I wouldn't call her a friend. Why?"

"She's attacked the Rokeby Venus. Says here, in the paper,

that she said she tried to destroy the picture of the most beautiful woman in mythological history as a protest against the government destroying Mrs Pankhurst, who is the most beautiful character in modern history. It doesn't make sense, does it? Even when she explains why she would do such a thing. How can destroying one beautiful thing put right destroying another? People who love the painting support the women's cause. You're one of them. So am I."

Harriet could feel heat creeping up her neck. Eight years ago, when they had seen the great Velasquez together, she had been captivated by the freedom of the brushwork, the sensuousness of the woman's skin, and the sheer modernity of the three-hundred-year-old painting. And here was Mary Richardson justifying destroying it and maintaining that people in Britain cared more about a painting than about women voting. The rationale was uncomfortably similar to the one Harriet had used herself to justify burning down the boathouse. Men cared more for their boats than they did about rights for women. She had actually said that to Inga.

But the boathouse had been a male preserve that excluded women, and the men would quickly replace their precious boats. Once that painting was destroyed, it was gone forever.

Emma said, "The National Gallery conservator thinks he can restore it. The slashes are narrow. They can attach new canvas to the back." She passed the paper to Harriet. "Page six, first column."

"You know I don't support this, Emma. Don't you? Not in any way. It's dreadful."

"Of course I know that, Harry. But when it going to end?"

"Well, the government could end it tomorrow by bringing in a limited franchise bill like the ones that have already passed."

Emma wiped away a tear.

"Remember how we loved her when we first saw her? Have

I ever told you I don't think there's any reason to think she's Venus at all? She's a real woman, not an abstraction. And she's looking at someone looking at her through the mirror. The angles are all wrong for her to be looking at herself. That little Cupid, tied up with ribbons, is the god of love showing her a lover through the mirror. That's what I think. Eyebeams meeting. Reminds me of you and Tom."

Harriet blushed and laughed.

"I meant it in the nicest way, Harry."

"I'm sure you did."

Harriet turned her attention to the long column of small print. Seven slashes across Venus' back with some sort of chopper before the attendant could stop her. The attack had been murderous. Deeply personal.

Emma drummed her fingers on the table for a bit, then picked up Sylvia's empty cup and took it to the sink. When she turned back her face was solemn.

"Harry, did you ever mention anything to Gwen about Tom working for the manufactory?"

"No, I thought we agreed it would come better as a suggestion from you, rather than me sounding like I'm begging."

"I did suggest it, and she said she would think about it, but I never heard anything else. I don't know what's going on with Gwen. She's so bound up in the manufactory these days it's like nothing else matters. You said Tom was writing around the dispensaries and I left off saying anything more. But I suddenly thought, it's been nine months and you've said nothing about Tom getting new work. So, I asked her again, last week. She said she'll talk to you after dinner tonight."

"Tonight?"

"Strange, isn't it? After so long not saying anything. She's been planning something, I'm sure of it. She was quite brusque with me and I'm not sure I should be telling you. But there, I've done it."

"You are the most amazingly sweet sister. You know that, don't you? And clever too."

"Don't be silly. I'm just a lone woman trying to make ends meet."

"And doing a fine job of it."

Gwen pushed her chair back.

"Take a stroll around the garden with me, Harry."

There was command in her tone. Emma, Robert and Wesley rose too.

Gwen's silver belt fastening caught the light as she walked.

Harriet said, "That's a lovely buckle. Is it new?"

"An extravagance. I need to give the impression the business is affluent."

Gwen sat on one of the wrought-iron chairs under the pergola. Harriet followed her example. Emma took the third. Robert and Wesley remained standing: Robert erect, with a glass of port in his hand, Wesley leaning against a pillar. In the low evening light the daffodils shone in nodding glory, but the air had a bite and Harriet was glad of her jacket.

Gwen folded her hands in front of her.

"I hope you have not discussed the possibility of Loxley Lace taking him on as an in-house physician with Tom, Harry. Apparently, Emma didn't warn you not to."

"No, I haven't."

Emma said, "See, there was no need to be so fierce with me, Gwen. There's no harm done."

Gwen glanced at the two men. "We are sorry, Harry. Tom is a fine doctor by all accounts, and we know he is a fine person, but the manufactory cannot afford the luxury of employing a doctor to administer to the hands."

Harriet raised a hand and attempted to speak. Skilled hands were valuable. A healthier workforce would pay for itself. Surely she could convince Gwen of that.

"You see, Harry, the salaried staff have all taken a cut recently, in order to have the funds to keep the skilled hands in work. It would be wrong to favour family with a newly created position. You do see our point, don't you?"

Harriet's jaw clenched tight. If that was the way Gwen saw things it was no wonder she had avoided voicing her thoughts. Since Gwen knew Tom had been trying the dispensaries she must have been hoping she wouldn't ever have to tell her that he was an unworkable element in the financial equation.

She looked from Gwen to Robert to Wesley. Gwen's face bore an expression of earnest sympathy that admitted she could have made a different choice, but wasn't going to. Robert was staring at the ground, as if he didn't agree but was staying silent. Wesley's eyes were on her, his expression unfathomable.

Only Emma looked surprised and upset.

She was glad that it was she who had asked for help from her family and not Tom. Now only she had been refused it.

She didn't join them in the Drawing Room. She went upstairs, checked on Sylvia and kissed her cheek, then went into her own bedroom.

It was stuffy from the warm day. She opened the window and flung herself on the bed.

There was a knock on the door.

"Are you alright, Harry?"

Emma.

"Not really. I need some time alone."

"You sure."

"Quite sure, thanks."

She heard Emma's footsteps going slowly back along the landing, sighed, sat up and took off her shoes and stockings. Her calf sported an island of shiny pink flesh. She rubbed it. She had taken such risks.

Tom had been true to his word. He had been looking for leads in the world of the charitable dispensaries, even expanding the search to Ireland. There had been no more panic, although he sometimes seemed worried and downhearted.

She lay back on the bed. If Ireland was possible, was Canada such an outrageous idea? Together, not Tom alone. If she could learn to treat wounds, and it hadn't taken Inga very long, they could open their own dispensary. She could even train to become a nurse. She could put her biology degree to some use.

At the sound of the door opening, she rolled onto her side and leaned on her elbow.

"Oh, there you are." Tom shrugged out of his jacket and hung it on the back of the trouser press.

"Did you eat?"

"Not yet. I'll forage for something in the kitchen later. I've been using the telephone at the surgery to butter up my old colleagues from Bethnal Green, the ones with new jobs in dispensaries. Didn't want Wesley overhearing any of my self-promotion."

He perched on the edge of the bed and put a hand on her ankle. She moved over and lifted her skirt up to her knee, showing the lace edges of her petticoats. Talking about Canada could wait a while.

Chapter 37
The Socialism Thing

April 1914

Tom's expression was fixed, as if he were trying not to let emotion spill over. Harriet put down her sewing. Alarmed as she had been that day when he'd run back from his parents' house to tell her bad news, she hoped he was about to reveal his feelings.

"Is Sylvia with Mabel?"

"She's upstairs. It's her afternoon sleep time."

"Yes, of course. Look, will you come up with me? This needs to be private."

Harriet stood and picked off the threads caught on her skirt. Not their usual need to be private. Not from his face and tone.

Tom sat in one of two chairs on either side of the little desk in their bedroom. Harriet moved a pile of drawing paper from the other.

He said, "I had a long conversation with my father this morning, and I'm going to leave the practice–"

"Have you found another position?"

He opened his mouth slightly and gazed at her but didn't speak.

"Well?"

"It's complicated. I don't know where to start. No, I haven't got another position, is as good a place as any, I suppose. And I'm not likely to–"

"Oh, Tom. The socialism thing. It seems wretchedly hard."

"Not the socialism thing. Never has been, actually. You see, I spoke to a lot of people while I was trying the dispensaries. After a few weeks some of them got back to me. As good as their word, they'd approached the senior doctor with my name. Then replies came back from the trustees. An absolute no. I was not to be considered in any way, nor was my name to be mentioned again."

"Oh, my God!"

"One of them, a real brick, was able to ferret out the real reason why. Not only why, but where the information came from."

He leant his forehead on his hands and stared at the desk. Harriet made herself stay silent.

He looked at her. There was a hardness to his eyes.

"When they asked for references from Bethnal Green his trustees were forwarded a letter from a Mr Wesley Brown, who is well acquainted with Doctor Thomas Bardhill of Nottingham. Said doctor is known for receiving women patients in private and after hours. He is a man of notorious sexual lasciviousness and not to be trusted alone with any female. That's the gist of it."

Harriet gasped. She felt as if she had been struck in the chest by something hard and unyielding.

"That malevolent traitor... I've been so unbelievably wrong about him. How dare he?... I know he's never really liked you but to do something like that–"

"And so clever. Because, let's face it, love, there's just a grain of truth. Someone in Bethnal Green must have told on us."

"Not Will. Never."

"No, not Will. Couldn't be. The housekeeper, perhaps. All Wesley had to do was ask. One of my father's patients opened up. He took me out for a drink. My apparent sexual intemperance has also been broadcast all around the gentleman's clubs of Nottingham. Men say their wives and daughters aren't safe with me."

"What absolute rubbish. How could they think such a thing? And the source is Wesley? Did this man say?"

"He didn't know. So I spoke to Robert. I've always felt Robert likes me and Robert has more contact with Wesley than any of us."

Tom paused and pinched the bridge of his nose. She waited.

"Robert said he was sorry, but it was true. He'd overheard several of Wesley's conversations and challenged him on them. But it wasn't because of me. It was because of my father. Oh, Wesley dislikes me alright, but he hates my father. You see, it was my father who diagnosed your sister's illness and had the family send Wesley away to be cured. For years, Wesley has lived under the shadow of you all knowing about it. He is bitter. He's hurting. He thinks that every day you all sit in judgement on him, and in his mind it's my father's fault. By defaming me he has a way to destroy my father's practice. If I leave the practice, perhaps, just maybe, my father can recover enough to be able to retire in comfort."

Harriet rested her chin on her hand. Robert? Why hadn't Robert told them, or done something? "Robert has authority over Wesley. Robert, along with Father, was the person who told Wesley that he had to stay away from Eleanor until he was declared clear of the infection. Why didn't Robert tell you, or your father? Why didn't Robert try to counter the rumours?"

"Because Robert is vulnerable himself and Wesley made it clear that he knows it and will use what he knows if Robert stands up for me."

"Robert? How? Robert is the nicest person. The nicest of us, I'd say, after Emma."

Tom got up and paced around the room, a habit of Will's when he was agitated, but not something she had seen Tom do before. After a few moments he came back.

"Because Robert is an invert. A man who likes men instead of women."

"A...?" she had no word. "Like a Sapphist? But a man? Robert?"

To her surprise, Tom smiled. Was it amusement or relief?

"I might have guessed. You and your New Woman friends. I was worried you'd be aghast, shocked, horrified, completely floored. How wrong could I be?"

"What was that word?"

"Invert."

She had heard of affections of one man for another, normally considered perversions, although clearly not by Tom. Robert, so charming and handsome, and no lady friends. Why had she never considered it?

Because her mind didn't work like Wesley's. She had no need to think of such things. She had always known Robert for who he was to her, her beloved, somewhat distant, oldest brother.

"Did you ever imagine this about Robert, Tom?"

"Yes. But it's not exactly dinner-time conversation, is it?"

"Not even between us?"

"No. Although I suppose we've just passed that barrier."

Her thoughts were tripping over each other. She could scarcely grasp them. Robert was at the forefront.

"Do you mind me asking, just how do you know about Robert?"

He sat down.

"Well, he's a handsome man, well known around the town and the heir to a third of one of the city's most prominent businesses. And he's nearing forty. Why isn't he married?"

"And that's how Wesley knows?"

"What I said is only speculating, not knowing. Wesley knows because he saw Robert entering a certain establishment in Low Pavement. And, well, when I spoke with Robert I'm afraid I lost my temper with him and berated him for not standing up to Wesley like a man. He broke down then and told me himself."

Tom pulled a handkerchief from his pocket and dabbed at his eyes.

"I was unduly hard on Robert."

"Perhaps you were. He's gallant and good-looking but he's never been forceful."

"My love, since the Labouchère amendment, gross indecency, as defined between men, has become a criminal offence. It's what put Oscar Wilde in jail."

"Labouchère! That self-important hypocrite. The same man who talked out Bamford Slack's suffrage bill? I might have guessed he would come back to haunt us."

Tom said, "I should speak to Wesley. Make him stop."

"Isn't it too late for that? The damage is done."

"I should at least tell him what a thorough-going blackguard he is."

"To what purpose? You can't threaten him with anything. And, if you try, he can hold exposing Robert over you and me as much as he can over Robert himself."

"Then you think I should offer him sympathy?"

"You did say he was hurting."

She watched him for a few moments before saying, "My love, you are a man of peace. You can't, and shouldn't, attempt to fight Wesley, in reality or verbally."

He looked up, his face blotched from where it had pressed on his knuckles.

"I'll tell my father about it."

"Good idea. With his connections in town, he can use them to undo some of the harm that's been done." She pursed her lips. "And you know who else has power over Wesley? Gwen. Gwen and Robert outnumber Wesley at the manufactory. They could make life difficult for him if they wanted to."

He shook his head. "No, let's not set family members against each other. My father will recover if I'm out of the way."

She sighed and took his hands in hers.

"The odds are stacked high against you, aren't they, my love. Thanks to that vicious weasel Wesley.... I think we should reconsider Canada."

He laughed a short self-deprecating laugh.

"I was beside myself that day. I don't know that I truly meant it."

"But I have thought about it since. You see, in Canada, I could train as a nurse and assist you. I do already have a biology degree. It would be nice to use it. And if we could raise charitable money we could open our own dispensary. We'll still have my income from the trust to see us through the first few years."

"Could you train as a nurse? A married woman?"

"I don't know. Maybe things are different there. But if they're not we could start out by pretending we're not married. We can say you're a widower and I'm your housekeeper. Have a second wedding later. It's a new world. Anything's possible where nobody knows you."

The look of astonishment on his face, followed by his snaggle-tooth smile, was almost enough to have made the preceding conversation worth it. He got up from his chair and she did the same.

He said, "'Vicious weasel Wesley'? That's quite tongue-twistingly alliterative. Endearing."

"Not at all. They're nasty little creatures with very sharp teeth."

"But little. Very little. Little like this narrow land we live in."

He put his arms around her. She leant into him and sighed. "Canada is big and empty. Sylvia can grow up in a different world."

She felt him hardening against her.

Sylvia wailed from the next-door room and she laughed.

"No peace for the wicked doctor and his shameless mistress."

Chapter 38
Not My Secret to Share

August 12th 1914

F or a while it had seemed that the assassination of the
Archduke Franz Ferdinand in the distant Balkans would
be a matter for Austria and Serbia alone, then all of a sudden
Germany was invading Belgium and Britain was at war. It had
turned out to be the one crisis the Great Powers didn't choose to
avert. Everybody was talking of glory and it was all horribly like
Tom had said it would be.

Harriet found Gwen alone in the garden, sitting on one of
the metal chairs and staring into space.

"We're bringing our departure forward. Soon it will be too
late. All the ships are being turned into troop carriers."

Gwen looked up, weariness in her eyes.

"I'm sorry. I feel so guilty about you having to go."

Harriet sat down. She could imagine the discussion Gwen must
have had with Wesley and Robert about employing Tom. Wesley
would have opposed the very idea. Robert would have said little and
Gwen would have been thinking of the future of their business.

Did she have the right to burden Gwen with one more thing?

With Tom out of the picture, Wesley would lose one line of attack on Doctor Bardhill but he could well seek out another. And Robert would remain vulnerable. But if she told the whole story to Gwen, how would she react, especially when she took in the realities of men loving men? Harriet had not recoiled until she had thought through what Tom meant by gross indecency. It was not a picture she wished to contemplate. And Gwen had an ambivalence towards, almost a hatred of, the idea of sexual relations, a horror brought about by the behaviour of Wesley himself.

But Robert was still Robert. And, as Harriet had thought more, she had accepted more. Sexual congress was bodily, wet and very strange. His was a different route to pleasure. And, to be frank with herself, she didn't know what Robert did in that house on Low Pavement, and it wasn't her business.

Gwen said, "Is there anything I can do to get you to stay?"

"No. I'm sorry. We've committed ourselves to this way forward."

Harriet tipped her head back and looked at the moon and the evening star now showing in the sky. The evenings were still long and light but would soon start drawing in. Perhaps this quiet moment was her opportunity. Robert's secret wasn't hers to share, but maybe there was some other way to break Wesley's hold over him. She couldn't leave knowing Wesley might end up in control of the family. She could start by telling Gwen the part of the story that was hers to tell.

"Gwen, Wesley has been preventing Tom getting employment. He's been saying Tom is a danger to his women patients. That he assaults them."

Gwen gasped and then hissed. "The beast. I might have

known. Wesley is capable of anything. Too bad he's so good at selling lace. But why, for God's sake?"

"To destroy Doctor Bardhill, the senior Doctor Bardhill."

"Doctor Bardhill?"

"Because he uncovered Wesley's perfidious activities and made him stay away from Eleanor. And I'm afraid he might turn on Robert because Robert still has a duty to remind him to get tested each year. Wesley is seething with hatred. I'm worried about him and what he might do to the family."

"Oh my God! The miserable wretch."

Gwen paused and frowned.

"I can encourage him to join the army, instead of trying to persuade him to stay because I need him, which is what I have been doing. I can have a sudden burst of indignation over Belgium. Both Wesley and Robert have been talking about volunteering. Wesley's certain it will all be over by Christmas. He says that with the French army and our navy the Germans are outclassed, and they will soon be fighting Russia on another front. I don't really need Wesley to sell lace. In fact, I have no idea how I will obtain the supplies of coal needed to keep the lace manufactory running at all. Lace production isn't going to figure high on the government's list of essential industries. And cotton comes in by the now-dangerous sea."

The dangerous sea that Harriet was about to risk crossing with her child. Was she doing the right thing? Tom was even more determined now the decision to go meant leaving a warring Europe behind, but should she be staying to support her family? Should Tom be staying to help, if the other men were going?

"You said other manufacturers are already making war materials and that the hosiery industry here is getting so many orders for socks and balaclavas it can't recruit workers fast enough. Can't you do that too?"

"The jacquard machines are complicated and specialise in weaving wide material. I'm looking into adapting patterns to produce the cotton bindings for blankets. There's going to be a huge demand for blankets for the army. But it won't be enough to keep the manufactory at full capacity. Still, if Wesley's right, we'll only have to survive until Christmas."

Harriet wasn't so sure about that. Her conversations with Tom about the nature of modern warfare, once massive economies like France and Germany were involved, had made her quite sceptical about the idea of fighting ending by Christmas.

Gwen said, "It will at least give Doctor Bardhill time to refute Wesley's allegations and to re-establish his list. How dare he say that about Tom! And you, by implication. And now I know, I can watch out for any attempts to undermine Robert and nip them in the bud. Meanwhile, let's just let him go and seek glory."

Harriet recalled how she had broken down under Wesley's attacks over Emily Davison's death and what a bully he had been, how hateful he could be, and how he had infected Eleanor and caused her to have her womb removed and never shown any remorse.

Wesley could go off and seek all the glory he wanted.

Not a charitable thought.

She whispered, "I'm sorry, Father."

"What?"

"Nothing Gwen. Just thank you."

Chapter 39
The Horses Are Waiting

August 18th 1914

Harriet slipped an old photograph of her family, one of her and Tom and Sylvia, and her prison medals, into the pocket in the lid of the trunk that they were taking on the train. The SS Canada was sailing the next day, the only second-class passage to Montreal Tom had been able to book. The other luggage had already been sent ahead to Liverpool docks. The fine studio photograph of her and Tom and Sylvia had been a gift from Sylvia Pankhurst, back when the world was still the right way up.

Harriet recalled the young clerk at Victoria railway station, the first time she had travelled by train without a chaperone. *Trunks are forever ending up in lost property.* Her thirty-six volumes of Sowerby's English Botany were in the trunk. She sighed. Sowerby shouldn't face the dangers of a sea voyage and all its connecting stages. Art was both timeless and fragile. She would need all her wits about her to keep Sylvia in her sight at all times, let alone the onboard trunk. She removed Sowerby's

English Botany and gave the books to Emma. It made room for clothes she had been going to leave behind.

Both families had gathered in the hallway while they waited for the wagon. Sylvia was sitting on the trunk, kicking her heels. Harriet bent to still the banging feet and whispered, "The carrier will be here soon."

As long as the streets were clear he would. Nottingham had burst forth with marching reservists and blaring recruitment bands rounding up men in their hundreds. Getting anywhere had become a nightmare. She and Tom had brought their departure for Liverpool forward a day because of the unpredictability of trains now they were being requisitioned for troops.

She felt suspended between farewell and leaving. Tom was talking with his father. Emma was trying to wipe her eyes without anyone noticing. Mabel, the maid who had come with them from the vicarage, who had been so enthusiastic when asked if she would like to help Harriet set up house in Montreal, was shuffling her feet and looking as if she might change her mind at any moment.

A sharp knock on the door and Mabel moved towards it, but it burst open before she could take more than one step in its direction.

"Harry! Tom! Thank God you're still here." Will dropped his bag on the floor and seized Harriet by the hands, gripping them tight, pulling her towards him and kissing her on the cheek. "Dear Sis."

When he released her from his grip, she stepped backwards, thrown off balance. Tom caught her arm and said, "We didn't think you'd make it back from France in time, old chap. It's wonderful to see you."

"It's wonderful to see you too, my friend. I'm so glad I am in time. Can you get a refund on your passage? You mustn't go. We have to stop it happening." Will flung open his arms. "The world needs every man to halt the German juggernaut."

No-one spoke. Will let his arms drop and smiled. "I'm sorry. I've been rushing for two days. I'm a little over-excited. This is the situation; this I know from the diplomatic chatter in Paris. With the German victory at Liège, Belgium is gone. Belgium! The country that all the great powers pledged would always remain neutral. Britain must stand by France now and drive the Germans back." Will grabbed Tom by the arm. "So you see, my friend, you have to stay."

Tom put his hand on top of her brother's. "I will always admire you, Will, for your insight and your passion, but Harriet and I have made our decision to try our lives in Canada."

Harriet stared at Will. He couldn't seriously be suggesting they change their plans, could he? He wasn't himself. He was overwrought, and probably short of sleep.

Will said, "The army will need doctors. You, Tom."

Wesley hissed, "You're a damned coward."

Eleanor gasped and put her hand to her mouth but neither she nor Harriet's other sisters spoke.

Harriet's blood pounded in her ears.

"My husband is no coward, Wesley Brown, whatever lies you might think you can spread!"

Her voice splintered the air of the hall. She locked eyes with Wesley until his lips twitched and he looked away. Her hands were shaking. She clasped them together in front of her and looked at Gwen. Gwen nodded. Gwen had taken care of Wesley. He was reporting for basic training in a few days.

"He's right there," Robert spoke softly. "The country will need every one of us."

Harriet glared at Robert in horror, not just at what he had said but at the realisation that he would also be leaving to fight.

She searched for the words to express her feelings but Tom spoke before she could garner them.

"You know I won't join the armed forces, Will."

"Why not, in God's name? It's what men do."

"I am a healer, not a killer."

Will had not let go of Tom's arm. "The army will need doctors. You can heal."

Tom pushed his hand away and stepped back.

"An army doctor? Can't you see the dreadful irony in that? A healer patching up deliberately broken bodies? Bodies broken by the very organisation that pays his wage. Stitching them together to send them out to be broken again. Can't you see how wrong that is?"

Harriet turned towards her mother. Mother nodded twice. What was she trying to tell her? That she was on her side? Would always be on her side, but had to be on the side of all her other children as well?

There was a series of knocks on the door. Eleanor, Gwen and Emma walked quickly over and hugged her, one after the other. No-one else moved.

Sylvia whimpered and Harriet picked her up. She glanced at Mabel and gestured with her head towards the door, but since Mabel seemed rooted to the floor she walked over and opened it herself.

"Wagon for the station, ma'am. Three people, one an infant, and one trunk."

"Thank you. The trunk is just inside the door, if you please."

Harriet crossed the hall to where her mother and her aunt were sitting.

"Goodbye, dear, kind, Aunt Beth. Mother, I love you dearly. I will be back to see you. As soon as I can. Sylvi, give Granny a kiss. There's a good girl."

Her mother clasped her hand in hers and whispered, "Go with God, my dear child."

Harriet bent to kiss her mother's hands, stood, chewed at her lip and swallowed hard.

"Tom, Mabel, are you coming?"

Tom walked over to his parents and put his arms around his mother.

Will took her arm. "Can't you talk him out of this? He'll be known as a coward."

"He's not a coward, Will. And it was our joint decision."

"I don't want you to go, Sis."

"It's not forever."

Tom joined them. He held out his hand to Will, which he took in silence.

Harriet lifted her chin and went through the door. Throwing out her arm to one side to balance against Sylvia's weight, she descended the steps of Loxley Hall and walked towards the waiting horses.

Afterword

The First World War, when all combatant nations are counted, saw the mobilization of 65 million soldiers. An estimated 9.7 million military personnel and 10 million civilians were killed. Emmeline and Christabel Pankhurst, both ardent Francophiles, turned their formidable public speaking talents to supporting the war effort. Sylvia Pankhurst and Emmeline Pethwick Lawrence were outspoken pacifists. The non-militant suffrage societies under Millicent Fawcett persisted in their quiet lobbying for the enfranchisement of women.

The UK Representation of the People Act 1918 became law on the 6th of February, 1918, eight months before the armistice ending the war in Europe, when the need for an overhaul of a property and residence based system had become acute with so many men 'resident' in the trenches in France. The Act extended the vote to all men over 21 and abolished all property and residential restrictions. It also extended the right to vote to women over the age of 30, with property restrictions. The electorate increased from 8 million to 21 million, 8.5 million of them women.

Afterword

The UK Equal Franchise Act 1928 extended the right to vote to all women over 21, with no property restrictions.

Historical Characters in Order of Appearance

James Henry Yoxall (1857-1925) was the MP (Liberal) for Nottingham West from 1895 to 1918. He was General Secretary of the National Union of Teachers from 1882 to 1924.

Alice Maud Mary Slack, later Lady Fletcher, (died 1932) was a suffragist and the wife of Bamford Slack. Unlike the other historical figures, just about everything she does in this book is the author's invention.

John Stuart Mill (1806-1873) was a giant of the nineteenth century. A philosopher, political economist and politician, for the purpose of the women's suffrage movement he is best known for being one of the most influential male proponents of gender equality and for his amendment to the Reform Act of 1867, where he proposed the enfranchisement of all households regardless of sex, arguing that the term 'man' included women and had been formally acknowledged by Parliament as doing so.

Emmeline Pankhurst (1858-1928) was the founder of the Women's Social and Political Union (WSPU), which she led, with her daughter Christabel, from 1903 until she suspended its

activities upon Britain's entry into the First World War in
August 1914.

Estelle Sylvia Pankhurst (1882-1960) was the second
child of Emmeline and Richard Pankhurst. An artist and a journalist, she worked with the WSPU until informed by Christabel
in January 1914 that the working-class women's federation she
had founded (The East London Federation) was not compatible
with the aims of the WSPU.

Adela Constantia Mary Pankhurst (1885-1961) was the
youngest of the Pankhurst sisters. Often overlooked in discussions of the WSPU, she was an accomplished public speaker, an
activist in the north of England and served several prison
sentences. Disagreements between her and Christabel over the
direction the WSPU was taking led to her emigrating to
Australia in 1914.

John Bamford Slack (1857-1909) was a Methodist
preacher and the MP (Liberal) for St. Albans from 1904 to
1906.

Sir John Fowke Lancelot Rolleston (1848-1919) was an
MP (Conservative) for Leicester from 1900 to1906.

Henry Du Pré Labouchère (1831-1912) was an MP (Liberal) for Northampton from 1880 to 1906. He was a publisher
and theatre owner and is best known for the Labouchère
amendment of 1885, which made 'gross indecency' between
men a crime.

James Keir Hardie (1856-1915) was a founding member of
the Labour Party. He was elected the first ever Labour MP in
1892 and was MP for Merthyr Tydfil from 1900 to 1915. He
was an outspoken supporter of the Pankhursts and of universal
adult suffrage. He and Sylvia Pankhurst were probably lovers.

Elizabeth Clarke Wolstenholme Elmy (1833-1918)
campaigned for significant pieces of legislation that preceded
the period of the militant suffragettes, including The Married

Women's Property Act 1882, the Guardianship of Infants Act 1886, and the repeal of the Contagious Diseases Acts in 1886. She was the first woman to speak publicly about marital rape, and spent over five decades championing humane, progressive reform.

Christabel Harriette Pankhurst (1880-1958) was the eldest child of Emmeline and Richard Pankhurst. She had a degree in law from Owen's college, Manchester. Together with Emmeline and Sylvia, she was one of the founder members of the WSPU, which she dominated throughout its existence.

Annie Kenney (1879-1953) was a Lancashire cotton-mill worker and an early member of the WSPU. Together with Christabel Pankhurst she was involved in the first militant action of the WSPU, getting arrested for causing a disturbance after being ejected from a political meeting in Manchester.

Sir Edward Grey (1872-1933) was MP (Liberal) for Berwick-on-Tweed from 1885 until 1916, and Foreign Secretary from 1905 to 1916. In 1914 he was instrumental in persuading the cabinet that Britain was honour-bound to defend France and must prevent Germany controlling Western Europe. He is remembered for saying, 'The lamps are going out all over Europe, we shall not see them lit again in our lifetime'.

Winston Leonard Spencer Churchill (1874-1965) is best known for his leadership in the Second World War. From 1901 to 1904 he was MP (Conservative) for Oldham. In 1904 he crossed the floor to sit as a Liberal MP. In the 1906 election he became the MP for Manchester North West. In 1908, at age 33, he became President of the Board of Trade in Asquith's government. He lost his Manchester seat in the compulsory by-election following his appointment as a cabinet minister and was found a safe seat in Dundee. As President of the Board of Trade, he worked with Lloyd George to promote a 'network of state intervention and regulation' to improve the conditions of working people. He was Home Secretary from 1910 to 1911 and introduced a number of prison reforms including a ruling that allowed women suffrage prisoners to wear their own clothes in prison. He was in favour of women voting but only if the majority of the male electorate supported the idea.

Herbert Henry Asquith (1852-1928) was a successful lawyer, Chancellor of the Exchequer for the Liberal government from 1905 to 1908 and Prime Minister from 1908 to 1916. He played a major role in drafting reforming Liberal legislation and in curbing the powers of the House of Lords. He was opposed to women voting, feeling it would not improve the government of the country and was reported to be bemused by the passions aroused on the topic.

David Lloyd George (1863-1945) was one of the twentieth century's most famous radicals. He was a lawyer and MP (Liberal) for Caernarfon from 1890 to 1945. He became President of the Board of Trade in Asquith's government in 1906 and Chancellor of the Exchequer in 1908. He was a lifelong Welsh nationalist and in 1916 became the only British Prime Minister ever to have Welsh as his first language. As Chancellor of the Exchequer he is best known for The People's Budget, which is recognised as the founding legislation of the modern welfare state. His views on women's suffrage appeared to vacillate.

Doctor Catherine Alice Raisin (1855-1945) was a leading geologist, head of Bedford College Geology Department from 1890 to 1920 and head of the Botany Department from 1891 to 1908.

Dorothy F rances Montefiore(1851-1933) was a suffragist and a founding member of The Women's Tax Resistance League. In 1906 she refused to pay her taxes, citing no taxation without representation, and barricaded herself in her house against the bailiffs for six weeks, frequently appearing to address the crowds in the street.

Heinrich Herman Robert Koch (1843-1910) was a physician and microbiologist and is one of the founders of modern bacteriology. He discovered the bacteria responsible for tuberculosis and for anthrax.

James Sowerby (1757-1822) was a naturalist and an illustrator. His English Botany in 36 volumes was issued over 23 years, until its completion in 1813. With 2392 hand-coloured plates and brief descriptions in plain English, provided by the naturalist James Smith, *Sowerby* became a hit.

Sir James Edward Smith (1759-1828) was a botanist and founder of the Linnean Society (a learned society studying natural history and taxonomy). He initially declined to have his name on English Botany, despite having written the text, because he felt being associated with a mere illustrator would damage his social standing. He changed his mind after *Sowerby* became spectacularly successful and his name is on later editions.

Emmeline Pethwick Lawrence (1867-1954) became involved in the WSPU in its early days in London. She was their treasurer and a solid administrator. With her husband, Frederick Pethwick Lawrence she provided the WSPU with its London headquarters at Clement's Inn for five years, and also provided a home to Christabel Pankhurst. In 1912 she and Fred were ousted from the WSPU by Emmeline and Christabel Pankhurst.

Fredrick Pethwick Lawrence (1871-1961) published Votes For Women for the WSPU. He was a lawyer and a wealthy man and frequently bailed members of the WSPU held in police custody.

Lady Frances Balfour (1858-1931) was a leading suffragist opposed to the violent militancy of the suffragettes.

Millicent Garrett Fawcett (1847-1929) was the leader of the National Union of Women's Suffrage Societies (NUWSS),

Britain's main suffrage organisation, and a co-founder of Newham College, Cambridge. Unlike the WSPU, the NUWSS continued to campaign for women's suffrage during the First World War.

Doctor Elizabeth Garrett Anderson (1836-1917) is best known as the first woman in Britain to obtain a licence to practice medicine. She was the elder sister of Millicent Garrett Fawcett, a suffragist, and active in politics. In 1870 she became the first woman to be elected to the London School Board and in 1908 she was elected Mayor of Aldeburgh, the first woman in England to become a mayor.

Philippa Fawcett (1868-1948) was the daughter of Millicent and Henry Fawcett. She was a mathematician and an educationalist, founding numerous schools in South Africa.

Jane Maria Strachey, Lady Strachey (1840-1928) was a suffragist organiser and patron of Elizabeth Garrett Anderson's New Hospital for Women and of Girton College, Cambridge. She circulated petitions calling for votes for women at the time of John Stuart Mill's famous amendment to the Second Great Reform Act of 1867.

Israel Zwangwill (1864-1926) was an author, feminist and Zionist.

Mary Leigh (1885-1978) was the drum-major of the WSPU band. She was one of the first suffragettes to go on hunger strike and one of the first to be force fed, in Winson Green Prison while serving a sentence for throwing slates from the roof of Bingley Hall, Birmingham.

Charlotte Augusta Leopoldine Marsh (1887-1961) was a trained sanitary inspector who became a WSPU organiser. She was arrested in Birmingham, along with Mary Leigh, and was also force fed in Winson Green Prison. She spent six months in prison after the window smashing campaign in

March, 1912. From 1913 until the First World War she was WSPU organiser for Nottingham.

Frank Mundell (1870-1932) wrote books focussing on heroism for the Sunday School Union.

Edith Nesbit, aka E. Nesbit (1858-1924) was an author, political activist and co-founder of the Fabian Society. Her children's novels, such as *Five Children and It, The Railway Children* and *The Phoenix and the Carpet* remain popular.

Sidney James Webb (1859-1947) was an economist and social reformer. He co-founded the London School of Economics and was an early member of the Fabian Society. He was married to Beatrice Webb.

Martha Beatrice Webb (1858-1943) was a sociologist, economist, social reformer and early member of the Fabian Society. She was married to Sidney Webb.

George Bernard Shaw (1856-1950) was one of the most significant playwrights of the twentieth century. He was also a political activist and an early member of the Fabian Society.

Doctor Philip Boobbyer (1857-1930) was Medical Officer of Health for Nottingham from 1889 to 1929. He fought a long fight against the pail closet system of human excrement removal, believing it responsible for the endemic typhoid in Nottingham. He argued that when Leicester, a nearby city of similar size and type of population, introduced communal water closets in poor areas both the incidence of typhoid and of deaths of infants due to diarrhoea were substantially reduced.

Emily Wilding Davison (1872-1913) has become one of the best known of the militant suffragettes. She studied English at St. Hugh's College, Oxford, achieving first-class honours. She later took another degree course at the University of London. She was at times, a governess, a teacher and a writer. She was arrested, went on hunger strike and was force fed on numerous occasions. Her militant activities were extreme, including throwing herself from a prison balcony, getting herself shut into the Palace of Westminster overnight, setting fire to post boxes and attacking a person she mistook for Lloyd George with a bull-whip. On June 4th, 1913 she ran onto the track during the Derby horserace and was struck by the king's horse. What her intention was is still a matter of debate. She never recovered consciousness.

Charles Edward Henry Hobhouse (1862-1941) was MP (Liberal) for Bristol East from 1900 to 1918 and Chancellor of the Duchy of Lancaster (a cabinet post) from 1911 to 1914. He supported radical social policies, including a national minimum wage, but was provocative in his opposition to women's suffrage.

Mary Raleigh Richardson (1883-1961) was a militant suffragette who joined the WSPU in 1909. She was involved in window smashing at the Home Office and several arson attacks. She was imprisoned and force fed on numerous occasions. On March 10th, 1914, in the National Gallery, London, she slashed and severely damaged a Velasquez portrait of a reclining nude, known as the Rokeby Venus. In a press statement she said, 'I have tried to destroy the picture of the most beautiful woman in mythological history as a protest against the government for destroying Mrs. Pankhurst, who is the most beautiful character in modern history'.

Archduke Franz Ferdinand (1863-1914) was the heir to the Austro-Hungarian Empire. He was assassinated on June 28th, 1914, while on an official visit to Sarajevo, the capital of Bosnia-Herzegovina, which had been annexed by Austria in 1908. His assassination was followed by a declaration of war by Austria against Serbia, which it held responsible for the Arch-duke's death. The event is traditionally held to be the precipitative cause of the First World War.

Acknowledgments

It takes more people than an author to create a book and this is where they receive my heartfelt thanks. I couldn't have done it without them.

My writing group, Claire Noonan, Monica McHenry, Allyson Johnson, Richard Probst and Steve Noble read Strait Lace chapter by chapter over many months and kept me up to the mark.

My beta readers, Katie Steinmetz and Larry Brown, generously read my manuscript and shared their thoughts.

My editor, David Imrie, provided thoughtful and detailed assessments that helped me shape a promising series of vignettes into a novel.

My proofreader, Barbara Kaiser, generously gave her time and expertise.

My cover designer, Anna Dahlberg, created the beautiful cover.

And a special thanks goes to Elizabeth Crawford who graciously answered my email about suffragette medals and to Mari Takayanagi at the House of Commons Archives who helped me with the appearance of House of Commons notepaper in 1905.

The following authors have also played their part in the formation of my story:

Elizabeth von Arnim, *The Benefactress*
Diane Atkinson, *Rise Up, Women, The Remarkable Lives of the Suffragettes*
Diane Atkinson, *The Suffragettes in Pictures*
Christopher Clark, *The Sleepwalkers, How Europe Went to War in 1914*
Elizabeth Crawford, *Katy Parry Frye, The Long Life of an Edwardian Actress and Suffragette*
Elizabeth Crawford *The Women's Suffrage Movement, A Reference Guide 1866-1928*
George Dangerfield, *The Strange Death of Liberal England 1910-1914*
Andrew Davies, *Leisure, Gender and Poverty, Working-Class Culture in Salford and Manchester, 1900-1939*
Kathleen Dayus, *Her People*
Millicent Garrett Fawcett. *Women's Suffrage: A Short History of a Great Movement*
Alison Gernsheim, *Victorian and Edwardian Fashion, a Photographic Survey*
Jill Liddington, *Rebel Girls*
Jack London, *The People of the Abyss*
Trevor Lloyd, *Suffragettes International, The Worldwide Campaign for Women's Rights*
Hilary Mandleberg *Edwardian House Style, An Architectural and Interior Design Source Book*
Joyce Marlow, *Votes for Women, The Virago Book of Suffragettes*
Frank Meeres, *Suffragettes, How Britain's Women Fought & Died for the Right to Vote*
Susanna Moody, *Roughing it in the Bush*
Christabel Pankhurst, *Unshackled*

Emmeline Pankhurst, *My Own Story*

E. Sylvia Pankhurst *The Suffragette Movement, An Intimate Account of Persons and Ideals*

Ronald Pearsall, *Edwardian Life and Leisure*

Martin Pugh, *The Pankhursts*

Jane Purvis, *Christabel Pankhurst, A Biography*

Antonia Raeburn, *The Suffragette View*

Andrew Rosen, *Rise Up, Women! The Militant Campaign of the Women's Social and Political Union* 1903-1914

Rosemary Taylor,. *In Letters of Gold, The Story of Sylvia Pankhurst and the East London Federation of the Suffragettes in Bow*

David Turner, *Victorian and Edwardian Railway Travel*

Michael Whitfield, *The Dispensaries, Healthcare for the Poor Before the NHS*

Douglas Whitworth, *Nottingham, A Century of Change*

Christopher Wiley and Lucy Ella Rose, *Women's Suffrage in Word, Image, Music, Stage and Screen*

Strait Lace was inspired by a story about Helen Watts, a daughter of the vicar of Lenton and a suffragette. In the 1980s a Bristol history teacher set his students a project. One student, choosing to write on the suffragettes, placed an advertisement in the local paper seeking information. To her, and her teacher's, surprise a worker at the Avonmouth docks responded telling her of a lost trunk they had in their possession containing suffragette papers. They were letters and speeches belonging to Helen Watts from her time as a suffragette activist. The trunk was supposed to be going to Canada, or possibly returning, either way it never got back to Helen.

The schoolteacher was given permission to read and copy the

documents. The copies are now in the Nottinghamshire archives.

I owe my knowledge of this delightful snippet of historical mystery to Elizabeth Crawford and her Woman and Her Sphere blog

https://womanandhersphere.com/2015/06/19/suffrage-stories-helen-watts-and-the-mystery-of-the-unclaimed-trunk/

Harriet Loxley is a completely fictional character bearing no resemblance to the historical Helen Watts, other than being a daughter of a vicar of Lenton.

About the Author

Rosemary Hayward is the author of *Margaret Leaving*. She now lives in Santa Cruz, California and Seville, Spain but was born, bred and educated in England, including some years spent in Nottingham.

She has a monthly newsletter, Your Next Book, where she shares comments about books from her bookshelf. You can sign up here: https://www.rosemaryhayward.com/subscribe-to-news letter

For comments on all things reading and writing check her FaceBook page.

For her latest book recommendation check her website, www. rosemaryhayward.com, or her Instagram.

For images that inspired the Loxley Hall Books check Pinterest

- facebook.com/RosemaryHaywardAuthor
- instagram.com/margaretleaving
- pinterest.com/hayward0738
- amazon.com/author/rosemaryhayward

Also by Rosemary Hayward

Margaret Leaving

Historical Mystery set in 1970s England

Shipping to the United States

Shipping to the UK

Margaret Leaving is at Amazon.com

Printed in Dunstable, United Kingdom

69097419R00251